PASSION BENEATH THE STARS

"What a beautiful night!" Jess cried, forgetting everything but the wonder before her.

"A clear night at sea is an incomparable sight," Rhys answered quietly. Though he had seen many such spangled heavens, he could appreciate its effect upon Justine. He himself was unable to tear his eyes from her shadowed face. He had been unable to look at anything else all night.

With an easy movement Rhys set one hand on the deckhouse wall, imprisoning her with his body. Jess pressed back against the wall, all at once terrified, and thrilled with an excitement that started at her toes and ran electrically through her whole body.

Rhys laid his other hand on her silky throat, his fingers stroking, soft as down on her tingling flesh. Lowering his head so slowly that Jess felt suspended in a glowing void, he met her lips.

At his kiss the flame came alive, with a sweetness Jess had never known existed. His mouth moved over hers, sensuously exploring its shape and outline, drawing from her lips pleasure, like nectar from a flower, waking in her a growing warmth and urgency.

Jess let her arms slide around his neck . . .

THE BEST IN HISTORICAL ROMANCES

TIME-KEPT PROMISES (2422, $3.95)
by Constance O'Day Flannery
Sean O'Mara froze when he saw his wife Christina standing before him. She had vanished and the news had been written about in all of the papers—he had even been charged with her murder! But now he had living proof of his innocence, and Sean was not about to let her get away. No matter that the woman was claiming to be someone named Kristine; she still caused his blood to boil.

PASSION'S PRISONER (2573, $3.95)
by Casey Stewart
When Cassandra Lansing put on men's clothing and entered the Rawlings saloon she didn't expect to lose anything—in fact she was sure that she would win back her prized horse Rapscallion that her grandfather lost in a card game. She almost got a smug satisfaction at the thought of fooling the gamblers into believing that she was a man. But once she caught a glimpse of the virile Josh Rawlings, Cassandra wanted to be the woman in his embrace!

ANGEL HEART (2426, $3.95)
by Victoria Thompson
Ever since Angelica's father died, Harlan Snyder had been angling to get his hands on her ranch, the Diamond R. And now, just when she had an important government contract to fulfill, she couldn't find a single cowhand to hire—all because of Snyder's threats. It was only a matter of time before the legendary gunfighter Kid Collins turned up on her doorstep, badly wounded. Angelica assessed his firmly muscled physique and stared into his startling blue eyes. Beneath all that blood and dirt he was the handsomest man she had ever seen, and the one person who could help beat Snyder at his own game.

DANGEROUS DESIRE

ASHLEY SNOW

ZEBRA BOOKS
KENSINGTON PUBLISHING CORP.

ZEBRA BOOKS

are published by

Kensington Publishing Corp.
475 Park Avenue South
New York, NY 10016

First printing: May, 1990

Printed in the United States of America

SAMARKAND NAMES AND WORDS

Rhys Llewellyn
Justine and Justin Maury
George Sporn
Yarmid Ali
Ulugh Khan
Wusu
Prince Tai of Tsinghai
Princess Tsingsia
Faud Monsel
Qashgai tribe
Basseri tribe
Habib Jabbar
Jamshid
Timurid

Rayys (a suburb of modern Teheran)
Bokharta (the Emirate)
Bukhara (the capital city)
Tien Shan mountains
Habadad
dishdasha (men's robe)
kaffiyah (men's headdress)
khobuz (Arab bread)
mashrabia (open-work screen in Samarkand)
lassi (yogurt drink)
kumiss (fermented mare's-milk drink)

One

The sign over the shop was faded and weathered from the constant assault of salt spray off the harbor. Justine squinted up at it, trying to make out the blurred name above a dim outline of a teapot tipped over a dingy cup.

"Peter Romaine, Dealer in Imports," she read aloud. "This is the place, Moriah."

"And 'bout time, too," her servant grumbled behind her. "Your Papa goin' to skin yo' hide, he find out you been down here in this slatterny place!"

"Pooh," Justine replied, twirling her sunshade as she closed it up and reached for the door handle. "He'll never know if you don't tell him. Besides, you know Papa. He might complain, but that's all he'd do. Now hush your fussing and follow me."

A bell jangled above the door as Justine swept into the tiny shop. Its merry caroling was a sharp contrast to the dingy room in which she found herself. Lifting her skirts above the grimy floor, she glided around the stacks of crates and boxes that crowded the room toward a counter at the far end. Above it two shelves, tilted precariously

7

against the wall, were lined with assorted jars, pots, and brightly decorated china plates and saucers. Justine leaned against the counter and squinted up at them while Moriah stood close behind her, her dark face scowling beneath a colorful turban. With wary eyes Justine's servant scanned the tiny shop as if expecting a swarm of pigtailed pirates to come descending upon them, ready to carry off her beautiful mistress. It was almost a relief when a door behind the counter opened and a small man wearing a black coat and a dirty, limp jabot poked his head around to see who had entered his shop.

"Not 'spectable," Moriah went on in her low, rich whisper. "A lady don't come to no place like this. A lady don't go wanderin' round the wharfs, like some common trollop!"

"Oh, do hush, Moriah," Justine said with exasperation, turning toward the proprietor. "Would you be Master Romaine," she asked the gentleman who, on seeing the bright young woman in a striped taffeta skirt and feathered bonnet gracing his little shop, ventured out through the door.

"That I would, Ma'am," Romaine said, all but rubbing his hands together. "Forgive my astonishment, but it is not everyday that such a vision of loveliness graces my humble place of business."

"That don't surprise me," Moriah muttered.

"How can I serve you, Madam? I have the finest wares and delicacies of the Far East, just arrived from the Orient. A painted tea pot? A Jappaned box? The very best Behoea tea? Willoware from Canton? What would please the lovely lady?"

"I don't want any of those things," Justine said, brushing the dust from the counter off her white lace gloves. "I have looked over the whole of Philadelphia

8

trying to find just the right snuff box—something in 'cloisonné' with scenes of China on it. It's a gift, you see, for my father. He's about to leave on a trip to the Orient, and I want him to have something that will remind him of me every time he uses it. Have you anything like that?"

Peter Romaine rubbed at the stubble on his sharp chin, wishing this wealthy customer had come wanting something more easily obtained.

"I might have just the thing," he said, straining to remember just what was in the crate he had unpacked the day before yesterday. "If Madam will only give me a moment . . ." He went scurrying off back through the door into the mysterious recesses at the rear of the building, while Justine tapped her slippered foot and pulled in her skirts from the dusty floor.

"I tole you we shouldn't have come down here," Moriah began, taking advantage of the silence. "No snuff box worth gettin' murdered for. We be lucky we get back to yo' Fourth Street house alive."

"I'm going to find this box, even if it kills me, Moriah. You could have stayed home, you know. You didn't have to come following me and complaining every step of the way. I declare you're worse than a parcel of ministers preaching at me every minute of the day."

"Master Maury skin me alive if'n I let you go off into this part o' town by yourself! Miss Jess, you too stubborn for yo' own good. It's goin' to get you in trouble one of these days, I swear it is, yo' headstrong ways."

"Pooh. You've been telling me that since I was two years old. It's bad enough seeing Papa sail away in two days' time for heaven knows how many months, without having you fussing over me as well. Have a little pity, pray."

The genuine grief that settled in Justine's eyes at the

thought of her father's departure brought a measure of release from Moriah's scolding. Father and daughter were almost too close, the servant thought, and had been since the death of Justine's mother ten years before. This long voyage that Justin Maury was about to embark upon was sure to have more than its share of dangers and perils. Perhaps she was being too hard on the child. She was debating how to say something more sympathetic when Peter Romaine came bustling back behind the counter.

"Would something like this suit?" he said, as he carefully lifted three small enameled boxes from loose gray paper and laid them before Justine. The girl's eyes widened as she touched each one. Her venturesome trip to the docks had at last paid off handsomely.

"They're very lovely," she said, picking up each one to examine it more closely. Only one had a painted scene on its lid, and its picture of a turbaned man against a flowing tent with a background of sand dunes spoke more of Arabia than of China. The other two were simple worked decorations around a large oval of color on the lids. "How much is this one?" Jess asked, opening the Arabian box.

"Very reasonable, Ma'am, at seventeen shillings."

"Oh, that is far too dear," she said at once, placing it back on the counter. "I wouldn't dare spend so much."

"But it's only just arrived from Persia itself," Romaine said hurriedly, pushing it toward her. "Look at the fine workmanship. And the exquisite colors."

Justine tilted her head, catching her full red underlip in her teeth. "All the same . . ."

She reached for her parasol as if to leave and Romaine said quickly, "Well, perhaps I could allow it to go for fifteen."

"Twelve," Justine said crisply.

10

"Madam," Romaine wailed. "I must make some small profit on the enterprise. Fourteen."

"Not a penny more than thirteen five."

Romaine eyed the little box with a fatalistic sigh. "Oh very well. Thirteen five, but it's as good as robbery."

"Pooh! You know you didn't pay more than ten shillings for it. And you probably paid less, if you received as many as forty at a time."

"No, no, ma'am. I assure you, it is the only one like it in the world."

Justine laughed, her voice rich with delight at besting the proprietor. "Perhaps. Anyway, I like it, and I think Papa will, too. Wrap it up, please, and Moriah give the man his thirteen shillings."

"Thirteen five," Romaine added, placing the snuff box in its paper nest. "And I hope your father has a safe and delightful trip."

Justine was already at the door, leaving Moriah to fish out the coins and take possession of the box. She nodded her thanks at the little man behind the counter and stepped outside, trying to push from her mind any thought of the voyage that her father was about to undertake. It was too painful. The thought of not seeing him for all those months, the worry that stretched ahead, never knowing where he was or how he was . . . she could not bear to think about it.

The bell jangled behind her as Moriah came scurrying out.

"There, you see, Moriah. I stood out here on this terrible wharf for one whole minute, and no one kidnapped or raped me."

"Miss Jess! Don't yo' talk about such things!"

"No one even hit me on the head and tried to take my reticule. Aren't you disappointed?"

11

"Now you stop that, Miss Jess. You know ol' Moriah only wants to keep you safe for the Master."

Opening her sunshade, Justine twirled it over her head and gazed out at the long wharf stretching toward the harbor, its deck crowded with the overhanging jibs of the ships at anchor. In truth the area was not a very pleasant place. Garbage, the litter of imports and exports, crowded the stacks of barrels and crates. If one looked closely, Jess thought, one could probably catch the water rats scurrying about. Two doors down from the import shop, a tavern gave out its raucous noises—caterwauling, loud shouts, a woman's forced laughter. Scabby children eyed them from farther down the street and dirty sailors lounged about, perusing her in her clean finery with curious and shifty eyes. She shivered, all at once as eager to be gone as her servant. Yet still she stood.

"Look at all the ships, Moriah," she said more kindly. "Do you suppose one of them might be the *Boeadecia*?"

Moriah took her arm and gently propelled her toward the end of the wharf where their carriage stood waiting. "Now don' you think about that, Miss Jess. You still gots two whole days afore your Papa leaves. Don' even think about that ship."

Willingly Justine let herself be led toward the haven of the carriage. "I wish there was some way I could keep from thinking about it," she said, so low that Moriah could barely make out her words.

How this city has changed! thought Justin Maury, as he pushed his way through a knot of officers in scarlet coats loudly laughing and jostling one another. One had to risk one's neck to execute the streets of Philadelphia since Gen. Howe and his army took over the town.

12

The walkways were bad enough, but the broad avenues—clogged with wagons, drays, carriages, carts, and the splendid mounts of the British cavalry—were a hazard to create terror in the bravest of men. It required the daring of chivalry simply to get from one side of Chestnut Street to the other.

Justin doffed his tricorn hat at a call from one of the passing officers, decked in scarlet with gold lace. His broad mouth drew up into a satisfied smile. There was something very nice about the pleasant reception he received when he walked the streets of Philadelphia these days. It was a contrast to those dark two years before the English arrived. Well, why shouldn't he enjoy being respected? He had earned the right. All those months of being cut dead by old friends who resented his loyalty to the Crown still rankled. He had endured their slights, their resentment, their endless arguments. He had even survived the audacious threats of the Sons of Liberty—that worthless collection of ranting knaves. Through it all he had remained staunchly faithful to England and resisted all pressures to join their misbegotten "revolution." Now it was his right to enjoy being surrounded by a British army and British society.

And surrounded he was. He scanned the crowded evening streets as he ambled along toward home, still marveling at the varied mixture of people. Surely that was Peggy Shippen and Becky Franks sitting there in the Shippen's fine coach, flirting with several of the young and handsome officers in Gen. Howe's retinue. Their families also had remained faithful to old "Farmer George," and at the same cost. Now their young daughters, along with his own lovely Jess, were reaping the benefits. Of course there were others who swelled the ranks of the pedestrians: the not-so-respectable women

13

who always followed an attractive army, dolled and painted and openly soliciting favors. And there were the refugees, loyalists from the outlying districts fleeing the repressive zeal of those so-called patriots who had swarmed into the countryside once it was apparent that the British would take Philadelphia. They were always easily recognized: uprooted, shabby and proud, trying to find homes and work for themselves in the crowded town. He had been told that the situation was even worse in New York.

All at once the crowd milling around him jelled into a knot of people blocking the walkway as they grouped around an entertainment taking place near the street. Maury was not a tall man, and he had to stand on tiptoe to peer over the heads of the crowd to make out the figure of a small fellow, dressed like a gypsy, with a monkey cavorting on his shoulder. The monkey was wearing a ridiculous pointed cap which he doffed at the crowd, squealing as he jumped from his owner's perch to a lantern post near by, swinging around it like a tree. The crowd laughed, urging the creature on while Maury paused, mildly amused.

There it was again, that dark face, glimpsed so quickly that he wasn't even certain it had actually been there. Just for an instant, it stood out from the crowd, staring at him from across the dusty street. Then a phaeton rolled by, and when it had passed, there was nothing there at all.

A violent anger swelled over Justin Maury. Pressing his lips and clenching his fists, he waited only an instant to calm the rage, then darted into the street. Damn the man—if man it was, and not a spectre! No, it could not be a ghost. Nor was it his imagination. That terrible face had been only too clear, twice today and three times yesterday. Always just a glimpse, yet disturbingly real. The black eyes, the strange, evil visage, heightened by

14

the bronze skin, the weird apparel, especially the dirty gray turban wound around the head, almost obscuring the black fringe that sprouted from it.

Dodging the traffic in the street, he made it to the opposite walkway, searching first one way and then the other for any glimpse of a foreigner. Nothing. Only housewives with baskets, an occasional sedan chair, and the ever-present officers. Was his mind playing tricks on him?

Yet he knew he had not imagined that horrible face. Once perhaps, twice even, a spectre brought on by concern over the trip that he was to face in two days' time. But five times? No. That could not be his imagination.

Justin tore off his hat and dabbed at his brow with a lace handkerchief. It was time to face his anxieties, he concluded as he started again toward his house on Fourth Street. He had pushed them to the back of his mind long enough. He sensed, without exactly knowing why, the presence of real danger hovering over him—and perhaps even his family—and that must be faced. He did not really care what happened to him, but nothing must be allowed to harm his beloved daughter, his lovely Jess.

"A good day to you, Mr. Maury," a voice said, interrupting Justin's deep contemplation. He looked up into the smiling face of Major Carmichael, one of the general's aides who had been paying attention to his daughter for the last several weeks.

"Good evening, Major," Maury answered without enthusiasm. His euphoria of a few moments ago had completely dissipated. "I did not realize you were back in the city. When did you return?" Vainly he tried to force his mind back along the everyday channels of conversation. When had this officer said he was leaving

15

for a routine mission into the countryside? He hoped it was recently.

"Why, sir, I've been back a week now. Were you not aware that on two afternoons I shared a delightful tea with your beautiful daughter?"

"No, no. I must have been busy. There has been a lot to do lately." Justin said lamely. "Jess must have mentioned it but—circumstances, you know. I have much on my mind."

"Of course, you would. My little excursion did not take long. The Americans have tried to bottle us up here in Philadelphia, you know, but of course they have failed. However, that ragtag mob they call an army is sitting far enough outside the city to allow them the advantage of rousing the countryside against us."

"And yet I've heard that they are in a pretty desperate way out there."

"Far worse then desperate. They cannot last much longer. Sir, I can only say I would suffer no such hardships for any cause, especially one so misbegotten as theirs."

Maury, who knew well how little food and shelter General Washington's army had at their Valley Forge cantonment, was almost embarrassed to look into Carmichael's well-fed, fleshy cheeks. I don't suppose you would, he thought. The gnawing anxiety that permeated his soul drove him to want to get home even at the risk of being impolite, but before he could make an excuse, Carmichael spied the Shippen's coach still standing on the opposite side of the street and suddenly lost all interest in Master Maury. With a hasty request that he be remembered to "the beautiful Miss Justine," he hurried off leaving Maury to make his morose way onward. Lowering his chin into his lace jabot, Justin kept

16

his eyes on the ground, hoping he would be able to get home and see that Jess was safe. He was fairly sure that his sensible daughter would not be overly concerned about the attentions of a foolish fop like Major Carmichael.

"Try some of this Madeira. You can taste the island itself in its smoothness."

"Something you picked up in passing? Did it really come from Portugal, or was it waylaid off a British packet?"

Rhys Llewellyn smiled knowingly as he poured the amber liquid into two pewter tumblers. Flecks of light from the swaying lantern above the table gleamed like sequins on its smooth surface. Rhys handed a glass to his friend and lifted the other. "To the British master of the packet, *Birmingham*. May his disappointment over losing a case of vintage Madeira be tempered by my pleasure in owning it."

"Here, here," said Alexander Greydon, downing the glass. He smacked his lips over the heavenly liquid. "The spoils of war can sometimes be a consolation. It's a good thing, or men would never be induced to fight."

"Sit down, Alex," Rhys said, indicating a chair in front of the table, while he himself draped his long frame over a bench built into the cabin wall behind it. "You can't know how surprised and delighted I am to see you. When I heard that you'd been captured after the battle of Brooklyn, and were a prisoner in New York, I assumed you would spend the rest of the war there. What happened? Were you able to escape?"

Greydon, nearly a foot shorter than his companion, settled comfortably in the chair and crossed one hosed leg over the other. "I wish that I had," he answered with

17

a note of bitterness in his voice. "The truth is much less dramatic and immensely more embarrassing. I'm on parole, you see. Brought on by the earnest pleading of my dear mother, who once knew General Howe personally and went herself to New York to plead my case before him. I've never been so chagrined in my life!"

Rhys gave a deep-throated chuckle. "So that's why you're walking the comfortable streets of Philadelphia, instead of freezing and starving out there at Valley Forge. I wondered at it when you came aboard."

"As well you might. I'm forced to endure the stares and insults of an occupying army while I long with all my soul to join my compatriots out there in the wilderness. At least my Mama is happy."

"Well, there must be some consolation in the fact that you're not a prisoner in New York anymore. Was it pretty awful?"

"Not for the gentlemen officers, though the lesser fellows in the sugar houses and prison ships of the city have it pretty bad. We were quartered with the Dutch farmers of Brooklyn, and while accommodations were certainly primitive, as long as we stayed within the bounds of the village, we were allowed a little freedom. The worst problem was boredom and knowing you were cut completely out of the real action."

"Here. Have some more Madeira. It's a great antidote for the blue devils."

Accepting another full tumbler, Alex settled back and studied his friend across the table. He had known Rhys Llewellyn since they were boys together, plying their small skiffs along the weed-choked inlets of the Schuykill River. Tall, well-formed, with strong shoulders, thin hips, and long, muscular flanks, Rhys had always been a commanding figure. Now time and experience had altered his handsome, interesting face in a way Alex had not expected. The shock of black hair had edgings of premature lightening around his brow. His eyes, always a startling, intense sea green, had darkened and seemed even deeper-set, emphasizing the sweep of his thick brows, the strong cheekbones, and the long lean lines of his face. The firm chin and wide, expressive mouth were more somber, as though the spirit behind them that was once so fun-loving and curious had grown tempered and guarded. Even, perhaps, a little cold.

"So, tell me about yourself," Alex ventured. "How many prizes so far this year? More than any other captain, I expect."

Rhys frowned and looked away. "Oh, not so many, though it's true I've had my share. It's made me uncommonly wealthy and, I trust, also added no small amount to the depleted coffers of the treasury of the Continental Congress. Also, it drives the British crazy."

"So I've heard. Which reminds me—how the deuce did you manage to sail into this harbor without being thrown into chains? Are they aware at headquarters that Capt. Llewellyn of the *Boeadecia* is the same pirate who waylays their warships?"

"They're finding it convenient to forget that for the present. I've given all that up for a time. This voyage was commissioned for the China trade, because they need good, reliable ships. It will be a welcome relief to get away from the war for a little while."

Greydon sat down his glass and leaned his elbows on the table, staring intently at his friend. "As a matter of fact, that's just what I wanted to talk to you about."

Rhys set his empty glass on the table and pushed it away. "I was afraid of that," he said, sighing with resignation.

19

It was half an hour later before the two men left the close darkness of the cabin and climbed to the upper deck. The ship was lying at anchor in the harbor. The sun had almost disappeared behind the spires and roofs of the town, laying shards of gold across the water. The gray sky above the masts of the schooner melded in the west into a brilliant palette of roses and blues billowing around the fiery red globe of the setting sun.

Rhys barely noticed the heavenly display as he motioned to one of his seamen to ready the launch to take Greydon back to shore. Standing by the opening in the taffrail, he paused, so preoccupied that he neglected to extend his hand in farewell.

"It just doesn't sit well, Alex. I'm sorry, but I just can't do it."

"Don't refuse outright, Rhys. Think about it tonight, and hold off your decision until tomorrow morning. I'll be at our old docking area near Swede's Ford at five o'clock. Take a launch up the river and meet me there. I'll escort you the rest of the way. No one need ever know you've been gone."

"You don't understand. I've agreed to make this trip with no political strings. I don't want to go dancing back into all this intrigue and danger. I've had more than my share of it. I deserve a little time off."

Alex leaned into his friend's face, speaking in a voice barely above a whisper. "For God's sake, Rhys, we're not talking about a minuet. This is war. Your country's need is very great. Men like you are our only hope. You can't just turn your back and walk away, claiming you need time off. I saw men's heads loped off by cannonballs on Long Island. I saw our countrymen speared to trees by Hessian bayonets in Brooklyn Heights. *They* deserve the rest they got. We who are able are still needed."

20

"Fine words from a paroled gentleman of affluence."

Greydon's pale face flushed with color. "That was unfair, Rhys. You know I would gladly offer my sword to my country, if I were not hemmed in by the demands of honor. I will excuse you that comment, if you'll only do as I ask. Besides, I don't believe for a moment that you offered to make this trip purely for profit and the chance to get away for a time. You have some ulterior motive, I'd swear an oath on it."

"You're wrong, Alex. I've seen enough of battle and blood to last me a lifetime. I do intend to go back to it, but only after some time away."

"Then at least listen to what these men have to say. I'm begging you, Rhys. You cannot know how important this is. It was God's own providence that you arranged for the *Boeadecia* to sail just at this time."

Rhys stared out at the water, his dark brows knitted in a frown. He knew Alex Greydon to be not just an old friend but one of the finest gentlemen he had ever known. That was the problem. He had come so far from the gentle and cultured roots they had both once shared that he felt he had lost himself somewhere back in the cannon fire and spilled blood of his last ship. Now the last thing he wanted was to consider going back into another demanding situation. Yet, one could not easily refuse Alexander Greydon.

"All right," he said, laying a hand on Greydon's shoulder. "I promise, I'll think about it. But if I don't show up at five tomorrow morning, don't waste time waiting for me."

The warm brick facade of the house on Fourth Street welcomed Justin Maury as he walked up the low steps to

21

his front door. Its classic lines, the glimpse of candlelight behind the curtains on the twelve-paned window, the brass knocker polished to a gleaming patina, the skylight over the door, the soft red of the brick itself—there was a homey comfort about it all. Though not a large house as town houses went, it was the home to which he had brought his wife, Margaret, after their marriage, and it still evoked memories of her. They had intended to move on to a larger home when the children started arriving, but, with its usual irony, life had not worked out that way. There had been only the one child, Jess, his daughter. After Margaret was carried off by scarlet fever when Justine was eight years old, he had never wanted to live in any house that Margaret had not shared with him.

He entered the front door and laid his hat and cane on the table in the hall. At the sound of the door closing, he heard a familiar quick step on the landing above and looked up to see his daughter peering over the railing at him.

"Papa! You're late. I was beginning to get worried."

Maury held out his arms and Justine flew down the stairs into them, hugging him with her usual exuberance.

"Gracious, child. You'll squeeze the life out of me. I'm only a few minutes late, after all."

Justine stepped back, with her arms still on her father's shoulders. "Yes, Papa, but you know how important every minute is to me now, with you going so far away in two days' time. I was certain you had stopped at the London coffeehouse and were involved in some political argument that would keep you through supper."

Maury tipped up his daughter's lovely chin and smiled into her eyes. How dear she was to him! "You know I wouldn't do that. At least not without sending you word. Come now. Is supper ready?"

"It's practically on the table. Moriah had Jody make you one of her wonderful custards. She knows how much you love them." Linking her arm through her father's, Justine led him into the small dining salon at the rear of the hall.

"All of you spoil me dreadfully. I don't know how I'm going to manage on ship's bread and ale for a year."

He pulled out the chair at one end of the oval table and Justine seated herself prettily, her striped taffeta overskirt billowing around her. She rang the tiny bell for Moriah while her father took the chair at the other end. The polished mahogany of the tabletop shimmered in the light of a candelabra in the center. On either side two small bowls of dried flowers gave off a scent of May roses and bayberry. While Moriah appeared to hand out the dishes, Justin admired his daughter's features, softened by the candle glow and the rosy light from the window behind him. She had pulled her hair back carelessly and tied it with a grosgrain ribbon, making her look even younger than her eighteen years. Tiny tendrils of chestnut curls draped her face. Her long lashes as she looked down at her plate lay heavy on her cheeks. He could see Margaret in the soft curves of her lips, the sweep of her brows, and the classic cheekbones. But the curiosity and challenge in her gleaming green eyes, and perhaps something of the strong line of her chin, were all his.

"You look very pretty tonight, my dear," he said as he heaped Brunswick Stew on his plate. "The major should be here to see it."

Justine looked up sharply. "The major? What major?"

"Why Major Carmichael, of course. I ran into him on Chestnut Street on my way home, and he specifically asked to be remembered to you."

23

Justine tossed her gleaming curls. "Oh, him. That silly man. I've had to bear his company for more than a week now, and although I've done my best to discourage him, he will persist in hanging around. I find him very tiresome."

"He's from a good family. And I'm told he is quite high in General Howe's estimation. You might do worse."

"Oh, Papa. He's boring and fascinated with his own opinions. I should certainly hope I could do better."

"Well, Jess, my girl, I confess I had rather hoped you'd find one of these dashing British officers to your liking. It would make me feel so much more confident to know you were taken care of while I'm gone."

"Now, Papa, we've been all through this before. I can take care of myself very well. And if I do find the need of friends, I have a whole city-full at my beck and call. I've known these people all my life. They'll watch over me, as if I needed it."

"But, if the Congress should move back in . . . If the British should leave . . ."

"We survived that once before, didn't we? I'll just grit my teeth, and make myself as uninteresting as possible. You mustn't worry about me. Besides, aren't you making this trip partly to help win the war and keep our country strong for the Crown? It's too important for you to be fretting about things at home. You must concentrate on your work."

At the mention of his trip, a pall seemed to settle over Justin once more. He picked listlessly at his plate, seeing again that dark face that had seemed to follow him around the city the past two days. It was unsettling. More and more he felt that some evil presence was closing around him, and that he must take steps to keep it at bay. But what? He might have confided in his daughter long

24

ago, but he felt that would not have been fair either to her or to the cause he served. Now he wondered if it would not be wise to at least bring in one other person. Someone who might be able to pick up the pieces, if anything happened to him.

Some of his unease conveyed itself to Justine, who was more than usually sensitive to her father's sudden depression. She laid it down to the fact that they were facing a long separation, and pushed her plate away, filled with her own private grief. Once the meal was over, she kissed her Papa on the top of his head, leaving him to a glass of port and a pipe, and took herself off upstairs to try on a new dress which had only been delivered that afternoon from the seamstress. It was her father's custom to work in his small study behind the parlor during the evening, until they sat together for a chocolate before bedtime.

The dress turned out to be just right, perfect for the Shippens' ball in two weeks' time. With Moriah's help she got out of it and while Moriah carefully put the gown in the press, Justine stood and analyzed her figure before the mirror. Tucking in her waist—already as small as she could make it with the aid of her stays—she turned this way and that, pleased with her profile. She had been blessed with full, rounded breasts, a slender waist, and rather solid hips—only to be hinted at beneath her several petticoats. She was wondering just how low she dared work her neckline, when she heard her father calling from the top of the stairs. Throwing a dressing gown over her undergarments, she stepped to the door.

"Might I have a word with you, Justine, just for a minute."

It was always an ominous sign when her father called her Justine. Jess pulled the sash on her robe and opened her door wider. "Of course, Papa. Do you want me to come to the study?"

"No, here in your room will be fine. Excuse us, Moriah."

The servant, full of curiosity, nevertheless hurried out, closing the door behind her. Maury pulled up a slim ladder-back chair, whle Justine perched on the edge of her bed. She did not at all like the worrisome look on her father's face.

"You know, my dear, that I must make this trip even though every inclination of my heart is against it."

"You've explained that to me, Papa."

"I know. But I will say it again, because I want you to understand and to forgive me for leaving you here alone in this city. I hope to bring back cargo for the Loyalist merchants in the colonies, which will insure their economic health and their loyalty to the Crown. That is my main reason for going."

"I understand, Papa, truly I do. And as for forgiveness, how could I not forgive you for trying to do everything you can for the cause we both believe in. I wish you would not talk of forgiveness."

"You're a good girl, Jess, and a great comfort to me. But there is one other thing." Justin reached inside his coat pocket and drew out a thick folded parchment sealed with a heavy daub of wax. "I want you to take this letter and put it in some safe place until I sail. Will you do that?"

Justine took the letter, wondering what there was about it that so distressed her father. "Of course, I will. But wouldn't it be safer in your desk downstairs."

"No. I think that would be too obvious. And, Jess, if anything should happen to me before the sailing . . ."

The color drained from her face. "Papa, what are you

talking about?"

"Don't be alarmed. I'm only thinking of the usual risks we face when we step into the streets. If by chance an accident should befall me in which I would be incapacitated, promise me you'll take this letter to British headquarters and give it to a Colonel Augustus Hughes. No one else. That is very important. Don't turn it over to an orderly or a sergeant or anyone else to give to Colonel Hughes. Promise me that you'll put it into his hand yourself."

"I don't understand, Papa. What is there about this letter that is so important? Why are you so concerned? You're not in any danger, are you?"

"No, no. I'm only trying to think of everything. Promise me you'll do what I ask, and then I can rest comfortably, having covered every contingency. Will you?"

Jess threw her arms around her father's neck and hugged him. "Of course I will, Papa. I promise. Please don't worry. You only make me more anxious."

"Thank you, my dear. I feel much better. Don't forget—Colonel Hughes' hand and no other."

"I'll remember, Papa. Are you ready for some chocolate now? I can be down in a minute to join you."

Maury was already at the door. "No, I think I'll forgo it this evening. I'm a little tired, and I still have some correspondence to face in my study. Why don't you just run down and say good night when you're ready for bed."

"I will, Papa. And don't worry about the letter. I'll find a safe place for it."

Maury nodded and gave her a forced smile. When the door closed behind him, Justine sat back on her bed and stared at the evil-looking thing in her hand. She felt certain that it was somehow connected to her father's worry and depression. There was something going on that she could not understand at all; something her father was not telling her. Yet she felt she could not press him to confide in her. Certainly he would, if he thought there was anything she should know. She must somehow put on a good face and get through the next two days. Surely once he was on his way, these blue devils would be lifted, for him if not for her. She laid the letter in her writing box, turned the key, and slipped it under her bed. When she caught her reflection in the mirror, she wondered what had happened to that smiling, light-hearted girl of only a few moments before.

"I'll simply have to make him talk to me about what's worrying him," she thought, as she untied her stays and slipped off the confining bodice. "Tomorrow morning I'll insist that he sit down and go over everything about this trip with me. I'll let him know how concerned I am, and how much it means to me that he trusts me."

Her resolution put some of her anxiety to rest, and she called Moriah back in to help her with her nightdress and brush out her long hair. Half an hour had passed contentedly and she was almost ready to go down and wish her father a good night, when she thought she heard the faint tinkling of shattered glass.

"What was that?"

Moriah's hands stayed over Jess's long locks, and they both turned toward the door. In an instant Justine had thrown it open and was standing in the hall looking down over the railing at the landing below. "Papa?" she cried anxiously, thinking even then that she was perhaps worrying needlessly.

A moan, so low she could barely hear it, was the only answer. "Papa!" Jess called and flew down the stairs to the closed door of her father's study. She knocked quickly and called again. Inside she could hear another faint moan followed by a loud crashing sound. "Moriah, this door is locked from the inside," Jess called frantically, shoving her shoulder against the unyielding wood. "Quick, get Toby to force it. Hurry!"

Moriah went running off through the kitchen to fetch the footman, while Justine, her anxiety growing, shoved repeatedly against the door. Before the two servants came hurrying back down the hall, she had managed to push it far enough that the lock gave and it broke open, careening her into the room. In an instant she saw what she had most dreaded—her father lying on the floor facing her, his eyes looking up, pleading as he clutched at his chest. Around him the contents of his desk were scattered haphazardly. A drawer, broken in pieces, lay cluttered among the shards of glass from the window.

Justine rushed to kneel beside her father. "Papa, are you hurt? Where? Oh, my God, Moriah get help. Hurry!"

Cradling her father's shoulders in her arms, she rocked back and forth, crooning. Weakly Maury lifted his hand, and Justine, following its direction, glanced at the window. Her blood froze. A face—a terrible, evil, dark face, glared back at her, and then was gone in an instant. She had only an impression of brown skin below a gray turban, the glint of a gold earring, slanted, angry eyes and a slash of a mouth. Then it was gone, leaving her cold and reeling with horror.

"Oh, Papa," she cried as she felt her father slipping away from her. She gripped him tighter, pressing his body to her. "Papa, we'll get help. Hold on. Please, for heaven's sake, hold on!"

He was trying to speak in a breathy, sighing kind of voice. She leaned closer to his lips and caught the word *letter*, then laid her cheek against his, her tears spilling

29

over them both. "Don't try to talk, Papa. Stay quiet until we can get help. Hold on. Please, hold on!"

Even as she spoke, she felt his body go slack. Horrified, she realized he was slipping from her grasp and there was nothing she could do to keep him. Clasping him tighter, she fought to keep his spirit there by physical force until the doctor could arrive. Then, she realized she was cradling her father's body; his spirit had broken free. Sobbing bitterly, Justine clutched Maury's body to her breast, rocking back and forth, making unintelligible sounds. She was not even aware when Moriah and Toby ran in, Doctor Singleton on their heels. The doctor had to force her fingers from her father's shoulders and pry her away in order to examine Maury. Moriah tried to hold and comfort the distraught girl, but Jess was beyond comforting. It was too sudden, too much of a shock. One moment all her life was as it should be—orderly, comfortable, loving. Then, in an instant, all was shattered. The father who had kissed her only half an hour before lay dead on the rug at her feet, his blood seeping in a spreading arc on the carpet.

Dr. Singleton carefully turned Maury's body over and laid it face down on the rug. Only then did Jess see the knife for the first time. It was buried up to the hilt in her father's back. Light glinted off the ornate black worked figures on the silver handle.

"The force of the blow suggests it was thrown from a distance," Singleton said with appalling objectivity. He pointed toward the broken window. "Probably from there."

His words were the last thing Jess heard before the darkness closed around her and she collapsed in Moriah's arms.

30

Two

By early morning a thick fog had rolled in to envelop the river. As the narrow longboat glided silently up the Schuykill, Rhys sat in the bow with his cloak pulled tightly around his shoulders, feeling as though he was traveling through a dreamlike region of the river Styx. He still could not believe he was actually responding to Greydon's offer, against every dictum of common sense and caution. He yanked his hat down close over his eyes, still groggy from lack of sleep he could not close off the nagging voice at the back of his mind that warned against becoming involved all over again. Yet there had been an urgency in Greydon's pleading he simply could not refuse. No harm in listening, he told himself for the tenth time. It did not mean he was committing himself to anything he didn't really want to do.

The boat veered lazily toward a shore hazy with mist. Rhys could hear footsteps on the dry leaves before he actually made out the shrouded form pacing the bank. Once Greydon spotted the boat, he eagerly waded out to help pull it into shore.

"I knew you'd come," Alex said in a quiet voice as he extended his hand to help Rhys out of the wobbling boat.

"Then you knew more than I did."

"I've got two horses tethered over in the woods. Ask your men to wait. We won't be long."

After a word to the boatmen, Rhys and his friend were soon astride their mounts, cantering along a deserted road that was shrouded in the early mist of morning. They rode less than half an hour before reining in at a dingy tavern which stood forlornly at a crossroad that cut through the thick surrounding woods and pastureland. Three soldiers waiting beside their tethered horses looked up curiously at them as they walked up onto the porch. Rhys kept his surprise to himself as Alex led him through a grubby taproom occupied by one or two men in farmers' smocks, up a low flight of stairs, and down a dark hall to a private room at the rear of the building. An open door revealed a small room with a ceiling so low Rhys's hat almost swept it as he entered. Across the room a welcoming fire burned in a hearth. Before it stood a small round table covered with pewter dishes where three men rose as one as Rhys and Alex walked in. All three looked toward the new arrivals with guarded, expectant faces.

Rhys swept off his hat as Alex made the introductions. He had recognized Gen. Washington right away, not so much because of the uniform and gold lace, as from having heard so much of his extreme height and sharp, granitelike features. James Madison was a surprise. Rhys had not expected such a well-known power in the Continental Congress to be quite so short and stocky. Of the third man, Robert Morris, he knew nothing except that he was rumored to be the wealthiest merchant in the Colonies.

"Thank you for coming, Capt. Llewellyn," Madison

said, shaking Rhys's hand warmly. "Won't you share some breakfast with us? You've come a long way this morning."

Accepting the offer, Rhys drew up a chair. He was surprised when Alexander Greydon politely excused himself and left the room, carefully closing the door behind him. He was hungry and enjoyed the meal, quiet as it was. Rhys sensed the whole time that he was being scrutinized, even as the three men made polite small talk about the state of the war and the government. There was an undercurrent of guarded concern in their conversation, as though they did not really trust him. He recognized their obvious attempts to draw him out and deliberately gave them a fairly thorough account of the prizes he had captured in the two years since the Americans had lost New York.

"You've done very well," Gen. Washington commented, and Rhys somehow sensed this was high praise coming from one usually so taciturn. Of the three men at the table, the general had been the quietest, though Rhys sensed he had been watching and listening intently to everything that was said. "How many ships have you lost?"

"Two, sir. One in battle and one in a storm that unfortunately fell upon us while we were about to capture the HMS *Pearl*. It was some consolation that the *Pearl* went down to the bottom along with my ship."

Morris pushed his plate away and leaned forward on the table, his face suddenly grave. "You appear to be a superlative seaman, Captain. And you are undoubtedly a man who has enthusiastically served your country. We have Capt. Greydon's assurance that you are devoted heart and soul to independence for these Colonies."

"That is true," Rhys answered simply. He felt certain

33

now that they wanted to trust him, though they still felt some reservations.

Madison spoke up. "Have we your word, sir, that anything said in this room will remain forever between ourselves? It is vital that even if you do not wish to accept our proposal, you never repeat what you are about to hear to anyone. Vital to our cause and our country."

"You have my word as a gentleman," Rhys answered. The three men gave each other guarded glances. It was a label they understood and would never question. Abruptly Morris stood, walking to the mantel over the fireplace. He made as if to take a spill for his pipe, then changed his mind and turned, thrusting his hands deep into the pockets of his expensive coat. Rhys wondered that a man of his obvious power and wealth should appear so nervous. His own curiosity was so piqued by now that he could not have walked out of the room, even had they dismissed him.

"Capt. Llewellyn," Morris began, then abruptly stopped and coughed, throwing a wary glance at the general across the table.

"You might as well trust him, Robert," Washington said quietly. "We've really no other choice."

That seemed to settle it. Morris pulled out his chair and sat down facing Rhys, his voice very quiet.

"Capt. Llewellyn, as you know we are in desperate straits at the moment in our war for independence. We are facing a crisis of great magnitude. Our noble cause is close to becoming lost for lack of funds to support it. What the British army cannot achieve in victory on the field is now apt to be won in the counting houses of the country. England has strangled our trade, interrupted the free flow of commerce between the states, indeed has fostered deep divisions between our own people. Some of our best citizens refuse to support us, looking more to their purse than their conscience."

"I've heard this, sir," Rhys answered cautiously. "I've also heard that certain men are making their fortunes from this rebellion. Supplies are ordered and rot by the wayside. Payments are deferred to those eager to line their pockets. I assure you, I've seen my own share of prize monies diverted to others who did nothing whatsoever to win it."

Out of the corner of his eye, he saw Gen. Washington's jaw tighten. The usually dispassionate eyes which the general turned on Rhys flashed with a sudden terrible anger. The general's temper was legendary, and Rhys smiled at himself for almost being taken aback by it. Slow to be aroused, his anger was known to reach some truly astounding heights when given full vent.

"That is unfair, sir," Washington answered in a tightly clipped voice. "There are such men and they do create scandalous wastes. But I assure you, the men in my army who bear the full brunt of this war often walk through the snow with no shoes, shiver from lack of warm coats, starve from poor food or none at all. As for pay, they've received so little as to create near-mutiny among the ranks."

Rhys spoke hurriedly. "I meant no disrespect to you or your men. I know you have all worked heroically to bring independence. I only wanted to put things in perspective."

"Naturally there is corruption," Morris said evenly. "There always is in time of war, men being the fallen beings they are. But most of us have given as deeply as we can to support our cause, and still it is not enough."

Morris stopped, coughing nervously. Rhys turned to him, waiting, sensing that Washington was still making an effort to control his anger.

"The truth is, Captain," Morris went on, "that we need funds desperately. I have some contacts along the trading routes which I used frequently before the war. I have accordingly arranged that a great sum of gold shall be sent to us as a loan from Prince Tai of the Chinese province of Tsinghai. Naturally, he is not doing this out of charity. He dislikes the British and their monopoly on trade with the West, and he believes that our independence will open up a lucrative field for him."

Madison leaned toward Rhys eagerly, enthusiastic now that Morris had broached the subject. "The problem, you see, is how to obtain the money. We need a reliable man to go for it and bring it safely back. Someone we can trust implicitly. Someone we can depend on utterly."

"That is why we thought of you," Morris added. "You have a reputation for daring and initiative."

"And you know the sea-trading routes."

"This trip is likely to involve some overland traveling as well. However, with your extensive experience on the oceans of the world, you must be familiar with most foreign ports."

Rhys looked from one man to the other.

"Overland? Where?"

"We're not very sure at this point. All we know is that you are to contact an Arab named Yarmid Ali on the Street of the Tailors in Baghdad."

"But that's not a port city."

"No, but it is not far from one. Bayrut, I believe. Surely you've been there."

Rhys looked from Madison's eagerly enthusiastic face to Morris's deadly serious one. He sat back in his chair, not believing the naïveté of these men, so accomplished in their own fields. "I've been to Bayrut. A dirty, smelly, rat's nest of a port. The best thing about it is the sense of relief one feels at having reached it without being captured by Algerian pirates."

Morris ignored Rhys's outburst. "This Arab," he went blithely on, "will advise you how to continue on from Baghdad. I believe Prince Tai's province is not too far from the city—or so I'm told."

Rhys pushed back his chair and stalked around the table to the window, where the first strong light of morning was dappling the curtains. "Gentlemen, the best way to China is by sea. It would be folly to go overland. Why it must be—at least a thousand miles." With a start he realized that he wasn't so certain himself just what lay between Baghdad and the western reaches of China. But it had to be a pretty fair distance.

"Ordinarily yes," Morris said. "And perhaps that is what this Yarmid Ali will suggest. But he is our only contact, and we will have to follow his suggestions."

"Can this Yarmid Ali be trusted?"

"We have been assured that he is utterly reliable. Naturally, there was a price involved."

Madison broke in, his face wreathed with smiles, as though he already counted on Rhys's acceptance. "You can see why secrecy is so important, Captain. And why we need someone upon whom we can completely depend."

Rhys drummed his fingers on the windowsill. "I don't know, gentlemen. Of course, I am anxious to do what I can for my country. But this? You're talking about a very long, difficult voyage involving certain perils. If the British should learn what I'm really after . . ."

"How can they learn of it if none of us tells them?

37

Think, Captain, what this money will mean to us. Our victory would be assured. We could go on fighting, resisting tyranny for twenty years, if need be, eventually wearing England down."

"Perhaps the captain would like to know if there is anything in our proposal for him," Gen. Washington said with a touch of irony.

Rhys smiled and returned to the table. "As a matter of fact, I would. I'm not accustomed to risking my neck without some promise of a reward."

Madison's face fell. Robert Morris, his lips tight, leaned forward to rest his elbows on the table. This was the kind of talk he understood well, even though he had hoped that the captain's idealism would not be quite so pragmatic.

"You'll have a tenth of the whole," he said with reluctance. "It will divert funds that might be better used, but if it will encourage you to help us, it will be worth it."

"Twenty," Rhys answered.

"Sir!" Madison reeled back. "That is unconscionable."

Morris smiled at his colleague. "It is simply business, James. Simply business. Twelve, Captain."

Rhys studied the three men. Though he didn't for a moment doubt the truth of Gen. Washington's description of his suffering army, yet it was obvious that these three men were not starving or going coatless. And yet, to be fair, he told himself, it was these three who were sure to be strung up to the nearest tree if this war was lost. And he had always been unable to resist a good challenge.

"All right, gentlemen," he said, leaning back in his chair. "It goes against my better judgment, but I'll bring you back your treasure."

A thin, satisfied smile touched Washington's taut lips. "For fifteen percent and nothing less," Rhys added.

Justine stared at the letter in her hand, turning it over and over, as though it was some peculiar object she had never seen before. How strange it was that she had forgotten it until now. All morning she had sat in her bedroom, staring with unseeing eyes at the flowered carpet, trying to absorb the reality of her father's death. The doorbell below jangled incessantly with well-meaning friends coming and going, paying their hushed, polite respects, and still she refused to move, to see any of them, to try to accept their sympathy or explain what had occurred.

"It ain't right," Moriah sputtered each time she climbed the stairs to urge Jess below. "The Masta, he ought to have his fambly watch with him. Yo' oughten to be there, seein' peoples when they comes. It just ain't right."

After a while Justine didn't even bother to answer. She sat with numbed mind, forcing thought away, trying not to wonder where Justin Maury would be buried, how she would manage alone in this house, how she would live. She would allow none of those questions to touch her conscious mind. Then at last Moriah came up and told Jess that her father would be buried the next evening. The city of Philadelphia had learned to quickly dispose of its dead after the last fierce epidemic of yellow fever. Something of all this broke through to Justine, and after Moriah went away, she suddenly remembered the letter.

Rising stiffly from her chair she walked to her writing box and lifted out the letter, turning it over in her hand. What had her father told her? This letter was important.

It was the last thing they had discussed together. He wanted her to do something with it . . . if anything happened to him!

Yes, that was what he had said . . . if anything happened to him! Jess clutched at the bodice of her dress, reeling from the sudden pain in her chest. She carried the letter back to her chair and pressed it against her breast. She wouldn't cry. No time yet for tears. Something had to be done. Something important.

Headquarters. British headquarters. The letter was to be given to a Colonel Hughes. Yes, that was it. Hughes. And to no one else. "You must put it in Col. Hughes's own hand," her father had said.

Very well then. Here was something she could do. Something important that would help her father. Something he himself had asked her to carry out in the event he . . .

She reached for her bonnet behind the door and was tieing it under her chin when she looked down to see that she was still wearing her bloodstained nightdress from the evening before. Something about that disturbed her. She couldn't go out on the streets to Army headquarters wearing a dress stained with her father's blood. She would have to change. It was only right to do so. Very methodically she set about removing her night robe and exchanging it for a morning dress from the press. Though her actions were deliberate and unhurried, it never seemed in the least strange to her that she was wearing a plaid callimanco underskirt with a pale-flowered chintz dress. Or that her chip bonnet was the one she usually wore to the dry goods stores on Second Street. She did remember to run a brush through her hair, but completely ignored the half-hour of fussing that was normally required for going out in public.

40

She went downstairs, determined to slip out of the house without seeing anyone. She could hear a low murmur of voices in the back parlor, and dimly she knew that she would be dragged back to take charge once the servants knew she had come downstairs. With a cunning that was almost innate, she crept down the hall, slipped through the front door, and started down Fourth Street to British headquarters, her mind fixed on one thing and one thing only—to dispose of the letter as her father had asked her to do.

The walkways were crowded with people, a few of whom recognized Justine. She looked past them, her eyes fixed on some unseen object ahead, unresponsive to their greetings. They let her pass, conscious of the grief she must be feeling, and a little appalled by the change in her usually vibrant, careful appearance.

A short walk soon brought her outside the imposing entrance of the elegant house the British had taken over for their senior officers. She walked up the stairs and turned the gleaming brass handle on the wide front door. A hallway swept through the house to long French doors at the other end, where a sunlight-dappled garden was just visible through the lace curtains. A young man in a silver brigadier wig and neatly pressed uniform rose from a small mahogany table in the hall and stepped in front of her.

"May I help you, Miss?" he said, blocking Justine's way and preventing her from entering the room beyond. She caught a quick glimpse of a fine drawing room now crammed with escritoirs and tables, around which other uniformed young men were busily working.

Jess looked up at him with eyes almost glassy. The young subaltern stepped back briefly, wondering if this lovely young woman was of a right mind. "Can I be of service?" he said again, gently taking her arm and leading her away from the drawing room door. "Was there someone you wanted to see?"

"Yes, that's it," Jess said quickly. Suddenly her emerald eyes flashed with purpose and reason. Digging into her reticule she grasped the letter without actually taking it out. "I need to see Col. Hughes," she said excitedly. "Col. Augustus Hughes. It's very important."

"Col. Hughes? Why, I don't believe he is in at the moment. Is there something I can do for you? Would you like to leave a message for him?"

Jess laid a hand on the man's arm, digging her fingers into his sleeve. "No, no. I must see the colonel himself. How long will he be?"

"Why, I'm not at all certain, Miss."

She looked around with a growing sense of panic. There were several chairs standing along the wall and she fixed her gaze on one of them.

"Then I must wait. Yes, that's what I'll do. I'll wait until he gets back." Deliberately she tightened the strings on her reticule and headed for one of the chairs where she sat primly down.

The young man coughed uncomfortably. "But, really, Miss, it might well be some time. Don't you think it would be better if you left your card? I'll make certain that he receives it."

"No, no," Jess said, folding her hands in her lap. Her father had been very specific about that. She must hand over the letter to Col. Hughes and to no one else. It was important that she do just what he had told her. More important than anything else. "I'll wait," she said and pursed her lips together stubbornly. The young man studied her a moment, then with a shake of his head disappeared into the drawing room, closing the double doors behind him. A few moments later he reappeared, asking Justine to accompany him through the larger room into a tiny alcove, where an older officer in a uniform elaborate with lace sat behind a table piled with papers. The officer rose as Justine entered and offered her a chair while the young subaltern silently left them together.

"Are you Col. Hughes?" Jess asked, thinking he must have returned by way of a back door.

"No, Madam. I am Major Fitzmorton. I understood you felt some necessity to speak with the Colonel. He is not here at the moment, but I assure you I have the authority to handle any business you might have with him."

Her face crumpled. Another delay! Why wouldn't these men let her near the one person she needed to see? "No, no," she said, twisting the strings of her reticule. "I must speak with Col. Hughes and no one else. It's very important, you see."

"Really, ma'am. You can trust me as you would the colonel himself. I assure you . . ."

"No!" Justine cried. At her obvious anger the officer, taken aback, walked back to his seat at the desk. He was beginning to wonder at this young lady's deep distress. Obviously an affair of the heart, although he would have thought that the dour Col. Augustus Hughes was the last man to upset so lovely a creature. "I'm really very sorry, but you see there would be no point in waiting for Col. Hughes. He is in New York Town at the moment, and we do not know when he will return. It may be tomorrow, it may be next week. It may even be next month. So, you see, you really ought to tell me anything you would have told him."

Justine sat back, staring at the man. "Next week . . ."

43

she whispered, trying to assimilate this information. She had never expected that the colonel would not be here to receive the letter. What should she do?

The officer smiled at her, trying to appear sympathetic without quite knowing how to handle her. "Of course, you might stop in tomorrow. Perhaps we shall know by then exactly when he will be returning. If you would like to leave your name . . ."

"NO!" Justine cried, jumping to her feet. She would not leave her father's letter in this officer's hands. She would not give it to anyone other than Col. Hughes. Her father had been adamant. She would just have to wait. "I'll come back tomorrow," she said, turning to the door and speaking so low the officer could barely make out her words. He went after her, grasping her arm. "Are you certain I can not help you?"

She looked blankly up at him and shook her head. He watched her wend her way through the crowded drawing room, ignoring the admiring glances of the men, intent only on reaching the front door. An affair of the heart, the officer thought again. It had to be. Certainly there was nothing he could do to help that. He'd never liked Hughes much anyway.

Back in her room Justine sat again in the chair near the window still wearing her bonnet and light cloak. The letter was in her hand, burning like a glowing coal. She stared at it in fascination, consumed with the thought that it was all that was tangibly left of her beloved father. Then, very quickly, she tore at the seal and broke it open.

The words were dim in the light, so she carried it to the window, holding it up to the afternoon sunshine, scanning the pages. She took several minutes to decipher its meaning, then, still confused, she went back to her chair to finger it, her mind racing.

So the trip had not been planned for trade after all. There was enough information given in the letter to inform her that her father was actually leaving on a mission of some significance to the king's government. "Proceed to Baghdad," it read. Baghdad! Where on earth was that? "There to contact one Yarmid Ali on the Street of the Tailors." Yarmid Ali. It sounded like an Arab name. Why would her father have anything to do with an infidel? "Be appraised of where to go further from there." And the last intriguing sentence: "At all costs this money must not fall into Rebel hands."

It appeared to be some plot to prevent the rebels from gaining the means to carry on their rebellion. And her father had been assigned this worthy task, this fine, noble task that would keep his country from falling into the hands of a gang of treasonous, so-called Patriots. Her heart was near to bursting with pride when she thought of the mission her father had taken on with such secrecy. And she might never have known if he had not been . . . had not been . . .

She clutched at her heart. He was dead, and now, at last, she understood why. Someone had wanted to prevent him from carrying out this crucial work. Someone who was now, no doubt, rubbing his hands with glee, thinking he had stopped Justin Maury from fulfilling his mission.

Her lips pursed and her emerald eyes took on that stubborn darkness that Moriah had long ago learned to dread. They would not win, Justine thought. They would not prevent her father from carrying out the task for which he had so nobly died. She herself, the true daughter of his spirit, would see that his work was accomplished. She would complete his mission!

Some small voice in the back of her mind whispered

45

that this was an insane idea—more insane than any little caprice she had ever committed to vex her father or the servants. Think again, Justine, it cried. You know nothing of the world outside Philadelphia. You have no credentials, no knowledge, no backing. You don't even have a chaperone. And, you are a woman. For a woman to set out on such a crazy adventure was unheard of. Calm down. Be rational. Take a second hard look . . .

Justine's eyes darted to the letter still in her hand, scanning it. The name on the letter of embarcation was clearly printed, JUSTIN MAURY. All she had to do was add an *E* to Justin, and who would ever know the difference? This was providence showing its hand. God must have meant it to be this easy. As for those other considerations . . .

With renewed purpose she ran to the press and began sorting her clothes. There was much to be done. She would have to speak to Brewster Chapman, her father's solicitor, and give him her power of attorney to handle the house and the servants while she was gone. She would go there directly, before the—the burial service. Yes, and she must put in an appearance downstairs. Let everyone think she was going about the normal business of grieving. Don't mention anything to Moriah—she would be sure to wake the dead with her screaming.

Her mind raced with a new clarity, examining each devious means she might use to get her way, without alerting anyone who could try to stop her. It would be best to appear at the *Boeadecia* early in the morning, just before sailing time. Slipping out of the house would not be difficult. She would tell Moriah that she was worn out with grieving and to let her sleep. Of course, she wouldn't be able to take much with her, but that was all right. The important thing was the trip itself. What did it matter

46

how she looked.

Money! What could she do for money, for it was absolutely necessary to have some for such a long journey. But then Justin had been planning to leave himself tomorrow morning. There must be money and letters of draft on his bank in his desk. She would have to search for them, but she felt certain they were there somewhere. That is, if the assassin had not taken them!

Her heart gave a lurch as the terrible scene from her father's study came sweeping back. But she steadied herself with a new purpose. Surely the murderer hadn't time to search her father's desk. Somehow she felt certain that all the preparations Justin had made for his trip were still there. It was part of the whole plan. She was meant to go. She was meant to carry on her father's work. It was her destiny.

Carefully she selected the dresses she wanted from the jumble around her and put everything back, laying the ones she would take with her carefully on top. Then, very deliberately, she straightened her dress, splashed some rose water on her face, smoothed back her hair, and went downstairs to face the sympathy of her friends.

The first gray shafts of dawn were gilding the roofs of the houses clustered along Fourth Street, as Justine slipped through her front door, closing it silently behind her. For a moment her gloved hand lingered on the brass handle and a sadness clutched her, making her eyes smart with unshed tears. The pang of sudden grief that stabbed at her chest was worse than anything she had suffered last evening, standing beside the family plot in Christ-church Cemetery. Then she had been able to steady herself with her resolute purpose and new determina-

47

tion. But now, she was saying farewell not only to her father but to her home, and all the world she had ever known. And who knew when she might return to them again.

Yanking her hand away she pulled the hood of her brown camlet cloak over her head, hiding her face. There was no time for such thoughts now. There was no time for anything except hurrying down to the wharf and getting herself aboard the *Boeadecia*. Sentiment could not be allowed to get in the way of her mission.

Carrying her cloth portmanteau, she moved along the street, half-running, hoping she might come across a farmer in a wagon who would give her a ride part of the way. But there were few people about. Now and then a soldier would appear out of the damp mists like a ghost wandering the earth, to stare at her curiously as she passed. One of them offered to help her, but her single-minded sense of purpose and the way her cloak hid her face discouraged him. The fog was a welcome presence, hiding her within its elusive fingers, closing her off from a curious, interfering world.

The wharfs were a brisk contrast to the streets, a busy jumble of travelers, boxes, crates, sailors, and first mates checking manifests. Justine moved silently among them, searching for the lighter that would convey passengers out to the *Boeadecia*. She found it near the end of Crooked Billet Alley, and blessedly there were few people clustered around its scrawled sign. Drawing herself up to appear more sure of herself than she actually felt, she took out that page from her father's letter that was her admittance on board.

An officer of the ship, wearing a ruffled shirt beneath a black leather stock and a worn blue coat, examined the letter. He looked up at her, then back at the page, his face a study in confusion.

"Justine Maury?" he said. "We weren't expecting a woman."

"I don't know why not," Justine answered in her haughtiest voice. "Women do travel, you know."

"But . . ." The officer quailed a little before her flashing eyes. After all, it wasn't his business to say who sailed with them and who didn't. "I don't think it was ever made explicit . . ." he started, but Justine snatched the letter from his hand and began folding it to return it to her reticule.

"You must accept people who have paid for passage, mustn't you? Mine is paid in full, I trust."

"Well, yes. But . . ."

"Then there is nothing more to be said. Kindly have one of your seamen carry my box and direct me to the lighter."

The mate looked around, peering through the haze that still hung heavy over the water. "And your maid, Miss?"

"She'll be arriving shortly," Justine said quickly. "I'll go on ahead."

Shaking his head, the mate made a decision to let the captain handle this. "The lighter's over there, Miss, by the pier. Be careful on the ladder. It's a little wobbly from the outgoing tide."

"You needn't worry, my man," Justine said with great aplomb. "I'm never seasick." That was actually true, but only because she had never in her life been on the sea to become sick. However, he needn't know that, she thought as she swept toward the pier, followed by a wizened little sailor with a greasy pigtail, clutching her portmanteau to his chest as though it were an albatross. Another sailor standing by the pier helped her down the

49

ladder and into the boat where Jess pulled her skirts around her and yanked her hood farther down over her face. The longboat wobbled in the water with a sickening series of lurches, and she clutched at the seat to steady herself as she felt her stomach turn over. The gray water around her slapped at the boat's side, and Jess caught the floating miasma of assorted garbage thrown there from the wharf. Overhead a seagull glided effortlessly, squawking at its mates. All the sense of adventure she had hoped to feel suddenly congealed into pure fright, but she quickly steadied herself against it.

This was not an adventure—it was a mission. And she was going to see it through, just as Justin Maury would have done. She could do it, she was certain she could. She had courage, she was intelligent, she was determined.

But, oh, dear Lord, she thought, please don't let me be sick even before I reach the ship!

Rhys anxiously paced the quarterdeck of his ship, scanning the heavy mist for the last trip of the lighter. The tide was beginning to move and he wanted to sail with it. Damn, it always seemed that they cast off later than he intended. As usual, it was the passengers who held them up. Although there were not many on this trip, they still managed to interfere with the smooth operation of his vessel.

It was strange to be starting on a trading voyage instead of one where he would be seeking out enemy ships and prizes. There were no passengers on those trips. Everything was focused on order, efficiency, and speed. They were a fighting unit, coordinated to search and destroy and take prisoners. He looked out over the decks of this new ship, the wide midsection, the sweeping

50

clutter of the poop. A fat, wallowing housewife of a ship he had beneath him on this voyage! Broad of beam, ungainly and cumbersome, who would chug through the water like an old winded sow. A far cry, this, from the sleek man-of-war he had grown accustomed to, slicing like a spear through the waves. Even the guns they carried on the *Boeadecia* were antiques. He would miss the long row of twenty pounders, flanking port and starboard. He only hoped this ship would not meet up with any trouble on the high seas.

Yes, it was like going back in time to the days before the war to be commanding a merchant ship again. And if they did not get underway soon, he might as well stay in Philadelphia.

He walked to the taffrail and began shouting abusive orders to the men below who were tying the longboat to the ship's ladder. Surely this must be nearly the last of the passengers. His first mate was still on the quay, to be ferried on the last trip of the lighter and then, with luck, they might cast off.

Absently he watched the shrouded figures clambering aboard deck from the ladder. He had turned away to scan the harbor in frustration when his gaze was pulled back to one of the passengers, who had just been helped onto the deck.

A woman! It couldn't be. He walked to the railing and peered down. It most certainly was a woman, swathed in a gray cloak with the hood over her face and her skirts whipping around her as she reached out to steady herself with one white hand on the mast. He was about to say something to the sailor who had brought the lighter out when an explanation rang clear in his mind. Of course, she had come out with one of the passengers to say good-bye. It was unusual, but it did happen occasionally. He

51

had seen it a few times himself when he was a mate on a merchant ship. He started to turn away, but without knowing why, stopped and watched her. She did not claim the arm of one of the other passengers as he would expect, but instead walked to the rail and looked back toward shore. The wind, giving one of its small frantic twists, caught at her hood and pulled it away from her face, then snatched at her cloak and sent one end cascading over her shoulder, revealing the figure beneath. Rhys stared transfixed at the beautiful profile, the chin tipped resolutely upward, the long graceful neck, the streaming chestnut-colored hair falling down her back, the ripe fullness of her breasts cunningly revealed by the press of her thin frock. Something in him stirred. He tried to pull his eyes away, back to the business of his ship, but was unable to. For a brief moment he was locked, a prisoner of the beauty incarnate before his very eyes. The girl's white hand resting on the railing moved to her throat, and for a moment he felt the poignancy in her gesture. Then, abruptly, she turned away, yanking her cloak over her face and around her body, and Rhys was freed.

Angrily he stalked away from the railing. What nonsense, to be so captivated by a brief glimpse of girlish beauty. It probably came from the knowledge that he was facing a long, hard lonely trip and a mission he still was not sure he should have undertaken. He must concentrate on the business at hand.

Leaning over the railing, he shouted at the seaman in the longboat to get back to the quay and bring out the first mate. "And take all these shore people with you," he added, none too gently. "We want to leave on this tide!"

And carry that vision of a girl back to shore, he thought angrily. Leave me to sail my ship!

Three

A heavy rain the night before had turned the dusty streets of Philadelphia to a morass of mud that clutched possessively at the wheels of Col. Hughes's military carriage. It was bad enough along the outskirts. Once the driver had turned down Chestnut Street and headed toward the busiest section of the town, their slow progress was made even more halting by a jumble of pedestrians and assorted vehicles, all similarly bound.

Inside the cab Hughes cursed, sank farther into his military cloak, and scowled at the leather window curtain. When had anything ever been easy in this accursed city, he wondered. Or, for that matter, in this accursed country! Ever since he stepped on to Coenties Slip in New York, it was as though fate itself conspired to thwart his every endeavor. Even the weather was barbaric. So hot in summer that it might as well be the outer reaches of hell, in winter frozen and miserable. Fate and the weather!

And yet Col. Hughes did not really believe in fate. It was man himself who made things happen, or failed to make them happen. He had long ago concluded that because most people were fools and cleverness was rare, one could usually turn matters to one's advantage.

A clever man could even conspire against the elements to get his way in the end. Unfortunately, that fool driver, Appleton, was not clever. Not only was he trying to fight the traffic and the mud, but he had also neglected to remember that today was market day and thus the streets were twice as busy.

The carriage ground to a complete halt and Hughes leaned forward to yank down the window, poke his head out, and peer through his glass at the congested swarm around him. A farmer in a round felt hat and coarse linsey-wolsey smock sat on a buckboard of a dilapidated wagon next to the carriage staring down in boredom at the colonel. Behind him a sleek chaise was turned halfway across the road by the press of mounted men and drays. Hughes banged his ivory-tipped cane on the side of the cab and yelled at his driver, a private of the Fourth Foot, who was struggling to control the colonel's nervous grays.

"Get this thing moving, Appleton!" Hughes ordered. "What's the matter with you! What's wrong up there?"

"I'm sorry, sir," Appleton called over the noise of the winnowing horses and cursing drivers. "It's a parcel of sheep being driven to market along Sixth. They've completely blocked the road. We'll move as soon as we can."

"Bah!" Hughes slammed his cane against the side of the cab once more for good measure and slumped back in his seat. Sheep! Wouldn't you know. It was a country of sheep! Stupid animals blindly following a leader over a cliff. The carriage gave a sudden lurch and pulled ahead, away from the wagon that had been blocking Hughes's view. Through the clutter of mounted riders and smaller drays he saw that the walkways of the street were as jammed as the road itself. Men in knee breeches and long coats, many of them shabby and worn, jostled with Quakers in severe black suits and round hats. Women with mobcaps under their straw hats, their ample skirts bobbing as they walked, shifted the wide baskets under their arms and called comments to acquaintances. Children darted among them, some dressed in the neat clothes of the better class, others, urchins in dirty smocks and torn stockings. As always, the ever-present scrawny dogs and rooting pigs scavenged for scraps in the gutters.

Disgusted, Hughes yanked up the curtain and sat back enveloped in the close solitude of the carriage. Benighted people in a benighted country. The Crown should have handled this problem long ago with the severity and force that would have prevented having to send so many men to these inhospitable shores. A firm hand would have solved the problem of independence before it had ever got off the ground. Let every member of the Continental Congress be taken out and hanged, then see how popular rebellion would be.

The noise outside the carriage lessened slightly as the driver turned off Chestnut onto one of the less crowded side streets. It would take longer, but at least they were moving, Hughes thought with satisfaction. There was much to do at headquarters, much that he had left unfinished when he made this unexpected trip to New York. His thoughts lingered for a moment on the city to the North. Hughes's thoughts never rambled—so disorderly a process was distasteful to one so meticulous and methodical. Disorderly, however, was a good word for

New York City. If anything, it was worse than Philadelphia. At least this Pennsylvania town had not yet cut down all the trees to use for firewood. There was a shortage of everything in New York, everything except people. More refugees with nothing to their name, less food, less housing. Having one fourth of the city burned before it was occupied only aggravated the situation. Even his own colleague, General Clinton, ran his army more sloppily and with less control than Howe's here in Philadelphia. He would not have thought such a thing was possible before his visit.

Musing as he was, it was with some surprise that he realized they had at last drawn up before British headquarters. Hughes pulled his cloak around him and waited for Appleton to jump down and open the door. With a last-minute touch to straighten his fine silver brigadier wig, the colonel sat his hat on his head and stepped from the carriage, throwing orders at his driver about the care of his valuable grays.

It seemed to the colonel that there was a slightly increased level of activity at headquarters this morning. Nothing indicating a single-minded devotion to duty, of course, that would be too much to expect! Just a slightly higher level of noise, a few more scarlet-coated aides moving around the halls, tables whose polished mahogany tops were more deeply covered with ledgers and papers, secretaries bent over their quills with ink-stained fingers flying. It gave Hughes some satisfaction to see. At the same time he hoped that perhaps some of this efficiency derived from seeing him stride through the door.

He had a room at the back of the second floor that was for his exclusive use and he went straight there, pausing only long enough to tell his aide, a major from Sussex whose name he could never remember, to set up an appointment for him with General Howe later in the day. Then, setting aside his hat and cloak, he sat down at the long polished oak table that was his desk and tackled his correspondence.

He was still sorting through the pile of letters that had arrived on two packets while he was gone, when he was interrupted by light knocking at the door. Without waiting for response, it opened and one of the young officers from the floor below stepped in. Hughes recognized Major Armstrong, a Light Infantry staff officer and one of the few men at headquarters whom he respected. Though not exactly a friend—for Hughes had very few acquaintances who could actually be called friends—the two officers got along well enough. The colonel found it expedient to have one or two people at headquarters who would speak to him with some confidentiality, for it helped to keep him abreast of what was going on under the surface.

"I heard you were back," Armstrong said. "Actually I should have known from the way everyone was jumping to business down there when you came in. Not interrupting, am I?"

"Yes, but come in anyway. You can fill me in on what's been happening while I was in New York."

Armstrong pulled up a chair, but looked to Hughes for permission before sitting on it. "And how was the city? I hope you had some oysters at the Queen's Head. That would at least have made the trip worthwhile."

"Oh, it was worthwhile, though I didn't take time for entertainments. New York is a depressing place. Worse than Philadelphia for scruffy loyalists, crowded prisons,

57

and rebel spies. I was glad to leave. What's been happening here?"

"We've had our usual attempts to make the winter bearable. Soirees, balls, theatricals. The pretty daughters of the sympathetic Americans have done a lot to keep the officers occupied."

"They may as well, since it appears there hasn't been any fighting to speak of. I don't suppose it occurred to anyone higher up that that is the reason we are here."

"If you mean the general, no. He has been enjoying himself as much as his junior officers."

"In the arms of Mrs. Loring, no doubt."

Armstrong looked around as though he thought someone might be listening. "Who else? But I tell you," he added, lowering his voice, "there is rumor, as of yet completely unfounded but very rampant, nontheless. We think the general is going to be recalled."

Hughes managed a weak attempt at surprise, though he had known for two weeks that Gen. Howe had indeed asked to be recalled to England. He also knew that Gen. Clinton was going to replace Howe as Supreme Commander of His Majesty's Forces in America. The prospect was not encouraging. He was quite aware that Armstrong suspected he knew all about the recall and had probably come up to his office to wheedle information from him. Naturally the major was going to be disappointed.

"What do you think, Colonel?" Armstrong ventured. "Will we stay in Philadelphia another winter or two? Can we hold both cities? The bets are on consolidating our army here and making a big push south come spring. But I wonder."

"You'll have to ask Gen. Howe," Hughes said cryptically. "And while you're at it, you might ask him for me why we've sat here most of the winter and allowed a rebel army that's smaller, poorer-fed, poorer-clad, and poorer-armed to sit unmolested a few leagues away. I'd like to know his answer. But enough of speculation. What do you have for me?"

Armstrong, recognizing that the colonel had had enough of this unaccustomed small talk, began leafing through his papers. It took them half an hour to go through every one, with the major briefly summarizing each and the colonel issuing a reply or setting one or two aside for more thorough examination. Finally Armstrong rearranged them in a neat pile and rose to leave. He was halfway out the door when he stopped.

"Oh, by the way. There was one strange event while you were gone. Remember Justin Maury, the Loyalist solicitor who entertained us at his home two or three times?"

Hughes looked up, his face guarded. "Yes. What about him?"

"He died unexpectedly about a week ago. It was a strange business. They called it an accident of some kind; related to a robbery. It took everyone by surprise, right enough."

Beneath the table Hughes's fingers groped for the undersurface where he gripped its rough wood while his impassive face revealed nothing of the shock he felt. "How do you know this?"

"Oh, it was in all the broadsheets. A few of our men attended the funeral. They had been quite taken with the daughter, I believe. She's a very beautiful girl, you know."

"I never noticed," Hughes said absently, his mind racing to other concerns.

Naturally you wouldn't, Armstrong thought. "Well, anyway, just thought you'd want to know."

"I do. Thank you," Hughes murmured and watched the door close behind the major. He sat staring at it unseeing, wondering how he might go about investigating this matter. Maury dead. He could scarcely believe it. Not that Maury's death in itself mattered so much. He was a clever enough fellow, but there were a hundred like him around the country. But his death put in jeopardy a whole series of plans that Hughes himself had carefully drawn and executed over the past two months. A key component of that plan was now missing, ruining the whole, and he must do something quickly to correct it.

But first he must know why and how Maury died. This was a matter for George Sporn. A colonel in the British Army could never go safely ferreting about the city—his presence and his uniform would be too noticeable. Besides, if there was someone behind all this, as he suspected there might be, Hughes himself must at all costs not be identified. Sporn would not be noticed, and if he was, no one would pay much attention. Take off his uniform and give him a dirty shirt and shabby frockcoat and he would look like a hundred other rustic yokels from the countryside. He would get him on the job right away.

The colonel reached for his hat and left the room, not even bothering to close the door.

Late that evening George Sporn slipped quietly into the elegant Georgian house that had been appropriated for the colonel's use during the British occupation of Philadelphia. A servant, moving as silently as a cat, took him straight upstairs to Hughes's bedroom where the colonel sat in a dark flowered-silk banyan with a black satin turban around his head. Although they were alone in the room, Sporn spoke in hushed tones, leaning close to the colonel's chair.

"It was as you suspected," Sporn said in his heavy London accent. "Master Maury was murdered right enough. Stabbed in the back, as neat as you please."

Col. Hughes frowned and leaned away from Sporn's unpleasant breath. "Do they know by whom?"

"Some stranger, was all. Broke a window while Maury was at his desk study and skewered him like a pike on a spear. Ransacked the room, but didn't have time to look too good since the daughter and one of the maids heard the noise of the glass."

Hughes looked up sharply. "Nothing was taken?"

"They couldn't find nothin' missing. The authorities ruled it was a robbery attempt that failed."

Hughes rubbed a finger along his smooth chin. Why hadn't the letter surfaced? Had Maury hidden it so well that no one could find it? He would have to go round and call on the daughter.

"What about that other matter?" he asked.

"You were right about that, too, Colonel. I asked all over the wharves and sure enough there was a peculiar foreigner seen down there a week or so ago. He was keeping a room at the Skull and Bones, one of the taverns frequented by thieves and sea dogs. No one had seen much of him, because he got sick right away. They said they thought he had a fever of some kind and no one wanted to go near him for fear it might be catching. Then he died."

"Died? When?"

"Last night or this morning, they weren't sure. But he was taken away to be buried at once, in case it was the Barbados fever. In Potter's field on Washington Square, I think they said."

"If he died this morning, he might not yet be buried. I want to see that body, Sporn. You say it's at the Potter's field?"

"That's what they told me, though how much credit you can give those people I wouldn't want to say."

The colonel was already pulling off his robe. "Meet me downstairs. And tell my batman to have my horse saddled. We're going out there tonight."

Sporn gulped. "Tonight, Colonel?"

"I want to see that body before it's put underground. Get moving, man. Do I have to tell you a second time?"

But the wizened little man was already out of the room. By the time the colonel's horse was brought around, Hughes was waiting on the front step, a heavy wool cloak over his scarlet coat. Sporn led the way on his scrawny mount carrying a lighted lantern before him; the colonel leaped easily into his saddle and followed. He knew the Square that was Potter's field, having made it his business to be aware of all the places in this city that might be of use to him. The streets now were a sharp contrast to what they had been that morning. They were nearly empty of pedestrians and only an occasional carriage churned the still soft clay of the empty road. By the time they reached the outskirts of the town where the dreaded graveyard for the sick, indigent, and American prisoners was located, they had the road to themselves.

Hughes had to pound on the door of the sexton's ramshackle house to rouse the man from his evening solitude. Unaccustomed to visitors after dark, his gap-toothed face was a study in disbelief as he stared at the tall imposing form of the colonel barking orders at him, as though he was Satan himself come up from hell.

"Did you have any burials today?" Hughes asked without bothering to introduce himself. He let his rank and uniform speak for itself.

"One or two. Why?"

"Was one a foreigner? It's important."

"Might be."

Hughes pulled out a purse and removed two coins. The cemetery Sexton's tiny eyes took on an avaricious glow in the dim lantern light.

"There's a foreigner in the keeping room, along with two paupers. Didn't have time to get 'em down today. Do it first light tomorrow."

"Where is the keeping room?"

"Back by the gully. Be careful of the dog. I keep 'im for protection, but sometimes I think I need something to protect me from him. Hee hee," the man laughed through his gaping teeth. Taking a thick cudgel from behind the door, he led them through a cluttered yard amid newly turned graves to the rear where the ground sloped down toward a gully. A ramshackle shed stood near its edge, close enough that they could hear the gentle gurgling of a creek at the bottom of the gulch. The sexton pushed open the door and raised the lantern to throw a shrouded light on the bare interior. There was no furniture at all. Nothing but three long forms lying on the dirt floor, each covered with a dirty cloth.

The keeper hung the lantern on a peg near the door and walked over to one of the shrouded figures. Sporn lingered reluctantly on the outside, but Hughes followed the man into the low room. Roughly the keeper shoved one body aside with his boot, then reached down to grab a corner of the cloth whose contours suggested a long, flat figure. He snatched back the cloth and the colonel bent to peer at what lay revealed. Behind him George Sporn shrank away from the door. Pursing his lips, Hughes pulled out his glass and examined the dark face not two feet away.

"Couldn't bury 'im in Christian ground," said the keeper confidentially. "'E's an infidel. You can see it plain."

Though Hughes didn't bother to answer, he silently agreed. The dark face with the swollen tongue protruding from gray lips was certainly that of an infidel, though he guessed it was not Arabic. Skin the color of walnut, slanted eyes still staring dumbly up at the beamed ceiling, prominent cheekbones, a slash of a mouth frozen open by the protruding tongue. It looked like a face from some nether regions of hell.

"Ain't you afraid of what killed 'im?" the sexton breathed, studying Hughes's concentration curiously.

The colonel threw the man a withering glance that quieted any further conversation and returned to examining the corpse. When he was satisfied, he slipped the ribboned glass back into his waistcoat pocket and turned for the door, leaving the keeper to throw the dirty cloth back over the gross, unseeing face.

With a slight wave of his hand, Hughes summoned Sporn, on the outer side of the shed, to follow him back into the road.

"I hardly expected a man of your violent tendencies to be so unwilling to face a corpse," the colonel said as he untied his mount's reins.

Sporn shivered. "Gives me the creeps, this place," he

muttered. "I don't mind a fight, and I'd as soon kill a man as look at him. But this place is full of ghosts. Got no use for ghosts."

Though Hughes felt none of Sporn's fear, he leaned on his saddle and breathed deeply of the night air which did seem especially clean and clear away from the graveyard.

"At first light tomorrow I want you to go down to the wharf and book passage for three on the swiftest ship in the harbor set to cross the Atlantic. Make very certain it is the swiftest."

"Three, Colonel?"

"That's correct. For me, you, and Lester Clarke. He may be slow-witted, but he's big enough and vicious enough to be welcome in a fight. And we will probably be facing quite a few confrontations where we're going."

Hughes vaulted easily up into the saddle and pulled his horse around. "First light, Sporn. Don't delay a minute."

"I'll be at it, sir," Sporn muttered, and lumbered up on his mount. "By the way, where are we going?"

Hughes was already cantering down the road. "Baghdad," he threw back over his shoulder, just loud enough for Sporn to hear.

To Rhys's surprise the weather turned favorable almost at once, and with a full fresh wind in her sails the *Boeadecia* soon left the Chesapeake behind and plowed full into the Atlantic swells. By the next morning, when he stood on the quarterdeck watching the first rosy rays of dawn paint the horizon, he began to feel better about this trip than he had at any time since his conversation with Robert Morris two days before. But then he always turned hopeful once he had a good ship under him and swelling mounds of silver sails above his head.

Rhys stretched with satisfaction, lifting his rib cage and breathing deeply of the sweet, washed air. On the deck below sailors moved busily around, engaged in their morning chores. The fragrant odor of frying bacon wafted up from the galley stove below the fo'c'sle. Above his head men moved about on the rigging like squirrels scurrying among trees, purposeful and happy. The sea took on a silver sheen where the sun touched it, and the gulls, still following the ship's enticing promise, cawed joyously as they glided around the snapping sails.

Walking over to the taffrail, Rhys peered down at the scene below. He was about to turn away when he spotted a figure standing by the rail, shrouded in a gray cloak with a hood covering her face. She was staring at the sea where the sun was just beginning to climb the horizon. Rhys gripped the rail, bending toward the woman, unable to speak for surprise.

"Rogers!" he shouted at the first mate, who was standing by the mainmast. "Get up here! Right away."

Rogers scrambled up the steps to the quarterdeck. "Is that a woman?" Rhys cried, pointing one horrified finger at the figure whose skirts lifted gently around her. "A woman on my ship?"

"Why, yes sir. I thought you knew . . ."

"Knew what? We had no woman on the manifest. How the hell did she come to be here?"

"It's Miss Maury, Captain. Didn't you see her yesterday when she came aboard?"

"I saw a woman, but I thought she was seeing someone off. Where was she yesterday? Why didn't I see her when we were close enough to turn back?"

"I believe she was ill in her cabin, sir. I went down

once to check and she was pretty miserable."

Rhys's face began to take on the familiar black cast that his sailors dreaded. "You went down to check on her! You knew she was aboard, you knew she was settled in her cabin, you knew she was seasick and you never bothered to say a word about it to me!"

Rogers smiled sheepishly. "I was afraid you'd take her back, Captain. Her papers were in right order, and she was determined to sail with us. I didn't think it could hurt. How often have we had such a pretty lady aboard, Capt. Llewellyn? Not often, as you well know."

"I've a mind to slap you in the brig, Rogers. You know I don't like to carry women on my ship. She'll have a whole parcel of maids and boxes, and she'll have all the male passengers, not to mention my sailors, carrying on like schoolboys. I don't like it. Not one bit."

He turned his back on his first mate and stalked silently to the high point on the deck over the vessel's stern. The woman had moved from the railing, throwing back her hood, revealing the long chestnut mane that fell down her back and Rhys recognized her at once. How could he forget!

"That's a strange thing, sir," Rogers added, cautiously following the captain. "She doesn't have any maids. Not one. She told me her woman would be following, but she never showed up. And as for boxes, well, I only saw one."

"Oh, wonderful," Rhys muttered. "One lone woman, no chaperone or maid, and no baggage to speak of. She's probably running away from an overbearing father and a hateful marriage. And it will be all our fault for taking her when she's found. Really, Rogers. I thought you had better sense. One sight of a pretty face and your wits fly right out of your head."

67

"Well, sir. You do have to admit she's pretty."

"Get on with your work!" Rhys snapped, dismissing the man. He was too irritated to talk more about it.

Later, the first opportunity he got, he returned to his cabin and pulled out the passenger list, spreading it out on the small teak table where he took his meals. He could swear that the name had been JUSTIN MAURY, yet there it was in plain view—Justine. He would never have agreed had he known. There was nothing to do now but accept it, and hope that she could be transferred to the first respectable ship they came across.

Rhys Llewellyn could not know all that was going through Justine's mind as she stood by the rail of the *Boeadecia* and watched the sun transform a soft gray world to gold. There was such beauty about the sky and ocean, such a feeling of freedom and release, such an ecstasy in the light lifting of her hair by the warm, soft breeze that for a moment she was almost happy. Then she heard the harsh cry of the captain screaming orders and looked back at the deck of the ship and saw it suddenly as her prison for the next few weeks. She was all at once terribly conscious of the fact that she was a lone woman in a world of men and strangers. She had hoped—when she thought of it at all—that there might be a few other women present on this sailing, but as of yet she had not seen a single one. She was marooned here, her world the open decks and cramped little cabin of this schooner, carrying her to an unknown world fraught with terrible risks. For a moment her courage failed her, and she had to grip her hands to keep from running up the quarterdeck stairs and pleading with the captain to take her back to Philadelphia.

But no. She had taken this on willingly, and she would

68

see it through. For her father's sake, she must see it through.

By that afternoon her stomach had returned to almost normal, and she began to get the feel of the ship under her feet. She realized then how famished she was, for she had not been able to look at food for more than twenty-four hours. The evening meal was still hours away, so she fastened her camlet cloak around her shoulders and climbed up the companionway to the deck, determined to charm one of the sailors into finding her something to eat.

She was relieved to recognize Rogers almost at once. He was bending over the bulwark watching some work being done on the chain plates from the channel shelf below. Several other seamen stood nearby, passing over tools when called for by a workman on the other side of the hull. Justine walked over to them and touched Rogers on the arm to get his attention. A broad smile creased his face when he looked up and saw her and he swept off his hat.

"Good afternoon, Miss," he said eagerly. "I hope you're feeling better."

"Yes, thank you, I am. Very much better. But I was wondering if—"

"Goddammit, Rogers!" a voice from the far side of the hull interrupted her. "Hand me that hacksaw. Can't you keep your mind on your work for two minutes at a time!"

"Excuse me, Miss," Rogers muttered and turned, leaving Justine in mid-sentence. As she watched, a hammer came flying over the railing, narrowly missing her slippered foot. She reared back, gasping as a man's upper torso appeared above the bulwark. He appeared to be a seaman with a shock of disheveled black hair,

69

rolled-up shirtsleeves, and a lean face grimy with sweat.

His gray-green eyes widened with surprise when he saw her standing close beside him, then went dark with anger. "What the devil are you doing here?"

"Really," Justine managed to stammer. "You very nearly hit me with that thing. You should be more careful."

Something about the arrogance of the workman touched a raw nerve in her. Accustomed all her life to servants who were both loving and respectful, she could never abide rudeness in the lower classes, who ought to know better. "Can't you speak to this man, Mr. Rogers," she said curtly. "He ought not to be allowed to address your passengers in such a fashion. It is extremely bad manners and very disrespectful."

"Well, ma'am," Rogers answered, hiding his face with his hand. "That is . . . well, you see . . ."

"You'll need a firmer hand to run this ship, I should think. I came up here to ask you if I might have a little tea and toasted bread now that I'm feeling more myself. I certainly did not expect to be assaulted with a hammer!"

"Yes, ma'am. Of course, ma'am."

Justine was surprised to see the sweaty workman resting his arms on the rail cap and smiling, indeed, almost laughing, at her. "Why don't you remind the lady that tea will be served in the captain's cabin this afternoon for all the passengers," the man said in a voice dripping with arrogance. "Perhaps she will find the company there more to her liking."

"I would find almost any other company more to my liking," Justine said huffily, outraged at the audacity of this lout of a sailor. It was all the more upsetting, because up until now she had been treated with the utmost courtesy and respect by those few seamen on the ship she had encountered. "Mr. Rogers, I shall be happy to accept your invitation to tea later this afternoon, and I will be pleased if you would see that I had a little something to hold me until then."

"It will be done, Miss. I'll have Hawkins bring a tray to your cabin."

"Thank you," Jess said, turning away. "It is very nice to know that some people on board the *Boeadecia* have agreeable manners."

She was half way down the companion ladder before Rhys found his voice. "By my faith, I believe she thinks you are the captain of this vessel, Rogers," he said as he leaped easily back on deck. "The unmitigated gall of it!"

Rogers managed a wry chuckle. "I don't believe ladies are accustomed to seeing ship's masters in shirtsleeves working over the chain plates, sir. That may have something to do with the misconception."

Rhys reached for a towel and began wiping his forearms. "That's because they never encountered a captain who could handle anything on his ship. It would seem Miss Maury has a lot to learn, for all her gentlewomanly ways. You'd better see to that tray before she turns her unladylike wrath on you."

"Yes, sir, Captain Llewellyn. Right away, sir."

By mid-afternoon Justine was feeling her old self completely and ready to face the other passengers. The tray that Seaman Hawkins brought her had done much to restore her good nature as well as her enthusiasm for the voyage. Long before teatime she had changed her frock and brushed back her hair, and was ready to go back up

71

on deck. The wind had picked up from the morning, and the sails above her head crackled and fluttered with its heady caress. The prow of the ship dipped and rose, lifting its figurehead—a crude painted carving of the great British woman warrior—from its frothy jabot of foam. Porpoises cavorted gleefuly in the wash of the waves alongside the hull, and Justine bent over the railing watching them, smiling at their antics. She had forgotten about the captain's tea until Hawkins stood at her elbow, admonishing her that: "Please, Miss, the captain says he would be honored to have you in his cabin, if you would be so pleased."

She went down the companionway to the upperdeck, prepared to be impressed at the palatial rooms set aside for the ship's master but was quickly disappointed. It was a small cabin for one so exalted. A row of windows, like a tiara, framed the rear, making the cabin awash in a dappled light as though it was underwater. There was an elaborately embroidered curtain drawn across what must be the captain's bed, while in the main part of the room, a bench ran along one wall facing a long table of East Indian teak covered with a linen cloth and almost engulfed by a huge silver urn. On the other side of the room stood two large carved oak chairs, dark, massive, and ornate, like relics from the Restoration, Jess noted wryly. They were the only ostentatious touch in the cabin, and strangely at odds with a man so unimposing as Mr. Rogers.

That gentleman himself appeared suddenly at her elbow, leading her into the room. It was crowded with several men in coats of various colors, with a sprinkling of others in blue uniform tunics spotted with bright brass buttons.

72

"I think you've met Mr. Dunbar," Rogers said as a short, stout gentleman in a gray bagwig turned his pink cheeks toward Justine. She remembered him from the morning before, when he had introduced himself to her on deck. A merchant from Baltimore, as she recalled.

"I heard you were not feeling well," Dunbar said, beaming at Justine. "I trust you are better. We missed your lovely presence on deck today."

Justine made the proper responses while her eyes sought around the room for the rest of the passengers. They appeared to be mostly of Dunbar's ilk, self-satisfied, well-to-do men, of trade rather than politics, pleasant enough, but not very interesting. But that was all right. A quiet, bland voyage would probably be good for her. It would help her settle her shattered nerves and temper her grief.

"I don't believe you've formally met our captain, yet," she heard Rogers saying. They had worked their way across the small cabin to the embroidered curtains that hid the bed. Above it the light from the window gave a silver glare so strong that Jess had to hold her hand before her eyes to see. Her surprise in learning that Rogers was not the ship's master was eclipsed by the dark form that loomed before her. Taller than any man in the room, she had an impression of huge shoulders, dark hair drawn back in a queue, a lean face whose features were blurred by the shadows, a form that seemed to swallow her up, half-threatening, half-fascinating. Then the man stepped from behind the light, and she saw his face and gasped.

"You!" she stammered as she recognized the arrogant workman who had nearly hit her with a hammer. Rhys gave her a formal bow, the corners of his lips lifted in a

73

smile that was almost mocking.

"Good afternoon, Miss Maury," he said formally. "I regret that we had no opportunity to meet before this." He turned to Rogers, indicating by his glance that he wished them to be left alone. His first mate, skilled in reading his captain's mind, hurried off, giving Jess a moment to regain her composure.

Rhys went on: "Actually we have met before, haven't we? This afternoon, I believe."

"You were very rude," Justine snapped. "Especially in not telling me who you were."

"I was very busy. And you, as I recall, were in no mood to listen." He could hear the irritation in his voice, yet he was powerless to suppress it. It was distracting to be standing there looking down on so much loveliness. Now that she stood so close to him, pressed in by the crowd in the room, he found it increasingly difficult to keep his mind on the high objective plane he had intended. Such classic lines in her face, such delicate, smooth skin, cheeks pale, yet flushed as she fought her embarrassment. Lips so beautifully shaped and luscious, eyes so large, framed with heavy dark lashes that only accented the deep emerald green of the irises. He could drown in such rich, delicious depths, drown in their enticing beauty as into the Caribbean itself. He was tall enough that he could see the deep fissure where her breasts disappeared beneath a foam of frothy lace and his blood began to simmer in a disturbing way. His irritation was as much at himself for being moved, as it was at her for being so fascinating.

He could not know that Justine was fighting her own demons. Her briefly satisfying idea of a quiet voyage was being turned on its head. The physical presence of this

74

man was overpowering. She fought against searching his features, so masculine and yet at the same time so intelligent and aware. It was not just that he was handsome—which he certainly was—there was a disturbing physical reality about him, as though the air between them had suddenly come alive, touching her body with a warm flame. This was something that had never happened to her before, and she felt uncomfortable at the helplessness it evoked. And she was outraged at the way he so obviously enjoyed peering down the front of her dress. All her irritation at his arrogance came swelling back.

"I could hardly be expected to suppose it was the captain of the *Boeadecia* doing such menial work. Don't you have ship's carpenters and joiners for such things? Is it customary for the master to be down on his knees pursuing laborer's tasks?"

Rhys's mocking smile increased. "I like the feeling of knowing there is nothing on my ship I cannot handle as well as or better than my crew. Besides, I never found it hurt a man to get down on his knees occasionally. Or a woman either, for that matter."

"I go down on my knees before my God," she answered haughtily, "but to no man alive. Especially not to one as arrogant and overbearing as . . ."

Again Rhys gave her a formal bow. "As me, Ma'am? Miss Maury, let's be very clear about one thing. There was nothing to indicate from my passenger list that I had a woman coming aboard. I was as shocked to find you up on deck as you were to find me repairing the chain plates. I don't like the idea of carrying a woman on such a journey, especially in such times as these. We are likely to run into antagonists at any time on the high seas—

75

British or American. Either one would take this ship without so much as batting an eye, and with only twenty-six-pounders aboard, we are ill-equipped to defend ourselves. If we are fortunate enough to cross the Atlantic safely, we still must run the gauntlet of Barbary corsairs in the Mediterranean Sea. I find it very difficult to understand why a woman—particularily one who claims to be a gentlewoman—would even be along on such a trip."

"You think I should be sitting at home in my parlor doing my tatting with the drapes drawn and the shutters closed. Well, Captain . . . Captain—"

"Llewellyn," Rhys said helpfully.

"Captain Llewellyn, you'll find that I am not that kind of lady."

"No, I hardly thought of you as a lady at all, Miss Maury."

Justine gasped. It was so unusual for anyone to speak to her rudely, that she found herself at a loss for words. That the ship's captain would do so, when she had expected him of all people to be respectful and supportive, was difficult to accept. She could feel her cheeks burning with indignation, but she was determined not to do or say anything that would attract the attention of the others. The best solution was to leave this detestable man alone to run his ship and repair his axles. She would content herself with the company of the more pleasant gentlemen on board.

As though he had read her thoughts, First Mate Rogers suddenly appeared beside her, offering her a cup of tea. She took it gladly, asking him in the most pleasant way she could manage to help her find some cakes to go with it. She did not glance back as she worked her way across

76

the room from Captain Llewellyn, and she was careful during the rest of the party to avoid speaking to him. Rogers was pleased and flattered that she seemed to enjoy his company, and he hovered around her and waited on her like a pet servant, being careful not to glance in the direction of his master. Only one time did he even mention the captain, and that was to apologize for not making it clear to her long before that he was not in charge.

"That was very naughty of you, Mr. Rogers," Justine said quietly. "I might be terribly embarrassed, if your Capt. Llewellyn wasn't so unpleasant."

Rogers smiled sheepishly. "Oh, the captain's all right, ma'am. He's a little brusque now and then, but there's no better man to be with in a fight."

"That's understandable. He's belligerent as Attila the Hun!"

"He'll get you to your destination if any man can, Miss Maury. And that's what matters, isn't it?"

Justine sipped her tea, taking her time to answer. The idea of two or three more weeks on this ship under the oafish guidance of a man like Capt. Llewellyn was unsettling, to say the least. But what Rogers said was true. It was getting to Baghdad that mattered, for that was the only way she would be able to carry out the work that her father had left her to do. This disburbing man must not be allowed to alter that by one little jot.

"Well said, Mr. Rogers," she said, smiling sweetly at the first mate. "Well said indeed."

Four

Justine saw little of Rhys Llewellyn for the next two days, partly because the weather turned treacherous and confined all those who could serve no useful purpose on deck to the cramped confines of their cabins. Her sea legs, tenuous at best, disappeared altogether, and Justine lay in a miasma of gray misery, watching as the walls of her little room rose to perpendicular heights, then went diving in the opposite direction. Now and then Hawkins appeared with a cup of steaming tea that she was unable to keep down, accompanied by comforting assurances that this little blow was nothing but a brief squall, and they would soon be back to rights again. Jess did not believe him. By the end of the second day of the storm, she was convinced there would never be anything left in life but sickness and wallowing. The earth had regressed to its primordial origins, and the next million years would be more of the same.

While she lapsed into a fitful sleep, in the early hours of her fifth day at sea, the storm abated and the seas resumed their gentle rocking. She woke that day feeling much better, though extremely weak from lack of food. Dragging herself up on deck she spoke to one of the sailors, asking for the comforting tea and toast that so wonderfully filled the void between sickness and health, and then took a moment to stare out at the treacherous ocean that had given her such a miserable three days. The sky was slate gray, the color of Pennsylvania stone and almost as heavy, it was still so laden with moisture. Small waves with edgings of white lace made the dark sea restive, as though it was loath to give up its raging. In the rigging the inconsistent wind fell still, then came screaming in sudden bursts of frantic gyrations. But the ship had settled into a moderate roll, and the creaking and groaning of her timbers were now only a mild murmur.

Justine spent most of the day stretched out on her bunk, noting the footsteps over her head as the sailors went about their work, and listening to the muffled commands from the quarterdeck. Near evening she caught the quiet sound of songs from the men on the rigging—something she had not heard since before the storm. It was time to rejoin the human race, she decided, and rose to dress and fuss with her appearance once more. Her clothes hung a little on her thin frame, and she felt certain her cheeks looked gaunt. But with a little fair weather and a renewal of her appetite, that would soon be remedied.

As she returned to the upper deck, the setting sun cut a rosey swath across the sequined water. The sea was very still now and the wind, as though weary from its previous exertions, had dropped to a lethargic calm. Even the air had grown suddenly warmer, and Justine wondered if perhaps they had been pushed south by the storm.

"Good evening, Miss Maury," a brusque voice said behind her as she stood by the bulwarks staring out to sea. She turned to see Captain Llewellyn coming down the steps from the deck above. Though he did not exactly remove his hat, he touched it lightly with his hand—as much a mark of respect, she supposed, as she was likely to get from him.

"You survived our little blow, I see. I hope it was not too uncomfortable for you."

"It was terrible. But yes, I did survive, even though there were a few moments when I hoped I wouldn't. Were we pushed off course at all, Capt. Llewellyn?"

"A little, but we'll make it up. I've found it's best not to fight the wind when it takes you. It never lasts too long, and you can always get back where you want to be later."

"Was the ship much damaged?"

"The *Boeadecia*? Oh no, not at all. She's not much built for speed, but she's solid and strong, and it will take a better gale than we've just been through to break her up."

An awkward silence fell between them. Jess turned her face back to the ocean, wondering what she could say to this man that would sound halfway polite. She expected him to walk away, but he lingered, standing beside her and examining the waves with a strange intensity.

"I thought perhaps, if you were feeling better, you might like to have a little supper in the captain's cabin tonight. It is customary on a voyage of this sort to offer the passengers several chances to get acquainted. I'd be honored to have you join us."

Jess looked sideways up at him through slanted eyes. "You surprise me, Captain. Somehow I did not expect your courtesies to extend to a 'detestable woman,' especially one aboard your ship. I would be pleased to come, but I warn you, after eating nothing but toast for the past three days, I'm famished. I hope your cook is prepared."

Rhys smiled back at her, ignoring her barb about the detestable woman. "I'll make sure we have enough. In about an hour then?"

He was gone before she could reply, leaving her to look after him and wonder at his invitation. She had not expected anything so gracious, nor even that he would speak to her so pleasantly. She was not prepared to change her opinion of him, for underneath his polite exterior he still exuded arrogance and contempt, yet she was prepared to accept a truce for the sake of the time they must spend together on this small ship. And she was ravenously hungry. The captain was bound to set the best table on the *Boeadecia*. She would be quiet, mind her own business, and concentrate on eating.

An hour later, attired in a blue satin dress with paste buckle shoes, she sat at Rhys's table and quietly listened while the gentlemen around her pursued the process of getting to know one another. They had all been strangers when they came aboard, and Justine recognized the prodding and testing that went on beneath their polite questions and answers. Her appetite had not been quite what she thought it would be, and she was quickly satisfied with the bland but hearty food the young cabin boys handed around. By pretending to be shy and unsure of herself—the only woman on a ship full of men—she was able to draw her own conclusions about her companions, conclusions that were a good deal more realistic than the impressions she had received at the tea party a few days before.

"Is this your first trip to China, Miss Maury?" Dunbar on her left broke in, once more trying to draw her out. The cheery little merchant felt he had some prior friendship from having met her the day they sailed, and refused to be discouraged by her silence.

"Yes, it is," Jess answered without any further explanation. The less said about her destination, the better, she felt. Though she noticed one of Capt. Llewellyn's crescent eyebrows edge upward at her answer.

"I've had the pleasant experience of traveling with a woman to the East once before," Dunbar beamed. "She was the wife of the ship's master and quite accustomed to crossing the world back and forth. It makes it so much more delightful for dull merchants like ourselves to have the charming presence of a lady on board. Don't you agree, Captain?"

Rhys mumbled something unintelligible while Jess dipped her head to hide her amusement.

"I wonder we are not going round the horn, Captain Llewellyn," said the fellow opposite Justine, sitting in one of the heavy ornate chairs. His name was Agar, and he was once from New York but now lived outside Philadelphia. His features were commonplace and ordinary, except for a large red wart on one side of his nose that Jess found it hard not to look at when he addressed her. He also was in trade, though this was his first venture overseas.

"That would be the quickest way to China, of course," Rhys answered. "And most of the time that is the route I would take. However, on this trip we have several other ports to touch at. By the time the *Boeadecia* returns to Pennsylvania, she will have been pretty nigh around the globe."

"Of course it's a waste of time for men who only wish to pick up their tea and ginger jars," Isaac Simsbury said from the end of the table. "But I for one am eager to see something more of the world. I've never visited Egypt or Greece, the cradle of our civilization."

"You won't see them on this trip, Mister Simsbury," Rhys said. "We'll pass them by, but we won't stop."

"Just to pass them is a treat."

Simsbury was by far the most interesting of the four other passengers, Justine thought. It was obvious from his speech and the people he knew that he had once been very well-to-do, but had lately fallen on hard times. He had shrewd, intelligent eyes and a kind mouth, but his appearance was marred by a heavy stoop of his shoulders and his rather shabby clothes. Jess liked him, but felt she would be wise not to reveal too much of herself around him. The fourth gentleman was the one she found least appealing. His name was Perry, and he was a merchant from Baltimore. Extremely gaunt with a long, sharp face and hooded eyes, he seemed to be always taking the measure of the others, as though trying to decide whether or not he could gain anything from knowing them. She especially disliked the way his narrow eyes seemed to linger over her.

Their meal had been consumed over pleasantries for the most part, until it was nearly over. Then Simsbury raised the subject of revolution, and the conversation took on an emotional undercurrent. It began innocently enough with Dunbar asking Isaac Simsbury when he had turned to importing Chinese artifacts. With color darkening and features contorted, he told them of how he had once run a successful business in the Dutch town of Albany. "Not your fancy wares but good substantial products the local farmers could use, as well as some fine English imports to grace the homes of the wealthy manor houses of the Hudson Valley." And then one fateful night they came swooping down on him. "The Sons of Liberty," the cursed mob, the dregs of the town and countryside. Lazy and wretched themselves, they used the excuse of his, Isaac Simsbury's neutrality, to wreck and burn his store, frighten his family near to death, smash his stock, run off his cattle, and bring him to the same ruin they had made of their own lives. "And this in the name of liberty!" Simsbury cried, his voice rising. "I'd like to liberate them right out of this world! This accursed rebellion has been the ruin of many good men, and I hope its architects all hang by the time it is over."

"Come, my good fellow," Dunbar interjected. "Surely you are too harsh. While it is true some innocent people have been hurt, surely you must agree that many men of principle and integrity believe fully in what they are doing."

John Agar pushed back in his chair, his face grim and his lips tightly drawn. Even the wart on his nose looked aflame as he lost no time in letting them know where he stood. "I hope to God that I am one of those men," he snapped. "I am sorry you suffered, but you must remember that others have suffered at the hands of the country and the government that you consorted with. England was happy to send silver and china to our shores to grace the tables of the manor lords, while at the same time grinding the poor man under her painted heels. A

84

republic, hard won as it will be, shall be infinitely better for the majority of Americans than all the fine English wares in the world."

Justine could stand it no longer. "Why, you speak treason, Mr. Agar," she said, her cheeks flaming.

"Treason, Miss Maury," Rhys said quietly. "Is it treason to wish to throw off the chains of a tyrant? Is it treason to fight oppression and injustice with all your strength? I suspect the only treason in that is to yourself."

"Well said, Captain," Agar boomed.

"Treason to King and motherland," Justine snapped back at him, forgetting all her resolutions of remaining quiet. "Rule by the mob is no substitute for order and law. This rebellion has tried to attach grand and noble ideas to its cause, but at heart it is just what the Crown has said it was all along—rebellion against a lawful government."

"We are all English," Simsbury added, leaning over the table in his enthusiasm. "We are turning our backs on our heritage."

"I'm not English," Rhys snapped back. "I'm Welsh. And there has never been overmuch love between the two."

"Well, I do think you made a good point, Captain," Mister Dunbar said in his gentle way, obviously trying to be the peacemaker. "I am an American, of course, but I can see that both sides have a valid argument. It is quite confusing at times. I saw a man actually tarred and feathered once in the streets of Boston, and it is something I never want to see again. On the other hand, I have read Mister Paine's pamphlets and they are very convincing. Very convincing, indeed."

"Twaddle, Dunbar," Simsbury cried. "Pure twaddle."

"And you, Mister Perry," Rhys said, turning to the one person who had offered no opinion. "What do you think about the revolution?"

Perry gave a slow smile and looked around the table as though they were all beneath his contempt. "I haven't made up my mind yet."

"Humph. You would not be allowed to get away with that in Boston, Mr. Perry," Agar offered, drumming his fingers on the table.

"Perhaps I would be burnt out of business, as Mr. Simsbury was, by a patriot mob."

"You might be run out of town by a gang of lawless Tories," Agar answered.

"Either way, it appears I lose. That is why I prefer to keep my opinions to myself, at least until I see which side is going to win."

Justine gasped. "Why, sir, that is ignoble!"

"Perhaps it is just good business," Rhys offered, in his old mocking tone. Justine began to feel annoyed with all of them. What would her father say? How would he answer their criticisms and help those who supported the rebellion to see the error of their ways? She simply could not imagine.

"I wonder if you gentlemen would excuse me," she said quietly. They all rose at once to their feet, all concern.

"We have worn you out with our politics, I fear," Mister Dunbar said, helping her around the table. "Please forgive us, my dear lady."

"I think it is just that the storm left me feeling rather weak, and I'm sure you would all prefer to get to your port. It has been most pleasant, Captain. Thank you for asking me."

Rhys rose from his place at the end of the table. "Allow me to walk you to your cabin, Miss Maury," he said, moving to lightly take her arm. She was so astounded at this surprising offer, that for a moment she could think of no way to discourage him.

"That really isn't necessary," she was finally able to say.

"It would be my pleasure," Rhys said, smiling enigmatically. "Young Adams here will pass round the port. I'll rejoin you in a moment, gentlemen."

They murmured their good evenings while Rhys ushered Jess out the door before she could pull her arm away. To her surprise, his grip tightened as they started down the hall, his fingers urging her toward the door to the upperdeck.

"Captain—" Jess said, pulling back.

"It was close in the cabin, Miss Maury. I thought it would be good for both of us to get a little air before you retire. I won't keep you but a moment."

She sensed it was going to be too difficult to get away from him without making a scene, so she allowed him to lead her up the hatchway and out onto the upper deck where the cool air brushed her face immediately.

With his hand lightly on her arm, Rhys led her across the deck into the shadows of the deckhouse where they were unobserved by the sailors standing watch. She was close enough to the taffrail that the whole ebony bowl of the sky was clearly visible. Stars, like a sprinkling of diamonds across the heavens, pulsed with a silver beauty that made her catch her breath.

"What a beautiful night!" Jess cried, forgetting everything but the wonder before her.

"A clear night at sea is an incomparable sight," Rhys answered quietly. Though he had seen many such spangled heavens, he could appreciate its effect upon Justine. He himself was unable to tear his eyes from her shadowed face. He had been unable to look at anything else all night.

With an easy movement Rhys set one hand on the deckhouse wall, imprisoning her with his body. Jess pressed back against the wall, all at once terrified, and thrilled with an excitement that started at her toes and ran electrically through her whole body. His face was very close to hers, the features indistinct with shadows. She stared into his eyes, eyes that were challenging and tender at the same time, and said nothing. There was a stillness hovering between them that she instinctively refused to break with words of protest or outrage. It would be hypocritical, for she felt drawn toward him by a force neither could stem. And it would be beside the point, for she somehow knew that he would be the master of this situation, not she.

Rhys laid his other hand on her silky throat, his fingers stroking, soft as down on her tingling flesh. Lowering his head so slowly that Jess felt suspended in a glowing void, he met her lips. At his kiss the flame came alive, with a sweetness Jess had never known existed. His mouth moved over hers, sensuously exploring its shape and outline, drawing desire from her lips, like nectar from a flower, waking in her a growing warmth and urgency. Jess let her arms slide around his neck as he pushed his body against hers, his tongue flicking her lips, probing their entrance, tasting their sweetness. Dimly she was aware of the hardness of his body, the swellings and valleys pressed to her own. Weakly she slumped in his arms, all her resistance drained away. Her lips parted and his tongue went joyfully searching, touching the roof of her mouth, exploring her teeth, probing the cavity of her open lips. His hands massaged her back, her shoulders, and then, in a searing urgency, swept around her throat, and down over the bodice of her dress, closing and kneading her breasts. Jess moaned, all thought lost in an upward surge of heightened feeling. His hips crushed against her, pressing her against the deckhouse wall, slowly gyrating with a movement she matched with her own.

She could not breathe. With a sudden panic engulfing her whole body, she tore her lips away from his invading tongue, turned her head to the side, only to have him probe her ear with the same maddening searching blade of his tongue. She felt herself falling, drifting on clouds of ecstasy, all reason and thought drowned in a sea of pure sensation.

"No," she gasped, desperately trying to regain her self-control. Rhys gave a low moan and pulled away from her lips to bury his head against her neck, slowly regaining the control that, to his surprise, had been swept so quickly away.

"I've been wanting to do that all evening," he groaned.

Jess's labored breathing gradually quieted. She did not move away, nor did he. There was some measure of contentment in standing with their arms around each other, holding each other close against the darkness of the night, while the brilliant stars pulsated their silent anthems above them. When at last Rhys lifted his head to look into her eyes, she knew with a certainty not at all born of reason or common sense that her life was forever to be intertwined with that of this man. For an instant there was a sense of having loved him ages before, and of love to come ages after, but it quickly vanished as reality came washing over her again.

"Capt. Llewellyn . . ."

"I think you might call me Rhys after what just happened."

"Rhys . . . I'm not sure . . . that is, I don't really . . ."

Rhys let his hands drop and he pulled slightly away from her. "I know. That wasn't at all proper, Miss Maury. But I won't apologize. I've wanted to do that from the first moment I saw you. Your body is a flame, a beacon to a man like me. I have a fire of my own."

That arrogance again! Some of the magic slipped away at his words. "I hardly think this is behavior appropriate to the master of a ship. I am a passenger here, alone and unchaperoned."

"All the more reason to offer you my protection."

"Your protection?" Jess said, a little perturbed at just what that might involve.

Lightly Rhys went back to stroking her soft neck with the ends of his fingers. "You needn't worry. I won't force you. I want you to come of your own free will. I want you to want me as much as I want you. And it will do no good to say that you don't, for your body told me just a moment ago that you do, very much."

"Really, Capt. Llewellyn," Jess stammered, feeling more and more embarrassed at the hot passion that had possessed her a few moments before. "Not only do I not know you very well, but we are at opposite ends of the political spectrum. I could tell by your words at the table that you support this treasonous rebellion in the Colonies. I should tell you the whole thing is repugnant to me. With all my heart, I long to see the Crown restore

90

law and order and a proper English government. There is nothing in the world I want more than an America securely and happily serving her rightful King."

Rhys dropped his lips and kissed the luscious curve of her white neck. "I never allow politics to interfere with love," he murmured.

That was the last straw. Justine broke from his light embrace and stepped away to the taffrail. "I think I had better go back to my cabin now," she snapped, her eyes flashing.

He laughed, almost a mocking chuckle, and folded his arms across his chest. "Very well, my flaming Tory mistress. I'll escort you to your door. My friends below have probably drunk up half the port by now anyway."

"I can go alone," Justine answered and started for the hatch in a swirl of satin skirts. As luck would have it, her dainty slippers stubbed up against a coil of rope laid there earlier by the boatswain and she stumbled, nearly falling on the deck. Rhys reached out and pulled her to her feet, then drew her arm through his own.

"Ship's decks can be dangerous places," he said smiling with the memory of that long, deep kiss. "I'll see you safely below."

He left her at her door, receiving a curt good night for his pains. He was not disturbed by her reaction, for before him swept the vision of a long voyage with many opportunities like tonight's. He intended to have her in his bed before the trip was far gone, and the thought of it was as exciting as anything he had ever encountered at sea. He might as well take every advantage of her nearness, for when they reached their first port of call it would all be over, and he would most likely never see her again. How fortunate she was on his ship alone and not

91

crowded by a protective father, aunt, or even a maid hovering over her. It was as though the fates intended to give him this one idyllic crossing out of all the turbulent ones he had endured at sea. He would be forever grateful to them for that!

In her cabin with the door securely locked, Justine sat down on her bed, rested her elbows on her knees, and laid her chin in her hands. Her emotions were raging and she knew she would get little sleep. As arrogant and sure of himself as he was tonight, Rhys Llewellyn had touched some chord deep within her awakening a longing she had never felt before. Her common sense told her that it would not be such a bad thing to have the captain's protection, since she was a lone woman on a ship filled with men. It might even be to her advantage, warning off all the other would-be admirers.

But just how far would that protection extend? A thrill shuddered through her body at the thought of lying in Rhys's arms behind that embroidered curtain in the captain's cabin. Treacherous thought! What would her father say! But her father was dead, and once they reached port, she would likely never see Rhys Llewellyn again. Would it be so terrible to reward him for his care of her? Not a soul on board knew her as a proper young lady of Philadelphia. Let them think her wanton and lightfooted, what did she care? She had nothing before her but a dangerous and perilous mission from which she might not even return alive. Her sense of adventure broadened to include a spine-tingling liaison that no doubt would never be offered to her again.

Absently she began unfastening the laces on her bodice, smiling to herself.

*   *   *

After that evening the days at sea took on a gentle contentment, sliding by one after the other with a sameness that was never boring, a peaceful certitude that every dip and thrust of the ship carried them toward some distant port of the future, while they remained suspended in an engulfing womb of time. Two days after the storm, First Mate Rogers went rummaging in the hold and emerged bearing a creaky rocking chair, black with age and warped by the dampness of the orlap. Justine soon became a familiar sight sitting in her chair, while the work of the ship went on around her, growing familiar with the orders Rhys barked from the bridge that sent the sailors scurrying up the sheets to the tall masts above, or running for pails and soapstone to clean the decks, or any of the other myriad tasks that were required to keep the *Boeadecia* in shining condition. Her eyes often settled on that handsome figure walking the quarterdeck, examining the way he carried his tall form so proudly, the manner in which he seemed to always know exactly what was needed, and the overbearing commands he issued so easily. Rhys himself had little time to dawdle around her as the other passengers frequently did, since the work of the ship kept him busy most of the day and night. When his glance did meet hers, so openly brazen, knowing and inviting, Jess felt her cheeks turn crimson, and she would quickly go back to watching the porpoises cavort alongside the ship. She had avoided any opportunity to be alone with him since that evening when he kissed her, mostly because she had settled her own mind as to how she should behave. But the air between them seemed to come alive when he passed by her, and once when he bent to lay a hand on her shoulder, making some careless comment about the weather, her whole body was shot through with flame.

She was almost grateful to John Agar, who had decided that of all the gentlemen on board he was the one most likely to win her affections. He had much of Capt. Llewellyn's arrogance and none of his charm, but he kept the others at bay while he pursued his obvious suit. Jess was polite but unencouraging. She laughed at his pompous pronouncements and used his conversation as a means of watching the captain unobserved.

On the other hand, she enjoyed her time chatting with Simsbury and Dunbar, both of them well-traveled gentlemen of breeding and intelligence. Mr. Dunbar had adopted a fatherly interest in her which she found comforting, while Isaac Simsbury simply liked having a sympathetic ear for his tales of horror at the hands of the Whigs.

Very early she decided that she must invent some pretext for her voyage that would satisfy their questions. When Rhys casually mentioned that the Near East had become home to a number of French Protestant clergymen pursuing converts, she took this as an omen, and let it be gradually known that her father had recently died, and she was going to Damascus to live with an aunt who was a missionary's wife. It seemed to satisfy everyone's curiosity except Rogers, and to him she explained that Peter Romaine, knowing she was leaving for the Arab world, had commissioned her to purchase goods for his store. Blessed with good weather, a stout ship, an ever-strengthening sun that beamed down its warmth, a sparkling sea, and jeweled nights, Justine began to think that she had surmounted all her problems and was halfway to accomplishing her goals. Once she handled this Yarmid Ali in Baghdad, she would return home having successfully accomplished the significant task left her by her father's death.

Then, as though she had been deliberately lulled into thinking all was well, everything began to go wrong. Mr. Perry fell ill with a fever that slowly spread to the other passengers. While apparently not dangerous, it was a debilitating and miserable illness that laid a wary caution over everyone's good spirits. Soon there were three passengers confined to their beds. Jess, who was quite willing to help, was not allowed to act as nurse, so fearful were they that she would catch the fever. She was left to the rather distressing ministrations of Mr. Agar, who took advantage of the time to hover over her and press his suit. The wind died altogether, leaving the ship to wallow in a shallow trough for days on end, and aggravating the tempers of all on board. A careless slip on the top mast ratlines left two of Rhys's hardest workers laid up in their hammocks, and reduced him to tight-lipped fury. An air of tension settled over the bobbing ship as its sailors went about their work with quiet resentment. Justine received curt answers to her questions, and found that no one had the time to dally around her anymore. Even the porpoises disappeared, as though realizing this was no longer the playful voyage it had been.

In the late afternoon of a particularly long, boring day, Justine sat in her rocking chair looking out at the deadly calm sea. The weather had turned very hot, especially since there was little or no wind to cool the increasingly stronger sun. She had spent most of the afternoon watching the sailors work lethargically at mending rope and sails, too lazy herself to attempt polite conversation. She felt restless and bored, yet in a contradictory way, she could not summon the energy to try any of the tame activities which occurred to her to do.

She was tired of reading, uninterested in talking with the sailors, unwilling to wait on her recuperating fellow passengers, and unable to find anything she really wanted to do.

Except one thing. She had seen little of Capt. Llewellyn of late, he had been kept so busy with the mishaps on the ship. She was aware of his frustration over the tepid wind of the last few days, and the way it kept the *Boeadecia* wallowing in the water, for his barked commands and curt responses made that very evident. After a short time on the quarterdeck in the early afternoon—which had been notable for another display of his bad temper—he had disappeared into the depths of his cabin and had not emerged since. Why should he sulk alone, she thought, when he was no more miserable than the rest of them. Her lips lifted in a wry smile as she thought of bedeviling Rhys Llewellyn in the one place where he could not escape—his cabin.

Jess smoothed back her hair, retied the ribbon that fastened it at her neck, fluffed out her skirts, and made her way to the galley stove below the fo'c's'le deck. The ship's cook, who had already proved himself partial to her by taking a delight in fixing some of the special dishes she enjoyed, was stirring a pot over a pile of flaming embers whose heat kept her at a reasonable distance.

"What can you give me that would brighten this long day, Jasper," Jess asked with her prettiest smile. The man rubbed the stubble of beard on his chin and wiped a long spoon on the dirty white apron that covered most of his stomach.

"Well, Miss, there's not much till supper and the fish stew I'm working on now. There's a biscuit, mayhaps, or a bit of cheese. Nothin' much for the likes of a lady

96

like you."

"Come on now, Jasper. You must have something better than that. I thought I'd take the captain his tea. Surely you were going to send him something better than biscuits and cheese."

The sailor gave Justine a wink that bordered on lewd, which though it embarrassed her, she decided to ignore. After all, she had asked for it by telling him what she planned.

"Well now, that's a little different. As a matter of fact, I was saving a nice bit of currant cake for such a day as this, but I'd decided not to send it, since the master was so rude to everyone earlier today. In fact, I had thought to give it to you, to brighten your afternoon a little. Wobbling about like we've been doin' these last few days can't be too pleasant for you."

"I appreciate that, Jasper. But I think the cake will serve a more useful purpose if I share it with Capt. Llewellyn. Maybe it will soften his temper a little."

"Oh, I doubt that, Miss. But I tell you what. I'll give you a little Madeira to go along with it. If that doesn't help ease his bile, there's nothing that will. That and the sight of such a pretty lady as yourself."

A few moments later Jess made her way—with heart thumping a little stronger than usual—down the hall to Rhys's cabin. With one hand she balanced a tray holding a small round cake, two plates, two forks, a half-filled bottle of Madeira, and two long-stemmed wine glasses. It was rather heavy, and it wobbled in her hand as she stopped before the closed door and lightly knocked.

"What do you want!" came a muffled voice from within. "Go away!"

Justine refused to speak loudly enough for him to hear,

since she knew her voice would carry to the passenger's cabins where the invalids would be hanging on every word. Instead she waited a moment, then knocked lightly once more.

"Goddammit, leave me alone. I'm busy."

Pursing her lips, she stood silently another moment, then knocked one last time, resolved that if he responded with one more ill-humored insult she would leave the wine and cake by the door and not speak to him for the rest of the trip. She could hear him stomping to the door and then saw it jerked open, the full force of his anger turned on her. It was with some satisfaction that she saw him catch his breath and look a little mortified when he recognized her.

"I brought your tea," she said quietly, unable to resist a smirk of triumph at his discomfort. "Do you still want me to go away and leave you alone?"

"Sorry," Rhys mumbled. "I didn't realize it was you. Come on in."

"Am I interrupting you?" Jess asked as she set the tray on the table.

"Yes, but it's of no importance. This is a surprise. I thought by now you'd be laid up with the fever."

"You sound disappointed."

"Not at all. It simply seems to be an illness that spreads. I only hope the contagion doesn't engulf my whole ship. A good, stiff wind would make a lot of difference." He drew up one of the ornately carved chairs and Jess sat primly down and began to cut the cake. Rhys stood to the side and poured the wine into the two glasses. His mood already appeared to have improved, and Justine was guardedly congratulating herself on the success of her idea. After handing her a glass, Rhys raised his own.

"To a fresh wind and a fair voyage."

She sipped the fruity drink which made itself felt all the way down. She was desperately trying not to be too conscious of the warming presence of this virile man. He had thrown his coat aside for the comparative comfort of a striped waistcoat and long full sleeves. His tight breeches disappeared into the tops of high leather boots. His hair fell in waves over his wide forehead, and his eyes were alight with the same ardor she had seen that evening on the deck when he first kissed her. Her eyes lingered over the sweep of his high cheeks and firm jaw, and her whole body began to tingle. Deliberately she focused her eyes over his head at the ornately embroidered curtain behind him.

"Are we very far from Europe?" she asked in a voice that was not as nonchalant as she hoped.

"Farther than we would be if we could get out of this endless calm. A good breeze and we should sight Portugal within the week."

"Portugal!" Jess cried, her eyes shining. "It sounds so exotic, so other-worldly. Castles, palaces, knights in armour. I've longed to see them all my life, ever since I read 'Mort d'Arthur as a child."

Rhys's eyes lingered over her hair, swept back from her high forehead and tied at the neck with a blue ribbon, leaving the long curls to cascade down her back. "You ought to be going to France or England," he said, smiling. "Paris is a city that would suit you admirably." He tore his eyes away from her, frowning. "The Arab world is not a congenial place for a woman to be traveling. I wonder at you going there."

Jess turned her face to the side so that he could not see into her eyes. "It was my father's wish that I go to live

99

with my aunt."

"Oh yes, of course. Your aunt!"

There was that mocking tone of voice again. All at once Jess was aware that the captain did not believe her aunt existed, and with a little encouragement might get the whole story of her trip out of her. Quickly she rose and, still carrying her wineglass, began to peruse the cabin.

"What interesting things you have hanging on your walls here," she said lightly. "Do they all mean something?"

Rhys leaned his hips on the table and folded his arms across his chest, studying her as she concentrated on the objects that adorned his cabin. "I like to collect mementos from my voyages at sea," he said cryptically.

"What is this?" she asked, fingering a long object of polished bone with a sharp-toothed cutting edge on one end.

"That is a harpoon for catching whales. You tie a rope to one end and throw it into the animal's side, then hope he doesn't drag you to the ocean floor."

"It sounds very hard on the whale. And this?"

"That is the jawbone of a shark. Deadly-looking, isn't it?"

"Indeed," Justine said with a small shiver.

Moving to her side, he took her arm lightly to lead her around the room, pointing out the various objects on display: a vicious-looking cleaver from the Amazon basin, a tattered flag from the old pirate's lair at New Providence, a Spanish sword with an ornate gilt handle from the Caribbean, the beautifully embroidered blue and gold curtain from China. "And this thing, which you probably presumed to be a coconut, is my proudest memento. It's actually a head, a human head. The

Indians of Brazil have a nice little way of shrinking the heads of their enemies and keeping them as trophies. Lovely, isn't it?"

"Ugh!" Justine cried. "It's horrible. Cover it up. I don't even want to look at it."

"You learn to take such things in stride when you travel the world."

She crossed to the other side of the room and stood looking at him, her head cocked to one side, her eyes narrowing. "There's something wrong here. You can't have been to all these places and done all these things. You're not old enough."

"I started as a boy." When he could see she still did not believe him, he threw back his head, laughing loudly. "You are too shrewd, my lovely. The truth is, I got all these things from a drunken old sot of a sea master in a dingy tavern in Philadelphia. They actually represent *his* years at sea. I once had my own collection, of course. Nothing as grand as this, but important to me, but it went down in a storm with my last ship. The only thing here that is truly mine is this."

He crossed to her and picked a small framed print off the wall. It was so nondescript that Jess had not noticed it before, but as she looked at it closely, she was struck by its loveliness. It pictured soft green mountains surrounding a serene valley with one tiny thatched cottage sitting near the bank of a stream. A thin swirl of smoke drifted from the chimney of the house, giving the whole scene a sense of sublime peace and well-being. "It's beautiful," Jess exclaimed. "Is it your home?"

"It was my parent's home in Wales. They brought this picture to America with them and gave it to me, to always remind me of my roots." Gently he took it from her and

101

placed it back on the wall. He was standing very close to her, so near that she could make out the pores on his bronzed skin and the dark hairs on the back of his hand. She could have easily moved away, but her feet seemed to be fastened to the floor.

Rhys turned to her and very casually removed the glass from her hand, setting it down, and then slipping his arms around her waist. Jess's body gave a slight little shiver, as though she knew some significant moment had come to fruition. She did not resist as Rhys pulled her against his hard body.

"Somehow, I cannot believe that you came here this afternoon to eat cake and talk about the objects that decorate my cabin."

She strained back against his strong arms. "Perhaps I was just a little bored and wanted company."

"I know your ever-present suitor, Mr. Agar, is indisposed, but there is always the company of my sailors, whom you have kept quite enthralled."

"Ah, but you've succeeded in putting them all in such a fear of your terrible temper that they won't take the time any longer to talk to me."

Rhys chuckled. "That was my intention. It's nice to know my plan worked."

"Your plan! If you think—"

He stopped her words with his lips, hard on her own. Jess resisted only for a moment, then melted into him, entwining her arms around his neck, filled with the most delicious glow of happiness and growing excitement.

It was a long kiss, not so gentle as the one that night on deck, as though knowing she was here alone in the privacy of his room gave Rhys a driving urgency, a mounting need that, with such wondrous hope of

102

fulfillment, could not be stemmed. His grip was so strong as to be almost painful. He twisted her in his arms until her head was bent back on his arm, and with his hard, insistent lips explored her parted lips, her cheek, the nape of her neck, her earlobes, and the sensitive little hollow behind them. Justine had no thought of resisting. She allowed herself to be swept along on this soft, golden torrent, carried like an infant with no will or strength along this molten, gilded river of pure sensation.

He steadied her on her feet and laid his hands on her shoulders, gently sliding the sleeves of her dress down her arms. Her bodice strained against her full breasts, pinpointed with the tips of her erect nipples. Her back arched as Rhys bent his head, nuzzling her breasts, working the lacey neckline down with his lips. Expertly he slipped her bodice down and reached inside to pull out her full, straining breasts, cupping one in his hand, lifting the sweet, dark areola into his mouth. With his tongue he licked, swirled, tasted, and flicked against the pulsating erection, until Jess thought she would faint from excitement. Then she felt herself swept up in his arms, light as a feather in the strong vise that held her. He swept aside the Chinese curtain and sat her on the side of the bed, getting down on his knees before her. She hardly knew where she was, her pounding senses were so focused on his hands, his lips, the hardness of his firm body. She pulled at the laces of her bodice and he had it off, leaving her in her chemise. With an expert deftness that left her dimly wondering where he had learned all this, he had her skirt off and was undoing the tapes of her petticoats.

There wasn't a fleeting moment of embarrassment as Justine allowed him to remove her clothes, one by one.

When her breasts were bared, Rhys exclaimed, "God, but you're beautiful!" then went on to lift off her petticoats, taking the time to let his hands linger along the sweep of her thighs and her long, lean legs, smooth as silk in his hands. He bent his head and kissed her knees, gently searching up the length of her inner thighs, easing her legs apart until his lips were near the fountain of her maidenhood. Jess laid her hands on his shoulders to support herself against the torrent of feelings he awoke in her. His tongue sought out her sweetness, circling and drawing against her swelling flesh until she moaned aloud. Then he was gone, leaving her to drift back on the bed, sinking into its downy softness.

He had only stopped to get rid of his own confining clothes. She turned her head, watching with eager excitement as the shirt and waistcoat were pulled away, revealing a chest sprinkled with dark hair and not as deeply bronzed as his face had led her to expect. He sat on the bed and pulled off his boots but not his breeches. She was glad he had not done that yet, for she liked to see the swelling fullness of his manhood straining against the fabric.

He knelt on the bed and tentatively she touched him, running her fingers along the taut cloth and feeling the ridges beneath that stood out against the swollen flesh. She cupped her hand around him and gripped the hard shaft in her fingers. His hands tugged at the buttons of his breeches until he had them undone, pushing them down and off his legs. Then, kneeling over her as she stretched on the length of the bed, he eased upward until, with an ease and naturalness she had never expected, she took the pulsating phallus in her mouth, pulling and sucking on it as he had sucked her nipples.

She could feel his excitement growing. She was almost

disappointed when he withdrew and stretched beside her. Sinking down into the feather bed along with her, he laid his hand on her waist and bent to taste her breasts. Cupping one hand beneath, he lifted the swelling fullness to his lips and sucked gently at the nipple. Jess forgot all else, writhing in increasing excitement as he worked on her as a musician works upon a beloved instrument. When she thought she could stand it no longer, his arms went about her and he covered her body with his own, spreading her legs and thrusting into her with the driving shaft of his manhood. There was pain, but it was lost in the wildness that consumed her. In all the world there was nothing else but this searing need to be consumed, swallowed, made whole and completed by the other part of her being. Nothing but his body surging against hers, urging her to the edge of a precipice from which there was no return. She dimly heard her own cries and Rhys's panting. Locking her within his arms, he thrust into her until at last they were completely one in ecstasy's fire. They fell together over the edge and lay spent and exhausted across the bed.

Justine opened her eyes to a shimmering shower of light that reflected off the sea outside the windows and gave the enclosed bedspace the sense of being underwater. With a long sigh she turned to lie in the circle of Rhys's arms, stretched against his long body, resting her head upon his chest, entirely without strength and blissfully at peace.

Gently his hands caressed her hair and he lightly kissed her forehead. "You amaze me," he said quietly, but with an intensity that lingered from their coupling. "Like no other woman I've ever known."

"That's know in the Biblical sense, I suppose," Justine said laughing.

"All right. Like no other woman I've ever made love to."

His arms tightened around her and she rested her head in the delicious hollow of his neck and shoulder. She was amazed at how natural it all seemed, even though for her it was the first time she had ever been with a man. She felt no sense of embarrassment at her nakedness or at his. It simply seemed so right for the two of them—her pliant soft roundness against his lean, hard strength—to meld together like this, lying in the downy womb of the bed with the water and light shimmering over them, as though the rest of the world had ceased to exist.

And then in the quiet repose that wrapped them both, Rhys caught the familiar snap and luff of swelling canvas far above his cabin. The ship rose with a gentle tremor and woke to life, dipping her bows in the waves and lifting the stern where they lay to suddenly blot out the horizon he had been watching from his window.

He lifted his head, listening intently, conscious of every slight movement beneath him. "By God, I think it's broken at last."

Justine, sorry that their lovely quiet had been shattered, sat up on her elbow. "What is it? What's wrong?"

"Wrong!" Rhys cried, leaping from the bed to begin pulling on his clothes. "Nothing's wrong. It's the best thing that could be. The wind's returned."

The disappointment on her face brought him to a sudden stop, his shirt half on. Planting one knee on the bed, he bent to kiss her full on the lips.

"Sorry, my love, but duty calls. We'll continue this later."

Jess knew it would be useless to argue, so she laid back on the bed and watched with amusement as he threw on

106

his clothes, so anxious to get to the bridge that his jabot was carelessly tied and his waistcoat buttoned only at the top. When he flew out the door, she wrapped the coverlet around her and walked over to make certain it was locked, then moved back to lay on the bed and stare out of the window at the sunset, enjoying the gentle rocking of a ship underway at last. She was still amazed at the joy she felt. For the first time she understood what the word fulfillment really meant. She felt whole, filled up, completed, as though a part of herself that had been missing had fused together again for a brief time. Above her head she could hear the thumping movements of the ship's crew, and she fancied there was joy and relief in their steps as they went about their work. The snap of the canvas was growing in strength, and she knew that when she stepped on deck again she would hear that wonderful strumming of the wind in the sheets that was almost like an organ playing in church. On the horizon the colors of sunset had begun their nightly litany, blue, gray, rose, and gold all merging around a vermillion sun that hung in the sky like a brilliant carnelian. Yes, she was happy. For the first time since her father's terrible death, she was really happy.

"Too happy!" she said aloud and brought her rioting emotions under control. She had work to do and a mission to perform. This dalliance on a hot, boring, becalmed afternoon was pleasant enough, but it would not do to give it too much importance. She sat straight up in the bed, shaking herself. She had no intention of attaching her heart to any man right now, least of all one like Rhys Llewellyn, an obviously worldly man who had loved many women in his time, and a rebel to boot!

*   *   *

107

The breeze that carried the *Boeadecia* toward Europe was as energetic now as it had been lethargic before. They flew on the crest of the wind like the gulls soaring over the mainmast who soon appeared to herald the nearness of the shore. Justine spent most of her days on deck, making conversation with Mr. Dunbar, the only one of the invalids to have sufficiently recovered, exchanging glances with the captain that were full of invitation and promise, and encouraging stories of other voyages out of the sailors who had the good humor now to entertain her.

Some of her satisfaction was due to the intervening nights she had spent with Rhys, locked within his arms, deep in the mounds of his feather bed. Her resolution to guard herself against him had not lasted very long. In fact, it had not survived their first supper together two nights after the wind returned. Though they were as circumspect as possible, she supposed the crew knew very well what was going on—their veiled comments about how lovely and bright she looked were too obvious. The fact that Rhys was busy most of the day and night running his ship made their times together more precious and infrequent, and Justine had satisfied herself that she was strong enough to enjoy them for what they were—a pleasure lasting only the length of a voyage, with no future. Already she felt a terrible pang at the thought of parting from him when they reached port, but that was the price she must pay for the joy of their time together. And, in a way, that parting was what made all this possible, as though life on the ship was not the real world at all.

And then they sighted land. Justine was not the first to see it, though she had been poised all day, staring at the horizon, searching for the long dark outline of uplifted hills that signaled Europe. The thrilling "Land Ho" came from the watch in the crow's nest high over her head and brought her streaking to the taffrail. The thin strip of gray that was land looked like a painter's brushstroke between sea and sky, yet it sent a thrill through her entire body.

Rhys leaned from the quarterdeck and called her up the steps to view the shoreline through his glass. Standing close beside her, with his hand lightly resting on her shoulder as he helped Jess to focus the ungainly metal tube, they both forgot for a moment that they were in full view of the rest of the crew. It was a moment of closeness that Jess would come to treasure as one of the last instances of the peaceful, dreamlike quality of their trip.

"Now the fun begins," Rhys muttered as though reading her mind. "Let's hope this good wind holds, at least until we're past Tripolitania."

"What do you mean?"

"Once we're in the Mediterranean Sea, we're fair game for those blackguards that lie in wait for anything that will bring them a profit. They're out of Algiers and protected by its dey. Nothing is sacred to them."

"But surely we have nothing of much value in our cargo."

"Anything is of value, from the ship itself to the crew." He looked down on her, his eyes twinkling. "And you would have the most value of all."

Justine lowered the glass to look up at him, her eyes round with surprise. "I don't understand."

Rhys was suddenly very interested in studying the horizon. "You'd bring a good price for some sultan's harem," he said lightly. "A Caucasian beauty with copper hair and green eyes. Worth a king's ransom I shouldn't doubt."

Her hand went instinctively to her throat. "Somehow I don't think you mean that as a compliment. Surely you're not serious. I'm an American, a British citizen."

"You'll find that has little meaning in some parts of the world. And I'm deadly serious. But don't worry about it too much. The *Boeadecia* may not be the swiftest ship afloat, but she can outrun the made-over brigantines these pirates sail. I'll feel better, however, if you remain below deck for the next few days."

Justine took one last hungry look at the shoreline, slightly darker and wider now. "You don't have to tell me twice!" she muttered, handing Rhys his glass.

As it turned out, she did not quite hide in her cabin as she thought she might when Rhys first mentioned pirates. She could not bear to see the dark mountainous mass of Gibraltar pass by so closely and not be on deck to enjoy it. For the next two days their sailing was so peaceful that she began to spend all her time on the fo'c's'le deck, straining for the shape that would mean Sicily, and all the ancient glories of Rome. They were keeping fairly close to the shoreline rather than venture out in the open waters of the blue Mediterranean, more from caution than a wish to view something of the ancient world. Justine's fellow passengers, now all recovered from their bout with fever, joned her at the taffrail, soaking up the mellow sunshine and sharing her enthusiasm at being within hailing distance of historical places.

And then they sighted pirates. The watch called a warning of a ship approaching bearing all the marks of a corsair vessel—a fighting man's brigantine, stripped of quarterdeck, fo'c's'le, and mizzenmast, flouting fore and aft sails. A shattering broadside as soon as the deformed ship came within range confirmed Rhys worst fears. He

110

banished Jess to her cabin immediately and, taking advantage of a stiff wind, headed for the open sea.

The converted brigantine was fast, but Rhys was more clever. Maneuvering his ship to take advantage of wind and current, he managed to stay far enough ahead of the raider that her guns lobbed into the water ineffectually. Justine stood at the solitary little porthole of her tiny cabin and watched for the sails of the horizon as the ship dipped and turned. The creaking timbers of the ship grew into complaint as more sail was crowded on to push her through the water. Jess clutched at the walls of the cabin as the gyrations of the beleaguered craft sent her this way and that, always straining for some assurance from her window that the pirate ship had not drawn closer.

Rhys's suggestion that she might be of value to such men as these had frightened her more than she would admit. She knew little of the Oriental world and her knowledge of harems was limited to the few stories from Arabian Nights that her nurse had read to her long ago. Still, that was enough to set her skin crawling at the thought of a lifelong confinement among a group of women who existed solely as sexual playthings for one powerful potentate. A shiver ran through her at the thought. Her lovely world in Philadelphia seemed far away, yet never had the thought crossed her mind that she would not see it again. Their sailing had been so uneventful, so "other-worldly" up until now, that she had forgotten how threatening reality could be. Now it came sweeping back with full force.

She spent the rest of that day and night alone in her cabin. There was no one to even bring her a tray, and she was too cowed to go on deck and bother the crew in the middle of their dangerous work. Late in the evening Mr. Dunbar appeared with a cold supper and told her the

111

captain thought they were safe, but wanted to wait until morning before declaring the danger really past. Jess slept fitfully that night, and was still so fearful of the ship being boarded that she never removed her clothes. She wondered at Rhys not coming to her for even a moment, or at least sending her word of how they fared, but she laid it to his preoccupation. If he could get them out of this danger, she was prepared to forgive him anything.

She woke the following morning to sunlight streaming through the window, spreading a pool of gold on the floor. Something about the ease with which the ship glided gently in the water told her they were safe now, and she changed her clothes and combed her hair, taking care to look her best. When she went up on deck, she found the sailors going about their chores in a cheery manner, and an unbroken expanse of blue water whose serene beauty laid her fears to rest.

"Good morning," Rhys said, leaning over the railing of the quarterdeck, his hands clasped as he smiled down on her. He bore the effects of having been up for many hours. His jabot was loose, his hair unkempt, and a stubble of black shadow covered his cheeks. Yet she could read the relief on his face and the old invitation in his eyes.

"I presume we got safely away," Jess asked, looking up at him.

"Oh yes. It took some fancy maneuvering, but we managed. We've a good crew and a sound ship."

"And a clever captain, I think. Where are we now?"

"See that dark line over there to port. That's Greece."

Justine turned, her face suddenly suffused with delight as she pushed her streaming hair from her eyes. "Greece! Is it really Greece?"

112

"I can see that Greece is even more stirring for you than the thin line that was Italy. Yes, it's Greece in all its ancient glory. I wish we had the time to visit some of its historic places, but we do not. You'll have to be satisfied with this one little look."

Justine went scampering up the steps to the deck beside him to get a better view. Rhys handed her the glass without her asking for it, then sat back to watch her as she peered through it. The sun glinted in her hair like burnished copper, and the wind lifted her shawl around her shoulders, revealing the swelling curve of her breasts beneath her thin frock. He was bone-tired, but he felt anew the old stirring of his flesh at the sight of her.

"It's frustrating to see just this little pencil line," Jess said, closing the glass with a snap and handing it back to him. "Besides, I'm famished. No one had time to bring me anything to eat yesterday when I was hiding in my cabin."

"You're always famished," Rhys said laughing. The wind sent a long stream of her hair against her cheek which he gently pushed away. "This will be one of our last two nights before reaching Bayrut. I think a little supper with the captain might be in order. Can I interest you?"

Justine felt a tiny pang at the thought that their time together was drawing to an end. And yet, the idea of another glowing night in his arms, deep in the warmth of that feather bed behind the embroidered curtain was enough to set her blood singing.

"Oh yes," she whispered, smiling up at him. "I think I would like that very much."

Five

The mournful cry of a *muezzin* from a nearby mosque brought Justine to the window of her room in the small hostel where she had finally found lodging. It was run by a French couple from Marseille and catered to Europeans like herself, adrift in the exotic city of Baghdad. All around her the cries were taken up, echoing across the domed and peaked roofs of the city, like the lost wails of ghosts and spirits from some unknown reaches of the nether world. The strangeness of that forlorn sound—which in actual fact was the only ordinary daily call to prayer—always accentuated for her the utter foreignness of this peculiar world in which she found herself. Had she been plucked from her familiar home to be planted on the slopes of Venus or Mars, she could not have felt more out of place.

Her window looked out across the Tigris River with most of the city behind her. On the far shore she could make out the ungainly shapes of water buffalo being driven home by two women, covered head to foot in black robes, their long switches bobbing like some giant insect.

Near them, on the river, several round *kufas*—those large circular boats that looked like big clay pots floating on the surface of the water—were held by their ropes against the sluggish tide. Behind them the mud walls of a village reflected the waning sunlight in patterns of rose, gray, and gold. The eternal stench of the river assailed her nostrils through the open window, merging with the unpleasant aromas from the street below. That ubiquitous smell had been one of the hardest things for her to accept, that and the poverty she saw around her on her infrequent trips to the *suq* or marketplace. *Madame* Brochard, the French proprietress who from the moment she laid eyes on Justine had taken a motherly interest in her welfare, assured her that she should not go out at all, or at least, only when wearing a hat and veil and accompanied by a bodyguard. This was not at all in keeping with Justine's plans, but since she had not yet come to terms with this strange city, she had gone along with the Frenchwoman for the time being. Once she felt more sure of herself, she was determined to strike out on her own and find this Yarmid Ali who was mentioned in her father's letter.

She leaned against the open fretwork of her window and stared out at the lovely evening sky, now shimmering the muddy waters of the Tigris like liquid gold. Being here was like living in a dream, she thought. It had been that way ever since she left the *Boeadecia* at Bayrut. Somehow nothing had turned out as she had expected, certainly not this utterly, overwhelming sense of being lost—one young, friendless white woman among a horde of dark foreigners. She remembered how she had stood on the wharf when they touched port, frozen with fear, completely uncertain as to which way to go. Then Rhys had leaned down from the quarterdeck, waved to her and called, "Good luck." She was forced then to put a good face on it. Gaily she had waved back and begun looking around as though waiting for her aunt. When she spotted a European woman on the edge of the crowd, she headed for her, prepared to carry out her performance at all costs.

Even now she felt that the Lord must have been watching over her. Bridget Malone was a middle-aged, rotund, slightly homely Irishwoman with a round face under a flapping mobcap and straw bonnet. The shock and surprise of a perfect stranger greeting her like a long-lost friend was tempered somewhat when Jess whispered in her ear as she embraced her: "Please pretend you know me. I'll explain later. I need a friend!"

Ten years in the Near East had prepared Bridget for nearly anything, and she willingly went along with Justine's act, delighted by the intrigue of the situation. It was fortuitous that Justine had chosen her, for she turned out to be extremely kind, knowledgeable about the Arab world, happy to find "one of her own kind" among these foreign people, and delighted with the romance of Justine's bold journey.

Bridget had come to Damascus as a single lady to assist her brother, a Catholic priest who ran a school there. She took Jess under her wing, offering her a place in her little caravan train back to the city, and introducing her to the language, food, and currency of the area. She thought it appalling that Justine was determined to go on to Baghdad, but was unable to make the slightest dent in Justine's stubborn resolve. Yet, even now Jess shivered at the thought of how she would have managed had not this kind Irish lady appeared when she did. It was through her introductions to other Europeans in Damascus—mostly French men and women who ran the schools and hospitals—that she was given a letter of introduction to the Brochards in Baghdad. It had all worked out so perfectly, that Justine could only feel it was meant to be.

And now here she was, alone, yes, but so much more prepared to face the task ahead. She understood a little of the language, with careful thought she could handle some of the currency, she had a friend to translate when the rapidity of Arab speech got beyond her, and someone to orient her to the ways of the city. Now all she had to do was find this Yarmid Ali and convince him to turn over the money he was holding to her, instead of giving it to the rebels. If she could talk him into that, she could go straight back to Bayrut, take the first ship bound for America, and return home having successfully accomplished the mission her father had left her. She sighed happily at the thought.

The chorus of *muezzins* continued around her like a chorale, echoing across the city. The familiar babble of the streets, softened by the prayers, was taken up and repeated. And Jess's thoughts went drifting back to Rhys Llewellyn.

It had been difficult for her to say good-bye, especially after that last night they shared before the ship docked at Bayrut. They had eaten together, drunk wine, and then he had picked her up and carried her to his bed, drawing the embroidered curtain against the world for the rest of that enchanted night. Long hours in each other's arms, ecstasies of love washing over them again and again, sleeping only to wake to ecstasy once more—she had never dreamed such happiness could exist. Although

117

both had agreed that this would be their last time together, and they would probably never meet again, yet Jess could not shake the sense that a part of her self had somehow become intertwined with a part of his, and to wrench them apart would mean that she would never be whole again.

And yet, she chided herself, that was foolish. Splendid as it was, Capt. Llewellyn had probably forgotten all about her by now and was absorbed in sailing his ship around the Cape to China.

A sharp rap on the door brought her back from her daydreaming. "Enter," she called, and the door was pushed open by *Madame* Brochard's corseted little figure carrying a tray with a fat English china teapot and several little cakes.

"I've brought you tea," she said in English laced with a heavy French accent. "I thought we share it together, yes?"

"How nice," Jess answered, taking the tray from the woman to set it on a table near the window. "You shouldn't have carried it yourself. I would have come down."

Madame Brochard had been a very pretty woman once, and her bright little face still grew lovely when she smiled. She pulled up a chair to the table and sat down to pour the tea. "I thought we have another lesson, *mais oui?* Your Arabic, it could still improve. You must learn the bargain or these *vendeurs*, they steal all your money!"

Justine laughed. "I don't expect to be buying souvenirs, Madame. But you are certainly right that my Arabic is woefully inadequate. I would also like you to draw me a map of the *suq*. Especially the Street of the Tailors."

Madame's sharp eyes settled on Justine as she handed her one of the handleless cups. "A shoddy part of Baghdad, *Mademoiselle*. Not where a respectable young lady like yourself should ever go."

"Oh, but one of your porters can accompany me. I've heard wonderful things about the tailors' skills and the marvelous fabrics they use—silks, tulles, brocades. And after all, I have come here to take these things back to Master Romaine, the merchant in Philadelphia. I must find these treasures for him in order to justify my trip."

"Ah, I never understand you English! A woman in a city like this, doing a merchant's job. *Mon Dieu!* No Frenchwoman would ever dream of such a thing." Her eyes narrowed. "Nor do I quite believe any merchant would choose a woman alone for such a trip. But, *néanmoins*, I do not pry. You say you come to Baghdad to buy the cloths, without husband, brother, father, mother, or, *mon Dieu*, lover, and I take your word. Only I urge you to be cautious, *Mademoiselle*. This is a strange city, like no other in Europe, or even, I'm told, the Colonies. Now, bring me your paper and quill, and I draw you the map."

Jess smiled to herself as she moved quickly to the *escritoire* to find the materials that would finally take her to Yarmid Ali and the Street of the Tailors. She had endured much and come a long way, but at last she could see the end of her journey in sight.

Rhys pulled his cloak closer around his shoulders and yanked his tricorn hat down over his eyes. It was not so much that he sensed danger in the narrow, crowded streets of Baghdad, but that it was all so foreign and strange. He had already learned that it was safer never to

119

make himself too obvious in the crowd, and to always be alert for what was happening around him. After his first excursions into the streets, where he was crowded by beggars, ragged children with open sores, barefooted mothers carrying scrawny babies on their hips, the crippled and maimed of all ages, all crying *Baksheesh!* and pulling at his robes with their clawing fingers as they spotted a European and an easy target, he had learned to adapt an air of concentration that shut out the people around him. It usually worked pretty well.

He hurried through a mostly residential section, making his way toward one of the outlying *suqs* near the Street of the Tailors. The road was little more than an alley, narrow and twisting, lined with mud-brick houses whose impassive fronts with their heavy, closed doors shut out the world even as he had learned to. Above his head, overhanging the road on both sides so close as to almost touch, were the ever-present bay windows with their intricate latticed grillwork. He could feel unseen eyes peering down at him, increasing that sense of nameless anxiety that was so much a part of this city. Although he had learned his way around rather quickly for an Englishman, it had taken him much longer to locate this Yarmid Ali. The tailor's shop, it turned out, was not actually located on the twisting, convoluted tailors' street, but on one of the narrower alleyways off it. It made Rhys grind his teeth to think of the time he had wasted going up and down the Street of the Tailors before finally locating someone who knew of Yarmid Ali and could direct him to the right shop. Someday he would let Robert Morris and Alex Greydon know how their carelessness had complicated his life.

But now his one obsession was to reach this Arab and

learn how he was to collect the money intended for his government. Then, with any luck and a good wind, he would be on his way home.

He hurried on, still amazed to find himself surrounded by throngs of men in long *dishdashes* and checkered headcloths, and women shrouded in the sacklike, black *abas* that gave them a spectral appearance in broad daylight. He gave a slight involuntary shudder. Ever since the morning after the *Boeadecia* left Philadelphia, when he first saw Justine standing by the taffrail, this trip had held something of the quality of a daydream. Something inside him grew warm as he thought of the lovely auburn-haired girl who had enchanted him so on the long voyage to this strange world. His thoughts went back to that dreamy night as they neared Bayrut—their last night together. The passion, the joy, the utter delight of her enticing body that had been so willingly his through those long hours, was a memory to treasure the rest of his life. He wondered if she was content now living with that round-faced homely woman who had met her at the dock. Did she ever think of him, ever remember the magic of their lovemaking in the cabin of his ship? Would that night stay with her, too, during the years ahead when she would no doubt be married to some plump Frenchman and raising a family of her own in this exotic world? All he knew was that he would never forget her, no matter where this crazy adventure took him.

He had reached the bazaar now and the noise level increased as he made his way past the stalls and shops. The network of narrow streets was roofed against the hot April sun with a variation of stone vaulting, wooden arches, or strips of canvas. Each trade had its own street where merchants displayed their wares openly, enticing possible customers into their booths with their cries. This city, he had learned, lay on the great trading route between Asia and Persia and the assorted goods from those countries on display here was enough to make a Colonial merchant lick his lips. The brilliantly colored cloth, the decorative woven straps and harnesses for horses, the intricate patterns of rugs and carpets, the sea of burnished gold in the copper *suq*—where the noise of the hammering inside the shops was almost deafening—the smell of spices and the heavy aroma of Turkish coffee—it was like being set down in a fantastic world of Arabian Nights. Rhys had to get a grip on himself to remind his wandering mind that he was here for one purpose and one purpose only—to help insure that his country would survive the process of breaking away from English domination. And this Yarmid Ali whoever he might be, was a necessary part of this purpose.

It seemed an eternity of wandering before he finally came upon the Street of the Tailors. Even then the tiny side street off the main road was difficult to find, there were so many of them. The morning was far gone when at last Rhys stood outside a mud-brick building that surpassed its neighbors for shabbiness. The small door in the crumbling wall appeared to open into a cave, so black was the room beyond. There was no window on the ground floor, though above the doorway hung one of the ever-present bays, so tiny and ramshackle it looked as though it would collapse if anyone sat there. The shops were so crowded on both sides of the street, and let in so little light, that Rhys doubted how much one could see anyway. But at last he was here, and that was all that mattered.

Bending his head, he entered the shop, setting off a

mass of camel bells hanging over the lintel. As his eyes
adjusted to the darkness inside, he could see that the
interior of the shop was even less inviting than the
outside. Shelves lined two sides of the walls, haphazardly
stacked with bolts of cloth covered with a coating of
white dust. One long table was set against the third wall,
littered with ragged pieces of black silk and magenta-
colored sacking. In the corner nearest it, a dirty curtain
obscured a narrow door to the rear of the shop. Rhys
waited, looking around for what seemed a long time,
considering that his presence had been loudly announced
by the camel bells. He lifted a corner of the silk on the
table, and was fingering it absently when the curtain was
pulled back and a small man thrust out his head. He wore
a turban so large it dwarfed his narrow face. His pale eyes
were a startling contrast to his brown skin, but they held
a liveliness and sparkle that was not in keeping with the
rest of his features. When he saw a European standing in
the shop, he smiled broadly, and Rhys noted how one
corner of his lips lifted higher than the other, giving his
narrow chin a lopsided, imbecilic look. Rhys sighed to
think he was going to have to deal with this slow-minded
creature—one more barrier to finding Yarmid Ali.

The little man stepped into the shop, bobbing up and
down and rubbing his short beard as he welcomed Rhys
with a long babble of Arabic.

Rhys broke in: "Do I have the pleasure of addressing
Yarmid Ali of the Street of the Tailors?"

"Ah, *effendi*. You speak English," the man answered,
bobbing even more energetically. "I also. A little."

"I am looking for Yarmid Ali. If you are not he, would
you please tell me where to find him."

He was answered with another long stream of Arabic,

as the little man hurried to one of the shelves and began pulling down bolts of dusty cloth.

"No, I don't want to buy anything," Rhys said, pushing away the lengths of fabric that were being draped over his arm. "I want to speak to Ali."

"But, *effendi*, such beauty, such texture. And I create the European style with great finesse. See here, this color, it is just right for you."

"You speak English very well for an Arab. Don't pretend you don't understand me. Take this stuff away, and take me to Yarmid Ali. Here, I'll pay you two dinars to do what I ask. But I do not want to buy any clothes."

The Arab shrugged and reached for the money, slipping it inside his dirty robe. "Ali," he frowned. "You do not want to speak with him. He is unpleasant. Always grumbling, complaining, even—Allah forgive—violent. Very, very violent. He is not a nice man. Why should a fine person like yourself want to have anything to do with such a fellow?"

"I have business with him. I was sent here to find him."

"Who would send for Yarmid Ali but cutthroats and villains? It cannot be for anything good. You must leave. Go home, back to whatever country you came from. Have nothing to do with Yarmid Ali!"

Rhys was beginning to get annoyed. "I cannot go back. Whatever he is like, I have no choice but to speak with him. You will please either fetch him out or tell me where I can find him."

"Ah, *effendi*, he will only hit me again. He is a very bad man to work for. He beats me often for even the slightest little mistake. I do not like to bother him for nothing."

The sly devil, Rhys thought. He sees me as an easy

touch. "Would this make it more worth your while?" he said, pulling out several more coins. Almost immediately they were grabbed from his fingers with a professional ease.

"Please to wait here," the man said, and resumed his bobbing as he hurried behind the curtain. Rhys stood contemplating the shelves along the mud-brick wall for what seemed fifteen minutes, before the curtain was pulled back once again, and a cultured voice said, "Enter, please."

He had to bend to pass through the narrow doorway. Once inside he straightened and looked around, astounded. He had passed into a room that was worlds away from the one he had left. It was well lighted and airy, with lattice work over the open ceiling and one wall at the far end that opened on to a courtyard cool with spreading shade trees. The walls were lined with soft cushions of intricately patterned silks and brocades, while the floor was covered with several carpets in brilliant shades of blue and red. A copper brazier stood in the center with several hassocks scattered around it. A tray was set nearby with a copper pot and several glasses surrounded by plates of ripe apricots and an assortment of pastries. Rhys was so amazed by the transformation that he could only gape openmouthed.

"It is a surprise, yes?" said the little man beside him. "Enter please and accept the poor hospitality of my house. It is all yours."

Rhys turned to gape at the man. "Why, you rascal. *You* are Yarmid Ali!"

"I regret the deception," he answered with a lopsided smile that suggested he did not regret it at all. "It is sometimes necessary to know who seeks me, before I

125

offer them my hospitality. You will understand, I think, that not too many people come here wanting new clothes."

"I think I will have my dinars back, if you please," Rhys said testily.

Yarmid Ali shrugged and waved his hand. "But they were taken in good faith. And, after all, I did bring you to Yarmid Ali, did I not?"

Ali sat cross-legged on one of the hassocks and tucked his feet neatly beneath him. "I hope you will forgive my little trick, *effendi*. It is not so often that an English comes looking for me, and it is sometimes necessary to use caution before admitting my identity."

Rhys could well believe that. The rascally Arab probably had a number of people he had cheated out searching for his blood. He sat on one of the cushions opposite his host and studied him, while Ali fussed over the charcoal brazier. He was peculiar-looking for a Mesopotamian. Walnut-colored skin fading to almond where the neck of his robe pulled away, thin lips, lively eyes, a narrow pointed chin. He still wore the dirty blue *dishdasha*, but had exchanged the turban for a white headcloth held in place with several woven cords. All in all he seemed a strange person to be entrusted with anything as important as a treasure that could save the American States. For the first time Rhys wondered if Robert Morris and the others really knew what they were doing.

"You will, of course, share a glass of tea with me," Yarmid Ali said as he set the copper jug over the coals. Rhys had been warned about the significance of the laws of Arab hospitality, and he readily agreed, accepting a sugary pastry from the plate Ali handed him, even though it was the last thing he wanted right then.

"You have come a long way, *effendi*," the Arab said cautiously.

It was the opening Rhys had been waiting for and he leaned forward eagerly. "I bear a letter from Mr. Robert Morris of the city of Philadelphia in the American Colonies. Your name is mentioned in it."

"May I see it please."

Rhys dug in the pocket of his coat and handed over the letter, wondering if the man would actually be able to read it or would perhaps simply recognize his name. "I was told you could furnish me with information about a certain . . . important object I'm entrusted to find and bring back to America."

Yarmid Ali nodded, bobbing over the letter. "Yes, yes, that is true. I've been expecting you, or, at least, someone like you."

"If you have it here, I would be much obliged if you would turn it over to me, so I can be on my way. I'm prepared to take it back to Bayrut with me where I can get a ship home. Your responsibility will be ended, something I feel certain you will welcome."

Ali laughed and waved his hand. "You think I would keep something of such value here? Allah be praised, I would as well invite thieves in to carry me off."

Rhys hoped his disappointment wasn't too obvious. "Then you can direct me where to find it?"

The Arab's face fell. "Alas, I cannot even do that. All I can tell you, *effendi*, is where the treasure lies. After that, it will be up to you."

Rhys accepted a glass of the strong, sweet tea, suppressing a sigh. He had hoped that, with any luck, the end of his journey would be here in Baghdad, but obviously that was not to be. Well, to be honest, he had not expected to be quite that lucky. "I gather it is not somewhere in the city?"

Ali laughed again, showing uneven yellow teeth. "I fear it is not. Your travels will take you far, *effendi*, if you hope to bring back this ransom for your government. The treasure is in the keeping of the Emir of Bokharta, somewhere in his city of Samarkand. You will have to go to the emir in order to collect the money."

"Samarkand! I never heard of it. Where is it? A day's ride? Two days?"

Yarmid bent forward, laying one hand over his mouth to cover his mirth.

Rhys, who was beginning to think the man was playing with him, found his anger growing. "Look here," he snapped. "I have already come a long way and gone to a great deal of trouble to find you, only to be told with some glee that you cannot help me. The gentlemen who set me this task are deadly serious about its importance. If you are not the man I need, then perhaps I'd better try to find someone else." He made as if to rise.

"Sit ye down, Captain," Yarmid Ali replied in such coloquial English that abruptly Rhys stopped getting up. "Sit ye down and don't be so huffy. Ye'll not find anyone in this bloody city who can help ye, so you might as well put up with me. It's not that I'm makin' a joke at your expense, but that ye're so bloomin' cocky. It's an English trait, I fear, and one some Americans have taken to as well."

Rhys stared blankly at the man. "Why, you're not an Arab at all," he finally managed to stammer. "What the devil is going on here!"

"I'm as Arab as an Englishman-born can be, after ten

128

years of livin' in this den of infidels and thieves. And as a man with one foot in both worlds, I'm probably the only person who can really help you. So relax and drink yer tea. It's not Bohea, to be sure, but it's tea, and ye'll soon grow accustomed to its syrupy taste."

"I think you owe me an explanation."

"Well now, the truth is, I don't owe you a blessed thing, but I'll satisfy yer curiosity a trifle, just because I'm basically a good fellow. I landed in Bayrut ten years ago, after jumpin' ship from His Majesty's Navy. I figured I was owed my freedom, since I'd been pressed into service after one memorable night at a Plymouth pothouse. Somehow the government didn't see it quite that way, and I had to take on an Arab identity in order to keep my precious freedom. I got pretty good at it. To this day there are only one or two men know who I really am. Not even your fancy Mr. Morris knows he was dealing with an Englishman. He thinks I'm a crafty Arab who knows the language well enough to be useful."

"I thought you spoke English awfully well for an Arab," Rhys said, aware now of the tiny indications in the man's appearance that revealed his true origins. "You're a little too cocky yourself, from what I've seen of the local fellows. Most of them are quite cowed around me."

"That's because ye're taller than they are and richer, or so they believe. They may bow and scrape in your presence, but, believe me, privately they consider you beneath their contempt. I've seen both worlds very closely, and I know how minds work in each of them. But come now, let's get to the business at hand. Ye may be an important fellow back in the Colonies, Captain, but you don't know your geography. Samarkand is half a world

129

away from here, near the China border. It's a deal more than a two-day ride."

"But there's nothing in between. How can I get there? I sent my ship on to Canton, because I was planning to go back to Bayrut and pick up another one bound for America. There's no port in Samarkand, is there?"

Yarmid Ali threw up his hands. "Nothing in between! Captain, Samarkand lies on the Golden Road—the great trading route between Persia, India, and China. People have been traveling back and forth across it for centuries. But not on ships. The only ships ye're likely to travel on have four legs and a hump or two. They're called camels."

Rhys was already thinking ahead. "I want you to tell me exactly what to expect and what route to follow. I'll need to know whom to see about horses or camels or whatever will get me there. I see now that that was what Robert Morris intended, when he told me to contact you."

"Oh, I think he intended much more than that. I'm prepared to arrange a place for you in a caravan starting for Samarkand in two days' time. I'll go along as your interpreter and general all-round assistant. I've had enough of the Middle East, ye see, and I've a hankering for home. It's time I got back, even if I have to assume a third identity to be safe in England." He gave a satisfied chuckle. "You're going to be my salvation, ye see. I lead you to the treasure, and you help me get back home."

Rhys frowned. "Where is this caravan?"

"It sets out from the market Thursday morning. The leader is one Faud Monsel, a camel merchant by trade who has branched out. It is a small train as trains go, but we'll be safe within it."

Rhys stood up abruptly. "Thank you, Mr. Ali, or whatever your real name is, but I think I will make my own arrangements. I don't speak the language as well as you, but I do have sufficient funds to impress this Faud Monsel. I don't need you to talk him into taking me along."

For the first time Yarmid Ali looked genuinely startled, and Rhys took some satisfaction from that. He went on: "Since I first entered your shop, I've had nothing but deception from you. I have served as the butt of your humor and an object of your contempt. In short, I don't trust you—Arab or Englishman or whatever your nationality—and I have no intention of helping you to get back home, or to get rich at Mr. Morris's expense. In short again, thank you for telling me where the money is and how to get there—which is all I was supposed to get from you in the first place. Good-bye and good fortune, Mr. Yarmid Ali!"

"But wait a moment! Think, man, what ye're doing. Ye NEED me!"

"God forbid," Rhys exclaimed, striding to the low door. "If my country has to depend on the likes of you for its freedom, may we remain an English colony forever! Good day, sir."

He walked back through the bazaar feeling rather pleased with himself. He had the information he needed to continue his journey and get to the treasure. One thing he did not need was the help of a wily Englishman-turned-Arab who could never be trusted. There must be someone else in Baghdad who could speak English well enough to translate for him. He would spend the rest of the day finding that person, then take him along when he went to find Faud Monsel to book a place in the caravan.

Meanwhile Yarmid Ali with his deceptions, falsehoods, and divided loyalties, could go straight to hell!

Rhys could not know it, but he left the Arab Yarmid Ali suffering the throes of a depression that was decidedly more English than Arabic in nature. Where a good Muslim might shrug and say, "It is the will of Allah," the Englishman in disguise gave vent to his frustration by throwing around a few pillows and kicking the table hard enough to bruise one toe. All this was accompanied by a string of invectives first learned in the stews of London and polished by seven years as the lowest form of life in the British navy.

"You could have handled that better, Collie," the man muttered, when his anger at himself was finally spent and he could examine the interview more objectively. "But then, I never thought he wouldn't want to take me along. The poor fool, he doesn't know enough about this part of the world to fill a snuffbox, yet he thinks he can get along without me. Well, let him try. Any blockhead who thinks Samarkand is two days' ride from Baghdad will probably have the birds picking his bones in the desert before he reaches the Zagros Mountains!"

Ali was still sulking over his failure to influence Rhys the following morning, when Justine walked into his shop. The young Arab boy whom *Madame* Brochard had insisted accompany her was glad enough to wait in the cafe opposite the tailor's shop, particularly when Justine gave him a coin to encourage him to leave her alone. She stood, as Rhys had done the day before, looking around the dingy room in dismay, wondering again if she had done the right thing in coming. She hadn't long to wait, for when Yarmid Ali peered out from behind the red curtain, he was so astounded to see a young, beautiful English girl standing in his shop, that he walked right out.

"You must be Yarmid Ali," Justine said, without waiting for the usual courtesies. "I assume you must speak English or I would not have been told to seek you out. I bear a letter from the American colony of Philadelphia," she went on, handing the folded parchment to him. "You will see that it mentions me by name."

The wily Arab finally found his voice. "I wasn't expecting a woman!" he said in tones that suggested outrage. Justine had suspected she would be received with suspicion, if not hostility, and she was prepared.

"I'm sure you were not. That is one of the reasons I am here. Who would suspect a woman on such a venture? It is clever, is it not? Col. Hughes thought it so. Is there someplace we can talk."

Her efficient, no-nonsense manner had the desired effect, and Ali ushered her into the back room, holding the curtain aside for her, but still unsure how to receive her. The letter looked official and her name was certainly written there. But an Englishwoman! Going boldly about in this city where no Arab woman would dare to show her face! Standing in his sitting room, alone and unchaperoned, like the Queen of England herself! He didn't know what to make of her.

"Please, sit down," he said, drawing up a cushion.

Jess looked down at it and decided that there was no way she could manage to sit on it in anything approaching a ladylike manner in her wide, heavy skirts and tight stays. "I prefer to stand," she said with dignity.

133

"What we have to say to each other should not take long. You have some information for me, I believe. Just tell me what I need to know, and I will go on my way and bother you no more."

Yarmid Ali was beginning to recover enough from his astonishment to appreciate the humor in the situation. He was also beginning to see a way opening up that would allow him to follow the trail of this money. He made a sudden decision to take this bold, lovely lady into his confidence. "Wait here a moment, *Mademoiselle*," he muttered, and disappeared only to reappear a moment later with a chair high enough that Justine could sit in comfort. He seated her, then sank on a cushion, tucking his legs beneath him.

"First, I *am* Yarmid Ali, but I am not an Arab. I come from Fleet Street, London, in jolly old England, but have lived in Baghdad, disguised as an Arab, for the past ten years."

It was Justine's turn to be astonished. Nothing in the man's dress or appearance had aroused her suspicions, or led her to think he was anything other than what he appeared to be. And yet, who better to help the Crown prevent the rebels from gaining a fortune with which to wage war. It not only made sense, it was a brilliantly clever tactic.

"I see ye are surprised," he went on, "but not half so much as I was to see you standing in my shop. What can the government be thinking of to send a woman on such a journey. I don't call it clever, I call it insane!"

Justine began to stammer. "Well, really—"

"No matter," Ali said, waving one hand. "Ye're here now, and we must deal with you. But it is not going to be easy. That American who was here yesterday—"

"What American?" Justine cried.

"That captain. Llewellyn, I think was his name."

Jess's hand went to her throat as she caught her breath. "Rhys Llewellyn! Here in Baghdad? But why? I thought he went on with his ship."

"He mentioned a ship. Sent it on to China, I think he said. Do ye know him?"

"It was his ship that brought me here to Mesopotamia. But I had no idea that he was coming to Baghdad. What did he want with you?"

Ali began to look a trifle uneasy, as he realized he had revealed more than he should have. There would be a few more cushions thrown around again for this lapse. "He came bearing a letter from a merchant in Philadelphia, seeking the same thing you are. I told him just what I shall tell you. The money is in Samarkand, held in trust by the emir there. I don't have it and never had it."

The mention of the strange new city went right over Justine's head. "Was this merchant by chance named Robert Morris?" she asked. When Ali nodded, she jumped to her feet. "But he is a patriot! A Whig. Why would they send Rhys to you, the same man I'm supposed to seek out? Why . . . why, you must be working for both sides! You traitor!"

"Now, ma'am, those are harsh words. What would I, an Arab shopkeeper, care about England and the trouble she has controlling her colonies. I simply have the advantage of speaking and reading the English language. When a man seeks me out and pays me to carry out instructions, I don't ask where his loyalties lie. Why should I?"

"I think you have become more Arab than English, Yarmid Ali. Your time here has not improved you overmuch."

"That may be, ma'am, but the truth is, ye need me if

135

ye're going to go ahead with this wild venture. It's going to be difficult enough for that captain to get to Samarkand. For you to get there without my help is not just unlikely, it's impossible."

Justine picked up her skirts and turned to the door. "If you are helping Rhys Llewellyn, you can be of no service to me. Good day, Mr. Ali."

"Wait, madam. I'm not helping him. He didn't want my services. You, however, are most welcome to them. I have had enough of life in Baghdad. I'd like to go to Samarkand, and from there work my way back to England. Even the poorest patriot gets homesick sometimes for the green fields of home. Especially in a land of desert and wastes like this one."

Justine thought a moment and then resumed her seat. She had learned enough of life in this strange world to know that as a woman alone she would never be able to finish her work here. While this peculiar little man was not the help she would have chosen given a choice, he was all that was available for the moment and she could not afford to walk away from him.

"All right, Ali. If you will help me get to Samarkand and prevent Capt. Llewellyn from carrying this money back to the rebels in America, I'll help you get back to England. I'll expect you to translate for me, help me deal with the natives, and protect me from any dangers we might come across. I know little of this part of the world, and I need someone to depend upon."

"*Mademoiselle* speaks truly when she says she knows little of this world. Naturally I willingly undertake to do all she asks of me, for a small fee, something to compensate me for my time. Also, the expenses of the journey will be borne by you, of course."

136

"How venal you are, Ali. The fee will be very small, not only because I don't have a lot of money with me, but also because you want to go to Samarkand anyway, and I am doing you a favor by taking you on as a guide. As for the expenses, I shall, of course, take care of them. I warn you though, my purse is far from bottomless, and you'll have to be very careful."

Ali bobbed up and down in the best Arabic fashion. "I understand completely, madam. By the way, what shall I call ye? Ye've not yet told me your name."

"Justine Maury, just as it is in the letter," Jess said, recognizing his attempt to trip her up. "What is your English name?"

Yarmid Ali thought her question over before reluctantly answering: "Collier, ma'am. Collier Rigby, called Collie most of my life. And that's close enough to Ali for you to use. As long as we're in Persia, I'd better keep my Arab identity. It's safer that way."

"Very well, Collie. What is our first step?"

He looked her up and down. "The first thing we'd better do is to get ye out of that ridiculous European dress and into something that will not call up so much attention. An Arab *aba* will do fine. Then I'll go round and get us a place in the caravan that's setting off tomorrow morning. Have ye ever ridden in a litter?"

"Hardly."

"Well, it won't be comfortable, but I think you'll manage. I'd better say you're my sister or something. Maybe my wife."

"I think I'd prefer to be your sister."

"All right. Have it your way. The important thing is that you keep ye face veiled, hide ye'self in the folds of yer *aba* and avoid any confrontation with men.

137

Respectable Arab women never face strange men without veiling their faces. Nor are they ever allowed in the company of any men other than their family. We'd better say ye're hard of hearing, as well. We'll pretend that you're being protected and shielded, or it won't look natural. On the other hand it affords us the opportunity of avoiding their spoken language. No one will wonder at your silence."

"Why, all this sounds like imprisonment. Don't the Arab women here rebel?"

"*Mademoiselle* Maury, women in this country are regarded as little more than chattel, not as high as a pure Arabian horse, but a little higher than the donkey. You'd better get accustomed to it, as we will have a long way to go together.

Justine shook her head and reached for her reticule which contained her coins. "I'll never get accustomed to it. But that's not important. Here, this should help you get started. Bring the *aba* round tonight to *Madame* Brochard's hostel where I have rooms, along with instructions where to meet you in the morning. And don't fail me, Collie. My country is depending on me, and I'm depending on you."

He swept her a bow. "*Mademoiselle*, I shall collect ye tomorrow, covered head to toe in yer new *aba*. I feel in my bones that Allah will bless our endeavor. Just leave everything to me."

138

Six

Justine was dressed and waiting for Collie the following morning before the first singsong chants of the *muezzin* rang out from the nearest minaret. She stood swathed in the folds of the tentlike *aba*, wishing she had a mirror in which to see herself. It felt so strange to be without the usual tight laces and corsets, the bone frame of the farthingale, the heavy yards of brocade or damask that made up the overskirts, stomachers, underskirts, and bodices she had worn all her life. Collie had thought of everything, the embroidered velvet slippers, the undergown of loose cotton, the bracelets and anklets of beaten brass, and the kohl to circle her eyes. He even included a headband sporting a few coins, meant to give her the look of a fairly well-off lady showing off her dowry.

To all this Justine had added one thing—a purse holding all of her money—except what she intended to hand over to Collie for expenses—which she fastened around her middle. It would be invisible under the folds of her garments, but would give her the familiar feel of a tightly enclosed waist. All in all, she was very satisfied with her disguise and eager to get underway.

And yet, later, as she walked closely behind Collie into the *suq* of the oldest section of the city, she was all at once so overwhelmed with the strangeness of it all, that she nearly turned and ran back to the Hotel Brochard. Even at this early hour the bazaar was crowded. Ragged children clustered around her, holding out their hands and crying for a pittance. Collie pushed through them and the knots of beggars lining the streets as though they were not there. Shrouded women, housewives making purchases, bargained loudly with shopkeepers crouched among their wares in front of the cavelike stalls. Men in loose trousers and *kaffiyahs* made for the coffeehouses whose bitter aromas choked the air. Goats, donkeys, dogs vied with the vendors, hawkers, beggars, and occasional musician for space, crowding Justine with a rudeness she had never up till now experienced. To them she was just another woman, not an exotic rich European, and the change was almost frightening.

The noises of the hawkers crying their wares, the musicians scraping and banging their instruments, the haggling of the customers, and the enticing calls of the merchants made a din that was earsplitting. It added to the myriad odors that made her draw her veil closer over her face—oils, spices, perfumes, leather, pastries, and sweets, merging casually with urine, dung, charcoal fumes, and over all, the bitter ever-present coffee.

She was relieved when they finally reached the caravan, though the heavy odors of camel and the cries of their drivers only aggravated the noise and smells of the *suq*. It was a long train, if she could judge by the amount of camels the drivers were prodding to their feet. All of

140

them carried some kind of litter; sacks or crates which added to their huge, ungainly forms gave them the look of some monster creature from another planet—as indeed they were to Justine. "Is that what I'm riding in?" she asked in a very small voice when she saw the woven barrel-shaped litter astride one camel's back.

"Shh," he warned. "I'll do all the talking. You just follow my directions."

Though his abruptness was annoying, Justine saw the wisdom of it and held her tongue. There were several other women in the party, and she could see them climbing into these covered baskets and letting down a curtain to hide behind. She stood close to Collie's back, while he talked and gestured at one of the merchants whose rich clothes suggested he was the *Rais*, or leader of the caravan. Glancing around, her eyes all but covered by her veil, her heart gave a lurch as she recognized Rhys at some distance, talking with several soldiers and holding the reins of a small, sleek Arabian horse. She pulled her veil even closer and looked quickly away. Time enough later to face Rhys Llewellyn. Right now it was imperative that she join this caravan.

She was relieved when Collie walked in the opposite direction away from Rhys, motioning her to follow. He managed to get her far enough away from the others that they could whisper quietly in English.

"It's all arranged," he said, bending closer to her while he pretended to fuss with the strap of his sandal. "Ye're my sister, on your way to be married. That's so no one will be interested in you as a potential bride."

"Collie, I saw Capt. Llewellyn. He was leading a horse, so I suppose he'll be riding along with us."

"I'd better not let him see me, not quite yet anyway.

141

Let's get you hidden away, then I'll take meself off until we're well out of the city."

"Don't leave me," Jess cried, clutching at his arm. "I feel like I'm adrift among the barbarians. I'll never manage alone."

Collie smiled his lop-sided grin at her. "They aren't barbarians. They're perfectly honorable Moslem merchants. Just act shy and stay quiet, and no one will bother ye."

"But I can't ride in that basket perched on a camel's hump! I'll fall out!"

"Nonsense. Arab women have been traveling that way for centuries. Ye may be bored, but you won't be uncomfortable. Just hang on, whatever happens."

"Oh, thank you," Jess replied, her voice dripping sarcasm. "That's very comforting."

"Here are a few dates, a piece of *khobuz* bread, and a little water. When we stop later on, wait for me. I'll come right to ye."

As he handed her a parcel wrapped in a dirty rag, along with a small water-skin, he noticed two of the small, grizzled drivers near them glancing their way suspiciously. Taking Justine's arm he bundled her toward the litter he had purchased and helped her to climb aboard.

Although the camel was sitting, and the litter was only several feet off the ground, she had a difficult time climbing on. The floor was thick with cushions, yet she could feel the rough canes of the woven bottom. The sloping roof was only high enough for her to sit upright in the middle section with her legs tucked under her. The overpowering odor of the camel and the closeness of the litter, still bearing the lingering perfume of its last occupant, made her empty stomach turn over.

She settled in, let down the curtain, and was congratulating herself on having come this far successfully when the noise level rose several decibels, indicating they were ready to get underway. As her camel was prodded to his feet, she endured the first of the day's many traumas. Thrown from side to side, the rickety litter was raised high in the air, where it felt poised on nothingness. When amid the strident screams of the driver, the reluctant beast began to move forward, Justine clutched at the sides as her wobbly perch lurched from port to starboard and back again. She knew they were headed for the nearest gate opening on to the flat, barren desert that surrounded Baghdad, but she was soon so ill from the motion of her transport, that she lost all sense of where they were. It was only as the noises of the city receded and the heat inside her litter began to soar, that she knew they had left the city behind and had begun their long journey. As she wobbled back and forth in the folds of her *aba*-tent, she thought with some irritation of Rhys. He had been planning to come here all along to try and take back this money to finance a treasonous rebellion. All along he had lied to her and tricked her. And now he was riding a sleek horse and able to move about at will, while she was smothering and suffocating in this horrible contraption astride a camel's hump! Someday she would get even with him for this. That thought was her only comfort as the long day wore on.

Although Justine could only get the barest glimpse of the country that stretched away on either side from her jolting litter, and that only by peeking from behind her curtain when she heard no one close by, she soon grew aware of the frightening flat barrenness that surrounded her caravan. She had come from a country rich with high trees and thick grasses, cool and temperate, alive with brooks and rivers and crowded with green pasturelands. The hot, baked gravel-strewn plains that stretched in every direction were so desolate, so intimidating, so strange, as to seem almost unreal, except that the suffocating air inside her enclosed litter told her this was no daydream. Stunted thorn bushes were no substitute for cooling, majestic trees, and it was that lack of trees that she felt most strange.

The choking cloud of dust that accompanied their long train parched her throat but, she was careful to conserve the skin of water Collie had given her, for fear that there would be no more. It wasn't until they stopped that evening for their first night's rest that she learned her fears were exaggerated. She stood to one side while Collie unloaded their baggage camel and set up the tent that would be their traveling home. Though not nearly as large as some of the others which were springing up all around her, it was pleasant enough and very welcome after her day in the litter. The ground inside was covered with rugs and carpets in faded, soft colors, while a curtain down the center afforded her space for privacy behind it. In front of the tent, Collie soon had a fire going to cook bean patties and rice for their supper. She saw then that they carried a very large water skin along with supplies. She longed for nothing so much as to discard her disguise, but Collie warned her not to until she was in the privacy of her tent. Her muscles were so stiff from sitting and bouncing all day that she could barely bend when he brought her supper on a wooden tray. Feeling very awkward without spoons or knives, she ate daintly at the food, too tired to really appreciate it.

144

"Finish that and I'll have some coffee for ye," Collie said as he folded himself beside her and dug into a plateful of food. Just the thought of coffee raised Justine's spirits.

"You thought of everything, Collie. I don't know how I would have managed without you."

"Ye wouldn't have," he answered simply. "Ye'd have to hire a flotilla of servants and your own private camel train, and that would attract a lot of attention. I doubt you'd have made it twenty kilometers."

Though Justine was irritated by his arrogance, she had to agree with him. She was completely out of her depth now, immersed in a world that she knew nothing about. Her mission would have certainly floundered had it not been for his resourcefulness.

"I had occasion during the day to ride up ahead and look over your Capt. Llewellyn," he said, licking his fingers.

"He's not *my* Capt. Llewellyn."

Collie gave a delighted chuckle. "He hasn't got the sense you have, that's for certain, or he would have hired me first. Instead he's gone and bought himself two bodyguards that would have been right at home among Tamerlane's Mongols and an interpreter who's a blackguard! He'll be lucky to get to Rayys alive."

Jess looked up curiously. "What do you mean?"

"I recognized that Arab he hired. His name is Mustapha, and he's a scoundrel if there ever was one. He speaks a little English, which he probably picked up from travelers who hired him before he stole their money. He's known around the *suqs* as bad business, but, of course, the great captain wouldn't be aware of that."

"Then you must tell him," Justine said, setting down

145

her plate. "Take him aside and warn him."

Collie laughed. "Me! Never. I offered to help him on his way, and he told me he'd as lief hire a serpent. He's made his bed. Let him lie in it."

"But that's cruel and unfair. He's an Englishman, like us, after all. You can't just abandon him to savages."

"Why not? He as much as called me one of *them*. Besides, why should you care? You both want to get to Samarkand for the same reason, it seems to me. If you can get there ahead of him, you stand a better chance of finding this money for your own people. If he gets 'lost' along the way, so much the better."

"I think you've been in this country too long, Collie. And yet . . . perhaps you're right. I don't really want to see him hurt, but I'd like to beat him to that money." She pulled her robes around her and groped her way to her feet. Somehow Rhys Llewellyn did not seem like the kind of man who would allow a couple of villains and a crafty interpreter to get the better of him. "I'm going to change my clothes and lie down, Collie. Would you bring my coffee when it's ready. All I want to do is stretch out and sleep."

He nodded and watched her disappear behind the black curtain. It occurred to him that perhaps he had not been so clever, making himself bodyguard and nursemaid to a delicate Caucasian girl traveling through this violent Semitic world. And yet, after ten years on the Street of the Tailors, even this had to be an improvement. He hummed to himself as he fussed over the coffee.

On the afternoon of the third day of wending their slow, ponderous way northward, Justine was brought up out of a lethargic half-sleep by the sound of a familiar voice. She jolted awake, recognizing Rhys speaking

146

almost directly outside her litter. Very carefully drawing aside the curtain, so as to be able to peek out, she saw him astride his horse, talking with her driver, his back half-turned away from her. Unable to look around for Collie, she could only hope he had had time to hide somewhere. But she had a direct view of the infamous entourage Rhys had hired, and it was not reassuring. The two bodyguards, in long checkered *kaffiyahs*, flowing robes, and wide sashes with the handles of curved scimitars protruding from them, looked muscular and mean enough to handle any adversary. The small, wiry Arab who stood beside them had to be Mustapha. He kept glancing around as though watching for someone, and his eyes, even at a distance, appeared veiled and suspicious. Rhys must have been desperate for someone who spoke English to have hired such an unsavory person. She had a fleeting thought that perhaps she ought to speak to Rhys and tell him what Collie had said. And yet that would be the worst thing she could do to herself. He had no idea who she was or why she had come to Persia, much less that she was sitting only a few feet away. It would be much better to leave it that way.

After Rhys had ridden off, Jess waited anxiously until Collie appeared, walking casually alongside her camel. "Did you see the captain?" she whispered over the creaking of the harnesses.

Collie nodded. "He didn't see me, though. I was able to drop behind when I saw him coming. Ye didn't let on, did ye?"

"Of course not." She dropped the curtain and shifted on the lurching cushions, relieved that for the time being they were safe.

That evening Collie set up the tent farther from their

147

neighbors, and stayed close by rather than sitting and talking with the other men. It had been a roasting hot day, but with evening a sudden coolness descended like a curtain. Justine was not as sore as she had been the first day of travel, yet she still kept apart, sitting inside the tent near the divider, sipping the strong, sweet coffee, and letting the cool air seep up inside her voluminous robes. The fire had died down to embers glowing like orange eyes in the night, and the voices from the nearest tent were low and distant. She was beginning to nod off when suddenly Collie came crashing into the tent. Justine dropped her cup and scrambled behind her curtain without waiting to see what had happened. It was only when she recognized Rhys's voice, speaking with low intensity, that she peeked out through the curtain. He was bending over Collie and had him by the throat, pinning the smaller man to the ground.

"You bastard! What are you doing here? You're following me, aren't you!"

"For God's sake, Captain," Collie croaked, trying to pull away Rhys's hands. "You're choking me. Let up!"

"I'll let up when you tell me why you're here. You want to get your hands on that money yourself, don't you, you villain? I saw you today, and I recognized you too, before you went sneaking off. Didn't want me to know you were here, did you, you damned scoundrel."

"I can explain everything, if ye'll just let me up!" Collie gasped. Justine clutched at her robes and grew very still behind her curtain, praying Collie would not mention her name.

Rhys released his hands from the smaller man's throat and sat back, glaring at him. "It had better be a good explanation," he said. "I have friends now, and they would as soon remove a flea from their robes as remove

148

you from this Earth."

"Friends, Captain? I saw yer friends today. If these are the men you hired in my place, then I fear for yer judgment." Collie rubbed at his throat, while his anxious glance made certain the black curtain was carefully closed. He sat back, trying to appear relaxed. "It was just that I heard about those men ye'd hired back in Baghdad. I knew the kind of men they were and I feared for ye. So . . . I came along."

"Bah! Do you expect me to believe you joined this caravan out of concern for my safety? And without getting paid for it? You want that money in Samarkand for yourself, don't you? And you think I am going to lead you straight to it."

"Be reasonable, Captain. Who told ye where the money was in the first place? Yarmid Ali, no? If I wanted to track it down for meself, I could have done so long ago, while you were still crossing the ocean from America. What I really want is to leave the East and go home to England. And you are my best chance for that. That's the reason I joined this caravan. I thought ye might change your mind along the way."

"Never! I didn't trust you in Baghdad, and I don't trust you now. An Englishman in this country is in enough peril, even when he's armed with guards, money, and an interpreter. I certainly don't need an adventurer like you to add to my problems. Go back to Baghdad!"

Collie smiled maliciously. "*Effendi*, you have more problems than you realize. Your bodyguards—which, by the way, I applaud ye for hiring since they are necessary for yer survival—are of the Basseri tribe, and likely to have more on their mind than protecting you. Mustapha, on the other hand, is more dangerous than a snake. Ye'd better watch out for that one. Whatever he tells you, his real interest is your money."

"Naturally, you'd say that. It takes one to know one."
Abruptly Rhys rose to his feet. "I know what it takes to
make this journey, and I've made certain I have it. I don't
need you, and I don't want you following me about. If
you cause me any trouble or bother me in any way, I'll
have my Basseri take care of you. Is that clear?"

Collie shrugged. "I tremble, *effendi*," he muttered.

Rhys threw the end of his cloak over one shoulder. "I
have some influence with the *Rais* on this train, and if
necessary I'll have him force you to leave it. Just keep
that in mind."

He swept out of the tent and off into the dark which
had fallen with a sudden swiftness. Collie watched him
go, sitting cross-legged on the carpet and still rubbing at
his neck. "I think it is safe to come out now," he
whispered. The tiny lamps had not been lit, and the tent
was in almost total darkness as Justine slipped out from
behind her curtain.

"Such arrogance!" she muttered. "How could you
bear it?"

"He thinks he understands the Semitic world, because
he was told he needed bodyguards and an accomplice who
speaks English. Typical of the English mind. Well, let
him find out for himself. I've a feeling it won't take
long."

"Thank you for not mentioning me," Jess said, sitting
beside him. "I'd rather not let him know I'm here, if it
can be avoided."

"I thought it better if you told him, not me. I'm not
entirely certain he believed my story, but it may put him
off for a while. Ye'd better keep low, though."

"How can I keep any lower? But yes, I'll try. It's too
bad we didn't take separate caravans, however."

150

"That would have put him well ahead of us. I don't think we need worry about the captain however. At the rate he's going he's likely to do himself in without our help long before we reach Samarkand."

The next day Justine sensed before she actually saw that they were leaving the desert at last. There was something in the air which bore just the lightest touch of clarity and coolness, as though night was descending when it was still morning. She peeked through the curtains and saw that the undulating horizon with its slopes and ridges was not a heat mirage, but real hills far in the distance. Her heart gave a leap at the thought of trees and brooks and cool, rejuvenating air. Perhaps she might even manage a bath. The tiny splashings she had endured so far were so little after the heat of the day in her litter as to make her feel almost rancid.

And yet, once the caravan began climbing the steadily steep road that led into and through the Zagros Mountains that separated the Mesopotamian desert from the Iranian plateau, she saw that her hopes had been a little high. This was a country of rocky slopes, stunted trees, and great jagged gorges, as formidable in its own way as the desert had been. But it was cooler, and Justine was thankful for that.

It was the second night into the mountains that they stopped at a small village where the tribesmen welcomed them with true Arab hospitality. Much of their meagre living was made by servicing caravans with fresh food supplies, rooms in their tiny houses for sleeping, and entertainment in the form of story-telling and conversation. They even provided a form of music with their squawking and banging on primitive instruments as old

151

as the Bible. Though Justine's caravan had not been traveling for very long, the leader decided an extra day's rest would be helpful in facing the steep climb that still lay ahead. For Justine it was like a gift from heaven not to have to climb back into her litter for one whole day, even if it meant more time to sit among the women without speaking while she listened to their gossipy Arabic. She was not sure what excuse Yarmid had given them about her silence, but she was grateful they did not bother her, beyond picking at her robe occasionally or examining her bracelets.

On the afternoon of the day of rest, she finally managed to slip away from the rest of the caravan and follow a path she had seen the women taking earlier that day with their laundry. She found a stream bubbling over gravel and bordered with large flat rocks, so polished they had obviously served as washing boards. She had brought a few clothes with her, but they were not her main object in coming to this little pool. Though there seemed to be no one about, she followed the stream down into a grove of sheltering trees where she felt no one could see her from the washing pool. Sitting beside the brook she waited until she was certain she was utterly alone. Then, drawn by the clear, cool enticing water, she slipped off the headdress of her *aba*, ran her fingers through her hair until it cascaded down her back, and stepped into the stream with her skirts lifted to her knees.

It felt heavenly! The bottom was rough on her feet, but the cleansing water was like manna from heaven. She waded back and forth until she could stand it no longer, and throwing aside her *aba* completely, she sat in the stream and splashed water over her face and hair, reveling in the feel of it. She still wore the long, straight undergarment that was her dress, but it had become so stained with the heat of her travels that it was as good to wash that as herself. The wet fabric clung to her body, sculpturing the curves and indentations, outlining like a second skin the globes of her breasts and the pointed uplifted nipples. She leaned back, arching her body to the afternoon sun, letting her long hair drag in the cold water, licking the drops off her parched lips with her tongue.

"I don't believe it!"

The sound of his voice brought her spinning around. There he stood on the bank, hands on his hips, feet spread wide, a look of such stupefaction on his face that it might have been comical had she not been so appalled.

"I don't believe my eyes," Rhys said. "I knew there was some kind of skulduggery going on, but I never expected to see *you!*"

Jess thought of diving for her *aba*, but what was the use? "You followed me," she said lamely. "You're spying on me. You're no gentleman!"

"What the devil are you doing here? How did you get here? Something *is* going on, and I don't like it. This can't be a coincidence."

"Would you please be so kind as to hand me my robe," Jess said in her haughtiest voice, trying madly to think of what she could say to put him off.

"Do you mean this?" Rhys answered, picking up the *aba* with two fingers as though it was contaminated. "I don't recall you wearing such strange apparel on the *Boeadecia*. It rather adds to the mystery, doesn't it? Tagging along on a caravan through the wilds of Persia dressed as an Arab. Let me see now. You could never have managed that by yourself. Not that you aren't clever, but that kind of duplicity doesn't suit you." Still holding the *aba* he sat down on the bank, crossing his legs

153

under him Arab-fashion. "No, you wouldn't think of this by yourself. Who could have helped you? Why, of course. Who else. Yarmid Ali, the great impostor. And can it be, that you are the mysterious deaf sister I've heard was with him?"

"Will you please stop being so rude and hand me my dress!"

"And why not? Since Yarmid Ali is himself an Englishman disguised as an Arab, why shouldn't he have a sister who's actually an American disguised as an Arab. Allah be praised, it makes complete sense."

"I hope you haven't been telling the people in this train that Collie is an Englishman. You wouldn't stoop that low, surely."

Rhys laughed. "No, but only because I thought his disguise might prove useful to me somewhere along the line. But you! I still can't believe it. I thought I had left you with your missionary aunt in Bayrut. Or was that a lie, too?"

Justine was growing cold after the first glow of her bath. Standing up in the water, she waded to the bank and grabbed the *aba* from Rhys's hand, draping it over herself. "If you can stop being sarcastic for two minutes, I'll explain everything." She flipped her wet hair from under the garment and sat down on the bank a little distance away. The sun was beginning to wane, but it felt warm on her cool skin. "There's a perfectly simple explanation. Yarmid Ali, or Collie, which is his English name, is accompanying me on a journey to see something of the Eastern lands. I hired him."

"I never before appreciated what a shame it is that women over here cover their bodies with those bed-clothes," Rhys said softly, unable to tear his eyes from the clinging fabric on her body. He stretched out on

154

the ground, leaning on one elbow and pulling at the thin grass. "You don't really expect me to believe that you are some kind of tourist. If you wanted to see something of the world, there must be two hundred more hospitable places than these Arab countries. And a million more trustworthy guides."

"I've seen no reason to distrust Collie. He's been very resourceful and helpful to me. I couldn't have come this far without his advice."

"And just how far do you intend to go?" Rhys asked, his eyes narrowing. She could not tell how much he believed of her explanation, but she was encouraged that he seemed to accept some of it.

"You will keep my secret, won't you?" she said without answering his question and looking up at him provocatively from under her long fringe of lashes. "It is so dangerous for an Englishwoman traveling in this Arab world, even with someone like Collie to protect me. Promise me you won't tell them who I am."

Rhys studied her for a moment. Even with her hair plastered around her head, she was so beautiful as to stir his blood. The *aba*, dampened from her soaked underdress, clung to her body, emphasizing every swell and curve. The thought of having her near—with the promise of a renewal of all they had shared on the ship—gave him such delight that he barely heard what she was saying.

"I promise," he muttered, trying to remember what she had asked.

"Word of honor?"

He gave himself a mental shake. "Word of honor. But I don't like it. It was foolhardy for you to come on a trek like this. If you were determined to, why didn't you ask me to bring you?"

"I didn't know you were coming. I thought by now you would be on your way to China with the *Boeadecia*. Why are you here?" she asked innocently.

Rhys realized he had backed himself into a corner. But he'd be damned if he'd give her an explanation. It was none of her business. "Here," he said, extending his hand to help her to her feet. "You'd better wrap yourself up again and get back to the village. I hope you have some dry clothes. It's beginning to get cold."

Pulling her to him, he circled her waist, holding her close. For a moment he looked deeply into her eyes, hoping to read there an explanation that would calm his doubts about why she was here in this unlikely place. Then he kissed her, long and hard.

Jess willed herself not to respond, even when her blood began to warm from his embrace.

"Perhaps I'll see you later," Rhys whispered against her cheek. He was gone as suddenly as he had appeared. She waited a few moments, then made her way back to the village, convinced she had him fooled.

That evening the villagers and their more esteemed guests gathered around a fire after the evening meal for an entertainment. A traveling story-teller named Sohrab had arrived that morning and the entire village was eagerly looking forward to hearing him. Jess sat off to one side with the other women, all of them at a discreet distance from the men. Although the village women in their shabby blue dresses and white veils did not bother to cover their faces, she was grateful that the ladies of the caravan continued to be swathed head to toe.

Faud Monsel, the *Rais* of the caravan, appeared to be the most esteemed guest, though Rhys was also given a prominent position near the honored story-teller. There was much loud talking and laughing among the men,

156

punctuated by giggles and low gossip among the women. The food was lavish, but it soured Justine's proud Yankee blood that she and the other women had to wait until the men had finished eating before they were allowed to share it. While the women finished off the meal, the talking among the men settled into subdued arguments which gradually gave way to stories woven by Sohrab in his singsong voice. Without understanding a word of what was being said, Jess found some satisfaction in watching Rhys surreptitiously from behind her veil. He sat cross-legged, his arms resting on his knees and his burly bodyguards close behind him. His interpreter, with a thin ferretlike face, sat to one side, leaning forward to speak to Rhys on occasion and eliciting a smile or a nod from his master. Jess wondered if he was actually telling Rhys what was being said. There seemed a slight tinge of contempt in the way the other men glanced at each other and smiled at Rhys.

Well, it was his problem. Perhaps no one had told him that the Arabs considered Europeans barbarians.

At length she slipped away while the other women were intent on the narratives. The back half of the tent which was hers was a welcome spot of privacy and warmth against the cool night. She slipped off her *aba*, wrapped herself in the blankets Yarmid had brought along, and stretched out on the pile of rugs and cushions she now called her bed. She was almost asleep when she heard a soft scratching on the outside wall of the tent. She sat up quickly as a hand reached under the flap and lifted it high enough for a dark form to roll underneath, landing beside her.

Jess gasped as Rhys's hand closed over her mouth, stifling her startled cry. "Shh!" he whispered. "Don't cry out. We wouldn't want to bring the entire camp down on us, would we?"

"What are you doing here! Go away. You must be crazy to come to my tent like this."

His face was very close to hers, although she could not distinguish it very clearly in the darkness. "No one knows I'm here. That's why I came the back way. Once I saw you leave, I told them I was tired and had to go to bed. They took it as a further sign of weakness in a decadent Englishman."

"But Collie—"

"He's deep into the story-telling, trying to show them how Arabic he is. I'll be gone before he gets back. Mmmmmm," he said, nuzzling her neck. "I'd forgotten how clean and good you smell, especially after days of being close to nothing but horses and camels."

"Rhys, we shouldn't," Jess whispered as his hands began to drift over her body, stirring the old fires she thought had burnt away.

"Why not? No one need know. I didn't realize how much I've missed you, until now when I have you in my arms again." His hand slipped inside the loose robe she wore, circling her breast. Jess arched against him, lifting the hardened nipple to his lips, forgetting everything but the heat building within her, the feel of his lithe body against hers, the exquisite drift of his hands over her taut flesh. She had missed him, too, she realized with sudden surprise. The knowledge that he was the enemy she was sent to outwit had driven away all memory of the bliss she had shared on the captain's bed in the shimmering light of the *Boeadecia*. Now it came swiftly back, washing over her, tingling her blood with the expectation of his body melding into hers. There was a great emptiness inside her crying out to be filled up with him. Passion, sweeping them both along on its singing tide, drowned out caution, wariness, reason. It had been a long time for Rhys since he had lain with a woman, and the need for her drove him half-mad, bringing him swiftly to a violent erection. His mouth, his hands were all over her, tasting and drawing as he sought to draw her body into his. The softness of her worked on him like an aphrodisiac. Eagerly he clutched at her breasts, smoothed her silken thighs, strained to hold every swell and curve of her body in his fingers. She writhed beneath him, driven to a frenzy by the insistent urging of his hands and lips. And then, when she thought she could bear it no more, he shifted above her and drove home, raising them both to an ecstasy of showering light and fire that left them panting and exhausted.

She had just enough presence left to stifle his cry against her neck. When he collapsed, her arms held him pressed against her, rapt with the sense of two bodies melded into one, two separate people for a brief moment one person. Rhys shifted his weight at length, and she lay spent and weak stretched against him, his arm cradling her head against his shoulder. As their mutual passion subsided, reason began to reassert itself, and Justine once again remembered that this man was the one she must outwit for the prize that would save her country. Lightly she began to stroke his chest, tantalizing him with the soft motion. "The *Rais* seems to think highly of you," she murmured against his neck.

Rhys laughed. "He ought to. I paid him enough to bring me along. I only hope my money holds out until we reach Asia. These people require more bribes than the Barbary corsairs."

"Oh? I didn't know that."

"Oh yes. I've been warned already that at every little campsite along the way, there will be some local official with his hand out. The Turks are the worst, so I'm told, but they're all pretty efficient."

"What happens if you cannot pay?"

"Then you're likely to find yourself inside a mud-brick gaol for God knows how long."

"Is this true for the natives as well?"

"Yes, but it's worse for the Europeans, of course. Still, there are advantages. Did you know that we'll be traveling over the great trade route between China and Baghdad, the one Marco Polo took on that first trip to the Orient? It's only used now for small caravans like ours, but it was once one of the world's great highways."

"I didn't realize that."

He turned and looked at her quizzically. "You know so little about this part of the world, I wonder that you are here at all. Why are you?"

"I told you. I just wanted to see something of the East."

Though he did not answer, she could sense his disbelief. "Well," he finally said, kissing her lightly. "I had better get back to my tent before I'm missed. I'll come again when I can—unless, of course, you don't want me to."

For an answer Jess laid her arms around his neck and kissed him, darting her tongue between his lips. When he was able to, he pulled away, chuckling as he rolled beneath the tent flap, leaving her smiling with delight at the thought of what they had shared.

And yet . . . why hadn't she told him never to come again? He was after the same prize as she, and he would snatch it from her in a moment, given the chance. How foolish to melt in his embrace, only to wonder how to get rid of him once he was gone!

She was all at once conscious of a painful lump

pressing against her back. Feeling with her hand, she pulled out a rolled leather pouch which she realized must have fallen from Rhys's clothes. It was too dark in the tent to see what it was, so she carried it to the front of the tent where a tiny oil lamp was burning against the night. Jess gave a cry as she unrolled the case. It appeared to be some kind of purse which could be worn close to the body for safety, and it contained all of Rhys's papers and a large number of silver coins. She recognized them as Mesopotamian currency and worth a small fortune.

"What have ye got there?" Collie said, appearing suddenly out of the darkness. "Ye shouldn't be out here withour your *aba,*" he added anxiously, closing the tent flap and crouching down beside her.

"I didn't hear you coming," Jess whispered. "And I was too anxious to see what this was to think about the *aba.* Look, Collie. It's Capt. Llewellyn's papers and a great deal of money. Do you realize what this means!"

"How on earth did ye get that?" Collie exclaimed, looking at her quizzically. "Was he here?"

"Yes, he was here," she answered without any further explanation. "And he dropped this. He probably doesn't even realize it is gone yet. We've got to hide it and pretend we never saw it. This is the means we've been looking for to get him away from the caravan. Do you know where we'll be stopping next?"

"There's a village on the other side of this ridge. There's certain to be some kind of official there, and if the Captain doesn't have his papers and his purse, it might be a small bit difficult for him."

"I'll hid it in my litter. I don't wish him any harm, Collie. I just want to get him out of the way for a while, so I can reach Samarkand before he does. Praise Allah, or the lord, or whoever! This is the answer to our prayer."

161

Seven

The following morning at dawn, the caravan started off again, slowly and carefully picking its way down the other side of the rocky mountain. It was another two days before they reached the plateau beyond, two days in which Rhys first questioned, then all but accused Justine and Collie of stealing his purse with all his papers. Collie managed to throw enough suspicion on Mustapha, Rhys's interpreter, to make Rhys doubt they were guilty. Justine managed a crafted innocence that nearly convinced Rhys that he could not have lost his papers in her tent. Meanwhile, she secreted the purse among her small box of clothes and money, not daring to hide it on her body for fear Rhys might appear again in her tent. When he failed to do so, she could only wonder if his suspicion had somewhat cooled his ardor.

The heat returned with a vengeance once they left the mountains behind. Although isolated groups of Bedouins followed them from a distance—to disappear until another group took their place—the train was not stopped by any official seeking bribes or documents.

Justine noticed Mustapha lingering about her tent in the evenings when they made camp, and was beginning to think that they ought to replace the purse among Rhys's things, when at last they reached a small village of mud-brick houses baking in the sun. A nearby group of palms and a primitive waterwheel suggested a stream or well, and it was decided to make camp and rest for a day. The baggage was barely unloaded before a group of officials appeared, questioning the merchants. Justine recognized the Persians by their dress and pot-shaped hats, but the most officious man in the group looked a stranger. Collie, when he got a chance, whispered to her that he was a Turk, a tax collector for the Ottomans and easily the most greedy of the lot. Their luck had held.

She kept discreetly apart for most of the day, feeling a little guilty and hoping that perhaps Rhys might be able to talk his way out of any difficulties, in spite of having no papers or money. That hope went flying late in the afternoon when she saw the captain being led off by the Turkish official and two other men from the village reeking with self-importance. The bodyguards and interpreter were nowhere in sight.

Justine could make no sense of the turmoil she felt at the sight of Rhys being led off to jail. She ought to be glad, she told herself over and over, since it made it all the more possible for her to get her hands on the money in Samarkand before he could get there. And yet, it seemed so underhanded, so unworthy. She hadn't asked him to come to her tent, she argued with herself. She hadn't stolen the purse, it had fallen into her hands, almost like an act of God. She was merely taking advantage of a heaven-sent opportunity. And think of what was at stake—nothing less than an end to the treasonous

163

rebellion in her country.

Unable to rest easy, she sent Collie into the village that evening. He came back to tell her that Rhys was indeed in the local gaol, a rather grim place that consisted of a beehive-shaped brick building with little air or light. He would have to stay there until the Turkish official left for Tabriz, taking Rhys with him.

Justine spent a restless night. At least five times she made up her mind to go to the gaol first thing in the morning and turn over Rhys's purse, only to talk herself out of it. She dragged herself up at dawn, enveloping her body in her *aba* and listlessly helping Collie pack up their rugs and tent. Then, closing the curtains of the litter around her, she allowed herself to be carried away from the village without a backward glance at the mud huts, already gleaming yellow in the strengthening sunshine. All day she sat sunk in a deep depression she could not shake off.

"I thought it was what ye wanted," Collie said irritably, while they ate their evening meal of the eternal bean patties and rice.

"It *was* what I wanted, but I can't help feeling badly about it. He might die in that place! The heat, the way they treat foreigners. I wish there had been another way."

"I don't think you need worry about Capt. Llewellyn. He can take care of himself. Having no official papers or any money should merely sharpen his wits. And remember, it's the prize ye want at the end of the line. He's going to try to take it for himself, and once he learns that ye're after it too, well, don't think he won't try to put you out of the way."

"I know," Justine groaned. "I just wish there had been

164

another way."

"We were lucky to get this one," Collie said unsympathetically as he licked his fingers. "Now, ye'd better get some rest. We ought to be nearing Rayys by tomorrow. It's a fair-sized town, I've heard, and we'll probably spend several days there. You should enjoy it."

Justine clucked her tongue. "Oh yes, I'll have a wonderful time sitting with the rest of the women behind screens and closed doors. What a country! It might as well be the Dark Ages."

In spite of her bitter words, she felt a sense of relief when her camel finally wobbled through the gates of Rayys. It was exciting to be back in a real town, even one so exotically different from Philadelphia. Rayys was a caravan crossroads, and its narrow, twisting streets were jammed with camels bearing litters and baskets, drivers herding them with their long thin sticks, farmers with donkey carts laden with produce for the town bazaar, pedestrians and travelers, all vying for the tiny spaces in front of crowded sun-dried brick houses and shops. Massive gates, affording tantalizing glimpses of trees within, closed off the homes of the more wealthy, while the poorest citizens, oblivious to the noise and tumult of the streets, dozed in doorways and nooks in the walls.

Even the noises brought nostalgic memories of home. The constant braying of the donkeys and camels, the bleating of goats who roamed everywhere, the snarl of stray dogs, the cries of the vendors and hawkers mingling with the commands of the drivers—the tumult kept Justine with her eyes to the curtain, peering out at the crowded streets with a smile on her lips. The smells reminded her of Baghdad—the spices and strong coffee aromas mingling with animal dung and overripe fruit.

165

They passed by the ever-present mosque with its high minarets, and soon after pulled to a stop at the town market. As Justine crawled down from her litter, she saw that nearly half of the caravan had continued on into the streets winding off the large square.

"I'm going to check out the local caravansary," Collie said by way of explanation, as Jess sat cross-legged in the shadow of the camel. "You never know what they're like in a strange town, and we can't afford any surprises. You wait here for me."

"Can't I go with you? I don't relish being left alone like this."

"There are plenty of people about, and no one will bother ye. They can see ye're with the caravan. I'll be right back."

He disappeared into the crowd before Justine could object further, leaving her to inch back against the camel and draw her veils closer around her face. Gradually, as the people milling around her seemed to take no notice of one more veiled woman sitting quietly beside her transportation, she began to relax and look around, fascinated by the procession of Middle Eastern types who passed. For the first time she saw courtesans and whores openly parading. They went unveiled, large rings with little half-moons in their noses, their breasts partly exposed by the low décolletage of their robes, jewelry on their wrists, necks, ears, ankles, and even their toes jingling as they walked. Farmers from the outlying villages were everywhere, hawking their produce. From a coppersmith's shop directly across from where she sat, the banging and tapping of the apprentices in the back added to the noisy din of the streets.

Justine noticed that an unusual number of the

pedestrians seemed to disappear into a tall building with low steps leading to a wide door that stood nearly behind her. It was a moment before she recognized what this was—a bathhouse, and a very popular one judging by the number of people who entered and left. Justine licked her lips. While she was in Baghdad, she had never dared think of entering such a place. But after the long dry days of traveling under the hot eastern sun, it now seemed the most enticing thing imaginable. She knew little of bathhouses, except that they were popular places for men and women, and she wondered if there was any privacy at all in them. She made up her mind then and there, that if there was any way she might safely use one, she was going to do it.

Her attention—which had been riveted on the bathhouse door—was drawn suddenly to two men standing twenty feet away under a fig tree, intently watching her. All at once, all the pleasure Justine had felt at being in a town again was transformed into a stark fear. She looked quickly away and tried to ignore them, but it was difficult to do. They were Persians, judging by the pot-shaped hats they wore, both bearded, both with that wiry and emaciated look of the underfed. Her quick glance had picked up their too-interested looks, and she could almost hear the quiet snickerings in their conversation. Their attention was a little too lusty and a little too interested for her peace of mind, and it was with a great surge of relief that she saw Collie making his way back to her across the square. She jumped to her feet and stood very close to him as he began urging the camel to its feet, hoping she looked like an obedient wife of a nondescript traveler.

"Where are we going?" she asked quietly as they made

their way from the bazaar.

"Not to the caravansary," he replied. "It's worse than any third-rate hostel in London. Crowded, dirty, noisy. By nightfall half the town would know there was an Englishwoman staying there. I've found a house for us. Habib Jabbar—a friend of a friend. One thing about these Arabs—they stab you in the back with as little thought as they'd strangle a chicken, but if you're a friend of a friend of theirs, their hospitality knows no bounds. Ye'll be safe there."

When they finally entered the iron gates off one of the winding side streets of Rayys, Justine found herself in a courtyard, cooled by shade trees and surrounded on four sides by rooms opening off the yard. With the gates closed behind them, and a gentleman in a turban bobbing them an effusive welcome, she began once more to feel safe and happy. Although there were many men living in the house, there were few women, and the story Collie gave out about her deafness spared her their attention. She had a comfortable bed in a room with several others, good food and kindness, and for two days she enjoyed the rest and comfort of the place. She saw little of Collie, who carried the burden of the hospitality offered by their host and, of course, she could not converse with the women or even pretend to understand their gossipy conversation. She soon grew weary of watching the merchants enter to spread their wares in the courtyard, though she did enjoy looking over the beautiful fabrics and enticing jewelry they displayed.

By the third day, with one more stretching ahead before the caravan resumed its journey, Justine decided she could not spend another twelve hours of daylight by herself within the walls of Habib Jabbar's house. She had

168

to get out among the people and excitement of the town.

"Absolutely not!" Collie said when she asked him to take her. "It would be crazy. This isn't Baghdad where ye can get lost in the crowds. Rayys is just large enough that most of its men know what is going on most of the time. Ye'd be tripped up somewhere and give yerself away."

"But you would be with me. I'm terribly bored here, Collie. I have to get out for a while. Who knows when we'll be inside a real town again, and it's lonely and quiet out on the desert."

"Ye want to get to Samarkand, don't ye. That's all that matters. Be patient, Justine. Besides, I can't go with ye. I . . . have other business."

"I've noticed you have quite a lot of 'business' in Rayys. What is it? Those courtesans who are all over the place? Gambling? The coffeehouses?"

Collie's brows inched upward. "Ye ought not to know anything about such things. Let's just say that I, too, enjoy the opportunities a town offers."

"Then you ought to understand how I feel."

"Yes, but I speak the language, and have had ten years to learn how to merge myself into their culture. I promised to get ye to Samarkand safely, and that I cannot do if ye go traipsing around the streets of Rayys. Now be a good girl and wait here patiently. It's only one more day."

She pursed her lips stubbornly as she watched him leave. How like a man in this country! No consideration at all for a woman's feelings. It was unfair. She had watched the respectable women of the town that day she waited in the marketplace. They went about swathed in their black veils, but they were free to buy and haggle and gossip with one another. They might not be able to

169

patronize the coffeehouses like the men, but they had some measure of freedom. She had none.

Her overworked sense of injustice drove her to a bold decision. She would go out anyway. By now she knew the gestures to indicate she couldn't hear or speak. They would just have to be her cover, for she would go insane facing another long day with nothing to do and no one to speak to.

After waiting for a moment when there was no one about, her nerve almost failed her as she slipped out of the gate nearly an hour later. She had a general idea of the direction of the market square and she set off, her veils pulled tightly around her face, hardly daring to meet the eyes of the people she passed on the street. For an hour she wandered about, eventually entering the bazaar from one of the sidestreets. It was as noisy and crowded as she remembered, but no one seemed to take any notice of her and soon she was happily wandering among the shops and displays unconcerned about the crowds.

And then she found herself in front of the bathhouse.

Justine stared at the welcoming edifice, thinking longingly of the steamy pools inside. How wonderful to submerge herself in the cleansing, comforting water. What a memory to carry with her back out into the desert.

No. It would be foolish. She hadn't the slightest idea how to handle the mechanics of getting a bath. She'd give herself away for certain if she tried. Turning reluctantly, she almost careened into two men who had stopped behind her. Quickly she pulled her veil close around her eyes, but not before she recognized them as the two who had been eyeing her while she waited for Collie two days before. She turned back, panic rising alarmingly in her breast, and hurried the opposite way, right up the steps of the bathhouse. At the top she glanced back to see that they were following her. Without hesitating Justine dove into the depths of the building and found herself in a long dark hall where the plaster walls were damp with steam. There was a small group of women ahead of her, and it seemed prudent to attach herself to them. She knew bathhouses had separate sections for men and women, and if she could only get safely into the women's quarter, she reasoned, she might be able to bluff her way from there.

The cavernous halls echoed with the chatter of the women. Smaller halls led off from either side, and nooks and crannies off those. Here in the entrance there were men and women mingling together, and Justine, in her hurry, failed to notice that some of the women were prostitutes, openly following the male patrons. She became separated from her group of *aba*-clothed respectable ladies and almost panicky when she saw they had disappeared ahead of her down one of the side halls. Pushing through the crowd to try to find them, she suddenly felt herself grabbed from behind and pulled into one of the smaller rooms. A hand closed over her mouth as she tried to scream, panic clutching at her. Fingers tore at her clothes, she felt the warm moist air on her bare thighs as her robes were shoved up over her body. The veils twisted around her face and head, but her eyes were clear enough to see the bearded, laughing repulsive face of the man who was holding her down. He was laughing, exposing rotted teeth and exuding a horrible breath close to her own. Sickened, only dimly aware of the other man forcing her thighs apart with his rough hands, her panic was swallowed by an all-consuming outrage and anger.

171

Tearing the veil from her lips, she screamed at the top of her lungs, over and over, flailing her arms and kicking with all her strength. She caught the man trying to rape her in the groin. He howled with pain and fell back, sending the other man into gales of hysterical laughter.

And then the laughter stopped. She heard a crash as the door was sent smashing against the wall, and the grasping hands on her body were yanked away. There was another man in the room, knocking her assailants about, smashing them with his fists and kicking them through the door. Justine rolled over against the wall and shrank into it as the two men who had dragged her into the room were thrown out of it. Only when the man who had rescued her slammed the door shut and turned to face her was she able to realize she was safe. Her veils were still twisted around her head and face. Pulling them away she looked up at the man towering over her, his hands on his hips as he stared down at her, his mouth curved in a mocking smile.

"Rhys!"

She stared at him, gaping like a simpleton, unable to believe her eyes. "It can't be you."

"No doubt you thought I was still locked in the depths of a stinking gaol back in the desert. I hope you're not disappointed."

In spite of his harsh words and biting tone, he reached down to offer her a hand to pull her up to her feet. When her knees trembled so she could hardly stand, he put a supporting arm around her waist. Justine clung to him gratefully.

"Of course I'm not disappointed. I'm so glad . . . I hated the idea that you might . . . I'm so glad to see you!"

Her arms went about his neck and she pressed against him. The truth was she had never been so glad to see

172

anyone ever before.

Rhys hugged her back, until he remembered how angry he was with her and with Collie, too. He stepped back. "What are you doing here? Surely that half-Arab Collie wouldn't have been crazy enough to bring you here."

Justine looked away, straightening her rumpled *aba*. "No. I came on my own. But how did you know? Were you following me?"

"Don't flatter yourself. I knew you were in this town. I know where you are staying. But it was coincidence that I was here today. When I heard a woman's voice screaming Help! in English, well, there couldn't be two American women masquerading as Arabs in this town. I decided to see what it was all about. Lucky for you I did."

His arrogant tone was beginning to dissipate the very real gratitude she felt for having been rescued. "But the gaol. How did you escape?"

Her nervous fingers twisted in the loose fabric. Rhys gently reached to help her straighten her dress, his voice softening. "Did you think all the money I had was in that purse? I bought my way out, of course."

"Purse?" Justine said lamely.

"Don't pretend you know nothing about it. I'm certain it was you and Yarmid who got me into that fix, though I'm still not sure why you don't want me to reach Samarkand when you do. But I'll figure it out sooner or later. In the meantime, let's get back to Jabbar's house where you'll be safe. Then I'll thrash Collie for letting you out alone."

"It wasn't his fault. In fact, he doesn't even know I'm gone. I just couldn't stand sitting around that house all day again. Oh, Rhys, now that I'm here, don't you think I could have a bath? I never wanted anything so much. Let me at least get in the water for a few minutes, before I have to go back."

She looked up at him, her large eyes pleading from under her long lashes. Rhys felt the old stirring in his loins. Even disheveled as she was and swathed in the loose *aba*, she was so beautiful that he wanted to take her right there. No, not in this room where those horrible men had tried to force her. There were better places in bathhouses for making love.

"All right," he said, tipping up her chin to kiss her lightly on the lips. "But only if you'll meet me afterward, in a little room I shall rent on an alcove near the women's baths. I guarantee you'll not spend the rest of this afternoon being bored!"

His tongue flicked her lips tantalizingly.

"That sounds even better than the bath," she sighed.

The echoing chamber of the women's bath was steamy enough that figures were not clearly defined. All the same, Justine got some hard stares from the other women as she slipped beneath the water, savouring its warmth and freshness. Her white body and long chestnut hair clearly set her apart from the others, and she only hoped they would assume there was a European visitor in the town trying out the bathhouse. Though the women chattered to each other, no one spoke to her, and she soaked for half an hour before finally stepping out to wind a soft robe around her body. Near the door she was met by a young boy with the soft feminine features of a girl who beckoned her to follow him. A curtained door was pulled back, and she found herself in a tiny room with a low couch covered with cushions and rugs. A small latticed window high above threw dappled shadows on Rhys's naked body stretched on the bed. To one side was a low round table with a smoking brazier and water pipe, a

174

brass jug, and two beaten copper cups. There was room for nothing else, but then, she realized, nothing else was needed.

She stood over the bed, her robe around her, and looked down at Rhys's glistening body. His hair was still wet, as was hers. He laid his hands beneath his head and smiled up at her, obviously relishing her perusal of his nakedness.

"You look very pleased with yourself," she muttered. And well he should, she thought. The long, muscular expanse of him, the tuffs of dark hair on his chest thinning to a hair's breadth in his taut middle then swelling out to encompass the vibrant, pulsing manhood that swelled even as she watched. His strong arms, tight hips, long, sinewy legs, his dancing eyes, and inviting smile—Justine had to hold herself back to keep from falling down across him.

No, she did not want this to go so fast. She savoured the time watching him, taking him in with her eyes, postponing the delicious moment of touching him, until she could no longer bear not to.

But Rhys could wait no longer. He reached out to run his hand lightly up her leg, then pulled at the robe, sending it cascading to the floor.

"Each time I see you without your clothes, I'm amazed all over again at how beautiful you are," he breathed, running his hand lightly up her leg. Her flesh began to tingle at his touch, every nerve suddenly alive. There was a tight agony of longing, beginning in the region of her stomach and spreading downward, growing warm as it moved. With an easy grace Justine knelt on one knee on the bed. Slowly Rhys allowed his hand to inch up her body, stroking, gliding, sensually leaving a warming trail behind. He closed over her breast, encompassing it

175

within his cupped hand as he pulled to his knees to face her, his other hand sliding around her waist.

Justine giggled as she slipped her hands over his shoulders. "You're greasy!" she laughed.

"That's scented oil," he murmured, nuzzling her neck. "I had a rubdown with the masseuse in your honor."

Her back arched as his lips honed in on her breast, tasting the taut nipple. "You can do that here?"

"It's one of the more civilized aspects of Arab culture," he muttered when he could speak.

She gasped as his tongue flicked against her nipple, circling, sucking, pulling at its taut sensitivity. "Women, too?"

Rhys's lips slid from the sweetness of her breast down the long expanse of her torso, his tongue slithering into the fringe through which he sought the opening, the beckoning of her woman's vulnerability. Justine, her back arched against his gripping hands, felt her hips move upward to take him into them, her whole body trembling with anticipation. "Any massage you get in here is going to come from me!" Rhys murmured against her. She barely heard him. His tongue, working like an insistent serpent, flickered her flame into life and she clutched in agony at his shoulders, pulling him toward her. The heat grew within her until she was a throbbing flame of need crying out for completion. Her legs spread apart to welcome him, and she cried aloud as he sucked at her, driving her to distraction. Then when she could bear it no longer, he pulled away, circling her waist to pull her down on the bed, falling upon her.

"Take me!" she cried, "Please . . ."

"Oh no," he murmured, kneading her body with his strong fingers. "Not so quickly. You're going to beg for it."

His throbbing manhood was hard against her. Dimly she wondered how he could bear to withhold it, and she knew this was his way of getting even. He played her like an instrument, his hands, his tongue, even the tip of his pulsating, swelling shaft, working on her tingling flesh until she thought she could bear it no longer. Then, back in the recesses of her mind, she decided he was not the only one who could play this game. Weak and longing as she was, she twisted beneath him until he raised up on his knees. It was all the room she needed. Sliding suddenly downward beneath him, she caught his throbbing manhood between her lips and began to suck, lightly at first, then with serious pleasure.

Rhys gasped, at first with surprise, and then in ecstasy as her lips pulled at him. Her arms went around his hips, pulling her toward her insistent mouth, sending him into a frenzy of pure feeling. He groaned, thrusting up and down with his hips. Although Justine was working hard, she noted his excitement with satisfaction. She was feeling rather proud of herself, when suddenly he took the upper hand again. Pulling away from her, he tossed her on her back and fell against her, thrusting his throbbing manhood between her legs. Her knees spread and rose to welcome him, and as he shoved into her with a pulsating, expanding lengthening series of thrusts, they soared together over the edge of a blinding universe where all was fire and explosion, dwindling away in a shower of flaming sparks that ignited the darkness and melded two people for a brief moment into one satisfying whole.

They lay their clasped together while both gasped for their breath, letting their bodies settle back into an exhausted sweetness.

"Do you think we made too much noise?" Justine

whispered, close to Rhys's ear. "I mean, would anyone else know what we're doing?"

"Don't worry about it," Rhys murmured against her soft forehead. "Everybody around us is doing it, too. That's half what these places are for."

Justine giggled. "Imagine how the people of Philadelphia would react if a bathhouse like this opened on Second Street."

"It only proves that some parts of the world know more about pandering to man's nature than others. Philadelphia could learn a thing or two from Persia."

"Rhys," she said, suddenly serious. "I'm really glad you didn't have to stay in that prison. Truly, I'm glad."

He smoothed several long strands of hair away from her forehead. "I'm happy to know it. But don't think I've forgiven you that easily. We Llewellyns never forget an injury. It may take a while, but we exact our revenge."

There was so much mirth in his tone that she did not take his words very seriously. "And what is your revenge?" she said, chuckling.

His hands slid around her throat, pulling her lips to his, his tongue flicking against them, forcing them open to his exploration. "To begin with," he muttered, "you'll spend the rest of the afternoon in this room with me, submitting to my every whim, doing everything I demand."

Justine found her battered nerves heating up again, warmed by his knowledgeable tongue.

"Mmmmm," she murmured. "That doesn't sound so bad."

"I can't believe ye did such a foolish, stupid thing!" Collie raged, struggling to keep his voice low enough that none of the family members could hear him. Justine watched, amused at the way Collie's Arab mask fell away when he became angry, revealing the London street dweller underneath. It had to do with the way his small eyes bulged in his narrow face, and the red flush that flamed below his walnut-dyed skin. It amused her to see him choke his fury under a falsetto voice, and she pulled her veil over her mouth to hide her grin. He sensed it anyway and grew even redder.

"I'm serious, Justine. You endangered yerself as well as this whole trip. How am I ever going to get ye safely to Samarkand, if ye won't do what I tell ye?"

Jess shrugged. "It worked out all right, didn't it? I was bored sitting around here all day, Collie. I just had to get out. Besides, you have to remember I'm not some passive Arab woman who thinks she's blessed if her lord and master husband allows her to eat the crumbs from his table after he's finished. I'm a young lady of Philadelphia and proud of it!"

"You young ladies from Philadelphia could use a little Arab humility."

"Pooh! Come on, Collie, let's be friends again. The important thing is that I got safely back, thanks to Rhys. Imagine, Rhys here in this town all the time, and we didn't know it. I'm glad he got out of that prison, even if it does make it harder for us to get him out of our way."

"Ye're really sure it was the captain," Collie said, relenting his anger at the lovely animation on her face.

"Now how many American captains are there in Rayys that I could confuse him with? I talked to him. He brought me home."

Pulling off his headscarf to run his fingers through his short hair, Collie glared at her as he sank into a divan against the wall. "I wish I could share yer enthusiasm,

179

but I don't. I believe Capt. Llewellyn is much more of a threat than you realize. He's after that treasure, and if he gets to it before we do, we're not likely to see him or the money ever again. Ye're allowing your emotions to color your thinking—another example of how things get muddled when women get involved."

"Is it muddled emotions to want a man spared from rotting in some loathsome Arab gaol? Besides, he doesn't know yet that we're after the same thing. Don't worry. When the right time comes, I'll help get rid of him. I might even find a better way to do it."

Collie appeared unmoved. "I'll believe that when it happens. Oh well, except for an hour spent racing through the bazaar searching frantically for ye, I suppose no harm's been done. Get some rest. We'll be starting off again early tomorrow morning."

"Where are you going?" she asked as he replaced the *kaffiyah* and straightened the *agal* that held it in place. "To another party, no doubt, given by the host to entertain his guest. His *male* guest."

Collie shrugged. "When in Rome, my dear, do as the Romans."

Justine began removing her veils with a barely disguised sigh. "Oh well, I might as well enjoy my last night in a civilized bed. Tomorrow it's back to the litter."

By the next morning when the caravan reassembled to wind out of the town as the early rays of dawn were seeping in, Justine took her usual place on the lumbering camel, but kept her eyes to a thin slit in her curtains, seeking Rhys. The sun was up, and they were back crossing the sand and gravel expanse of the plateau when she finally spotted him, riding by at a distance. His two bodyguards followed closely, and though Mustapha was nowhere in sight, she was reasonably certain the

180

interpreter would be somewhere about.

Justine spent most of that first day dreaming about the afternoon in the bathhouse, and wondering if Rhys would come to her tent that evening. She was disappointed when he did not appear, but she thought surely he would come the next night or the following one. After four weary days of traveling and four sleepless nights in her tent, her disappointment had turned to annoyance, and she was beginning to wonder if it would not have been better for Rhys to have languished in jail after all.

That evening over their supper, Collie mentioned with studied nonchalance that he had spoken to Rhys, and that the good captain had in no way forgiven them for sending him off under a Turkish guard to rot in prison while they moved on to Samarkand. Justine hid her surprise, thinking that Rhys had certainly given her no indication he was still angry.

"I'm sure it's that Mustapha's fault," Collie said, breaking a flat round *khobuz* in half and swiping his food with his fingers, Arab style. "He probably fills the captain's head with all kinds of nonsense. Ye can be certain he makes himself look good and us look bad, and it's all going to lead to his own gain somehow, mark my words."

"Rhys . . . Capt. Llewellyn didn't talk like he was so unforgiving to me," Justine said quietly.

"That's because he obviously wanted something from you. He's not going to alienate a beautiful woman, especially one who makes ga-ga eyes at him everytime he rides by."

"I do not make ga-ga eyes at him! He is . . . was a friend after all. Why shouldn't I be friendly?"

"Because he is going to try to do ye out of a very large sum of money, as I keep reminding ye. If ye allow him to

181

think he can manipulate you anyway he wants, we're sure to lose whatever chance we had of beating him to Samarkand. Try to remember that, Justine, when ye're admiring how handsome he looks riding by on his fine horse."

"Mind your own business!" Justine snapped. "I know what is at stake, and I have no intention of allowing Rhys Llewellyn to trick us out of that treasure. I'm not that naive, after all."

Yet as she lay in her solitary bed of rugs and cushions that night, she could not help but think back over Collie's warning. Had Rhys only wanted to use her that afternoon in the bathhouse? Was there nothing more to his lovemaking than the enjoyment of her body? Was he still angry with her and looking for a chance to take his revenge? She would have sworn there was more between them than that, and yet she could not be sure. And if he *was* only using her . . .

Her sudden surge of anger at least drove away her longing for him. She clutched at it, drawing on its strength. If that was all she meant to the captain, then she would jolly well make sure she was not so easy to fool the next time. If that was the kind of game Rhys wanted to play, well, she would be as good at it as he.

After six days had gone by without Rhys once slipping inside her tent, Justine decided that Collie must be right after all, and her resolve hardened to protect herself against his wiles, should he ever try to use them on her again. Then, on the morning of the seventh day, the caravan came to an abrupt halt just as the morning sun was gaining strength. They had been slowly inching their way across the plateau for two hours, and still had three to go before reaching the next village where they planned to rest and restock their dwindling supplies. After sweating inside the litter for half an hour, Justine drew the curtains and motioned to Collie.

"What's the matter?" she whispered down to him.

"There's some kind of a snag up front, and we can't go on until it's resolved."

"Well, get me down from here. I'm sweltering inside this thing. At least let me sit in the shade and get some air."

A few of the camels around them had already been brought to a sitting position, not an encouraging sign, since it meant the other drivers assumed they would be stopped for some time. With difficulty Collie finally got Justine's camel on its knees and helped her out. Then he walked forward to see what the delay was all about.

He returned half an hour later, trying to be serious, but barely able to control his mirth. "It's our friend, wouldn't ye know. Those bodyguards of his. I could have told him he'd have this kind of trouble, but of course he wouldn't listen to me. Now his chickens have come home to roost."

Though she was dying to know what the trouble was, Justine was forced to keep quiet, as all around her the men of the caravan began to push forward, some of them followed by their women. When there was no one close enough to hear, she leaned toward Collie.

"What's the matter? Tell me."

"It's the old story in these parts. Tribal loyalties and tribal feuds. Those two ugly bodyguards are of the Basseri tribe and we are now crossing an area where a great number of Qashqai have set up nomadic homes. Sometime—who knows how long ago—a family of one tribe caused some injustice to a family of the other tribe.

183

Now Rhys's Basseri guards are refusing to set foot on Qashqai land, and the captain is having an apoplectic fit."

"But what's going to happen?"

"I don't know. The *Rais* is very unhappy about the whole thing, but he's had this happen before. He told Capt. Llewellyn he'd have to handle it or be left behind."

Justine looked ahead where the swirling dust, stirred up by several horsemen riding toward the caravan, hid the crowd gathered around Rhys. "Perhaps this will be the opportunity we were hoping for, Collie. At any rate, I want to see. I'm going to walk up there."

"I don't think that's wise, but maybe I'll go along with ye. Wait until I get someone I can trust to watch our baggage. And don't forget—you can't talk!"

Justine could hear the angry words flying before she reached the head of the caravan. It was the first time she had had occasion to be this close to Rhys's bodyguards, and she was struck by the savage, beefy look of them. The curved scimitars and knives that protruded from their wide sashes, the impassive cruelty of their hard faces, their massive arms, fierce eyes, and the grim slash of their mouths—they were like something out of a nightmare. They looked as though they could stomp a person to death and enjoy it.

Yet they were hardly more fierce-looking than the horsemen who reined up alongside. These, it turned out, were the representatives of the Qashqai family, come to challenge the presence of the hated enemies among the caravan. The angry words, like so much babble to Justine, flew between the two groups while Rhys and the *Rais* attempted to interject some touch of reason between them. Justine was almost enjoying the commotion, when it became obvious that the two sides were drawing off to

184

go at each other, and Rhys had elected to join them.

Collie, seeing the frantic look in her eyes above her veil, gripped her arm with a steadying hand. He laid a finger to his lips and shook his head at her, to remind her that she was not supposed to be able to hear or speak. Abruptly he turned her and pushed her back toward the middle of the caravan where their camel waited.

"It's not our fight," he muttered when they were out of earshot of the others, most of whom were pushing forward eager to watch the confrontation.

"He must be crazy! He doesn't have a chance of coming out of a fight with those barbarians unscathed. You've got to stop him, Collie."

"Ha! Even if I could, I wouldn't. You be a good girl now, and go on back to the baggage and wait for me. I want to see what happens."

"You men! That's all you care about. Fighting and bloodshed." She snatched her arm out of his grasp. "I won't sit and wait until Rhys is killed."

Collie gave her a sharp glance. If ever he had suspected that Justine's feelings for the captain ran strong, now he was certain of it. "If you go up there, Justine, ye're certain to go wading into the fight trying to help that man. Nothing would give ye away as a foreigner more quickly. A good Arab woman wouldn't dare to intervene in a situation like this. Now I'm telling ye—if ye want this thing to work ye're going to have to wait back here, or stand and watch quietly, whatever happens. Which will it be?"

Justine stopped, realizing the truth of his words. "I'll . . . I'll wait. You're right, I couldn't be quiet. At least back here, I'll be alone and can pray!"

"Good girl."

Eight

Faud Monsel was a tall man for an Arab, gaunt to the point of emaciation, with a long face that framed eyes flashing with energy and intelligence. It was probably those eyes, Rhys thought, that made him such an effective leader of the peculiar accumulation of men and animals that made up their caravan. At this point, Faud's intense gaze was heightened by the scorching anger he focused on Capt. Llewellyn.

"I begin to regret, Englishman, that I agreed to bring you," he said, speaking in a thick, heavily accented English. "It is nuisance that the men you hire refuse to move on. Now other men here, with any relation to the Basseri, all wish to fight. How do I drive on my train? Tell me that, Englishman!"

Rhys, who still felt all this trouble was a tempest in a teapot, tried to appear serious. "We shall simply have to face these Qashqai and defeat them. That should resolve the problem."

"And if you fail? I do not wish to delay my caravan over some tribal argument with its roots in a trivial event

186

of two hundred years past. I think I shall leave you and your guards and go on without you."

Rhys did not like the sound of that. "Then you will be leaving half the men of your train."

"Not quite half." Faud's English appeared to grow more clear as his consternation increased. The truth was that he had learned it in a Catholic school and spoke it quite well. But he had found long ago that it never paid to let Europeans know that. He studied Rhys with his hooded eyes. It was obvious the captain was anticipating the thought of a good roaring battle as much as any virile young Arab. The fools! If it were not that he could remember feeling that way himself, before he grew so accustomed to responsibility, he would leave all of them stranded on the plateau to make their own way across Persia.

"I give you half a day," he finally muttered. "This train leaves tomorrow at dawn for Samarkand. You must decide. Either you come with us, you and your guards, or you find your own way."

"Or leave my bones to be picked by the vultures," Rhys added cryptically.

"That also is a possibility." The *Rais* rose to his full height, pulling his robe around him, and stalked from the tent.

Rhys, sitting cross-legged on one of the rugs, watched him go. "He looked at me like he thought I was an idiot," he muttered to his interpreter, Mustapha, who was sitting at the back of the tent. "The arrogant bastard. Why can't he handle these Basseri tribesmen. What in hell do I have to do with their family arguments. He acts as though I'm enjoying this. All I want is to get on to Samarkand."

"The Captain wishes my opinion?" Mustapha said in an oily voice. Rhys was becoming accustomed to his mock humility, yet it continued to irritate him.

"And what is that?"

The Arab unfolded his wiry body from his sitting position and moved nearer Rhys, without appearing ever to stand up. Mustapha was as different from Faud Monsel as could be—small, ferret-faced, tiny eyes that never seemed to look directly into another's. He crept where the *Rais* strode, whined where the *Rais* spoke with authority. Of the two men Rhys infinitely preferred Faud, and yet Mustapha had given him no reason for distrust. He tried to concentrate on that as the interpreter leaned close, his garlicky breath right in Rhys's face. "It would be fitting for you to come up with some solution, seeing as it was you who told me to hire those two Basseri in the first place. You must have known something like this would happen."

Mustapha shrugged. "They are good guards, are they not? There is no one in Persia who does not have enemies somewhere. I suggest that even old hatreds might be susceptible to the ring of silver."

"God's life! Are you suggesting I can bribe these men to go on? I thought it was a matter of honor not to set foot on Qashqai territory."

"There are times, *effendi*, when even honor can be bent. Of course, it would take a considerable amount . . ."

Rhys smothered his rising distaste for Mustapha's manner of almost rubbing his hands together when money was at stake. "How much?" he said bitterly.

"Well, there would be the two Basseri, who must be induced to forgo the honor of killing a few of their

188

ancient enemies. And the Qashqai, of course, must be convinced to allow their old foe, the Basseri, to set their sandals on their own ground. And—"

"God's blood!" Rhys exclaimed, jumping to his feet. "I'll be ruined before I ever reach Tartary. Do I look like a walking silver mine? I've already paid out more than I should have to get out of that stinking gaol. I'm not made of money, you know."

"Perhaps *effendi* would prefer to join the battle tomorrow."

"Tomorrow? How do you know it will be then?"

"I listen and talk to the Basseri. They are sharpening their swords, hoping to dip them in Qashqai blood. They will be helped by some of the men in this train who also have old enmity for the Qashqai. But then, the Qashqai will also be bringing men from their other villages. It should be a good fight. Much blood. Many martyrs sent to Allah by day's end."

Rhys walked to the opening of his tent and looked out. The gabble and clatter of many tongues were noisy around him, as the men of the caravan sharpened their weapons and laid their bets on the coming confrontation. There was an excitement in the air, punctuated with laughter and bragging. It was crazy! He loved a fight as well as any man, and this one might be a pleasant diversion from the long dreary days of travel. But while they were hacking at one another, the caravan would be wending its way onward. He did not doubt for a moment that Faud meant what he said. Of course, he might catch up with them later, assuming he wasn't killed or wounded. But even if he emerged unscathed, it would mean traveling on alone, or in the solitary company of those two ferocious Basseri. Was it worth that?

His life had become so separated from the Colonies recently, that he had almost ceased to think of home much anymore. Now he remembered why he was here in this wild, crazy place. He had a mission, and it was his duty to see it through. That had to come first. If he separated himself from this caravan, he might never be able to get back to it, and who knows how he could find another one.

Reluctantly he turned to Mustapha. "How much will it take?" he said, reaching for the key to his strongbox.

It was Collie who told Justine about Rhys's settlement the following morning as the caravan prepared to embark once more. "The captain is looking rather long in the mouth," Collie said, not even trying to hide his glee. "He thinks everyone is laughing at him, and in truth, they are. It appears he has been fleeced once more."

"Do you mean it was all a hoax? That there wasn't any real enmity?"

"No, no. These Arabs can always find a reason to despise each other. The tribesmen would have fought each other some way. But where they can unite to do an Englishman out of his money, be assured that will come first. Poor Capt. Llewellyn. At this rate he may run out of funds long before we reach Samarkand, and that will solve the problem neatly for us."

Justine crawled up into her litter and pulled the curtains together. While she couldn't share Collie's mirth over Rhys's problems, she did feel relieved that he had not involved himself in an Arab battle. It served him right for not accepting Collie's offer to escort him to Samarkand in the first place. But, of course, if he had,

190

where would she be now? No, Collie was right. He brought this on himself.

The train continued to wind its slow way below the Elburz Mountains, through a strange mixture of barren, gravel-strewn plateau fringed with brown hills in the distance. Occasionally the hills were dotted with patches of green where enough water existed to cultivate simple crops—a tantalizing glimpse, Collie told her, of the wide verdant slopes that existed farther north near the banks of the Caspian Sea. But for the most part, the train kept to level ground, venturing into the sparse villages only to replenish water and food supplies. For the first time in her life, Justine began to realize how precious water was, and to sense how its need and the lack of it at hand had shaped the lives of the nomads and villagers living in this part of the world.

All in all, she could only admire the way the Persians had adapted themselves to their strange, wild environment. From the villager eking out a bare subsistence on the barren hills, to the camel who could live without a drop for weeks, to the lonely tribesman who rolled up his house and his furniture and packed them on his animals to move on in search of a new water supply—they had learned to deal with and live with this demanding, hot, inhospitable country with a superb nonchalance. When she remembered the great sweep of bay and river, the bounding, crystal creeks of home, the green pastures, and great over-arching trees, she could only admit that she could never cope so well herself.

That evening she sat in the opening of her tent to watch the stars come out. Collie had taken himself off to share a gossip and a game of Trictrac with some of the men in the train behind them. The sky was like velvet, and the air so clear that the stars seemed a scattering of diamonds across it. She was so busy admiring it that she was startled when someone suddenly swung down beside her inside the tent.

"May one wish the sister of Yarmid Ali a pleasant evening?" Rhys's mocking voice whispered. Justine turned swiftly.

"What are you doing here?" she hissed. "Are you crazy! You know I'm not supposed to be able to talk."

"Just make some suitable gestures, and I'll do the talking. I came to see Collie. Where is he?"

"Go away. He's not here."

The sound of jewelry jingling interrupted her. She pulled her veil around her face as a woman swathed in a black *aba* and carrying a jug ambled in front of the tent. Justine could feel rather than see the woman's curious eyes fixed on them both.

Rhys leaned forward and yelled at her: "Yarmid Ali. Where?"

Mouthing some incomprehensible sounds. Justine jabbed a finger toward the rear of the camp. The woman passed, and Rhys slipped farther back in the tent where he would not be so noticeable. He also reached out and extinguished the small oil lamp near the entrance, making the brilliant heavens appear even closer.

"It's beautiful, isn't it?" he said, noticing how Justine's eyes went back to the sky. "Part of the magic of this country. I suppose that is why some men love it out here. Personally, I perfer the rivers and the green pastures of Pennsylvania. Do you ever think of home?"

"No," she lied. She inched away from him, conscious of his strong masculinity. If he touched her, she knew she would fall into his arms, and she did not want that.

192

She was half-convinced that his lovemaking was merely an attempt to use her for his own pleasure. And, she reminded herself, they were enemies, after the same goal, but for entirely different reasons. "Go away," she whispered. "You're only going to add to our problems."

"I don't see how you have any problems. And mine have affected the lightness of my purse—which, by the way, still hasn't found its way back home."

"I don't know anything about your purse."

"So you say. I still haven't quite figured out why you wanted me left behind in that gaol, but I'd settle for an apology. Why don't you just admit you were responsible, and we can be friends again."

"Why don't you go jump in the lake!"

Rhys gave a low chuckle. "I would if there were one nearby. It might be a relief from the endless sun and gravel." He studied her dark form by the tent opening, wondering at her nervousness and hostility. Certainly it was not what he expected, considering the way they parted that afternoon in the bathhouse. And yet, perhaps it was just as well. He did not entirely trust her, and he was still irked at the trick she and Collie had played on him.

"You're very cool this evening," he commented dryly.

"Why do you want to see Collie?"

Rhys watched her without answering. How to say that he had come to distrust Mustapha and his guards, and would feel safer with another pair of eyes and ears working for him. How to admit he had come seeking the conversation of his own kind? She was not likely to be sympathetic, considering her mood.

He rose and pulled his coat around him. "May one wish the sister of Yarmid Ali a pleasant good night," he said formally, giving her a sweeping English bow. He walked out into the darkness with Justine's eyes following him.

Why had he come here tonight, she wondered. Obviously it was not to make love to her. She was disappointed and yet relieved. How to sort out the conflicting emotions she felt for this attractive, challenging, frustrating man? How was she going to manage to get him out of her way without doing him any real harm? It was more than she could resolve tonight. She began picking up the supper utensils and moved back to her end of the tent. She would worry about it tomorrow.

Rhys went back to his tent after deciding not to seek out Collie after all. He had managed on his own so far well enough. He was certain he could handle things the rest of the way.

Two days later he woke at the first call of the *muezzin* through the camp. Throwing on his clothes, he walked outside in the brisk, dark air and was curious that no one was about. Both Mustapha and his bodyguards had disappeared. He had been in the camp long enough now to prepare his own breakfast of flat bread and strong, sweet coffee. By the time it was consumed, Mustapha had come ambling up to begin the daily process of rolling up their baggage.

"Where the devil have you been? We'll be leaving shortly, and we've got all this gear to tie up."

Mustapha shuffled forward. "Forgive me, *effendi*, but I have been seeing to your welfare."

"My welfare? If you want to see to my welfare, then start packing up this baggage. Where are those guards?

They're never around when you need them."

"It is because of them, *effendi*, that I have been away from your tent. Forgive me, Lord Captain, but those guards have deserted you."

Rhys stared at the man. "Deserted? What the devil do you mean?"

"You will recall, *effendi*, those horsemen who appeared on the horizon last evening. These Basseri, may the dogs lick their bones, recognized them as members of their tribe. They have ridden off to join them. Together they plan to go back and take vengeance on the Qashqai for the injustice done the honor of their family."

"You mean after taking my money they've ridden off and left me! God's blood, what kind of honor is this!"

Mustapha began rolling up the rugs from the tent. There was an attitude of fear about him, as though the messenger feared being punished for his bad news. And yet, the slight smile that hovered about the corners of his lips suggested to Rhys that he was actually enjoying all this. It was all Rhys could do not to grab him by the neck of his robe and heave him through the tent flap.

"It is our way, *effendi*," Mustapha went on unctuously. "Family is all."

"Family! Allah deliver me from family! First they hold up the entire train for this tribal nonsense, and now they run off and desert for it. And after I've paid them most generously, too. I'll never understand you people."

Mustapha worked energetically at the tent strings without looking directly at Rhys. "Do not worry yourself, Lord Captain. In two days' time we shall be nearing the caravansary at Hadabat. It is a busy place where many caravan roads cross. Perhaps Mustapha shall be able to hire other guards from the people there.

195

Of course, it will require the use of the Captain's gold—"

Rhys angrily pushed the coffee and its tray toward the Arab. "Of course. What else! Get this gear stowed away. I'm going to get my horse."

By midday, amid great mirth, the word of Rhys's humiliation had spread through the caravan train. No one enjoyed it more than Collie, who took great glee in recounting every detail to Justine that evening.

"Will he be safe without those guards?" was her only disappointing comment.

"Safe enough, at least until we reach Hadabat."

Justine was aware that no one in the caravan was more anxious to reach the great caravansary than Collie. For days the other travelers had been extolling its pleasures, until the anticipation was nearly enough to overshadow the satisfaction he felt over Rhys's being bamboozled by his guards.

"It's a great place," he told Justine when she asked about it. "They say it has all the things that make for relaxation after a trek in the desert—good food, musicians, dancing, women . . ."

"All the things that make for relaxation for *men,*" Justine said cryptically.

"I'm sure ye'll find a few diversions, too. There will probably be merchants from all parts of the Eastern world. Things to admire and buy. And lots of other women."

"Oh certainly. I'm not supposed to be able to talk, remember? And even if I could, from what I can tell, all Arab women ever discuss is their dowry, their husband, or their children. I shall have a lot to say!"

Collie reached over and patted her arm. "Justine, ye always have a lot to say, even when ye can't talk."

196

And yet all the following day she found her excitement growing at the thought of entering the caravansary at Hadabat. All the pleasurable anticipation she had felt on entering the town of Rayys began to reawaken. When, the next morning, a dark shape rose on the flat horizon, indicating the oasis in the distance, Justine readily joined in the excitement that swept through the train. The walls rose like an abnormality on the barren plain, too straight and solitary to be a natural hill. With the visual tricks that the desert played, they appeared much closer than they were, and it took most of the day to reach them. Justine passed the hours remembering Rayys and the vitality and life there that was so thrilling after the solitary plain.

Yet Hadabat was no town. She recognized the difference even before they lumbered their way between the open gates in the high sun-dried brick walls. It had been built on the wasteland of a flat gravel-strewn plain to service the caravans who crossed here from the west, the east, and the south. It consisted of one large two-story building of sand-colored brick surrounding four sides of an open grassy square. Outside, a few trees and parched fields gave way to the desolation beyond. But inside, the square was crowded with people much as Rayys had been. Like Rayys, Hadabat attracted farmers from the outlying areas bringing produce for the travelers. Merchants, landlords, an occasional gendarme mingled with the hordes of men and women from the trains. Donkeys, camels, stray dogs, and the occasional fine horse of the well-to-do added to the confusion.

One of those fine horses belonged to Rhys. He sat there looking over the crowds, very conscious of one segment of the population which Justine had failed to

197

notice—the large number of gaily decorated, half-dressed women who brazenly wandered among the new arrivals, inspecting even as they themselves were inspected.

"Are those harlots?" he said, dismounting and handing the reins to Mustapha.

"But of course, *effendi*. They are the women of pleasure here to service the men of the caravans. You would perhaps wish me to engage one for you."

"No, thank you," Rhys said hurriedly. He did not especially care for the shopworn appearance of the women, or the diseases which usually accompanied them. Then he had a sudden thought.

"Do these women ever arrive with the caravans?"

"Oh yes, Lord Captain. Many live here, but others come and go. And occasionally a great courtesan will come through, on her way to the cities to ply her trade there."

"Hmm," Rhys said thoughtfully. "Mustapha, there is something I want you to do for me. Now listen carefully . . ."

Once the camels were seen to, Collie and Justine went to seek out the best known proprietor to engage a room. Hadabat was very crowded, and it was obviously going to be a luxury to hire a private room, yet Justine was determined to have one, whatever the cost. After all the time in her wobbly litter trying to be so careful not to reveal who she was, she felt she had earned a little place in which to be herself for a few days.

Yet even she was appalled at the final cost. Moreover, it turned out to be quite a shabby room, considering the

198

huge amount she paid for it. It was very small, with one latticed window high up on the wall, a low table, a brazier, and two worn rugs on the floor. Yet it was almost worth it for the bed. It was a real bed, low to the floor and covered with a lumpy mattress and a few shabby pillows. But a real bed! She thought longingly of returning to it and resting for hours and hours.

They went down to the cafe, where to her surprise she saw other respectable women sharing a communal meal of lamb stew, flat bread, and strong, hot tea. Collie controlled his impatience throughout the meal, anxious to return Justine safely to her room and be off to his own diversions. He had his eye on a particular whore who this afternoon in the square had favored him with a provocative, inviting smile. She was one of the more alluring lasses, with strong white teeth, flashing black eyes, and half-concealed breasts that hung like ripe melons on her spare frame. He could hardly wait!

With the leisurely meal finally finished, they went back up the dark stairs to their room. Collie lit a small lamp that hung from the ceiling, while Justine threw off her *aba* and stretched out on the bed, sighing with pleasure.

"Collie, if you intend to sleep here, you'll have to use the rugs on the floor. I'm not giving up this bed for anyone."

"Don't ye worry about me. I don't plan to sleep here at all." He pulled off his headgear and began to comb his hair, while Justine smiled at his feeble efforts to primp.

"Why, Collie! And just where do you plan to sleep?" she asked mischievously.

"Never mind. Ye shouldn't know."

"Collie, I'm shocked. But seriously, what about me? I

199

can hear all the music and talking from downstairs. This is a lively hostel. Will I have any trouble?"

"Ye'll be safe as a baby. I'll stop in every now and then, just to check on ye, if that will make you feel better."

She was about to tell him not to bother, when there was a loud banging on the door. "Now who could that be?" Collie said, looking up from the tiny mirror he had taken from Justine's baggage. "Wait," Justine cried, reaching for her *aba* and engulfing herself within its folds. Collie put his fingers to his lips to remind her she wasn't supposed to be able to talk, and went to the door, opening it slightly. Through the crack Justine could just see an Arab man standing in the hall, loudly talking and gesturing with his hands. Collie answered in Arabic, his voice rising in frustration as the exchange continued.

To Justine's surprise the man suddenly tried to shove his way through the door, but Collie, enraged by now, grabbed him by the collar and shoved him back into the hall, slamming the door behind him.

"What on earth was that all about?" Justine whispered.

"I don't understand," Collie muttered, staring at the door as though the answer could be found inscribed there. "He wanted someone called Tepe. He was told she had rented this room."

"Tepe? But who . . ."

"I don't know who she is. But she must be someone famous. I couldn't convince him there was no one here by that name."

Justine shrank back against the wall. "Did you tell him he was wrong? He tried to force his way in here!"

"Of course I told him." He was interrupted by a second banging on the door. "If that fellow has come back again I'll . . ."

Cautiously he opened the door a crack, while Justine tried to melt into the wall beside her bed. Once again she glimpsed an Arab outside, but it did not look like the same man as before. The heated exchange began again, with Collie growing increasingly frustrated and finally slamming the door in the man's face.

"I'll be damned . . ." he muttered. "He says Tepe is a famous courtesan. Evidently she has a reputation that's spread from Damascus to Bukhara. I never heard of her. I'd better go ask the landlord about this."

"No! Don't you dare leave me here alone!"

Even as she spoke the banging resumed. This time it was two men, and from the sound of their argument, they were determined not to be turned away. Justine, growing more anxious by the moment, got down on the floor, ready to roll under the bed if they came barging into the room, as it seemed they were threatening to do.

"Ye've got the wrong room!" Collie screamed, slamming the door and throwing his shoulder against it to hold it shut against the two men outside who, undiscouraged, pushed against it. "Quick, Justine! Shove that table over here!"

"That's not going to do much good," Jess cried as she pushed the table toward him. Collie reached for the one chair in the room and piled it and the table against the door, even as another series of loud knocks resounded from the hall.

"Use the bed," Justine said, beginning to pull at the frame.

"We don't need that much," Collie answered. This time he did not open the door, but called through it in Arabic, "You've got the wrong room!"

Justine could make out the angry voices on the other side, arguing with him through the door. When the men

201

outside began shoving against it, opening it a crack, she looked anxiously at Collie. "Well, perhaps the bed wouldn't hurt," he muttered, and she ran to pull it across the room. With the furniture piled in front of the door, and Collie standing over it, answering the knocks that came rapidly, one after the other, she began to feel a little more secure.

"This is crazy," Collie exclaimed. "It's a misunderstanding. I could solve it, if I could talk to the proprietor, but I don't dare leave you to do it."

They both looked longingly at the high window. "Perhaps you could take me with you," Justine suggested.

It was a tempting thought, until he recalled the gleeful anticipation on the faces of the men in the hall. "I wouldn't trust taking ye outside this room tonight," he said, bitterly. "Tomorrow we can get it straightened out."

Another series of loud knocks came crashing against the door. "You won't leave?" Justine whispered anxiously.

Collie sat down with his back against the bed frame, his ornate leather knife shaft cradled in his hands.

"Not now, anyway. Perhaps in an hour or so they'll learn their mistake and leave us alone." And he might hope his pretty little whore was still available.

Late the following morning, Justine made her way down the stairs to the cafe to drink a cup of the hottest, strongest coffee she could buy. Her eyes were so heavy she could barely see, and every muscle in her body was exclaiming its fatigue. The cafe was nearly empty, and she gratefully slumped over the table, her *aba* drawn close around her as she nursed her coffee.

"May one wish the sister of Yarmid Ali a pleasant good

morning," said a mocking voice at her side. She looked up to see Rhys standing there, smiling down at her. "I trust you had a refreshing sleep," he added, pulling up a chair beside her.

"No, I did not!" she muttered.

"Why, I'm surprised. A real bed in a private room. You ought to be fully refreshed."

Her eyes narrowed as she studied the gleeful glint in his dark eyes. "You!" she said, not even bothering to disguise her speech. "It was you who did this!"

Rhys fussed with the sleeve of his coat. "Did what? I confess I don't know what you mean."

"You know very well what I mean. Someone gave out to the men in this place that there was a famous courtesan staying in my room. Tepe. I suppose you made that name up."

"Tepe? I believe it means 'peak' or something like that. Very appropriate for a courtesan. I wish I had known. I might have visited her myself."

"You . . . you bastard! Collie spent the whole night sitting in front of a barricade, trying to prevent these lust-crazed men from forcing their way into my bed. I had to sleep on a rug on the floor, though there was little sleep involved. Everytime I dozed off there was another pounding on the door."

"How unfortunate. And you were looking for a little civilization after your long sojourn across Persia, too."

"You are despicable! How could you play such an underhanded trick on us. It cost me a fortune to engage that room."

"As much as it cost me to bribe my way out of an Arab gaol?" Rhys answered sarcastically. "Come now, no harm was done. Just rent another room tonight, and perhaps they'll leave you alone."

"And what rumor will you spread about me tonight? That I'm traveling with a satchel filled with emeralds and pearls?"

"You wound me to the quick. Of course, you can solve all your problems by spending the night with me in my room. That would, I presume, also leave Collie free to enjoy himself."

"I'd rather die!"

"Have it your own way. There are plenty of other willing women about."

Justine rose unsteadily to her feet. "Why don't you go find Tepe. I'm sure she'd sleep with anybody. Even you."

"Well now, I would if I knew where to find her."

She leaned into his face, her eyes flashing with her anger. "Tepe had better disappear, Rhys. I'm not going to spend my entire time here trying to keep from being raped. You let these people know it was a mistake, and no such person exists or else . . . I'll find some way to get even with you."

"Oh, all right. It was only a harmless little prank. If you're going to be so crabby about it, I'll see that Tepe leaves Hadabat as easily as she entered it."

"See that you do!"

Wobbling a little from sheer weariness, she made her way back upstairs to the new room Collie had managed to hire for her once he felt it safe to leave her alone. It was at the other end of the hall overlooking the oasis and the desert and was actually quieter than the first room. Justine fastened the chair in front of the door and fell on the bed, drifting to sleep almost at once. It was only later, when she woke refreshed and able to look back on the night before, that she allowed herself to see the humor in it. Rhys had certainly managed to get even with her for not returning his papers and his purse. And now that they were even, perhaps it was time to casually allow those purloined items to reappear. The problem of what to do about *him* still remained, but since they still had a way to go, surely she would think of some way to detain him.

She thought longingly of his invitation. It was tempting, but no, she would not put herself in such a vulnerable position again. She must keep her wits about her and concentrate on getting safely to Samarkand.

Yet, she decided, there was still time to enjoy Hadabat. Though it was late in the afternoon by now, she washed up, put on her second *aba*, combed her hair, tucked it beneath her veil, and sallied forth to the square to see what life here was like. The crowds were as thick as before, but there seemed to be more merchants with their wares spread on rugs in long aisles across the open square. Justine took her time examining them all, since there was little else she could take part in. There were exquisitely embroidered fabrics from Turkistan and silks from China. Wonderfully intricate rugs from Kerman vied with beaten copper trays and utensils from Shiraz. Brightly colored harness for camels and horses hung beside inlaid leather worked into bags, belts, and satchels. She made up her mind that if she was going to go on masquerading as an Arab woman, she deserved to wear the jewelry they loved so much, and she passed all the other merchants to find those rugs that were covered with silver and gold ornaments in exquisitely worked patterns.

She was bending over one such display when Rhys appeared at her elbow.

"Would the sister of Yarmid Ali allow me to bargain for her?" he said rather loudly so those around them could hear. Then he looked at the merchant and pointed to his ears, speaking the Arabic word for deaf. Justine could hardly send him away without speaking, so she meekly nodded.

"Here's a lovely thing," Rhys said, lifting a head ornament of gold with several round disks dangling from it. The waning rays of the sun caught its shimmering brightness, glinting off it in rays of brilliance. "It would look lovely on you," he added, holding it up to her forehead. "How much?"

The merchant named a figure which appeared to leave Rhys appalled, and they embarked on a hearty round of haggling while Justine watched, annoyed and yet amused. At length he bought it, complaining at the way he was being robbed and, taking her elbow, moved her on to the next booth, chatting all the while.

Forced to listen silently, Justine could only nod her head like an imbecile child and let him lead her around the square. He appeared to be enjoying himself hugely as he bartered for necklaces, earrings, ankle and wrist bracelets, and even toe rings. The only time Justine managed to make her displeasure felt was when he seemed determined to purchase a large silver ring for her nose. He gave that up, and instead bought a long length of beautifully worked turquoise silk that shimmered like the ocean in the evening light.

"Perhaps it will remind you of the *Boeadecia*," he whispered as they walked back to her room to deposit her packages. Once they were out of earshot, Justine hissed: "That was not fair. You knew I couldn't object."

"Yes, but look at the pretty things you have. And how would you have ever been able to get them by yourself, when you aren't supposed to be able to hear or talk."

It was true of course, but she was reluctant to admit it. Instead she scowled at him and drew her veil closer around her face.

"Look here," Rhys said at her door. "I won't even come in, if it makes you feel better. But think for a moment. You have no one in this whole place with whom to be congenial except Collie and me, and Collie seems to be very happily involved with his own pursuits. I, on the other hand, have no friends either. Can't we call a truce and enjoy ourselves while we're here?"

She caught back her quick no and hesitated, drawn by the good sense of his comment.

"I could order supper, and we can take it out under the trees where no one would hear us. What do you say? Wouldn't that be better than barricading yourself in your room for another night?"

Justine hesitated only a moment. Why spend a lonely night in her room, when she could share it with the one person with whom she could be herself? "All right. I suppose it makes sense."

Shortly afterward they made their way through the gates of the caravansary and ambled among the stubbly growth of the outside gardens beneath the tall palm and date trees. In the distance they could see several half-robed men prodding oxen through the fields. Nearer the well two men in abbreviated rags worked a primitive waterwheel powered by a bored camel.

Rhys found a somewhat private spot where they were sheltered from the curious eyes of the workers by a grove of trees. Spreading a rug, he laid out their meal of buffalo cheese, dates, figs, bread, and tea. As a rare delicacy he had managed to add several sweetmeats and a sugary delicacy called *baklava*.

He broke off a piece of the cheese and handed it to Justine. "Do you ever find yourself remembering the sumptuous meals of Philadelphia?" he asked. "Sometimes I think I would sell my soul to taste once more turtle soup, syllabub, or Brunswick stew."

"Beefsteak pie, corn pudding, flummery . . ." Justine added.

"Oysters on the half-shell. When I think of the fish and game we took so much for granted, I could kill."

"If I never see another bean patty in my lifetime, it will be too soon."

Rhys stretched out on the rug with his hands beneath his head, staring up at the sky, filigreed by the tree branches. It was getting on to dusk and the brilliant azure blue had given way to the golden bronze of sunset. "It was such a comfortable life—Philadelphia—wasn't it. So gracious in many ways. So civilized compared to this primitive, backward country. Look at those men bringing up water from the well, for example. That's probably the way it was done when the Bible was young. They never learn any better ways and seem content to go on using the old ones forever."

Justine popped a pastry into her mouth and licked her fingers. "It seems to me that our Colonies are becoming more primitive. If the rebels have their way, the very things that made us so civilized will be thrown away."

Rhys threw her a sharp glance. "Not even civilization is worth tyranny."

"And I suppose a mob is not tyrannical. My father used to say that mob rule only allows the scum to rise to the top."

"I've heard of your father," Rhys said casually. "He was a solicitor, wasn't he? Rather thick with Dr. Shippen and Mr. Franks and all the Tory hierarchy. I suppose he was also a familiar figure at British headquarters."

"He was friends with Gen. Clinton and some of the others."

"So I suppose he welcomed the occupation of his hometown by a foreign despot."

"He welcomed the presence of the lawful representatives of our rightful King! Just because he knew Major Hughes and Sir William Howe doesn't mean he wasn't conscious of the military presence in Philadelphia. He felt it was necessary for the salvation of our country."

Rhys reached over and picked up a handful of sand, running it through his fingers. "Your father was a friend of Major Hughes? I've heard of him, too. He was responsible for the hanging of several good patriots whom he labeled spies. A fine man to have for a friend."

Justine turned her face away, aware that she had made a bad slip. "He wasn't a close friend—just someone my father knew slightly. We met most of the British officers at one time or another. We even entertained them in our home. I never heard that Major Hughes was associated with spies."

"No. Of course not. You wouldn't." Reaching out suddenly he pulled her to him, laying her down on the rug and bending over her. His face was very close. She was conscious of the thick lashes fringing his eyes.

"We are never going to agree on politics," Rhys whispered, nuzzling her ear. "There are better things to discuss."

Justine gave a low laugh at the tickling sensation in her ear that sent warm waves down her spine. "Perhaps it's better to discuss nothing at all."

His lips trailed along her smooth cheek and found her mouth. Gently probing with his tongue he outlined the lovely shape of her lips, seeking their warmth and sweetness with his own. She caught his full lower lip between her teeth, not hurting, but claiming it as her own. His tongue slipped between her lips, flicking and

209

exploring the inside of her mouth, lightly tasting, probing.

"I think it is truly remarkable how we are able to rise above our prejudices," Rhys said, chuckling.

"I believe that is because there is one thing that interests you more than politics," she laughed.

"And what might that be?" he asked, lightly trailing his fingers down the length of her throat and over the swell of her breast.

"You know very well," Justine said, breaking out of his embrace to sit up on the rug. "I feel as though everyone around us is watching," she said, throwing back her long hair. "Couldn't we go inside?"

Rhys rolled over, disappointed. "If you insist on being modest. I can't see why you're worried, though. It's getting dark enough that they couldn't see anything if they were standing over us."

"I don't quite know why it bothers me," Justine answered reflectively. "I always have this feeling that they are laughing at us behind our backs, somehow. As though there was something they know that we don't, and we're making rather fools of ourselves in their eyes."

Rhys began gathering up the food into the basket. "As long as we have gold to hand out, we needn't worry what they think. That's all they're really interested in."

"I don't think so. It's all mixed up with the strangeness and . . . well, mystery of this place. I feel somehow as though they belong here and I never will. As though they have come to understand and deal with the harshness and the beauty of this country in a way I'll never understand."

"That's because you weren't born here," Rhys said prosaically. "I'll wager, given a chance to change places, they'd fall all over themselves trying to reach the ship.

Come on, my modest girl. It sounds as though there is music and dancing going on inside the walls, and we may as well enjoy it, too."

By the time they made their way back to the square, darkness had fallen like a blanket laid over the world. Dancing shadows from the many torches set in the walls frolicked among the milling crowds in the open mall. The acrid odor of burning pitch mingled with charcoal smoke, fried onions, and sizzling meats. It almost made Justine wish she had not gorged herself on the picnic foods Rhys brought.

At one end near the entrance to the hotel, a large crowd circled around a dancer performing to the throbbing beat of a clay drum and the exotic warblings of several reedy, pipe-shaped instruments resembling hautboys. Justine and Rhys paused, as the crowd made way for them, fascinated by the gyrations of the woman in the center. She was buxom, with her large breasts barely concealed by a gauzy halter. Her legs were encased in transparent trousers of the same material that began halfway down her torso. Bangles cascaded everywhere over her, from ankles, hips, neck, arms, wrists, and over the veil that swept back from her forehead. Rhys was transfixed by a large, gleaming jewel in her navel which stayed stationary while her hips vibrated violently to the throbbing music. She slowly circled, her arms outstretched, her body vibrating like a string on a viol, her pelvis thrust forward, her shoulders straight as a board, a hypnotic half-smile on her rouged lips.

Rhys's hand clasped Justine's as they both watched, transfixed. The erotic beating of the drum increased in tempo, the dancer's moist flesh was dappled by the glistening torchlight. All of the exotic East was caught up in her dancing—the heat, the warm flesh, the emotional,

211

erotic drumbeat, the inviting sensuality of the woman, the abandon, the untamed wildness of the desert . . .

"Come with me," Rhys muttered, and pulled her away from the crowd. She ran after him gladly, as eager as he to reach the sanctuary of a closed room where they could throw off the bonds of propriety as easily as they threw off their clothes. The dance had worked on Justine with the same intensity as on Rhys. Her body was aflame, her anticipation almost painful.

She was surprised when he hurried her past the dark narrow stairwell to the rooms on the second floor and on toward the back of the building. His fingers lightly touched the small of her back, encouraging her on, a searing flame against her skin. Down a dimly lit hall, the light from oil lamps set in niches in the wall threw sharp shadows against them. When he paused to open a door and urge her through, she did not recognize whose room it was, nor did she care. The door closed behind them and his arms enfolded her. She stood trembling while his hands tore at her robes, pulling them away to fall in a tumbled heap on the rug. Inflamed, she moaned while his hands searched her body, his lips bruising her mouth. In his driving excitement he was not gentle. He was all over her where she stood, trying to taste, feel, stroke, and meld into her flaming body all at once. He fell to his knees, drawing her down with him. Justine gasped as his lips tore from her breast to slide over her cheek, her throat, along the sweeping curve of her neck and between the deep valley of her breasts, seeking the tight peak where he caught at a nipple, suckling wildly. Still kneeling, his hands slid down between her thighs and upward, thrusting into the moist mystery of her femininity. She heard herself cry out. She could not bear the pain that was also an exquisite pleasure.

She reached out to pull him against her, and it was more than Rhys could manage. Toppling her over on the thick cloud of rug, he fell on her, driving his manhood into her with a desperation and abandon he had never felt before. She arched her back and rose to meet him, drawing him into her depths, crying aloud as they both went crashing over the edge of the world, into a void that was sweet as it was wild and unformed.

Justine lay on the rug, feeling the weight of his body, drawing long breaths as her pulsating senses gradually eased. When Rhys shifted to turn over on his back—his own breath coming in short, heightened gasps—she turned her head and realized she was lying on no ordinary carpet. Thick and luxurious, it was a claret-colored brilliance, worked with master hands. She raised on her elbows and for the first time became aware of the room she had entered.

The gentle murmur of water—which she only now heard—came from a small but exquisitely carved fountain in the center of the room. The walls were draped with hangings of shimmering gold and silver cloth, worked with patterns of azure blue. A large divan lay on the far side of the fountain, overflowing with cushions and pillows. Above it, a gauze curtain swept from a small central gold ring to frame the sides of the bed. Open-worked lattices in the walls showed the darkened patterns of trees outside, while in the ceiling above them, more lattice work brought in the night sky, diamond stars twinkling against an ebony background. Near the door one small oil lamp flickered, throwing long shadows on the curtained walls.

"Is this where you are staying?" Justine said when she could get her breath to speak.

Rhys sat up, draping his arms across his knees. "Not

213

exactly. It's the best suite in the place, and the most expensive. I rented it for tonight."

"You . . . you *rented* it! Rhys Llewellyn, did you plan this whole thing. How could you be so sure I'd come? Or did you just intend to bring some woman here, and I was convenient."

Rhys reached out to sweep her long hair from her face. "Don't be foolish. Of course, I rented it for you. I was taking a chance on the magic of the desert and the music to soften your annoyance over last night."

Justine pushed his hand away and rose to her feet. Picking up her robe, she draped it around her and walked around the room, taking in its beauty. "That was a very underhanded thing to do," she said, trying to sound angrier than she actually felt. "It would have served you right if I hadn't come, and your money would have gone for nothing."

"It would not have been the first time on this journey," Rhys said, laughing. He stood up and walked to a niche in the wall to pour her a tumbler of boiled wine. His lean hard body glistened in the soft light, and Justine stared, admiring the sleek beauty of it. Walking over to the divan, he sat down and extended his hand to her.

"Come, my love. Be comfortable. We have the whole night before us."

In spite of herself, she smiled and moved to the bed. "If the first time was any indication, I don't think I'll last the night!"

"You're stronger than you think," Rhys said, lifting the thick rope of her hair to gently kiss her neck. "Here, drink this. It's been denuded of its alcohol to please the sensitivities of the Muslims, but it should keep up your spirits nonetheless."

She sipped the wine, then laid back on the shimmering

covers, stretching in satisfaction. Resting on one elbow, Rhys bent over her and pulled away the robe to admire the satin smoothness of her body. There was no urgency now, no driving need. He smiled down at her and let his hand roam gently in a slow descent along the curves and hollows of her neck and shoulders, down between her swelling breasts, and along the quivering flats and mounds of her hips. Justine closed her eyes and lay mesmerized by the light, feather touch of his hands along her skin. The gentle cascade of the fountain gradually grew to fill the night. She hadn't thought she could ever be aroused again after the exertions on the rug, but the magic of his hands began to work on her once more. She lay in a delicious lethargy until suddenly she felt a cold trickle on her breast, and opened her eyes to see him tipping the tumbler of wine over the nipple. With a cry she tried to sit up, but was stopped as he lowered his lips to gently lick the wine from the growing tautness. The warmth that eased in through the latticed window from the desert seeped into her body, glowing like a flame within her. His suckling was gentle at first, lightly pulling on the nipple as a child might. But the magic of its sweetness worked on Rhys as well, stirring the fires within him that had only shortly before lain like embers.

Justine moaned softly and stretched her body its full length on the bed. Rhys drank deeper of the sweetness of her breast, teething the jutting crown lightly. He tore his lips from it to search the swelling perimeters, driving into the deep valley and up again to grasp the other peak. With his hands he pressed the two together, as if to more easily drink of one, then the other. She moved beneath his hands, stirring with a growing glow that was fast becoming a raw ache. The muscles of her thighs tightened and her hips slowly rotated against him. Her

215

own hands went searching over the broad shoulders, down the smooth plane of his back, over the swelling of his hips. He moved beneath her hands as she had beneath his, exciting them both. She slipped one hand between them to grasp the pulsating shaft of his hard manhood and he cried out, loosening for a moment his hold on her breasts. Eager to give pleasure as well as to receive it, she lifted him between their two bodies and gently undulated against him. Rhys began to be overcome with that wild abandon of before, but he stilled himself to remain gentle. He reached around, grasping her buttocks with his hands and pressed her against him. Gradually he worked his hand between them, searching for the soft moistness between her legs. Finding it, he relentlessly massaged, bringing her to his own growing frenzy. When he could stand it no more, he wedged her legs apart with his knee and rose to enter her, hard now, but with a concern for her fulfillment that had not been there before. Justine was carried on the torrent, the cascade of water that seemed to roar through the room. Her back arched to receive him, and together they were swept along as one person up into the shimmering night where the brilliant stars went shining like meteors around them.

She fell back, sighing, utterly spent. Opening her eyes, she glimpsed the silver streak of a shooting star falling across the night sky. She was too breathless and too content to speak of it. Rhys lay beside her, one arm across her hips, his breathing slowly subsided and his eyes closed. She thought perhaps he had drifted into an exhausted sleep.

He stirred and turned over on his back. "Why are you here?" he said.

It was so abrupt after what they had just shared, that

216

Justine could barely believe she had heard him right.

"What?"

He laid his hands beneath his head and stared up at the sky. "Why are you really here in this forsaken part of the world? What's the true reason?"

"Do we have to talk about this now?" she said somewhat testily. All the comfort and joy of the moments before somehow had grown tarnished and she resented it.

"No, but I thought perhaps, considering . . . all this, you might be honest with me for once."

She sat up and reached for the goblet of wine. "I have been honest. I told you why I came. What more do you want me to say?"

"It has not escaped my notice that you and your English friend would like to separate me from the caravan. I can't believe I am a threat to anyone buying goods for a Philadelphia merchant, so there must be some other reason. For the life of me I cannot imagine what it is. Especially when we seem to get along so well. And we are very good together, you know, in spite of the fact that you're a deluded Tory."

This was adding insult to injury. "That's just the kind of remark I would expect from a fanatic Whig! It's not the loyalists who are deluded. It's the rabble-rousing republicans who want to throw away a good and decent government for a crazy experiment."

Rhys turned over on his side, and she could see he was smiling. "You're just trying to get me riled, aren't you?" she said with irritation.

"I'm just trying to face facts. You know, don't you, that when we win this revolution, all your kind are going to have to leave America. Maybe England will take you in."

"And maybe we'll win, and *you'll* have to leave!" she

217

said, poking at his chest.

"Oh, no. We shall all be hanged from the nearest gibbet."

"You've a poor idea of English justice."

"With some justification. How can you defend them? How can you . . ."

All at once he was aware of how beautiful she looked, the color high in her cheeks, her hair like a copper cloud around her face, the dim light shadowing the planes of her cheeks and the sculptured contours of her lips, parted in anticipation of flinging some argument back at him. He laughed, reached out, and pulled her to him, silencing her lips with his own. "My fiery Tory princess," he said when he could speak again. "I wonder if you know how beautiful you are."

Justine fought down her irritation. His face, so near her own, was too dear, too strong, and too handsome to fuel her anger at his words. Of course, it was also too proud, too arrogant, and far too full of mischief to let him know that. Even now she was not certain if he was just trying to tease her, or if he really meant what he said. She suspected there was a little of both.

"Rhys, you're impossible!" she murmured.

Very slowly he slid his hand down her waist, along her stomach and hips, to cup the silky, swelling softness between her legs. In spite of herself, she stirred beneath his touch. With her head in the crook of his arm, he laid her back on the bed and bent over her, gently massaging. Once again the heavenly lethargy took possession of her body under his insistent fingers.

"Impossible," she moaned, and gave herself over to his divine explorations.

Nine

Nasr ud-Din had been the chief proprietor of the Rayys bathhouse for nine years, and, Allah allowing, he would be for nine more. In that time he had had occasion to serve a few Franks, as he called the Europeans who showed up at his door. It was beneath him, of course, to serve barbarians and infidels as though they were equals, but he had learned to mask his contempt rather well, hiding behind a lethargic ineptitude which drove them wild. The more they raged and called him imbecile, the greater his secret delight. Since few came through Rayys—which was far off the more traveled routes that radiated like a wheel spoke out of Baghdad—his little trick had stood him well. Now, after nine years, he was near to losing his carefully schooled persona. He had finally met a Frank who drove him wild.

"Take this to that English at the end of the hall," he said, handing a stack of soft robes to Mani, one of the young boys who worked the bathhouse. "And don't take any bribes from him. Come right back."

"Must I?" Mani groaned. "I hate that Frank. He cuffs

me every chance he gets. He's always complaining, and he treats me like I was feebleminded."

"It would surprise him to know what we think of him," Nasr muttered. "The arrogant bastard acts as though he was visiting a slum. Always asking questions, bribing everyone in sight with his gold. Demanding this and that. Bah! The sooner he is gone, the better. If he asks you any questions, tell him anything that will send him away."

"He claims that everything we say are lies," Mani said, picking up the robes.

"He is very free with his insults, that English. But then, you cannot expect a backward race like the Franks to know the rules of hospitality. That one, though, he is dangerous. I see it in the cold eyes and the hard mouth. You keep clear of him. Just leave these and come back."

"With pleasure," Mani exclaimed, darting down the hall. Nasr watched him go, his eyes softening. He had a warm spot for Mani, one of the smaller boys who had been forced here when his parents died of a fever. At least the difficult Frank at the end of the hall seemed to have no interest in the boys. Perhaps he had too little kindness in his cold heart to care for anyone or anything. Allah be thanked for small blessings!

Col. Augustus Hughes looked up briefly from the table where a masseur worked over his oiled body, long enough to see one of the dirty little urchins that swarmed over this place like ants, slither along the wall of the room and dump a pile of grimy rags on a stool. Probably crawling with vermin, he thought, like everything in this place. He was mildly disappointed that it wasn't George Sporn, for he had been expecting him for over an hour now. Though it was better to waste time in a place like this that catered to the comforts of the flesh—far preferable to wandering the dirty, smelly bazaars where one was accosted on all sides by unwashed bodies mouthing incomprehensible sounds—still he was growing impatient. There were things to be done, cities to reach. He could not afford to waste time in this backwater of civilization much longer.

And yet his methodical nature rebelled against setting off half-cocked, without knowing for certain where he should go. That might lead to an even greater waste of time—something he could not afford.

The urchin had hardly darted back through the door before the eagerly awaited Sporn slipped in, looking, as always, completely out of place. Sporn was unable to appreciate the Eastern custom of bathhouses, and though willing to rob, maim, or kill when it was necessary, this place smacked to him of pure, unadulterated sensuality. It was a source of amusement to the colonel, and part of the reason he insisted Sporn meet him in this place.

Hughes sat up on the table and dismissed the masseur from the room with a contemptuous wave of his hand. "It's about time you got here," he snapped. "Where have you been? I've been waiting nearly two hours."

Sporn's eyes looked everywhere in the small room, except at the naked oiled body of his colonel. "I came as soon as I had anything to report. It takes time, Colonel."

"Throw me one of those rags they call robes," Hughes ordered. The business at hand was more important than his amusement at Sporn's discomfort. He tied the robe around his waist and waited.

"I found a man, Habib Jabbar, who entertained this Yarmid Ali in his house when the caravan came through here."

"So they were in Rayys. Good. Good."

"Yarmid has a sister traveling with him, and they both stayed there."

"She's probably along as some sort of cover. What about Llewellyn? Didn't he stay there as well?"

"No. Habib did not know of any Englishman in Rayys with the caravan."

"Well, we know he was here because several people in this bathhouse remember him. That's the thing about bathhouses, Sporn. If you want to know what's going on in one of these miserable cities, go to the bathhouse or the coffeehouse. It's gossip that keeps those places going. So, Yarmid and Llewellyn are with Faud Monsel's train. Now, all we need to know is whether they are going north to Bokharta or south through the Iron Gate to Balkh. We should be able to discover which it is farther along. You'd better go and tell Clarke to get our gear ready. We'll need some mounts and a few Arab guides. No, make that Persians. They know this country better." The colonel picked up his clothes. "Get going, Sporn, we've no time to lose."

"Yes sir. It's as good as done. But . . . Colonel . . ."

"What is it?"

"What about the woman? There were tales in Baghdad and here in Rayys of an Englishwoman in the train. Shouldn't we try to find out who she is?"

"I don't see the need. She could be anyone. Occasionally women do travel in this part of the world, although the kind of woman who would do such a thing makes me suspicious. She's probably not respectable or anyone of note. Besides, as we catch up with the train, we're likely to hear who she is. The important thing is to get moving again."

222

Sporn ducked quickly from the room as the colonel began pulling at his robe again. It was halfway off when he hesitated. The hot pool was very inviting and would serve to wash away some of this heavy, fragrant oil. He might as well take advantage of the opportunity while he was here. Once back on the road, there would be no such chance again.

With his robe hanging loosely from his shoulders he made his way to the pool. Steam rose from the water to moisten the cavernous ceiling. There were a few other men there, but not so many that he couldn't find a solitary corner. Slipping off his robe, he stood at the pool's edge just as Mani passed behind him. The boy slipped on the wet surface and fell, grasping at the colonel's legs for support.

"Don't touch me, you vile little rat!" Hughes snapped, yanking his leg away from the boy's hands. "Get away before I box your ears!"

"Sorry, *effendi*," the child murmured, scrambling to his feet. Hughes reached down and grabbed the boy by the loose collar of his robe and gave him a hard swipe to the head, just for good measure. "Guttersnipe!" he snapped, then dropped the child on the tiled floor and kicked him away from the pool. "I can't bear these people!" he muttered, throwing off his robe to step into the hot mineral water.

With his ear still ringing, Mani made his way from the pool and back to the front of the building where Nasr stood working an abacus.

"That Frank! I hate him!"

"He didn't bother you, did he?"

"Only to hit me and kick me. Oh, if he would only stay here, I'd find a way to fix him. I'd get even."

223

"Just stay clear of him. You didn't tell him about the woman, did you?"

"No, nothing. Once I saw he was seeking information, I wouldn't tell him anything. I only wish I hadn't mentioned the big Englishman."

Nasr gave a low chuckle. "I don't know what it's about, but I bet that Frank would give a lot to know those two spent the afternoon together here. Ah, Allah be praised. What times they must have had."

"It was me who had an ear to the door, not you," Mani said, smiling again. Nasr reached out and smoothed the boy's curls away from his brown forehead.

"Such an education you get in this place. But you earn your living and for that you can be thankful. And be thankful too that most foreigners are not like that Frankish colonel."

Throughout the hot morning, Justine sat in her litter dreaming with a soft smile on her face of the previous night. It did no good to tell herself that she was being foolish, soaring like a silly schoolgirl on wings of love and ecstasy. She knew that reality would come sweeping back sooner or later to dim the joy she had shared with Rhys in that glorious room at the caravansary. But not yet. The swaying, rocking motions of her camel and the stilted confines of her curtained carriage were reality. And they were transformed by the happiness of her memories.

But he was her enemy, too! He had made that quite plain. She worked hard at reminding herself that soon they would reach their destination, and, once there, she must use all her cleverness to outwit him. She told herself yet again that her country's survival depended on

224

her getting that money before Rhys managed to.

Then the memory of her body, aflame in his hands, would come searing back, and a satisfied smile would grace her lips. He was a skilled lover who had won her heart, and there was no way she could blot that out.

But she was also his enemy. When he realized that, would he balk at putting her out of his way? Was his dedication to the rebellious Colonies great enough to destroy her, if it meant achieving his goal? Somehow she suspected Rhys Llewellyn would not allow his feelings to cloud his judgment when it came to something so important.

A growing murmur along the caravan train broke into her thoughts. She pulled aside the curtain to see some of the drivers halting their beasts and running along the train, calling to each other. An anxiety, more felt than understood, swept along with them. Frantically she looked around for Collie, but he was nowhere to be seen. Her own driver stood at his camel's head, pulling at the bridle.

Justine yanked aside the curtains and made some gestures and noises at the driver. He pointed off to the horizon and continued working at the camel, forcing the animal to its knees. At first Justine could see nothing that would explain why the caravan had come to a stop. Then she began to make out a long dark spout rising from the surface of the desert into the sky. It wavered and shimmered in the heat, and it grew even as she watched.

The driver got the animal to its knees, while Justine clung to the frame of the litter, then he started to run off. In her anxiety not to be left alone, she screamed at him, bringing him back to her long enough to give her a hand out of the litter. Then he tore off toward the front of the train, leaving her standing alone. She looked around, wondering if at last she must throw off this masquerade of not being able to speak or hear. All around her the other travelers were hunching down behind their animals, pulling great swaths of rugs or cloths over them. Justine stood frozen, as the sand around her began to swirl, irritating her eyes and choking her throat. All around her the frantic calls echoed in Arabic, Persian, Hebrew. Where was Collie? The winds grew stronger as she watched, tearing her robes around her body and whipping her veils around her face.

"Collie!" she screamed, no longer caring who heard her. The wind whipped her words away. Her camel turned to stare at her with its stupid, bland expression, and she clutched at the frame and crouched beside the litter in the tearing wind.

"Collie! Where are you?" she screamed again. The dark spout of the storm, now grown to enormous proportions, seemed to loom over her. Sand, pebbles, and gravel from the desert floor bit into her skin and blinded her eyes. Panic such as she had never known gripped Justine, paralyzing her as she clutched at the weak frame of the litter. It seemed as if in an instant the world had gone wild. The desert, usually so serene and benign, had swelled up in fury and threatened to devour her and everything around her.

She thought she heard her name called, and for an instant wondered if she were hallucinating. Then a dark form loomed up from out of the swirling wastes. Hands clutched at her and a familiar voice pulled her down to her knees.

"Rhys!" she called as he gripped her arms and shoved her down against the camel's body. Reining in his horse, he pulled him down in front of them and yanked a heavy rug over their heads. Nestled between the two animals, cut off somewhat from the merciless, choking sand, Justine could only cling to him as he cradled her in his arms.

"What is it?" she screamed over the roaring of the wind.

"A dust storm. I was afraid you wouldn't know what to do."

"If you hadn't come . . ."

He pulled her head against his shoulder, protecting her from the blistering sand that battered at their cover. Even under the rug, her mouth and throat were gritty with sand. She buried her head against Rhys, grateful for his arms around her and the warm strength of his body, ashamed of the tears that mingled with the dirt on her cheeks.

They could not tell how long the storm raged around them though it seemed hours. Then, as suddenly as it had come, the storm lifted, the wind died, and the desert settled back to its normal imperturbability.

When at last Rhys pulled away the rug, Justine was aghast at the change the storm had brought to their train. Animals and cargo lay half-buried in sand. The horses, goats, and camels were dun-colored under a coating of the desert floor. Yet they appeared to have survived unharmed, except for some of the smaller animals that had to be dug out. Most of the travelers were familiar with storms like these and knew how to weather them, but Justine was still shaken. Even when Collie came running up, full of apologies and concern that he hadn't had time to reach her, she was too upset to berate him for failing her.

Rhys laid her robes around her shoulders, and, without speaking, mounted his horse to gallop back toward the head of the train.

"I would have died, if he hadn't come along," Justine finally managed to stammer to Collie.

"Thank God he did. I was at the very end of the train, trying to settle some gold I won off one of those Armenians at Hadabat. I'm sorry, Justine. Now look, our pack camel has run off, and God only knows where I'll find him. I promise I won't leave ye again."

Still shaking, she crawled back into her litter. "I'm going to hold you to that," she snapped.

It was only later, when the caravan was lumbering along as though it had never been interrupted, that she wondered if anyone had heard her speaking English.

By the end of that week, they reached Nishapur where the caravan separated. Those merchants and travelers heading for the Indian route broke off here to travel south through the ancient area called The Iron Gate and on to Balkh. Justine had learned little of what lay to the south except that it traversed wild passes through great mountains and finally emerged in the warm, jeweled plains of India. The northern route which led to Samarkand left Nishapur traveling northeast to Merv, then on to the ancient city of Bukhara, the first bastion of Turkistan. The terrain began to change as they traveled this road. Flat gravel plains gave way to hills, some of them verdant with green scrub and groves of trees. The air grew cooler and the nights cold. But there remained that mysterious aura of the desert, where the stars seemed so brilliant in the velvet night sky that you felt you could almost reach out and pluck them. The glimmering salt flats, the black rocks, and the unyielding harshness of the plateau had been with them so long now that she had grown quite accustomed to them. When they reached their first real brook—a thin trickle through a small rocky gorge—she felt a twinge of sadness at leaving the desert behind.

Their train was now less than half of what it had been. Faud Monsel still commanded, however, and under his competent guidance they wound their way toward Turkistan and the end of their long journey.

She first heard of Rhys's intention to visit one of the buried cities on an evening shortly after their group had separated. They were past the edge of the Salt Desert now, and it seemed unwise to say the least, to deliberately go back toward it.

"Isn't that a foolish thing to do?" she whispered to Collie as they consumed their evening meal.

"Foolish! It's crazy. Mustapha has convinced him that every European has to see these ruins. He's probably even told him there is some kind of treasure to be found in them. Of course, that's a lie. There's nothing there but a few old columns and some large stones with markings on them that no one can read. But the captain insists he must see them for himself."

"Was he able to hire new guards?"

"No. He trusted Mustapha to do it at Hadabat, so it did not get done. It's my opinion he puts far too much confidence in that weasely Arab."

"Shouldn't you warn him, Collie?" Justine said in a tentative voice.

"Nay, I've learned from experience that the captain takes my warnings very lightly. He'll discover for himself

229

eventually how little Mustapha is to be trusted."

"Yes, but will he be safe?"

Collie gave a low chuckle. "I'd no idea it mattered to ye so much. I think he'll be safe enough. Mustapha wouldn't dare harm him, especially when everyone knows they went off together."

Justine debated speaking to Rhys herself, but that was difficult to do, limited as she was by her disguise. In the end she accepted Collie's assurances and tried to put Rhys from her mind. The caravan was to spend one whole day resting at the next well, and it was from there that Rhys was to set out with his guide to view the ruins of one of the ancient cities scattered throughout the Eastern world.

She saw him briefly as he was leaving, when he rode near her tent. He waved at her, then cantered up to doff his hat and bow from his saddle.

"May the infidel wish the sister of Yarmid Ali a most pleasant day," he said formally, his eyes twinkling with mischief.

Justine looked nervously around. None of her neighbors were close enough to hear her speak, but, just in case, she went to stand by Rhys's horse, stroking his velvet nose.

"You shouldn't be going out there alone," she said softly. He leaned down to rub his mount's neck.

"It's safe enough. I have a knife and a gun with me. Besides, it's a chance to view a little history."

"And bring back a little treasure?"

"Perhaps. It also serves to break up the monotony of a long caravan ride."

Anxious to be off, he pulled up on the reins to turn his horse. "Be careful, Rhys," she whispered, looking up at

230

him. The concern in her large eyes made him hesitate, but only for a moment.

"Don't worry yourself about me," he answered, laughing, and cantered off with a wave of his hat.

All the rest of that long day she tried not to think of him. But when evening began to fall and he had not returned, her concern began to swell from an annoying twinge to a full-blown ache. As darkness began to envelop the camp, she sent Collie to Faud Monsel's tent, to see if Rhys was back. He returned shaking his head.

"I'm sure something has happened to him," she said, twisting her fingers nervously.

Collie began to unroll his bed rug. "Capt. Llewellyn is a grown man, and very able to take care of himself. I wish ye'd not get yerself so worked up."

"But that's just it. He knows he should be safely back in camp by nightfall. We'll be leaving before dawn tomorrow."

"Perhaps he means to come in early, or to catch up with us later in the day. Perhaps what he found there was so interesting, he could not bear to leave after only a few hours."

"That would not be like Rhys. I tell you, Collie, I know something has happened to him. I can feel it."

"Bah! You're letting the blue devils get the better of you, just like a woman. Come on, Justine. We have a hard day's ride tomorrow. Get some sleep."

But she retired behind her black curtain only to toss on her bed most of the night, unable to shake the forbidding mood that gripped her. By dawn, when the camp began to stir, she insisted on going with Collie to see Faud Monsel.

"The captain's tent has not been used," the *Rais* said in his dignified way. "But we cannot wait for him. He was

231

told that before he went out into the desert."

"I know, I know," Collie replied miserably. Justine plucked at his sleeve, trying to say with her eyes what she could not speak.

"Couldn't we wait for him at least until the sun is well up?" Collie asked. "Or perhaps send some men after him?"

Faud shook his head. "We have already lost much time. I warned the captain of this possibility. It was up to him to return here in order to continue with the caravan. And I have no men to spare, now that we are only a third of our strength, to go searching for him. He knew this."

Collie nodded and pushed Justine away from the men working around the *Rais*. They had only gone a few steps when Faud called them back.

"I shall see that the captain's tent and gear are loaded, in case he is able to find us later in the day. That is the most I can do."

Collie bobbed his head. "You are most gracious, *Rais*. Thank you." Then he shoved Justine back toward their camels.

"There's nothing we can do," he hissed under his breath. "You heard the *Rais*. If we want to reach Samarkand safely, we have to stay with this caravan."

She waited until they were near their camels and out of earshot of their nearest neighbors. Then she sat down on the desert floor, crossing her legs beneath her voluminous robes.

"I'm not going!"

"Ecod, Justine! What's the matter with you? How long do ye think we'll survive on our own out here, waiting for Rhys to amble in? Between the sun and the Bedouin raiders we might last an hour, if we're lucky."

"I don't care. I can't just ride off and leave him to some awful fate. How long can he survive between the desert and the raiders? He may need our help desperately."

"And he may already be dead. I told you about that Mustapha."

A cold finger ran down Justine's spine. "Oh, Collie, would he really kill Rhys?"

"Yes, he might, though it would be a stupid thing to do. Come along, Justine. The train is already beginning to leave."

Justine pulled at his arm. "Collie, I can't leave him. At least let us ride over to find him. If he's dead, then so be it. I'll gladly go on to Samarkand."

"Has it occurred to you that it would be better for us if he was?"

"Yes. But I have to know. I . . . I owe him that much."

Collie threw up his hands. "Allah deliver us from the wiles of women! All right, Justine. You hired me, and I'll do what ye want. Do you think you can ride a saddle on a camel?"

"No, but I'll do it anyway."

"Wait here then."

She never knew just how Collie managed it, but within half an hour they had divested their camel of its litter and substituted a saddle. Collie had a donkey to ride, while the rest of their baggage went on with the drivers and the caravan. She watched them wend their long, serpentine way out of sight with a feeling of panic, for they bore security and safety with them. Somehow the desert had never seemed so all-encompassing before, or quite so lonely as it did when she and Collie set out at a angle to the train, bearing southwest to the caravan's northeastern route.

Collie had obtained directions from one of the Arabs in the train who was familiar with the buried city. He managed to follow the scattered landmarks well enough that by the time the sun was directly overhead, they could glimpse the dark columns rising on the horizon. Justine, thankful to stop the thumping of her mount for a moment, pointed them out.

"Is that the buried city?" she called to Collie, who was doddering up behind her.

"It must be. There are no trees around here. And no water, either. I tell you, Justine, this is crazy. We'll be lucky to get back to that train alive."

But he could not dampen Justine's spirits now that they were actually in sight of their goal. "Stop your carping, Collie. We're nearly there. Come on, can't you hurry that beast?"

In her enthusiasm she urged her camel ahead, clutching to the reins for dear life as it lumbered over the sand. The columns took on their perpendicular shape as she rode nearer, and she pulled up, waiting for Collie. It was an eerie place, as dead as a corpse in the empty desert. A quiet lay over everything, with not even an occasional hare or bird to break the ominous silence. Up close the columns, a last vestige of the ancient world, rose to astounding heights and loomed over her. Huge hewn slabs lay scattered among them, as though thrown from the hand of a giant recalcitrant child. Even from where she stood, she could make out the carvings on their rough faces. Paved steps led to nonexistent streets, lined by the rubble of what must have once been houses. And over it all, the deadly, unmoving silence.

Justine's fears for Rhys were heightened by the sadness of the place. She felt in her bones that somewhere scattered among those sun-baked wastes they would find his body, already dusted by the encroaching sand. She fought down the thick lump that rose in her throat, as Collie came tottering up on his donkey.

"Pretty dead, isn't it?" he said softly, looking over the place. "Not a sign of life. I can still see the tracks though. Look here. That means he reached this place at least."

On closer inspection Justine recognized the churnings in the sand as the hoofprints of a horse. Her hopes rebounded. Perhaps that meant Rhys had a chance, although if the traitorous Mustapha had caught him when his back was turned . . .

"Well, Collie. We might as well know the worst. Help me down off this absurd camel."

They started on foot up the low steps that led into the rubble. It was hard going in places, especially when the road disappeared below a layer of sand. And it was much larger than she had expected. Nervously Justine called Rhys's name, an echo in the desert quiet, as around every corner she expected to find his butchered body draped over the ruins. The blazing sun forced them to rest frequently in the limited shadow of the stone columns. Her fears mounted as they worked their way into the mass of remnants from an ancient world with no sign of life anywhere.

At one point they split up briefly, but Justine was too fearful of being alone in this desolate place to go very far from Collie. They wandered for the better part of an hour without finding any sign of Rhys. At that point her fears for him, and the numbing sorrow she felt that he might be dead, finally got the best of her. She slumped on a square boulder lying among others on a tiled patio, and laid her head in her hands.

"It's no use, Collie," she said, her voice choked on unshed tears. "He must have gone back out in the desert and become lost."

Collie sat beside her, unusually grave. "Or it might be that Mustapha killed him and buried his body. In that case we'd never be likely to find it."

"Oh dear," Justine sobbed, covering her face with her hands. She was tired and hot and overwhelmed by the desolate atmosphere of the place. That, added to her dreaded certainty that Rhys was dead, did away with the tense constraint she had used as a front for so long. Collie laid a comforting hand around her shoulders.

"Don't cry, Justine. It is a bad end for a Colonial gentleman like the captain, but it's possible it will be all the better for us. Try to remember that."

"But . . . I have . . . had . . . such tender feelings for him," she said brokenly. "I wanted him out of our way, but I didn't want him to die. Truly I didn't."

"I know. I feel rather sorry about it meself. He was a man who was so full of life."

Justine laid her head on Collie's shoulder and allowed the tears to flow. It helped a little to vent her feelings, after holding them in for so long. She no longer cared if Collie knew that she loved Rhys, or that they had been lovers. The little Englishman let her cry against his shoulder and said nothing, knowing there was nothing he could say to comfort her. He himself felt terrible about the loss of a man like the captain.

"Ahem," said a voice behind them.

The quiet sound fell like a thunderclap. Justine gasped and looked around while Collie jumped to his feet, his hand on the knife handle that protruded above his sash.

"Who's there?" he called as Justine shrank behind

him, quickly pulling her veil over her head. Her heart was thumping wildly. The impassive stones stared back at her with no sign of life. Yet she had heard a human voice.

"Come out at once," Collie shouted, sounding braver than he actually felt.

"I can't," a voice replied. This time she could tell it came from behind a wide column on her right. It was also very familiar.

"Rhys!" she cried. "Is that you?"

"Who else would be hiding behind a pillar out here in this wilderness?"

"Why, you villainous rascal," Collie exclaimed. "Ye were here all the time! Why didn't ye show yerself?"

"Believe me, I have a very good reason. Besides, I was enjoying the conversation. Tender feelings and all."

"Oh! You brute," Justine said, stepping out from behind the shelter of Collie's thin frame. "You let me cry and go on, and all the time you were standing there alive! That's reprehensible!"

"Sorry I couldn't oblige you by providing my dead corpse. I prefer this, bad as it is."

Collie moved forward to peer around the column. "Just how bad is it? Why wouldn't you show yerself?" He walked up to where he could see Rhys, who was still hidden from Justine. "Oh! I see. Well now. Ha! Ha!" And to Justine's surprise, he doubled up laughing.

"I don't understand what is so funny about this," she said, still too annoyed to join in. She walked up to Collie just in time to see Rhys dart around the column away from her. He was stark naked.

"What on earth—" she said as the laughter began to bubble up from deep below. "What happened to your clothes?"

237

"Mustapha took them. Along with everything else I owned," Rhys answered, chagrin darkening his face. "The bastard! He stole my gun, my knife, my horse, my money, and even my clothes. Rode off with them bold as brass, leaving me here to roast. If I ever see that stinking Arab again I'll . . ."

Collie, who by this time was doubled up on the ground laughing hysterically, gave over to new gales of hilarity. With her anxiety rapidly giving way to the humor of the situation, Justine joined in, holding her sides. Everytime one of them would sober up a moment, they would glimpse the other's eyes and begin all over again.

"I'm so glad you appreciate the humor of all this," Rhys said sarcastically. "Would it be troubling one of you too much to throw me some rag from your clothing that I might use as a cover?"

"Here," Collie said, still laughing as he pulled off his outer cloak and threw it to Rhys behind the column. "Give him one of your sashes, Justine, to hold it together. After all, we can't have him getting sunburned, can we? Ha! Ha!" and he was off again.

With the tears streaming down her face Justine pulled off one of her ropes. She could not have said how much her tears were due to her laughter, and how much to relief—she was too happy simply to enjoy them. When Rhys finally stepped out from behind the pillar with the robe tied around him, the chagrin on his face nearly set them both off again. They were draped around the columns, holding their sides, as Rhys, deadly sober, sat between them.

"I'll remember your tender sympathies," he muttered. "If you could manage to control your mirth for a few minutes, perhaps we could discuss how to get away from this place. I've seen enough of it to last me a lifetime."

"Why didn't you start back to the caravan?" Collie asked, wiping his streaming eyes. "We would have met you on the way."

"Yes, and by then you would have had trouble trying to tell me from a boiled lobster. I thought the best thing was to wait where there was some shade. I hoped someone would come looking for me."

"Ye must have been cold last night," Collie said, giggling.

"Now don't start that again," Rhys commanded. "What about the caravan? Are they waiting for us back at the well?"

"No. They went on. Faud said they could not wait, and he could not afford to send anyone to look for ye. If it hadn't been for Justine, you'd be out here yet, waiting for the vultures to find ye."

Justine looked quickly away, embarrassed. She could not forgive herself for betraying her feelings so openly a few moments before. "We had better be on our way as well," Justine said, suddenly sober. "It's going to be difficult to catch up with the caravan, and the longer we stand here talking, the harder it will be."

The realization of the urgency of their situation did away with any lingering mirth. "Justine, ye'll have to ride pillion on that camel with Rhys," Collie said, turning her toward the entrance to the city. "Do ye think ye can manage?"

"I'll have to. We don't have enough time to take turns walking."

By now it was scorching hot, and the trip back across the wasteland in the direction needed to cross the path of the caravan seemed endless to Justine, even though she was perched behind Rhys with her arms locked around his waist. She was still too embarrassed that he had overheard her outburst of love to enjoy his nearness. He seemed just a little too satisfied about her indiscretion for comfort.

They rode as quickly as they could without distressing their animals, yet it was still late afternoon before they found the tracks in the sand and the clumps of camel dung that indicated the caravan had passed this way.

"If we push on, we might be able to catch them where their camped for the night," Collie said. "Can you make it, Justine?"

Although every bone in her body protested, she nodded. She knew how important it was to make it back to the caravan before night fell. Alone out here they were too vulnerable to the predators—animal and human—they might stumble across.

They pushed on, weary and thirsty but doggedly determined, expecting over every hillock to catch sight of the tents and fires of the caravan. The land slowly and subtly began to change, merging from flat gravel-strewn floor to a gently rolling plateau, in places covered with a harsh, stubble of grass. Even the air felt different as they began to leave the desert for the hills that marked the end of the Persian plateau and the beginning of West Tartary. Far off in the distance, an undulating gray line gave indication of real hills and trees. Justine was studying them eagerly when she happened to notice off to her right several tiny dark splotches scattered along the gray plateau. Thinking it might be jettisoned cargo, she pointed it out to Collie.

"The caravan may have decided to leave some of its baggage behind, but I'm dammed if I know why," he answered, peering ahead. "You two wait here, and I'll ride over and inspect it closer."

"Oh no," Rhys exclaimed. "You're not leaving us alone out here. We'll all go together, or not at all."

"Suit yourself," Collie shrugged and lumbered off on the donkey. Rhys slapped his camel's side, sending them after him. As they drew closer, he pulled up on the reins, sorry he had not heeded Collie's warning.

"You recognize them, too," Collie muttered, halting beside them.

"Yes. Jackals. We should have kept Justine back there."

"Jackals out here," Jess cried. "But why?"

"Something has obviously died. Something rather large. Now will you two stay here, and let me see what it is?"

"I've seen more wildlife in the last hour than the last week," Rhys said, "but I never expected anything like this. Justine, you stay here with the animals, and Collie and I will walk ahead. You'll be safe. We'll always be in sight."

Though she did not like the idea at all, it seemed preferable to walking up to whatever lay over the crest of that dark hill. Getting down, she gripped the reins of both mounts and watched the two men ease their way ahead.

"What could have drawn them here?" Rhys asked after they were out of earshot. Collie's face looked grim as he answered: "It might be a dead camel. Although that's a bloody lot of scavengers for one dead animal. Keep low and walk slowly. We'd better not announce our presence until we know what's out there."

The two men skirted a rocky depression and, crouching, eased around the brow of a low hill, where

241

they could look down on the scene spread below. "God's blood!" Rhys muttered. At the sound of his voice several of the skeletal creatures shied away, slinking off for the nearest cover. He could feel the hairs on the back of his neck come alive. Next to him Collie made a soft clucking sound.

The flat valley was scattered with crumpled forms, too small and grotesque to be dead camels. Rhys drew in his breath sharply as he recognized them as men's bodies, some still wearing robes that were familiar even through the massive bloodstains. Crouching, he inched closer to stare down at a figure splayed on the ground, its head half-severed from its body. Beyond lay several others, even more hacked and mutilated.

"Is it . . . ?" he said, looking at Collie.

"It's our caravan, yes. I think I recognize Faud Monsel's *kaffiyah* over there. It's pretty grim. Can ye go closer?"

"I thought I'd seen the worst men can do to one another at sea, but this is beyond all. I'll go."

Cautiously they moved into the mass of bodies. A heavy silence lay over everything, emphasizing the desolate horror of the scene. As it became apparent that there were no survivors among the dead, they grew bolder, drawn by a horrible fascination with the terrible carnage.

"They must have carried off the women and animals," Rhys said, whispering in the deathly quiet. "I don't see any among the bodies."

"They took most of the cargo as well, but they left the ordinary things. Look over here. Isn't this the *Rais?*"

Rhys glanced briefly at the gaunt body sprawled on the ground, its eyes staring up into the sun. Though it had been hacked unmercifully, there was enough of the face left to identify.

"Yes," he said, looking quickly away. "Poor devil. He was a good man. He had some of my things with him. Do you suppose they might still be here?" Avoiding the body as much as possible, he rummaged among the strewn bundles and clothes nearby, pulling away one of the rugs to reveal his coats, shirts, and breeches. "Providence be thanked," he said, and began yanking away at the clothes to draw out a small round cushion. With his knife he tore at the cloth and pulled out a small metal case.

"My strongbox," he said, smiling up at Collie. "Thank God they didn't take this. It's all I have left between me and pauperism."

He was pulling away at his robe, to put on his clothes, when Collie stopped him. "You can't wear those, you idiot. Haven't you learned yet that a European in this country is easy game. We don't know who did this, but they were obviously after something or someone. Here," he said, throwing Rhys a handful of Arab robes from a pile at his feet. "Put these on."

Rhys started to object, then, remembering his experiences at the buried city, thought better of it. Grudgingly he donned the long dress, outer robe, and even the headdress of a Syrian.

They looked around a few moments longer, trying to find anything of value that might have been missed, then had enough of the horror of the place.

"Let's get out of here," Rhys said, "and leave it to the jackals. Wretched creatures. They are as awful as this place." They were halfway back to the shallow valley where Justine waited, when Rhys stopped Collie. "What are we going to tell her?" he asked. "We'd better get our

243

stories straight. She ought not to know too much about all this."

"Ye'll have to tell her something. She's too intelligent not to suspect something is very wrong."

Rhys's eyes darkened. "What *is* wrong, Collie? Who did this? Was it an isolated Bedouin raid? I've heard they prey on caravans."

Collie studied the horizon. "It might be. But it looked a little too methodical to me for that. It was almost too neatly done. I don't know what there is about it, but something makes me very suspicious."

"What do you think we ought to do?"

Collie looked up at him, astounded. "Do you really want me to tell ye? Ye haven't been too anxious for my advice up until now."

Rhys fought down his irritation. "There hasn't been as good reason to up until now. And, to tell the truth, I'm bothered, too. I feel a sense of danger that I don't understand but which is extremely strong. Besides, Justine and I are alone now in this country, completely at your mercy. We have no choice but to trust you."

Collie smiled his satisfaction. "All right then, Captain. I think we should get away from here as fast as we can move. Before we left the caravan, one of the men told me his home village was somewhere to the northeast. We'll head for that, and hope we can find shelter and make plans. The important thing now is to put this place behind us as quickly as possible!"

Ten

They headed north across a series of increasingly higher hills toward the largest mound on the horizon. The terrain was strewn with boulders and stunted trees, but the rim of mountains far ahead seemed to promise forests and green growth. Collie, who was not nearly as confident of the location of Jamshid's native village as he pretended, was relieved when late toward evening they crested a hill and looked down on a valley surrounding a small group of cube-shaped houses with flat roofs and wooden-framed outbuildings. He was even more relieved to see mules being used in the fields and a few horses corraled nearby.

Cautiously they picked their way down the hill, keeping as much as possible to the border of low trees, where they could not be seen from the village. Halfway down Collie pulled the camel to a halt.

"Ye two dismount here, before the dogs catch our scent. I'll go on with the animals and see what kind of a reception we're likely to get."

"But we can't stay the night here, Collie," Justine

broke in. "It's already growing cold. We'll freeze to death."

"I misdoubt that," Collie said, leering at Rhys. "But in case it gets too uncomfortable, make for that open structure on the near edge of the village. It's probably full of hay, and ye can bed down there. Only, for heaven's sake, try to keep downwind of the dogs."

Rhys helped Justine down and handed the reins to Collie. "I suppose you'll be needing some money," he said, hoping he was wrong.

"I'm glad you mentioned it before I had to. I'm hoping to trade these animals for two or three of those horses, but it will probably take some close bartering. Money might help, though silks or a few pearls would be better."

"I've only money and damned little of that. But here, take this and get us those horses. It will take days off our trip."

Collie nodded and pocketed the money. Leading the donkey and the camel that had served them so well, he circled back to come down to the village away from where Rhys and Justine were hidden. They watched the tiny dark figures below as the villagers ran out to see what had brought on the hysteria of the dogs, and were relieved that Collie did not receive a hostile reception. After a time standing and gesturing, they all made their way into one of the more imposing of the houses, and the village settled back to a quiet routine.

Once darkness had descended on the hillside, Justine started shivering in the stark cold. Rhys led her down the hill and into the open-sided little building which appeared to be some kind of a stable, no longer used for animals, but heaped with grain and hay. They burrowed into the fragrant grass, ignoring the insects that were

246

disturbed by their presence, and kept very quiet but warm enough for the rest of the night.

Justine did not fall into a deep sleep until close to dawn, when she was roughly shaken awake by Collie, who laid a hand over her mouth to keep her from crying out.

"I've got the horses," he whispered. "Slip back up the hill, and I'll meet ye there as soon as I can get away. And don't be seen! These people are not fond of strangers. They only accepted me because I mentioned Jamshid's name."

"Was this his village?" Rhys whispered, brushing the hay from his sleeve.

"No, but they knew him. Get going now before I have to explain ye both."

Once Collie had headed back to the houses, they slipped out of the building and back up the hill, keeping low, thankful for the gravely soil and lack of dry leaves. They watched as Collie, mounted on one horse and leading two others carrying baggage, headed the opposite way from where they lay behind a mound of rocks. Still keeping low, Rhys led Justine over the rim of the hill, where Collie could double back and meet them without being seen by the village. Even then, it took most of the morning for him to reach them. The three little horses were much less glamorous seen close up. Even their simple decorative harness failed to soften their stubby, coarse coats and bony frames. But they were horses and not camels, and for that Justine was profoundly grateful.

"I got us some clothes, as well," Collie said, spreading out a bundle he untied from one of the saddles. "We're getting too far from Mesopotamia to wear these Arab robes. They'll stand out a mile once we're out of Persia."

"You mean I can throw away this *aba* at last!" Justine

247

exclaimed. "Thank the Lord!" She held up the colorful embroidered skirt Collie had brought her. There was a full-sleeved blouse and an embroidered vest, plus leggings and shoes with pointed toes. It was peasant-fare, made of coarse cloth but beautifully embroidered. It was going to be wonderful to feel like a woman again. Rhys had a tunic, boots, and a fur hat, shabby and far from new, but serviceable. They dressed quickly, bundling their Arab robes into the saddlebags, just in case they might be needed again. Justine mounted her little horse, wishing she might have had a real saddle and finding that riding astride was a strange experience. The horses turned out to be very surefooted in the rocky, hilly terrain—a fact they appreciated more as the day wore on and they climbed ever higher into the low mountains. Once, far in the distance, Justine spotted a tall peak covered with snow, and more and more green patches began to dot the hills. They both congratulated Collie for the way he had emerged from the village with mounts, food, clothes, and directions. Though Justine managed to keep from pointing it out to Rhys, she was very conscious of the fact that without Collie, they would never had made it this far.

The desolate emptiness of the mountains made them confident enough to build a fire when they camped for the night. With the horses tethered nearby, and a makeshift tent with one side open to the fire, they ate the bread, cheese, and fruit Collie had bought from the village, and felt some measure of contentment. When Justine wrapped herself in one of the blankets and fell asleep, Rhys sat closer to Collie, speaking in a low whisper.

"What news did you learn in that place? Anything that

248

explains what happened to the caravan?"

"Nay. They did not seem to know anything about it, and I wasn't going to be the one to tell them Jamshid was dead. There was one thing that puzzled me, however. Several of the men mentioned that a band of Uzbeks had come through recently. They were soldiers, very fierce and cruel. People in these little villages usually give them a wide berth."

"But aren't they close enough to the border here to be accustomed to soldiers passing through?"

"Not really, because this hill route is so far off the main caravan routes. Normally they would use the pass near Merv. Of course, it could mean anything from diverting from their usual paths in search of new people to bully, to looking for escaped prisoners. But . . ."

"But what?"

Collie shrugged. "There was something about the way that caravan was butchered that bothered me. It did not appear to be the usual way Bedouin raiders leave their victims."

"You've witnessed these scenes before?"

"No. But I've heard of them many times from others who have. It is just a nagging blue devil I have about the whole thing. If we're careful we may to be able to make it to Samarkand without crossing the path of these Mongol soldiers."

Rhys took a stick and stirred at the embers of the fire. "And if we do cross them?"

"Ye had better just pray that we won't. I've been pretty confident up until now, because we were dealing with people and places I know. Now as we get closer to Bokharta, I don't feel quite so certain. That's why I think we should try to be as inconspicuous as possible."

"I agree. And perhaps we'd better not mention these soldiers to Justine. It would only give her one more thing to worry about."

"Ye're very strange, you know. Sometimes ye watch over her like a big brother. Others, ye act as though ye wish she would disappear and stop bothering you. I cannot figure ye out."

Rhys smiled. "Nor I, you. What's your game, Collie? Why are you going to all this trouble to reach Samarkand?"

"I told ye. I want to get back to England."

"Bosh! If that was all you wanted, you could take any ship from Bayrut or Alleppo."

"And be arrested for desertion before I stepped off the gangway. No, this is a better way. Somewhere between here and Canton, Yarmid Ali can pick up another disguise and another name. When he returns to England, it will not be as Collie Rigby."

"And maybe pick up a little treasure as well, eh?" Rhys said, glancing at the little Englishman out of the corner of his eye.

Collie shrugged. "Others have found it in Asia. Why not me? Isn't that what keeps ye heading East as well?"

Rhys threw the stick into the dying embers. "We'd better get some sleep before morning."

They were entering a new country now. As they traveled ever eastward, Justine was enthralled with the strangeness and beauty of the land. After a long period of seeing nothing but sand hills and open plateau, the undulating hills and irrigation canals of Western Bokharta were like being transported to heaven. For the

250

first few days, they did not come across many people, but when they did at last descend to a plateau where a nomadic tribe was setting up a summer shelter, she was utterly intrigued. Because the climate was more temperate, they wore brightly decorated layers of garments, often beautifully embroidered. Silver ornaments—in noses, ears, around the necks, or sewn on the blouses of the women—marked them as well-to-do. The men had a dark fierceness in their black eyes as they brazenly examined her from under their floppy turbans. Though the camel was still popular, they saw many more horses, short, stubby little beasts with coarse coats. Most of the women wore their hair in large greasy puffs over their ears, which appeared as though they hadn't been combed out since infancy. Later she discovered that indeed they had not.

The women were just as intrigued with Justine. They recognized at once that underneath her ordinary dress she was not one of them. While Collie and Rhys sat with the men, trying to find enough common language to carry on a conversation, the women crowded around her, fondling her long chestnut hair, her pale skin, examining her thin arms. Frightened at first, she was encouraged by their smiles and laughter. They had beautiful strong teeth, but the brown faces of even the young girls were lined, and their eyes looked old. Later Collie explained it was probably due to the hard life they led, wandering the hills always in search of pastureland for their flocks of sheep and goats.

As they descended toward the Asian plateau, they began to see signs of civilization. Small villages were grouped around a canal with fields stretching on either side, and beyond them, arid plains. With the information

251

he had been able to pick up, Collie was able to lead them around Merv, one of the great caravan cities of Central Asia. Rhys objected to this, since it seemed wiser to him to link themselves up with another caravan if possible. But Collie was adamant. They were far too obviously strangers in the region not to be stopped and detained by the authorities. It was better, he thought, to travel as inconspicuously as possible until they could pick up some of the language and customs of the area.

When he began disappearing for long periods of the day, after pointing them in the right direction, Rhys's old suspicions began to return.

"I never trusted him," he muttered to Justine, after she commented wryly one morning that they had not seen Collie for several hours. "He's entirely too crafty for my money."

"But look how he's helped us up until now. I know I could never have come so far without him."

"Has it occurred to you that we are entirely at his mercy? He knows so much more about this part of the world than we that he could do anything he wants to get rid of us, and we would be completely helpless."

Justine bobbed along on her pony, looking anywhere but at Rhys. "Now why would he want to get rid of us?"

"I don't believe that story about wanting to get back home. He wants to use us for his own gain, I'm sure of it."

"Oh, Rhys. You're entirely too suspicious."

"All the same, it wouldn't hurt either of us to begin trying to learn something of the language around here."

Though Justine could not see that Rhys was making any effort to carry out his suggestion, she herself began paying more attention to her surroundings, working to

252

pick up little phrases that might come in handy, and watching the people more closely to try to determine how they saw things. Rhys's words had awakened her own undercurrent of suspicion, and there seemed to be a new menace in the lovely countryside around her. She began to distrust the friendliness of the peasants they came across, wondering if it was genuine. A few days later, as they sat around a campfire in the early evening, Collie confirmed her fears.

"We'll be approaching the city of Bukhara very soon now," he said, breaking off a hunk of the goat cheese he had brought them back for their supper. "We'd better decide how we're going to handle it."

"Why can't we just go around it as we did Merv?" Rhys asked.

"It wouldn't be wise. By now word has traveled along the routes that two Europeans are crossing the country, and they'll be looking for us. We'd better have some story ready."

"What authorities? Aren't we still in Persia?"

"No. We're entering the emirate of Bokharta. It was under Persian domination a few years ago, but now it is independent. They'll be highly suspicious of travelers arriving alone from the west."

"Is this the same emir who rules Samarkand?" Rhys asked casually.

"Samarkand is one of the cities in his emirate. Bukhara is the capital, but he may well have moved to his summer residence at Samarkand by now."

"How did you learn all this, Collie?" Justine asked.

"Oh, I listen and ask questions, when I know the right ones. One of us has to know something about where we are." He wiped his arm across his mouth, looking more

253

than ever like an Arab journeyman from Persia. "I think in the morning, you two should follow the road, while I forage for food and any information I can pick up."

Justine ignored the I-told-you-so glance that Rhys threw her. "But suppose we get lost?" she asked with real fear in her voice.

"How can ye get lost? We're nearing Bukhara on a caravan path that has been used for centuries. Just keep to the trail, and ye'll be all right. I should be able to catch up with you around noon."

"And what is this famous story we're supposed to be using?" Rhys asked cryptically.

"Just say we were separated from our caravan on the other side of the mountains, and we're trying to find another one. It might be wise to say we're headed for China rather than Samarkand. Let them think we're just passing through."

"I don't like it," Rhys muttered, but the following morning, when Collie rode off at dawn, apparently delighted to be on his own, he grumbled less than usual to Justine as they ambled down the trail toward the ancient city of Bukhara. Possibly that was because they were seeing more people along the road than they usually did—other travelers, farmers working the fields on either side of the road, small oasis villages where the children ran out to call strange phrases at them as they passed. Their brown smiling faces and the pleasant cultivated land slowly began to work its magic, and soon Justine was feeling more self-assured than she had at any time since they crossed the mountains.

Her complacency lasted until they ran into the border patrol. It consisted of a small group of horsemen, obviously soldiers, with scimitars in their sashes, cone hats, and fierce, Mongol faces. The slanted eyes and prominent cheekbones under the turbanlike brims of their hats awoke a dim memory that brought alive the hairs on the back of her neck, though she could not remember where it came from. Within seconds the soldiers had circled their horses around the couple and pulled their reins into their own hands.

"Look here!" Rhys snapped with anger. "Take your hands off me. I've got papers. Who's in charge here?"

One of the men rode forward and peered into Rhys's face. He was a horrible-looking man, with one eye missing from an old injury. It added an additional menace to his heavy brows, sunken cheeks, and hard mouth.

"You English," he said in a guttural voice.

"American English, yes," Rhys answered back, visibly relieved to hear his own language being spoken.

"I speak little English," the officer replied, with a smile that had no friendliness and nothing of humor in it. "You have papers?"

"I do," Rhys said, pulling out the bag he wore around his neck underneath his tunic. "For myself and my . . . my cousin here."

Still smiling the officer spread out their papers and looked them over. Even though it was apparent he could not read, he seemed a little impressed by the attached seals. With a brisk snap he rolled them up and put them inside his buttoned tunic. "You are arrest," he said and glanced at his men.

"What! Wait a minute—" Rhys called, as he was grasped by the men around him and his arms trussed tightly to his sides with a rope. "You can't do this! I'm a British citizen—"

"Rhys!" Justine screamed as one of the soldiers slid

255

from his saddle and jumped up behind her on her horse. Arms like an iron vise gripped her, as the heavy, pungent, unfamiliar odors of the man pressed against her, choked off her breath, "Rhys . . . Help . . ." she screamed again, but Rhys was helpless to do anything. He was tied to his horse so quickly and so tightly that he could only watch in horror as the officer spoke to the man who held Justine, sending him galloping on ahead.

"Don't you harm her," he yelled to the officer who had taken his papers, but the man only smiled evilly and directed his entourage to move on down the road. They ambled so slowly they might have been out for a pleasant walk, and all the while Rhys cursed Collie under his breath and tried not to think about where they had taken Justine. Fear and fury made his heart pump more quickly beneath the constricting ropes and he was relieved when at last they stopped near a collection of small dilapidated huts. Rhys was pulled roughly from his saddle and hauled inside one of the more sound buildings to face the officious officer once more.

"This is an outrage!" he snapped, his eyes blazing. "I demand to know why you are treating my cousin and me in this scurrilous fashion!"

"I don't understand your words, all of them," the officer answered, "but I tell you this. You are a spy, sent from Agha Mohammud Shah who like to own Bokharta again."

"That's ridiculous. I've never even met the shah of Persia. Why would I spy for him?"

"Why else English come through Bokharta? Only few years since Nadir Shah conquer this country. Not again will it happen. You are spy!"

Rhys pulled against his ropes in frustration. How

256

could he make this stupid official understand he was not a threat? And where in hell was Collie!

"My cousin had better not come to any harm," he said as threateningly as possible. "You'll have the British government to answer to, if she does."

"She is safe," the officer said, smiling again in a way that chilled Rhys's blood. "No harm."

"I don't believe you. Why should I?"

But the officer had had enough. With a few guttural words, he directed the guards holding Rhys to drag him away. They led him across a small yard to one of the huts in the back of the compound, where another guard stood at a locked door and, opening it, threw him in. With his arms still tied, Rhys rolled along the dirt floor helplessly, coming to rest against the far wall, blind in the sudden dark. Very slowly he pulled himself up to lean against the wall, and waited for his eyes to adjust to the darkness. Feeling, rather than seeing, another person nearby, he shrank back as a face leered into his. It was a broad, flat face, with little eyes deeply set in fleshy folds. The lips were fat, and a thin trickle of saliva drooled from them. The body bent over him was huge and beefy and shimmered with sweat on bare shoulders.

"My God," Rhys gasped as the man leaned into his face, his foul breath suffocating the air. The man reached out a hand and grasped the ropes around Rhys's chest, yanking them toward him. His other hand closed around Rhys's neck, casually choking off his breath. Rhys closed his eyes, fleetingly thinking how sad it would be to die here in this place, at the hands of some evil monster he did not even know.

"That's enough, Lester," a cool voice spoke from across the hut. "Let him alone."

257

With a thud Rhys landed on the ground where the monster dropped him. He waited for a moment until his voice was back to normal, then gasped: "Is there an Englishman here?"

"Yes. Untie the man, George. He cannot be very comfortable trussed up like that."

A second man appeared, much smaller than the monster, who moved with quick, wiry motions. He had Rhys's bonds undone in a few seconds.

"You can't know how happy I am to meet someone from home in this vile place," Rhys muttered, as he rubbed his hands to get the circulation going in them again. As his eyes adjusted to the dark hut, he could begin to make out the other men. The big threatening fellow had moved away to slouch against one wall, a dark hulk in the shadows. Against the adjoining wall two figures sat, one the man who had untied him, leaning his elbows on his knees and watching Rhys suspiciously, the other casually reclining, his face still in shadow.

"Not quite from home," the cool voice went on. "I believe you are from the Colonies, if I detect the accent correctly. My home is Hampshire. And, as you can see," he said, waving a languid hand, "we are three Englishmen, not one."

"I'm grateful to you," Rhys said graciously. "To two of you anyway. How on earth did you get to this place?"

"I suspect under the same circumstances as yourself. We are accused of spying for the Persian Pasha. I had no idea that politics were so complicated in this part of the world."

Rhys struggled to his feet and walked over to get a better look at this unexpected friend. "I am Rhys Llewellyn, sir, and pleased to make your acquaintance."

"Augustus Hughes," the man said, after a slight hesitation. "And these are my friends, George and Lester. Lester is the big one. His bulk gives him a threatening appearance, but he's actually rather harmless."

Rhys doubted that, yet he could see how a personal bodyguard of such girth might be useful in this part of the world. He could see the speaker now, and would have recognized him as English anywhere. A long face, thin, shapely lips, eyes brimming with contempt, haughty aplomb in every pore. He still wore a white wig, slightly askew but tied with a grosgrain ribbon. He lounged in shirt, waistcoat, breeches, and buckled shoes, the very picture of an English gentleman who had set his coat aside for the moment.

As Rhys was studying his fellow prisoner, the door was jerked open, and an old woman shuffled inside, carrying a bundle. She dumped it on the floor, squatted beside it, and began spreading it out.

"Well, Mr. Llewellyn, it appears you have arrived just in time for dinner," Hughes said. "How fortunate for you."

Rhys gave a quick look at the unappetizing blob of dun-colored paste which the woman began ladeling into three bowls. "I think I can forgo the pleasure."

"Nonsense, my man," Hughes cried. "This is our daily ration, and if you don't partake of it, you shall be extremely sorry by tomorrow noon. I suggest you give it a try, at least. It's really not so bad once you grow accustomed to it."

Rhys was beginning to realize how long it had been since breakfast. Dipping a finger in the bowl George held out to him, he tasted the mess. It tasted better than it

259

looked, so he forced a little down, watching in amazement as George and Lester lapped it up. Hughes, for all his brave words, only dabbed at the stuff.

"What happens now?" Rhys said. "Do we just sit in this prison until they decide to kill us?"

"They don't dare to do that without the emir's permission. I believe word has gone to Samarkand, and we are awaiting some reply. Let's hope it is in our favor. Meanwhile, they will allow us out under guard to walk around that yard out there in the evening. The rest of the time, we sit in this foul place and meditate on the fickle finger of fate."

"I must get out of here," Rhys said, thinking of Justine. "I must."

"We all must, but I fear we will not until that officer decides it is to his advantage to let us. Lester! Let that mongrel alone."

Rhys looked over to see that Lester was tormenting a thin cur that must have followed the old woman inside when she brought their dinner. He snapped his fingers and the dog slunk over to him once the big man let him go. Like friendly dogs everywhere, the animal responded to Rhys's casual stroking by licking his hand and nuzzling down beside him. Later in the afternoon, when the guards led them outside to walk around the yard a few times, the mongrel followed along behind Rhys, and nestled by him during the night. The honest comfort Rhys received from the dog's friendly ways had none of the ambiguous feelings he felt toward the other inmates of the jail. Even though they were countrymen who spoke the same language, he could not rid himself of the thought that there was something about them he distrusted. The big beefy one was obviously a simpleton who enjoyed cruelty. The thin, slight companion with a face like a jackal reminded Rhys of the worst kind of seamen he had known, impressed from the London stews. Hughes was the most enigmatic of the three. Outwardly friendly and smiling, there was a steely coldness to his languid gaze, like a predator teasing its prey before pouncing. The little mongrel with his nose resting on Rhys's thigh was a welcome contrast.

He made it through that night and the following day by forcing from his mind all thoughts of Justine. He had already determined that there was no way out of the small hut, for even though the walls had patches that admitted light, they were too well guarded to escape more than a few feet away. Any attempt at freedom would probably be met with even tighter security. Surely Collie was searching for them and would locate them eventually.

His hopes seemed justified when, on the third morning, he awoke to a familiar voice outside the hut. Jumping to his feet he peered through one of the slits in the wall to see a strange man talking excitedly to the guards across the yard. The creature was wizened and brown, dressed in the shabby clothes of a Tartar peasant, with greasy strands of hair protruding from underneath a felt, cone-shaped hat. Though he was speaking the local language like a native, Rhys would have recognized that voice anywhere. His heart gave a leap and he almost called out, stopping himself just in time, in case it was the wrong thing to do.

Hughes stepped up beside him to peer out into the yard. "One of the locals," he said in a bored voice. "Too bad. I thought perhaps it was a messenger from the emir."

One of the guards detached himself from the group and stalked to the door of the hut. Opening it, he pointed to Rhys. "You English," he barked and motioned for Rhys to follow. With great restraint Rhys kept himself from bounding into the yard and instead walked sedately out, blinking in the sudden light.

The guard turned to the stranger and spoke a few words. Nodding energetically the peasant approached Rhys, bowing and scraping and emitting a stream of incomprehensible sentences. "Master, master," he finally said in English. "What have they done to you? Oh, my master, your servant weeps with anguish at the sight . . ."

"Master?" Rhys muttered. He glanced up to see that the officer in charge had emerged from his office and was watching them curiously. "Yes, yes, you imbecilic serf!" he shouted. "Where have you been while I was kept prisoner in this vile hovel? I'll have you soundly thrashed." He continued laying it on thickly, while his poor servant appeared near to tears. Then, as suddenly as he had been allowed out, he was thrust back inside the hut and the door barred. It was the last thing he had been expecting. Cursing under his breath, Rhys watched through the peephole as Collie was led inside the officer's quarters.

"I take it you knew that man," Hughes inquired.

"Yes. He's my servant. Let's hope he can do something to get me out of here."

"Very fortunate of you to have a servant from the local populace. How did you manage that?"

Rhys hesitated. "I had contacts in Baghdad."

To his relief Hughes seemed satisfied and let him alone. Rhys spent the rest of the morning growing increasingly frustrated as nothing further happened to suggest he would be freed. And yet, he was confident something would. With that peculiar ability to disappear into whatever role he assumed, Collie had seemed the

262

very incarnation of one of the Turki peasants. Had Rhys not recognized his voice, he would never have known him. Surely he would find some way of getting them out of this fix.

His hopes began to rise again, so much so that when the old woman came shuffling in with their daily ration of mutton paste, he felt he could not stomach another drop of it. Instead he gave the unappetizing mess to the dog who lapped at it greedily. As the mongrel finished the bowl, the door was opened, and the officer in charge came striding in.

"You, Sir English," he said, bowing slightly and pointing to Rhys. "Come with me."

Rhys bounded up. At the door he stopped and whistled for the little dog, but when he looked back he saw the animal stretched out on the dirt floor.

"Perhaps he ate too much to move," Hughes said, trying not to appear too jealous or curious about where Rhys was going.

There was something not right about the way the animal tried to lift its head, whimpering at Rhys. He walked back to kneel and stroke it, and watched it die under his hand.

"My God!" he breathed. Across the room Hughes threw his bowl aside. "You come," the guard snapped at Rhys, who rose and followed him from the hut. Outside he looked up to see Collie standing by the far building and beside him, Justine, smiling at him from across the yard. With a cry she ran across the yard and into his arms, hugging him wildly. Rhys clasped her to him, weak with relief.

"Are you all right?" he finally managed to say.

"Yes. I was kept with the women. I'm fine."

The officer came striding up to them, bowing and

smiling as though they were honored guests. "We plan to send her as gift to emir of Bokharta," he said by way of explanation. "But not to be. So sorry to detained you, Sir Prince. We hope you are not been . . . in . . . inconvenienced."

"Sir Prince?" Rhys muttered, looking up at Collie. His erstwhile servant bowed nearly to the ground, bobbing with respect and babbling in the local dialect, while the officer handed Rhys his papers and called to have their horses brought up.

"You see, all well kept. We send you on way with our compliments."

"Am I to be allowed to leave then?" Rhys asked, trying to hide his puzzlement over the officer's new attitude.

"Oh yes, Sir Prince. And please, please give our apologies to Emperor for stupid mistake." Bowing deeply, the officer seemed not a little frightened of what Rhys might say or do.

"Let's get out of here," Rhys muttered and hurried to his horse. The three of them were in the saddle and galloping out of the yard, leaving the officer still bowing and apologizing, almost before he realized they were gone. They rode at a hard canter long enough to get well away from the officer's compound. Once out of sight, Rhys pulled up on the reins.

"All right, Collie. Explain! How did you manage that? What did you tell them?"

Collie pulled off his hat and brushed back his grease-streaked hair, suddenly taking on his old familiar appearance. "It's no mystery. You simply have to know something about the people ye're dealing with."

"Knowing something of the language certainly helps," Justine said as they began ambling their horses along the trail. "How did you manage that?"

264

"And where do you think I've been going these last days, when I left the two of ye to talk between yerselves. There's no way we're going to make it through this country without knowing how to manage, Collie my lad, I said to myself. So I set about finding out. I suspected ye'd walk right into some kind of trouble like that border patrol."

"You might have warned us," Rhys muttered.

"And miss the fun of seeing you brought down a peg or two? No, I figured ye'd both react with good old Yankee honesty and tell them all about yerselves, every word of it true. But that's not how you handle things in this part of the world. You see, there's only one thing that counts here and that is to be a big man. If ye're just an ordinary fellow on a tour through the country, you're a nobody, and could be up to who-knows-what kind of deviltry. But a big important man now, nothing he can do is going to be wrong. Or if it is, you had better not get in his way. So, I just convinced them ye were an important man—back in America anyway."

"Just who did you say I was?"

"I told them you were a prince, the son of the Emperor of America and nephew to the King of England. They don't know much about the Colonies, but they've heard of the King of England."

"Emperor of America!" Justine said, laughing. "Whoever heard of such a thing? How on earth did you get them to believe that?"

"I had a few important-looking papers fixed up. That's what took me the extra day before I could get ye out of there. I knew about their plans for Justine and that she was safe, and I figured it wouldn't hurt the captain to cool his heels for a while."

"Not hurt . . . ." Rhys sputtered. "Did you also work it

out that someone would poison my food? Oh, I can see by the astonishment on your crafty face that that is a surprise. But it happened. If I hadn't given that horrible mess to that poor cur, I'd be lying dead on the floor of that hut right now."

"No, that wasn't in my plan," Collie said, somewhat subdued. "Why on earth would anyone want to poison you?"

"I have no idea, but nothing about this place surprises me. It might have been intended for the other English gentleman sharing my jail, though I doubt it. That old woman particularly handed the bowl to me."

"Other Englishman?" Collie and Justine both said in unison.

"Yes. A Mister Hughes from Hampshire. He had two colleagues with him, too, both too stupid to be anything other than his bodyguards."

"Now that is a most peculiar coincidence," Collie said, his mind working rapidly. "I wonder how they came to be here?"

"He is also a visitor touring the country," Rhys added sarcastically.

"Mmm," Collie mused. "There seems to be an unusual number of English tourists in Bokharta this season. Ah, well. I feel sure we shall run into him again. There can't be many more Englishmen about."

While the three travelers skirted the capital city of Bukhara and neared ancient Samarkand, Colonel Augustus Hughes sat on the floor of the dark hut Rhys had left, lost in deep thought. He felt quite pleased that Rhys Llewellyn—the American courier sent to collect Prince Tai's gift for the Colonies—had stumbled across his path. He was even amused at the way the captain had tried to pretend he was only visiting so unlikely a place as

266

Bokharta out of curiosity. Although Llewellyn was a weak spy, he was exactly the kind of man the rebels would send on a mission of this sort—handsome, adventurous, probably an excellent swordsman.

No, it was not the captain's appearance that troubled him, but the sight of that girl here in this exotic country, where by rights she ought not to be. It had taken him most of an hour to remember who she was, his vision of her being so reduced by the peepholes in the hut's walls. When he finally recalled her as the daughter of the man who should have been sitting here in his place—Justin Maury—it gave him the worst turn he had had since embarking from Philadelphia.

What on earth was Maury's daughter doing here? Apparently there was some kind of relationship between her and the captain, judging from that fervent embrace he had witnessed. Supposing she had actually read the letter he sent Maury. What if she was a traitor, trying to help Llewellyn get his hands on the treasure for the rebels?

No, if that were true, surely Llewellyn would have known Hughes was a British officer, and it was obvious he had not. There had to be some other explanation, but what?

Hughes pounded his fists together in frustration. He could not yet imagine what Maury's daughter was up to, but one thing was clear. He must get away from this place and into Samarkand. The time for subterfuge was over.

He reached beneath his waistcoat and shirt to where his military papers lay hidden in a body belt around his waist. "Sporn!" he snapped. "Get the attention of that guard, and make him understand that I want to see the officer in charge immediately!"

267

Eleven

The last leg of their journey into Samarkand was fascinating. Long before they entered the city, they passed through lush orchards, fields, and gardens worked from soil irrigated by the canals built to bring the life-restoring waters of the great Amu Dar'ya River to the otherwise dry region. The fields were worked with Chinese laborers, the first time the travelers had seen so many of that unusual race at one time. Collie mentioned dryly that most of them were owned by the Moslems, rulers of the Uzbek tribe, the primary one in the emirate.

They visited briefly with a caravan on its way west from the city, two hundred camels long and carrying what to Justine seemed a treasure in exotic goods—silks, satins, musk, jewels, and even bundles of the lowly rhubarb. They wandered past ruins of once-great palaces and the decaying ramparts of what was once the outer fortification of the city. They paused to rest under trellises of thick vines heavy with fruit, and were given vegetables from the fragrant gardens where they stayed the night.

Because the city lay on a major ancient trade route, the natives appeared accustomed to strangers riding by, and met them with a friendly courtesy. The people themselves appeared to be a polyglot of tribes, and Justine soon grew accustomed to seeing Mongol, Chinese, and Aryan faces around her.

When at last they sauntered through the inner gates and into the city itself, it was almost a disappointment. Samarkand had seen its greatest glory four centuries before, and since then time and neglect had taken their toll. It still had the water system that was the marvel of the ancient world, bringing running water to every palace. But its houses and monuments appeared shabby, its narrow winding streets potholed and dirty. They were soon hopelessly lost in the rabbit warren of narrow alleys, passing decaying houses built cheek to jowl, some of them converted to industrial uses to augment the silk and iron industries that were still a part of the town. Often these alleys led to a dead end where they were forced to retrace their way, until Collie finally managed to obtain the correct directions that led them to the Registan, the great town square. Streets near this amazing area were wider and tree-lined. The square itself left Justine in awe. It was filled with wonderful buildings, most of them showing the ravages of neglect, but still beautiful. Collie, with his amazing ability to pick up information, pointed out Tamerlane's great mausoleum with its ribbed dome faced with brilliant multicolored tiles. The gorgeous turquoise cupola belonged to the Bibi Khan mosque, erected by the great Tamerlane to the memory of his favorite wife. There were other beautiful mosques and even an ancient observatory built by Tamerlane's grandson.

269

"And all this at a time when the kings of medieval Europe were still living in cold castles, and their subjects in huts with roofs of straw," Collie commented.

"And I thought this was a backward part of the world," Justine sighed, staring up at the brilliant turquoise cupola of the Bibi Kahn mosque. "How did you learn so much about it, Collie?"

"I hadn't been in the Arab world two years, before I began to realize there was a history here no one in our part of the world knows anything about. I still find it kind of fascinating that our civilized English gentlemen look down their aristocratic noses at a civilization that once far-surpassed their own."

Rhys slipped from his horse, leaning against his saddle as he looked about at the people milling around the square. "I'm not so certain it was that much greater," he said casually. "I know something about this Tamerlane, and he wasn't quite as civilized as you make out."

"Now how would you know that?" Justine asked, as he helped her out of the saddle.

"Collie isn't the only one who can ask questions, you know. I also studied the antiquities in my schooldays. The man was actually Timur the Lame, a cripple. He did conquer most of the Near East, but he was cruel in the extreme. He left behind great columns in the cities he felt were not responsive to his rule, made up of the heads of the people that lived there."

"Ugh!" Justine cried. "I don't want to hear this."

"It gets worse. You might as well be prepared, because these people have a reputation for the art of refined cruelty that makes our hanging a Tory spy seem like child's play."

Collie dismounted and went over to sit in the

270

welcoming shade of an Indian almond tree. "We'd better think about how we're going to proceed," he said as the others joined him. "I think we should find a place to stay first. Surely they have something resembling an inn or a caravansary in this town."

Rhys said nothing, though he was thinking to himself that his first item of business was to get an appointment with the emir. He was blissfully unaware of the fact that Collie and Justine were both thinking the same thing.

"Yes, I'd like to find a place where I could stay put for a while," Justine answered. "Preferably someplace with a bath. Or do they have bathhouses here?" She managed not to look at Rhys, though both their thoughts went swiftly back to Rayys.

"They once had a plumbing system here that brought water right into the houses, but I'm not certain it still works. Now, do the both of ye think ye can manage with the few words I taught ye? We don't want no more trouble with the authorities."

"There is one more important phrase I should know," Rhys said. "How do you say, 'your servant, sir'? You couldn't get along in America without that."

Collie clucked his tongue impatiently. "When will ye understand that no one here respects you for those polite pleasantries. In this part of the world only the peasants are your servants. Politeness counts for nothing, rudeness is strength. Try to remember that, Captain."

Rhys smiled at Justine. "Well, it might be refreshing for once to be allowed to express your worst—" he was interrupted by the horrified expression that came over Justine's face as she gazed out toward the square. Turning to look, he saw a great giant of a man facing them, his hands on hips and his feet widely spaced. He

271

was dressed as a soldier with a brass and leather plate covering his breast, a peaked hat with a fur brim, and a huge curved scimitar protruding from the wide sash around his tunic. Long greased moustachios fell from either corner of his mouth . . . a slash in his dark face. Standing behind him were four others, not quite as large, but every bit as frightening.

"It seems the authorities have learned of our arrival," Collie muttered and clambered to his feet. Justine slipped closer to Rhys, who put a protective arm around her shoulder, as they watched Collie bowing and chatting to the huge soldier. He hurried back to them, every inch the lowly servant.

"Are we being arrested?" Rhys asked softly, his fingers tightening on Justine's arm.

"Far from it. It appears the emir knew we were approaching the city and has sent his guard to bring us to him. He offers us his hospitality!"

"But—" Justine cried. Collie laid a finger to his lips. "I told him we were greatly honored and would accept. Nod your head, Captain, and look greatly honored!"

Rhys smiled broadly at the guard. "But, of course, we accept. With pleasure." Turning slightly, he whispered to Collie: "I don't suppose I say, 'your servant'?"

"Of course not. You look as though you expected nothing less than this," he muttered back.

Rhys did his best to appear as arrogant as Collie suggested as they remounted and followed the guard through the narrow streets. With three in front and two in back, they felt more like prisoners than guests, yet remembering Collie's advice, both he and Justine sat proudly and smiled benignly at the people they passed. It was not encouraging to note how the citizens scattered at

272

the sight of their guards, but they were careful not to betray any apprehension they felt.

Once they passed into the palace grounds, Justine's underlying fear was almost eclipsed by the wonders around her. The terraced gardens were thick with roses of every size and hue. Orchards of almond and apricot trees, heavy with half-grown fruit, beckoned with their promise of cool repose. Birds flew among the small pagodas standing near exquisite artificial lagoons and ponds, where great white blossoms floated on the emerald water. The rooms inside were even more beautiful than the gardens. Tiled mosaics in brilliant jeweled hues lined the floors and wove decorative patterns on the walls and ceilings. Ornately carved screens called *mashrabias* with intricate open-work brought the grounds inside, a natural background to the artistic creations of the emir's artisans. Justine padded openmouthed through the rooms, following Rhys and Collie through long passages until they came to a small courtyard where one of the guards rudely grabbed her and yanked her away from the two men.

"Rhys!" she cried as she was pulled into a corridor apart from the others. He tried to rush after her, but was stopped by a long spear thrust across his path by one of the guards. He looked at Collie, who only shook his head, then allowed himself to be pushed on by the guards.

With her fright swelling, Justine was hurried down a long corridor and shoved into a room. A door closed behind her and she heard a bar slide into place. She leaned against the door and looked around, trying to calm her fears and get her bearings. Gradually it dawned on her that she was standing inside one of the most beautiful rooms she had ever seen. The exquisite tiles, the crimson

273

silk cushions, the deep, beautifully patterned rug at her feet, the intricate open-work patterns in the *mashrabias* along one wall, opening onto a vista of the green-shaded courtyard beyond, all took her breath away.

"Welcome," a cool voice said behind the golden grill to her right.

A woman was standing behind the screen intently watching Justine, her face half-obscured by the intricate filigree. She was tall and regal, swathed in flowing pale blue gauze, her hair pulled tightly away from her flawless face. A single ruby blazed from a thin band on her brown forehead.

Justine stood dumbfounded as the woman moved smoothly from behind the grill. Seen up close she was older than she appeared at first glance—a matron with tiny lines etched in her painted face. Her large black eyes assessed Justine with dispassionate coolness.

"I . . . chief wife . . . Ulugh Khan," she said in halting English.

Justine nodded, "Madam," and remembering Collie's instructions stopped herself from making the usual curtsey.

The chief wife had obviously exhausted her supply of Justine's native tongue. She waved a languid, bejeweled hand and a bevy of young women suddenly appeared to cluster around Justine, fingering her long braid and her clothes, giggling and murmuring to each other. With the raising of one cool eyebrow, the chief wife brought them to an immediate silence. Jess, who had assumed they were the emir's lesser wives, realized they were actually servants as they began very gently but firmly to remove her clothes.

"Really . . . I'd prefer . . ." she tried to object, but

274

they paid her no mind. She was led along to an inner room where she was completely divested of every stitch of her clothing and pushed into a small pool of warm, scented water. Once she realized that the women meant her no harm, she let herself relax and began to enjoy their skilled ministrations. The chief wife disappeared while the serving girls worked over Justine with a quiet competence. She was bathed, massaged, and rubbed with a fragrant ointment. Her hair was washed and arranged in exotic braids and puffs with a long rope of pearls intertwined. Then she was carefully dressed in gauzy breeches of soft blue that reached to her ankles, while a long, open-sided emerald green tunic—so stiff with gold embroidery it could almost stand alone—was draped over her shoulders. Anklets, gold sandals, amulets, bracelets, and a single droplet of translucent pearl on her forehead set off her dress. Her eyes were lined with kohl, her lips with cerise. While she was being fussed over by the young women, other servants came and went offering her trays of grapes and pomegranates, bowls of iced sherbert, and tumblers of dark, sweet tea.

"And I thought they were going to cut off my head!" she mused as she was finally led away to be appraised by the chief wife of Ulugh Khan. That lady walked silently around her, scrutinizing every hair and fold of her dress. Only once did she speak, sending her servants scuttling. One of them returned with a cedar box beautifully decorated with gold inlay. Justine's eyes grew large as it was opened to reveal a tangle of twinkling jewelry. The chief wife rummaged her long fingers among them, and selected one large ring with a sapphire stone the size of a walnut. She handed it to the servant girl who slipped it on Justine's finger.

"Thank you," Justine nodded, remembering not to protest that such a gift was highly inappropriate.

The chief wife smiled her enigmatic, humorless smile, and with a nod of her head bade the women open the door. One of the soldiers standing there beckoned Justine to follow, which she did without so much as a glance at the chief wife and her entourage.

"I may begin to like this once I get accustomed to it," she thought to herself as she glided haughtily along the tiled halls.

She was led to an anteroom where two other people waited, a Persian prince resplendent in a long burgundy coat embroidered with silver, and his servant in spotless white breeches, tunic, and turban. Justine and the prince stared at each other for a moment, each impressed with the other's finery.

"Rhys!" she cried as it dawned on her who the prince actually was. "I didn't recognize you—you look so gorgeous! And Collie—I've never seen you look so clean!"

"I smell like a bloody rosebush!" Collie grumbled, sinking down on a large hassock in the corner.

"You're beautiful!" Rhys murmured, taking her hands and twirling her around.

"I don't feel a bit like myself," she said, smiling up at him.

"No, more like some exotic princess out of the Arabian Nights. What a wonderful transformation!"

"What would my friends in Philadelphia say to see me now," Justine laughed. "Look at all this gold, Rhys, and this sapphire ring. I've never had such jewels."

"They are made all the more lovely by your beauty."

Justine gave him a mock curtsy. "Thank you, sir. I

276

would express my gratitude to an even greater degree but it's the custom here to accept such compliments as though they were your natural right."

She was interrupted by a man appearing at the door. One glance told them that he was too fashionably dressed to be a servant. He also had that same look of latent power that Justine had recognized in the emir's chief wife.

"I am Timurid, minister to Emir Ulugh Khan," he said in guttural English. "His majesty wishes you welcome in our country. You please to follow?" He motioned them down the long hall. Rhys threw Collie a glance that said, "This is the moment," and set off, Justine right behind him. A further tangle of halls—several of them bordering a courtyard—brought them at length to a long room resplendent with silk hangings, lush carpets, and multitudes of tasseled satin cushions in various sizes haphazardly lying around. At one end of the room, lounging on a great pile of pillows strewed around a small dais, sat the Emir Ulugh Khan. They could feel his eyes on them from the doorway.

At once Timurid fell to his knees and laid his head to the floor. Collie was right behind him, pulling Rhys and Justine down with him.

"What ever happened to strength in rudeness," Rhys muttered under his breath with his head on the floor.

"It was left at the door." Collie muttered back. A few words from the dais brought Timurid to his feet again, slowly followed by Rhys, Justine, and Collie. The emir beckoned them forward , and they made the long trek to the foot of the dais where they could inspect and be inspected by the round little man who lounged there.

The emir studied them several long minutes. Then he raised a hand, so minutely Rhys almost failed to notice it.

"His Highness wishes to know who you are," Timurid said from behind them.

Looking at the emir, Rhys said, "Tell his Highness that we bring him greetings from a land far across the sea, the Colony of Philadelphia in America."

The minister spoke in the native tongue. The emir, without speaking, raised his hand once more.

"His Highness says he has heard of the Colony of America, and of the great nation of England as well. But he wishes to know who *you* are."

Rhys muttered under his breath, "His Highness has a remarkable ability to speak without using his lips."

"Careful," Collie muttered back.

"Tell his Highness that I am Capt. Rhys Llewellyn, Master of the ship *Boeadecia*, and this is my cousin, Mistress Justine Maury. This useless fellow behind me is my servant, Yarmid Ali of Baghdad."

Again Timurid addressed his master. The emir, after another long pause, fastened his eyes on Justine, leaned forward, and beckoned her forward. After an anxious glance at Rhys, she steeled herself to stride resolutely toward the dais. The emir bent to look closely at her, examining every detail of her face, her hair, and her dress. She was extremely uncomfortable under his intense scrutiny and her courage wavered until she looked back at Collie and Rhys. With his eyes, Collie warned her to keep her place.

"His Highness wishes to know if you found everything satisfactory in the women's quarters," Timurid said. "If there was anything that offended you in any way, he will make certain someone suffers for it."

"No, no," Justine said quickly, remembering the stern, cold countenance of the chief wife. "Everything

278

was wonderful. Perfect. I loved every minute. Really."

The emir smiled in a grotesque muscle contortion that did nothing to soften his unpleasant features. He was really quite repulsive, Justine thought, trying to lean away from his face—so near her own—without seeming to. He had a round head, nearly bald but for a long, thick beard and a fringe of greasy hair. His lips were fat, almost bloated-looking. High cheekbones, very prominent, accentuated the eyes which were tiny and almost lost in folds of flesh. When she could bring herself to look into them, she found them cold, calculating, and hard—the eyes of an alien race.

To her dismay he reached out a fat finger and ran it down her cheek, leaving what she felt to be a red streak. His touch was cold and horrible. Justine felt her knees giving way beneath her.

Running up behind her, Collie took her elbow, steadying her. He spoke in fluent Persian to the minister, who, shocked at anyone approaching the emir without permission, was about to raise the guard. "She is very tired and weak from the journey," Collie then said in English. "Please explain to his Highness."

For the first time the emir actually spoke, rattling off a few sentences to his minister. "His Highness understands and forgives Madam's servant for his indiscretion which, under a less magnanimous king, would require the immediate severance of his head from his body. You may retire, Madam."

Weakly Justine moved back to where Rhys was standing, leaning on Collie's arm. Then the emir beckoned Rhys forward.

Once again the emir leaned into a stranger's face, intently inspecting it. But this time there was no

279

contorted smile.

Rhys faced him boldly, looking into the hard eyes without flinching. "I am honored to approach the great ruler of Bokharta," he said and waited for the minister to translate. "I have journeyed over many waters and much land for this meeting. The emir's fame has reached even to my country, America."

The fat round head bobbed with approval at the translation. Rhys went on: "My cousin and servant are weary from the rigors of our journey. Perhaps his Highness will allow them to retire, so that I might tell him myself of the great reputation he enjoys in colonial America."

The emir's eyes shunted to Timurid, who, apparently, reading his mind, said quietly, "There will be time enough for that. His Highness wishes to know if the captain is a brave man?"

Rhys looked back at Timurid in surprise. "I consider myself so."

"Bravery is much admired in our world. The brave man suffers all hardship without complaint. He endures suffering and pain without flinching. He is the man most worthy of adulation, the man whose loyalty is never questioned. Are you such a man?"

Rhys pursed his lips, wondering where this was going to lead. "I consider myself so," he replied with as much arrogance as he could summon.

The contorted smile touched the emir's lips. Reaching out, he lightly ran his hand over Rhys's hair, carefully selected one lone, long strand, and with a sudden furious jerk, yanked it out by the roots. With great self-control, Rhys never removed his eyes from the emir's. He even managed a thin smile of triumph.

With a grunt his Highness slumped back on the pillows and waved them away. Timurid moved forward to back them out of the hall without turning their faces from the great eminence who watched them from the dais like a huge spider atop the mound of pillows. Once outside the room, Timurid faced them, smiling.

"His Highness is well pleased with his honored guests. You shall be given the best quarters in the palace for as long as you wish to remain. He wishes you to join him for his private supper tonight."

Rhys nodded. "Please convey our humble gratitude to your great emir. We will be honored to join him for supper."

Timurid was about to lead Justine back to the women's quarters, when Rhys stopped him. "Might not my cousin and I have a moment for a visit before she returns to her rooms—to discuss the generous qualities and great charity of your king?"

"A walk in the gardens perhaps?" Timurid answered, directing them through the open doors into the green beauty of the gardens beyond. "I shall send my servant to you in a short time, to direct you to your rooms."

Rhys bowed his thanks, and the three of them strolled through the latticework and along the shaded path into the gardens. It was cool and lovely, a sharp contrast to the tension they had sensed in the emir's throneroom.

Once he judged that they were out of earshot, Rhys exploded. "Damn the bastard! My head will pain me for a week!"

"You managed very well though," Justine said softly. "I couldn't have borne that without crying out."

"Crying out! It was all I could do to keep from burying my fist in his fat face."

"That would have concluded matters for us," Collie said sarcastically. "'Generous qualities . . . great charity.' Laying it on a bit thick there at the end, weren't ye?"

"Only to keep from saying what I *really* felt! What a horrible fat little bug he is! And to think, I came all this way . . . Ah well, it will be an experience to tell my grandchildren."

"If you live to have any. And by the way, I just loved 'useless fellow.' Much thanks I get for bringing ye this far."

"You're supposed to be my servant, aren't you? I was trying to be convincing. No doubt you've noticed that servants here are little better than chattel."

Justine made a clucking noise with her tongue. "Well, neither of you had to endure what I did. Ugh! That horrible man touching me. It gave me cold chills. How can his wives bear it!"

"He liked ye, no doubt about that," Collie muttered. "Sit here a minute on this bench, so we can take our bearings. There are a few things ye both should realize. First, be careful what you say in English. The emir understands every word."

Justine stared in surprise. "How do you know that?"

"I was reading his face the whole time, and I recognize the signs. He also understands Persian, so watch every word you speak around this palace. It will get back to him, every syllable.

"Second, do not let that friendly manner and grotesque smile fool ye. This is a very crafty rogue. Never forget that."

"You call it friendly to tear out one's hair by the roots."

"He was testing you. Taking your measure. He wants

282

to know the kind of man he's got to deal with."

Rhys threw Collie a look that warned him not to betray his real reason for being in the emirate in front of Justine. But he took careful note of the warning. He too felt he must take an accurate measure of this emir if he was going to bring off his mission successfully.

"Third, Justine, who were the women you met when ye were being all dressed up in this gorgeous finery?"

"Only servants and one of the emir's wives—the chief wife, she called herself."

"Yes, I thought so. That would be Zenobia, the first wife and the mother of the heir apparent. She's a force in this kingdom, as much as a woman can be a force behind the throne. She has a reputation for being even more crafty and cruel than the emir, and she is one of the few people who can get her way with him. Watch out for her. She's very dangerous."

"I think, if it is not too much trouble, I would like to go home now," Justine said in a little voice. "I don't really like it here."

"Courage," Rhys said, taking her hand and squeezing it. "We'll not stay long if I can help it. Just long enough to . . . to get away with dignity intact."

"And with our heads still on our shoulders," Collie added. He looked up as a soft step on the graveled walk announced the minister's servant coming to fetch them. "We'll talk again. At supper if not before."

Rhys raised Justine's hand to his lips and kissed it. Somewhat comforted, she followed the woman who accompanied the servant down the long halls back to the women's harem.

*   *   *

It took Rhys several days before he was able to speak to the emir alone. He endured the many meals—most of them accompanied by the nobles of the court and the eternal guards—with growing frustration. Time and again he begged Timurid for a private audience, only to be met with vague excuses. The emir's interest in Justine seemed to grow steadily, even as his interest in meeting with Rhys declined. Even when Rhys was driven to try to speak quietly to the emir while others were present, the emir only looked at the American dumbly, as though he did not understand. All three visitors were treated with great courtesy, but it did not take them long to realize that it was a manipulative kind and very false. Valuable time was slipping away, and Rhys felt certain that if he did not say something soon, Collie was sure to be there before him and make off with the money.

Though Rhys did not know it, Justine was suffering the same frustration. But she had managed to put Collie to work for her, and she felt certain that soon they would get their hands on the money and be off, leaving Rhys still trying to raise the subject. She had a few pangs at the thought of what he would think of her, but she was determined not to allow her feelings to get in the way of her country's need. That thought was all that helped her endure the repulsive attentions the emir forced upon her.

Once they tried to make an excursion into the city, simply to break the monotony of lying around the palace. They soon found that they were not going to be allowed to leave without a heavy "security" guard of soldiers, and that it was preferred that they not go at all.

"We're nothing but prisoners here!" she complained to Collie. For once her innovative companion had no answer. He had not been able to arrange a private meeting with the emir either, though he had tried every underhanded trick he could think of to bring it about. The truth was that the servants in the palace were so thoroughly cowed by the cruelty of this king, they were unwilling to be bribed by an outsider to risk his displeasure.

"Ye're more likely to get information in the harem," he said to Justine. "Ask questions. Make discreet comments. Maybe ye can at least learn where he keeps his gold."

"That's impossible. No one talks to me. I've seen Zenobia perhaps twice since that first day, and all she did was look over my dress. The serving girls still treat me as though I were a creature from another planet, and they giggle so much I cannot understand a word of their language. No, Collie. You've got to speak to the emir somehow, and let him know the real reason we are here."

"I should have pretended I was a gentleman like the captain. I certainly would have had more opportunity."

Then early one morning, Timurid appeared in Rhys's quarters and announced to him that the long-awaited audience would be granted later that day. With a growing excitement, Rhys dressed in the best finery they had given him and paced the apartment until close to noon, when Timurid appeared to lead him to the emir's throne room. There were a number of local nobles standing around who eyed Rhys suspiciously, and he was relieved when Timurid did not take him inside. Instead they passed through several more halls and ended up in a small room fitted up like a private study, with gold braziers, gleaming brass tables, hassocks and divans scattered around on rugs of brilliant jeweled colors. In the center, sipping a tumbler of tea, sat Ulugh Khan.

Timurid bowed himself out, leaving Rhys alone with the emir. Rhys watched him leave in surprise, wondering how he was going to carry on a conversation without a translator.

"Sit please, Capt. Rhys," said the emir coolly, smiling at Rhys's surprise. "Yes, you did not know I speak the English, did you?"

Rhys bowed his head to hide his own smile. "I am astounded, your Highness. All this time—"

"I think it better to let you believe I not understand. I am clever, am I not?"

"Your Highness's wisdom leaves me overwhelmed," and Rhys made him a gallant leg.

"You English, you so polite. But also weak, I think. I watch you all this time. Not like Uzbeks, I think. Too polite."

"We can be most cruel and brave when the occasion calls for it, I assure you, your Highness. I am grateful for this chance to speak to you. You see, I have come on a mission which I could not tell you of when the others were present."

"Your cousin? She does not know?"

"No, Sir Emir, she does not. It is a most secret mission, one that concerns the future of my country. I think you must understand what I mean, you are so clever."

The emir chuckled, his rolls of fat bobbing like jelly. "Indeed, I do understand. You come from the Colonies to take the great treasure sent by Prince Tai Tsinghai to support your revolution. Alas, Sir Captain, I do not have it."

Rhys was unable to speak for a moment. "But I don't understand . . ." he finally managed to mumble. "I was told you were holding it in trust for the Colonies' representative."

"The truth, Sir Captain, is this. Prince Tai, whom I know as the father of one of my wives, made a promise to give an amazing amount of money to your government. It was sent by armed caravan across the Celestial Mountains to my palace, where I was to hold it for safety. Unfortunately, evil men learned of the plan and set upon the guard in the mountains, bandits who would stop at nothing to obtain such a treasure. The guards disappeared, and the treasure with them." He made a hopeless gesture with his hands. "There is nothing I can do."

Rhys studied the man angrily, convinced he was not speaking the truth. No doubt he had stashed the money away himself, and now expected the Colony's representative to swallow such a story. This fat little spider with the sanctimonious look on his repulsive face. How little he knew of Rhys Llewellyn!

"Surely, there must be some way of tracking down these bandits and recovering at least part of the money. My government will be grievously disappointed, if they do not receive this help. The . . . the emperor is counting on it mightily."

"Yes, I understand you are related to the Emperor of America. I am the Emir of Bokharta. I understand the needs of kingship. I do not wish to displease that august ruler. But you must see—"

"The emperor will indeed be displeased, if he does not feel that his friend, the emir, has not done everything that can be done to support his country in their hour of greatest need. Could you not send an army after these bandits?"

287

"You . . . what is it? . . . anticipate my very sentiments. The army is already underway. I hope you will continue to enjoy my hospitality, until they can return successfully with the hoard."

Rhys silently ground his teeth. "The Emir is most kind. I am happy that at last we have spoken honestly with each other."

The Emir smiled his humorless smile. "Is not honesty always the best way?"

Rhys raged to himself all the way back to his rooms. Although he hesitated to share this news with Collie, he found he could not hold it in, even for the sake of policy. Collie shook his head silently. "I feared something like this. That fellow doesn't know what honesty is. I'm sure he was lying to you."

"I think he has the money hidden here in Bokharta. But if so, why keep us here? It would be smarter to send us on our way, or dispatch us and be done with it. By the time word got back to America, if it ever did, he'd have it spent."

"He's up to something. The best thing for the present is to play along with him and see what happens. But I'd watch my back, if I were you. I intend to watch mine."

"And we'd better warn Justine, too."

About the only time he was able to have a private word with Justine, was at the evening meal when they managed to put their heads together while the others around them were talking. But that evening, when he met her in the anteroom and took her hand to lead her into the brightly lit dining chamber, she stopped on the threshold, staring in astonishment at three strangers sitting near the dais where the emir lounged.

"What's the matter?" Rhys whispered. He too had recognized the men as his three companions from the gaol at the border. It did not surprise him to see Augustus Hughes in the palace—he had half-expected that he would show up eventually, English visitors being rare in the country. The other two were out of place to be sure in such surroundings, but he supposed Hughes wanted them near for safety's sake.

Justine pulled back into the corridor. "I know that man," she said under her breath.

"So do I. He is that Englishman I met in the gaol—Augustus Hughes from Hampshire in England."

"No. Oh, his name is Hughes, all right, and he may be from Hampshire. But he's also a colonel in the British army. I met him once in Philadelphia. What on earth is he doing here?"

"Are you quite certain?"

"Yes. He knew my father. He's not the kind of man one easily forgets. I really don't want to face him right now, Rhys. Could you make my excuses, please? Tell them I'm unwell or something."

"I'll take ye back to your rooms," Collie offered, and Justine gratefully accepted, leaving Rhys to deal with the visitors. They were halfway back to the harem, when Collie said softly: "All right. Who is this Col. Hughes?"

"He is the man who commissioned my father to come to Samarkand and prevent the rebels from getting their hands on the treasure. He must have come himself, when he heard of my father's death."

"I thought it was *you* who were commissioned."

Justine looked down at her hands. "I'll explain that later. Meantime, he mustn't know I'm here." Not until

289

she had a chance to speak to him privately anyway.

Collie shuffled along in his best peasant style, thinking to himself that now there were five people trying to get their hands on that treasure. One of them, the emir, unfortunately seemed to hold all the good cards at the moment.

"The captain has been told by Ulugh Khan that there is no money in Samarkand," he whispered. "It was captured by bandits in the Celestial Mountains, and he wants to keep us here until he can get it back. Watch yerself, my girl. Has Zenobia made any further attempts to befriend you?"

"No. I hardly see her. And I never see any of the other wives at all. It's really quite dull in the harem."

Collie smiled enigmatically. "Pray that it stays that way."

While Justine was still trying to figure out some way to speak to Col. Hughes privately, she was summoned one day into his presence. She had assumed she was on her way to an audience with the emir, but instead she found herself alone in a small anteroom off the gardens heavy with the fragrance of jasmine just outside. A man emerged from behind a curtain, and she found herself facing the colonel, still in civilian dress, but with that unmistakable arrogance of high British military officials.

"You may imagine my astonishment in seeing you here, Madam," Hughes said in his clipped voice.

"None more than mine at seeing you," Justine snapped, determined to put up a good front.

"I assume you read my letter to your father." It was not so much a question as a statement.

"My late father. He was killed under very mysterious circumstances, because he took on this commission from you. It seemed only appropriate to his memory that I try to carry it out for him."

"You American girls. Spoiled, headstrong, thinking yourselves capable of anything. How could you have imagined you could carry off a dangerous, difficult assignment like this one? It was asking for disaster."

Justine lifted her chin. "I've managed rather well so far. I have the assistance of a very capable gentleman who has brought me safely through many dangers. I intercepted the colonial courier and have kept him under close surveillance all the way from Philadelphia. That is more than you can say."

"I presume by a 'very capable gentleman' you are speaking of that Arab, Yarmid Ali. Like all Arabs, he's sure to be in this only for the money. As for Capt. Llewellyn, you would have served your country better to have slipped some poison in his tea before you ever reached Baghdad. In fact, I can't think why you haven't. Your father would have done so."

"That is not true!"

Hughes waved her objections aside. "Well, no matter. The point is what are we to do with you, now that I'm here to see this thing through." He walked over to her and tipped her chin up with his long fingers, inspecting her face. "You are very beautiful, you know. More so decked in Eastern dress and all those fine jewels than ever in Philadelphia. I must admit I wasn't aware of just how beautiful."

"Take your hands off me," Justine snapped and moved away. "I don't want your compliments or your advice. I've managed very well this far, and I intend to go through with this mission, all the way to China if I must."

The colonel gave her a sardonic smile. "And where do I fit in?"

Justine softened. "Let me be your partner. Perhaps I can help you. I hear things in the women's quarters, and I know Capt. Llewellyn well. I think I know his weaknesses as well as his strengths. He can be a dangerous man."

"Bah! A typical colonial adventurer. I can deal with the captain. However, I grant you the harem is a place where you might help. Very well, then. We shall work together until such time as I am able to finish this little enterprise. Then I shall see about getting you home."

Justine breathed a small sigh of relief. "I'll do all I can to help you, Colonel. I promise."

He raised her hand to his cold lips. "Good. Now get you back to the harem where you can keep your eyes and ears open for me."

She left smiling at him while he stood in the room, fingering his watch fob and thinking how indeed he had not realized what a beauty she was. As pretty a piece of mischief as ever he had seen, as the song went. A rustle behind him brought him around.

"I hope you enjoyed eavesdropping," Col. Hughes said to the emir as he stepped from behind the curtain.

"Most informative. And always I enjoy watching the beautiful cousin of the captain."

"She is lovely to look upon."

"Looking is for the other men. Possessing is for the Emir. She will make a beautiful and exotic addition to my harem."

"Yes, indeed. It is a bargain then? You get your new wife, and I get the treasure for my country."

Ulugh Khan shrugged his shoulders. "Once I am able to wrest it away from those bandits. I think I must have my new wife first."

"I don't think so," Hughes replied coolly. "After all, a wise man does not give away his bargaining chips before the game is finished."

"You are too clever," the emir answered, chuckling. "But I also am clever. What if I give the treasure to the captain?"

"I do not think Capt. Llewellyn would be so grateful to turn his cousin over to you for your harem," Hughes said, remembering the way Justine had rushed into Rhys's arms outside the jail. "That is an important difference between us."

"You win the point," Ulugh Khan said, still smiling. "That captain, he is a nuisance. Two times I try to dispose of him before he reached Samarkand. Now I keep him around in order not to cause his cousin distress."

"And when you make her your wife?"

Ulugh Khan rubbed a finger along his thick underlip. "Then he will have ceased his usefulness and will disappear. I do not bother overlong with unnecessary guests."

Hughes bowed and backed his way out of the room. The emir's threatening words and sharp little glances were a trifle too pertinent to his own situation to be of comfort.

Twelve

There was a subtle change in the atmosphere of the palace. Rhys could sense it, but he couldn't tell what had brought it about. When he looked up one afternoon to see Timurid strolling in the gardens outside his rooms, he hurried out to join him.

"I rather hoped to see you," the minister said casually, as he opened an exquisite silk square and began to throw the crumbs inside at the birds who clustered around him. "They are beautiful, are they not? They find a haven here in the palace gardens, safe from starvation, hunters, or predators. Would it were so for humans."

"It appears to be such a tranquil, lovely place," Rhys answered, falling in step with the minister. "As I learn more about it, I sense that beneath all this tranquility there is another kind of life . . ."

Timurid raised a finger as if to his lips. "It is better not to speak of it. I suspect that even the emperor's court in America has its share of intrigue."

"Oh, indeed it does. It appears to be a condition of palace life. Has the emir any word yet from his army in

294

the Celestial Mountains?"

"Alas, they have sent a runner to report that they have not been able to find or subdue the bandits who stole the treasure. It has made the emir very unhappy."

So that explains his change in attitude towards us, Rhys thought. Perhaps he has decided we are more of a liability than a trump card.

"The emir," Timurid went on, "feels acutely that he has failed in his trust to keep the money safe until it could reach your government. It has cost him great pain."

I'll bet it has, Rhys thought. His pain is likely because he hasn't been able to get it for himself. Though if he had, we should have all been sent to our heavenly reward long ago.

"It grieves me that the emir suffers on America's account," Rhys said cooly. They had wandered far into the paths of the gardens and were out of sight of its gleaming white walls. Timurid stepped casually into the shadows cast by a thorny acacia tree and turned to Rhys, speaking very softly.

"I like you, my friend, and thus I feel it imperative to warn you. Our emir, for all his greatness, is prone at times to loose sight of the long-term gain, in his impatience with immediate rewards. I, on the other hand, feel it would be to Bokharta's advantage to build strong and lasting ties with America. To that end, I wish to help you."

"You could best help my cousin and me by getting us away from here and on our way. We are practically prisoners in this palace, not free to wander the city, much less strike out for America. I am impatient to do something—try to find this money myself or, failing that, return home."

"I can understand. I, personally, feel it is best that you do leave and soon, even though the emir would like to keep you here. Reluctantly, I have determined it is in the best interest of my country to help you on your way. I have a plan of escape . . ."

Rhys found his hopes beginning to soar. "My government would be eternally grateful."

"I will come to you within the next few days. I caution you, however, trust no one else. Follow only me. Is that clear?"

"Very clear."

Timurid resumed his casual stride. "Good. We understand each other then. Be patient, my friend. All will be well."

Later Rhys spoke quietly with Collie. "Do you think Timurid can be trusted?"

Collie looked grave, but nodded his head. "The gossip among the servants is that Timurid is only waiting his chance to throw the emir off his throne and take it for himself. He's distantly related to the ruling family and believes he would make a better king—which he probably would."

"We must get word to Justine somehow. Do you think you can get in to see her?"

"I'll find a way. Make up a present of some kind that I can take to her. She has to be warned to be ready."

It turned out that there was no need for Collie to try to get to Justine, for she found him first. She too had felt a growing tension in the harem and the palace, though she set it down to the presence of Col. Hughes working his mischief against Rhys. Then abruptly one morning Zenobia, whom she had not laid eyes on for days, came striding angrily into her apartment. She stood regally staring lightning bolts of hostility at Justine and pointed to the sapphire ring still on the young girl's middle finger. Two of Zenobia's women jumped to pull it off, but it was a close fit and refused to budge.

While the women tugged painfully at Justine's finger, Zenobia pointed to a third servant who stepped forward holding a ferocious little dagger.

"NO!" Justine screamed, reclaiming her finger. "I'll get it off. Give me a moment." With the help of a little fragrant oil from a flask, she was able to slip the ring off her finger and hand it to the serving girl, who squirmed across the floor on her hands and knees to give it to Queen Zenobia. Still glaring, that lady turned on her heel and stalked from the room. Behind her, Justine heard her own servants giggling.

"Why?" she asked them.

One of the eunuchs, a tall fellow with a bald head and a constant smirk on his thin face, stepped forward. "You . . . new wife . . ." he said, smirking more than ever. "Queen not like."

Justine could only stare. "I'm to be . . . not the Emir . . . Oh, no!" she stammered. "Not for all the gold in Persia! Without realizing it, she was backing from the room, shaking her head, still unable to believe her ears. Once through the door, she shoved past the ever-present guard and began running in the direction of Rhys's room. With the soldier on her heels, she ran straight into Collie on his way to see her, and threw herself into his arms.

Calming her down enough so that her cries wouldn't carry to the rest of the palace, Collie led her outside to a bench near one of the pools.

"I'll kill myself, Collie. You and Rhys have got to get me out of here! Immediately!" she sobbed. He laid a

297

comforting arm around her shoulders.

"Don't worry, Justine. We've already made plans to escape. Ye'll never marry that fat old man."

Justine shuddered. "God in heaven, what a fate! It's like a nightmare! Why can't we leave *now?* I hate this place. I want to go home!"

"I know. And we will. Be patient a little longer."

"Where is Rhys anyway? Why doesn't he ever come to me?"

"He hasn't been allowed to. It probably has something to do with the emir having designs on you himself. The captain has been working mightily to get his hands on the treasure, so far without success. Had he gotten it, I imagine he would have taken off and left us to our fate by now."

Justine wiped her arm across her face. "He wouldn't do that."

"I'm not so sure. He wants that money for the Colonies, and he is just selfish enough to abandon us without a qualm, if he saw a way to get back home with it himself."

Justine gripped Collie's hand. "You make sure he knows what my fate involves! I'm serious, Collie. I'll kill myself first!"

He patted her shoulder. "Don't worry. It will be all right. But in the meantime, you'd be wise to take advantage of any chance you get to outsmart Rhys Llewellyn. Don't let your heart be swayed too much."

Justine nodded. "I know. Col. Hughes would kill Rhys in a minute, if he saw the opportunity. I don't want him to die—I just don't want him to get control of that money before we do."

"Well, at this point, no one is getting his hands on the money. Our best hope right now is just to get away from

298

this place."

"Make it soon, Collie. Make it soon!"

That evening Justine sat beside Col. Hughes at the elaborate evening meal. With servants coming and going, carrying trays of grapes, melons, and nectarines, boiled lamb, mounds of Turki bread and a pilaf of mutton, rice, and carrots, all to the accompaniment of exotic music on reedy, Eastern instruments, Justine sat and brooded, eating little, saying little, and trying very hard never to let her eyes meet those of the emir. She could feel them fastened on her, and deliberately she turned the other way, toying with her food, and staring at her trencher.

"You're very quiet tonight," Hughes finally said, leaning down to her. On his other side, Justine caught a glimpse of Rhys bending around.

"I must talk to you alone," Justine hissed. "It's urgent."

Hughes studied her a moment through his hooded eyes. "I'll walk you back to your rooms," he whispered and went on eating. When she rose at last, pleading ill health, both Hughes and Rhys stepped forward to take her hand. She gave it to the colonel, throwing Rhys an enigmatic glance that left him more concerned than he wanted to be, and walked from the room.

"That terrible emir wants me in his harem!" she whispered to Hughes as they made their way through the halls followed by the eternal soldiers.

The colonel caught his breath. Now how had she learned that? "Nonsense. He's said nothing to me about it, and I'm sure he would if he actually planned such a thing."

"Why should he speak to you? I'm supposed to be

299

Capt. Llewellyn's cousin."

"Did the captain tell you of this?"

"No. One of the eunuchs in my chamber told me. They know a few scattered words of English, and I was wondering why Queen Zenobia all of a sudden hates me so much."

The emir was not going to be happy with his chief wife, thought the colonel. "I'm sure he was making it up. Such a thing would be too farfetched, even for a place like this. As for Capt. Llewellyn, if he had heard of such a plan, he probably would say nothing about it, unless it served his own purposes. You must be very wary of that man, my dear."

"I know. And yet I cannot alienate him completely. He has a plan to help us escape. We're supposed to get away very soon. And I want to leave here, Col. Hughes. More than anything in the world!"

One eyebrow inched up the colonel's thin face. "How interesting. What are the particulars?"

"I don't know them, but I think there is someone in the palace working with us. All they told me was to be ready to leave when the summons comes."

"Perhaps they might make room for my friends and me," Hughes said obliquely. "I do not feel the climate in this place is conducive to health myself."

"I'll ask him when I get the chance. Meanwhile, you must let me know if you hear anything about the emir's plans for me. That horrible fat old man! I'd rather die than live my life out in this palace!"

"Don't worry, my dear. I shall see that nothing of the sort occurs."

He patted her hand in a fatherly gesture that Justine found comforting. He was, after all, her father's friend, and an officer and a gentleman while Rhys seemed everyday more of an unknown quantity. She glanced to her right, where through the lattice work of the screen she caught sight of a man working near one of the flower bushes. He was a laborer, dressed in a loose tunic with a thick white turban wound around his head. He turned and their eyes met, stopping Justine in midstep. She stared at the man—the short beard, the slanted eyes, and prominent cheekbones, the dark skin, the air of menace.

"Merciful God!" she exclaimed, gripping Hughes's hand. "That face! Now I remember!"

"What is it, Justine?"

"It's the face at the window, the night my father was killed. I've seen others in this country that reminded me of it but that . . . that's the very one. I'm sure."

"That's quite impossible, my dear. I myself viewed the dead body of the man who killed Justin Maury. He died of a fever shortly after your father was buried. That cannot be the man."

"Then it is his twin. Don't you realize what this means, Col. Hughes. That assassin must have come from Bokharta!"

"My dear, you are allowing your fears to get the better of your imagination. Look at the poor man. He's going about his work completely unconcerned, even as we discuss him. Put it from your mind, dear girl, and let the matter rest with me."

He was so insistent, Justine wavered in her conviction. Perhaps she *was* seeing things. Yet, for just that instant, it had all appeared so clear. The colonel seemed so confident, so sure of himself, it was a comfort to lean on him and feel that he would watch out for her future.

301

Especially now when she was so cut off from Collie and Rhys.

"Do me this one favor," Hughes went on, gently leading her down the hall. "When you hear more of the captain's plans, let me know what they are right away. I cannot care for our welfare if I do not know everything that is going on."

Still troubled, Justine nodded. "Of course. Yes, I'll get word to you at once."

Three days later Timurid spoke quietly to Rhys: "Tomorrow the emir is entertaining emissaries from a Mogul raj. There shall be feasting and dancing, the best Bukhara can provide. Be ready."

Rhys made an effort to calm his rising excitement. "Is a prince of India so important to Ulugh Khan?"

"This prince is. He is wealthy beyond measure. Our great emir would welcome trade with so significant a ruler."

Rhys casually waved his hand around. "Bokharta appears to me to be already enjoying great wealth. Is the emir that greedy then?"

Timurid laughed, looking at Rhys as a father might at an idiot child. "My friend, I see that you know little of the East. I once visited this same raj, and his wealth makes our poor Bokharta look like a barbaric pesthole. Ulugh Khan is no more greedy than other princes. It is a trait common to rulers. However, he must constantly support an army to protect our kingdom both from the Persians on the west and the Manchus across the Tien Shan. Not to mention Russia to the north. The great mountains afford us some protection from the south, thankfully. Ulugh Khan wishes to make a treaty with this prince. Thus the elaborate entertainment."

Rhys picked a luscious grape from a tray and popped it into his mouth. "I wonder that the emir does not seek to make a treaty with the British. They are uncommonly busy in India these days."

Again Timurid laughed. "Why do you think he has made Mr. Hughes and his unsavory companions so welcome?"

Although they were, as usual, surrounded by people coming and going, Rhys managed to whisper to Collie, "Timurid tells me there will be a great feast tomorrow for the Indian emissaries. Be ready. Tell Justine."

Collie nodded. Later that evening he accompanied Justine back to her rooms when she left the evening meal. He repeated Rhys's words, quietly and obliquely enough that even if the soldiers should hear or understand, it would sound like simple small talk. She bent her head to hide the thrill of hope his words gave her and spent the better part of the night planning the best way to speak to Col. Hughes. It turned out to be wasted effort, when she came across him striding the halls the following morning and invited him to walk in the gardens with her.

"You're quite certain this servant actually meant that you are to run away tonight?" Hughes said when she had told him of Collie's message.

"Oh yes. Otherwise he would not have spoken to me about it. I'm sure he meant that something will occur during this entertainment which will allow us to slip away. If you are prepared, perhaps you can come with us."

"You haven't mentioned my coming along to the captain, have you?"

303

"I've had no chance. If I had, I would know more about what's planned. I only tell you this because, as a fellow English citizen, I owe you some allegiance."

Hughes absently flipped the short fob ribbon on his waistcoat. "Of course, I am somewhat reluctant to leave without yet knowing the exact location of the money. That, after all, was our reason for coming here. On the other hand, I don't think this emir knows where it is either, and we shall certainly not locate it as long as we are prisoners in this palace."

"Exactly," Justine said, stopping to dislodge a stone from her sandal. "Rhys might know, however, and that is reason enough to see that no harm comes to him."

Hughes smiled down at her. "At least not until we're safely out of Bokharta, eh." He could see by the look in her eyes that he had hit a sensitive nerve. He had forgotten for the moment her feelings for this rebel captain, and it would do him no good to have her turn against him now in order to protect her lover. "Don't worry," he said cooly. "I only want to outwit Capt. Llewellyn, not hurt him."

Justine straightened and resumed her slow ramble. "I, too, wish to outwit him, and obtain that money for England rather than the Colonies. But I do not want to see him hurt. Remember that, Colonel. It is a condition of my trust. Otherwise I should leave you here without a qualm, while we make our escape."

Stupid women! Hughes thought. No wonder they are so useless in espionage. He gently patted her shoulder. "Of course, my dear. I understand completely."

Though Justine was slightly upset by her conversation with Col. Hughes, she quickly put it from her mind and became absorbed in the heady thought that at last they

304

would be free of this place. Nothing seemed to her so dearly wished as to no longer have the emir undressing her with his lascivious glances, fingering her gauzy garments, running his greasy fingers down her arms, her neck, her thighs, using her latest bauble as an excuse for inspecting her throat and looking down her dress. If she never laid eyes on his repulsive bloated body ever again, it would be too soon!

Yet, as the evening wore on, she began to wonder if she had indeed misjudged Collie's message. It was certainly a sumptuous feast, more grand and elaborate than anything they had been given in their stay at the palace. Serving girls came and went, bearing trays piled high with meats, vegetables, luscious melons, and delicate sweetmeats. Goblets of tea and *Lassi*, a yogurt drink sweetened with a tamarind syrup, were passed, along with pomegranate juice and almond water. With each new course, an elaborate gift was offered the raj—carnelian from China, pearls from India, emeralds from Persia. Through it all, dancers gyrated to the exotic, nasal sounds of native instruments, interspersed at intervals with other entertainers—acrobats, jugglers, trained animals, and demonstrations of weaponry skills. Justine tried to limit what she ate and drank, in order to keep her wits from becoming sluggish, but the evening wore on so long, and the emir was so grossly attentive, that she ended up drinking more of the *Lassi* than she planned. At length, disappointed and feeling almost ill from the rich food, she made her way back to her rooms. Rhys had already left, followed by Collie. It sickened her that through the entire evening there had never been a chance to speak to either one of them. Even Hughes, though he gave her several knowing looks, was unable to exchange a single word to raise her sinking hopes.

Her serving girls clustered around her to remove her elaborate robes, but, after slipping off the embroidered outer tunic, she sent them angrily away. In the garden outside her apartment, moonlight played tantalizingly on the marble columns and benches, and the soft air bore the heady fragrance of rose blossoms. Yet she could take no delight in any of the beauty around her. In fact, it seemed cloying and sickly, like being imprisoned in a sumptuous gold sarcophagus.

She was startled when a figure appeared in the shadows of the archway leading to the garden. Stifling the cry that nearly escaped her lips, she waited silent and still until he moved away from the columns and into the light. Justine's heart sank as she recognized the emir's chief minister, Timurid.

"Sir, you startled me," she said, her white hand going unconsciously to her throat.

Timurid smiled at her and extended his arm. "Would you walk in the garden with me awhile, Madam?" he said in his dignified voice. "The moonlight is so lovely. I find after a long and heavy meal such as we've just finished, a walk is most refreshing."

Justine hesitated, wondering what she would do if the summons came while she was with this man, a powerful friend of the emir's. And yet she could not afford to refuse him. It might make him suspicious.

"Of course," she said, walking through the archway and into the garden. "I had thought of going myself. It is much more pleasant to have company."

The ever-present guards moved to take their places a few paces behind, but Timurid spoke to them in his native tongue, sending them scurrying back inside.

"I've dismissed them," he explained, strolling beside Justine. "No need for soldiers when you are with me."

She fought to hide her anxiety. "It will be refreshing not to have them dogging my every step," she said cooly, all the while her mind working. This great man had never sought her out before. Why tonight? And where were they going? He appeared to be leading her toward the rear walkways adjoining the outer palace walls. She was about to protest that she was tired and wanted to go back when, as they passed beneath a small grove of trees that draped them in shadows, Timurid suddenly grabbed her arm and pulled her off the path, toward a small pagoda. She tried to cry out and found a hand tightly clamped across her mouth. Struggling she was half-dragged from one black shadow to another, well away from the women's quarters and into a part of the ground she had never seen before. Her mind was screaming by now, certain she was being carried off to the emir's apartments. They reached the pagoda, and she was thrust up into the arms of a man standing there.

"For the love of God, don't cry out," Rhys whispered as his arms went tightly around her. "Here, put this cloak around you and follow me."

Justine found she could breathe again. "Oh Rhys, I thought . . ."

"No time now," he whispered and, grabbing her hand, pulled her across the grass. Still mystified, Justine could see that Timurid was leading them, while in the shadows behind, Collie dogged their heels. She gave one thought to the missing Col. Hughes, then forgot him in the effort to match Rhys's silent steps.

At the wall they stopped, pressing against its rough surface and straining to catch their breath. By dodging

307

the patches of moonlight, they appeared to have come this far without being seen. The garden was still and silent, not a breath of air stirring. Justine reached for Rhys's hand and squeezed it. She could just make out his face in the moonlight, so near her own, smiling down at her. The hope of freedom was like a live entity between them. And so was the fear of being caught.

"Courage," Rhys whispered.

"Come!" Timurid commanded, and took off running along the shadow of the wall toward a dark depression a few yards away. They followed, keeping as close to the wall as possible, their feet silent on the thick grass. The depression—Justine saw when they reached it—was a small door, one she had never noticed before. Timurid fussed with the lock while the three of them stood looking furtively around, trying to catch any slight movement. The door had not been opened for a long time, and it creaked and groaned in protest as Timurid pulled at it, making an opening just large enough for them to squeeze through.

On the other side they were met with a great wall of darkness. The pungent odors of the city were enough to verify that they were outside the palace, but gave no indication of where or how to proceed.

"Which way?" Rhys said to Timurid, still standing inside the door. He stepped around it long enough to point. "Follow that street. It will take you to the east gate. The caravan trail should be obvious from there."

Rhys nodded and clapped a hand on the man's shoulder. "Thank you."

His whispered comment was lost as sudden noises exploded all around. From every direction the clatter of booted feet bore down on them. Out of the shadows,

308

armed men materialized, swords in their hands, pointed stilettos on their helmets.

"Run!" Timurid cried as he made to dart back through the little door.

Rhys did not answer. Grabbing Justine's hand, he pulled her into the darkness, running as fast as he could go. She half-ran and was half-dragged behind him, her fear choking her throat like bile. She looked around, to see Collie sprinting behind them as Timurid was grabbed by one of the soldiers. A white blade slashed through the moonlight, and she had an impression of a head falling one way, a body rolling another.

"Rhys!" she screamed, but he pulled her away, driving for the black haven of the street. Somehow they made it, diving into its dark womb, running blindly up alleys, into culverts, doubling back when they reached a dead end, climbing over low walls, and leaping across small garden plots behind squat, square houses. It was a nightmare, her breath tearing at her throat, the dying clatter of the soldiers behind them, fading only to reappear stronger around the next bend.

At one point they were forced to stop to catch their breath. "Rhys . . ." Justine sobbed. "Timurid . . . they . . . they . . ."

"Don't talk!" Rhys snapped. "Save your strength. We must keep going."

"Where the bloody hell is that gate!" Collie moaned beside her. "I feel like a rat in a maze."

"We'll find it. We must," Rhys answered grimly. He had heard Timurid's last cry and had a pretty good idea about what had happened.

In the black distance they saw a tiny bobbing point of light. Paralyzed for a moment, they all three caught their breath as it dawned on them that the light came from a torch borne by one of the soldiers. Rhys looked blindly around, grabbing Justine's hand and heading for the nearest black hole that he hoped was a narrow alleyway off the street. It was, though so blocked with refuse thrown from the overhanging houses that they stumbled as they ran, setting up the hysterical bark of a watchdog chained behind the walls. They could hear the cries of the soldiers behind them, and the clatter of their boots as the noise signaled where they were.

"This way," Collie whispered as Rhys and Justine nearly missed a tiny opening between the houses. Like a tunnel it weaved its way between the mud-brick walls, opening at last on to a broader walkway that bordered on the city's network of canals.

The soldiers had taken a shortcut around the tunnel and emerged farther down, where the canal bent gently toward the outer walls of the inner city. Collie and Rhys gave each other a meaningful glance and pulled Justine toward the canal.

"No! I won't—" she cried as Rhys dragged her over the low wall and into the water.

"You've no choice," he whispered as she sank into the murky mess, gasping silently. Like the other canals of the city, this one served as a latrine, and its warm water was thick with human waste. The ghastly smell choked her lungs and set her stomach churning. Alongside the two men, she sank until her nose was just above water and glided silently along away from the soldiers, trying desperately not to think about the garbage around her or the soft mushy bottom. Just as they thought they had escaped, their pursuers came clattering out of a side street ahead of them. They had only just passed beneath a cross walk over the canal and, without speaking, they glided back into its shadow, trying to not even breathe for fear of being detected.

The soldiers spoke briefly to each other, then walked down the road, passing just above the bridge where the three huddled in the water. One soldier stepped up on the bridge and paused to look down into the canal. He laughed and said something in the local language that set the others laughing, too. Rhys was trying not to think how helpless they would be if they should be caught while immersed in this sewer, when the soldiers at last moved on. He did not let himself breathe deeply until the sound of their boots was nearly out of earshot.

Justine leaned her face against his shoulder and choked back a spate of coughing. Supporting her with his arms, he wiped away some of the murk on her cheek. "Courage," he said softly. "It can't be much farther."

"We hope so anyway," Collie whispered. "If only I could have explored this city while we were stuck in that palace. I've got no idea where we are."

"Most of these canals merge. One of them has to lead us to a gate."

They slid out into the water and paddled a little farther, hoping every minute to see the high towers of the gate. Instead they ran straight into one of the pits, placed at intervals to catch the waste which could then be collected for the fields outside the city. There was nothing to do but climb out and take to the streets again. To add to their dismay, the moonlight suddenly emerged in full glory, shimmering on a huge dome that Rhys recognized as one of the monuments in the Registan. His heart sank as he realized that they had worked their way back into the center of the city near the great square.

Running footsteps clattered on the cobbles behind them. Grabbing Justine's hand, he ran toward the square, Collie fast on his heels. The narrow streets melded mazelike into one another, at length depositing them like a conduit into the great dark square, where the moonlight bronzed the domes and arches of Tamerlane's huge momuments. They made for a tamarind tree, low and heavy with shadow, and stopped to catch their breath.

"We can't hope to hide," Collie spluttered. "They'll smell us a mile away!"

"We could run under that fountain," Justine said between deep gasps, thinking how wonderful to wash off the crud of the canal.

"In this moonlight, they'd see us clearly. Nay, we can't afford to."

"What are we going to do? We can't dodge them forever," Rhys whispered.

Thinking hard, Collie searched for a solution. They had very few choices as far as he could see and not one of them looked encouraging. In fact, they all looked rather bad. How ironically disgusting to have come so far on his wits, only to be cornered in this crazy part of the world by a few barbarians with scimitars.

"The mausoleum throws a lot of shadow," he whispered. "Head for that."

They struck out across the square, darting between the shadows of trees, low buildings, and an occasional awning, stopping now and then to listen for the sound of running boots behind them. Once near the huge mouldering mausoleum, they saw that in order to reach it they would have to cross a broad patch of courtyard, golden with shimmering moonlight. It was risky, since

312

they would be so exposed, but once there they would be relatively safe.

They waited, gathering strength for the spring across the open courtyard. Just as they were ready to start, they heard the dreaded cry of the soldiers and saw them running from two sides of the square straight toward them.

Justine gasped.

"Run for it!" Rhys called and pushed her into the yard.

She could hear the triumphant cries of the soldiers as they spotted the three moonlit figures running across the courtyard. With her breath bursting in her lungs, Justine tore from the dark hulk of the mausoleum, horribly conscious of the sounds of the soldier's boots bearing down on her. She reached the shadows and collapsed against the tiled mosaics of the wall, gasping, looking blindly around for the next hiding place.

"Collie!" she heard Rhys cry, and she looked back to see that the little Englishman had tripped and fallen just outside the shadow of the wall and in full view of the soldiers.

"Go on! Get away!" Collie yelled, trying to scramble to his feet. Soldiers were running from all sides, converging on the square. One group of them broke away to surround Collie where he sprawled on the stones. She saw the naked silver flash of their swords glinting in the moonlight. Tearing away from Rhys's grasp, she tried to run to Collie. Rhys grabbed at her, pulling her back toward the far end of the wall, where an open archway led into the building.

"No!" Justine cried, struggling against Rhys's iron grip.

"Don't be a fool! We can't help him now."

But it was too late. A huge hulking form loomed up in front of her. Her arm was torn from Rhys's grasp, and she was lifted off her feet and thrown into the air. Screaming blindly, she was trussed with a rope and heaved over a shoulder like a sheep. Thumping against the wall, blind in the darkness, she was carried shrieking into the depths of the dark where, overcome with shock and horror, she fainted dead away.

Rhys watched appalled as Justine disappeared on the shoulders of one of the soldiers who had cornered him. He turned his back to the wall, facing a ring of guards, smiling their gap-toothed smiles now that the chase was over the the quarry cornered. Rhys looked around at them as they inched closer, their scimitars gleaming in the moonlight, the sharp stilettos on their helmets glinting in the bronze glow. Beyond them he could see the bloody mass that was Collie sprawled on the cobbles. As the soldiers moved in, Rhys was conscious of broad armour plates closing like walls around him, a deadly ring of predators ready for the kill.

He felt the cold wall against his back and knew he had nowhere to go from here. Well, he thought, if die I must, then it shall be bravely. It hadn't been such a bad life. Poor Justine . . .

He had no weapon to fight with, but he would do his best to hurt them before they killed him. He would throw himself against that hard leather wall of breastplates and kick and bite if nothing else!

As he braced himself for the blow, the soldiers who had surrounded Collie turned suddenly and ran toward the group facing him, swords raised and spears thrusting upward. The guards facing Rhys all at once had their backs to him and, to his astonishment, were fighting for their lives. The two groups fell on each other, slashing and grunting while Rhys watched, too weak to run, utterly confused. In just a few moments the palace guards had had enough and turned to disappear up into the darkness of the streets.

Saved! Rhys thought. Never mind who or why—just give them your heartfelt thanks! He slumped against the wall as one of the second group of armed men came running up to him, something dark in his hand.

"I'm grate—" Rhys started to say. The soldier raised his arm high, and Rhys threw up his arm to ward off the thick sack which was yanked roughly over his head. He choked in the suffocating darkness as a cord was pulled tightly around his throat. Desperately trying to call out, he felt himself falling as a sudden thudding blow to his head sent the night exploding into reams of drifting stars. They were the last thing he saw as the night engulfed him.

Thirteen

Light, bobbing up and down, shadowy, then brightly shining directly into his eyes so that he squinted and struggled to turn away. But his body refused to respond. He was helpless, a creature without bone or sinew.

Somewhere nearby the wind sang gently through tinkling glass. In the distance the soft tones of a lute played a strange, exotic, toneless melody. His eyes fluttered for an instant, and he was besieged with a riotous expanse of color, brilliant and shimmering, as if in the middle of some gigantic jewel.

"He is waking," said a soft musical voice near his ear. A heady heavy scent of jasmine surrounded him, part of the lovely voice. Rhys's eyelids fluttered, and with a supreme effort he opened them.

A face was bending over him, close to his. An exquisite face, like nothing he had ever seen before. White, white skin, as if sculptured in the purest ivory. Lips startlingly red and shaped like a tiny blossom on the pale face. Eyes barely open, slanted sharply up toward the black, black braid of hair that framed the face.

Had he died? Was this what heaven was like, this paradise of color, light, beauty, scent, and exquisite sound?

"You are not dead, Captain," the singing voice said close to his ear, as if its owner had read his mind. "Slowly now. Take a little boiled wine. It will help you regain your senses."

Rhys choked as his head was lifted slightly and the sweet liquid dribbled against his lips. He felt its healing warmth all the way down, giving strength to his wasted limbs. It helped to prevent him from sinking back into that haze of unconsciousness that his body longed for.

Opening his eyes, he struggled to sit up, and felt gentle hands lifting him against piles of downy cushions. As his mind cleared, he looked around, trying to sort out where he was.

It was a room, beautiful beyond belief. Flowers everywhere, inside and out through the open archways that led to a pavilion of some sort. Around him fell hangings of the most exquisite embroidery, golden dragons as tall as columns, cavorting against jeweled green- and blue-flowered backgrounds. Lamps burned from niches in the walls, and beside him a golden brazier gave out fumes of heady incense. He heard a low, musical laugh, and saw that it came from a woman bending over him, the same beautiful, exotic face he had seen in his dream.

"You are quite awake now?" she asked, and lifted a hand to his forehead. Instinctively Rhys shied away. The hand was as white as her face, but the nails, red as blood, were like talons, curved and over four inches long, every one of them.

She laughed again, amused at his reactions. "Do not be

317

afraid, Captain. You are among friends. I deeply regret that my soldiers were required to use such force, but it was necessary. You would never have come with them otherwise."

"You . . . you speak English?" Rhys managed to stammer, wondering if he was still in the throes of his dream.

The laugh again, like the wind singing through the glass chimes. "A little. I learned English in my homeland long ago. It is good to have the opportunity to use it again."

His head was clearing. He knew now he had not died, and was certainly not in heaven. This room was too much like those in the emir's palace, though infinitely more beautiful and differently arranged. "I don't understand anything," he muttered and groaned as he clutched his head. He had a lump there as big as a hen's egg, and it pounded horribly.

"Take a little more wine. Then I shall explain all." The beautiful woman nodded her head, and a servant lifted a golden goblet to his lips. Taking it from the servant's hand, Rhys drank deeply, then fell back against the cushions. "Who are you?" he asked quietly.

The woman, who he could now see was sitting on a silk hassock beside his divan, nodded to her servants, who silently made their way out of the room, leaving the two of them alone. She turned back to Rhys, her masklike face inscrutable in the flickering light of an oil lamp atop a thin silver column beside the bed.

"I am Princess Tsingsia. My father is Prince Tai of Tsinghai across the Celestial Mountains.

"But . . . isn't he . . . ?"

"Yes. He is the same friend of your Robert Morris who

318

has agreed to help support your revolution."

"No one told me his daughter was here in Bokharta. We are still in Bokharta, aren't we?"

The princess laughed again. "Yes, you have not been carried away from Samarkand. In fact, you are back within the emir's palace."

Rhys rubbed his head. "Is it the same day?"

"Nearly morning of the day you had hoped to escape from Bokharta. Alas, it was not to be."

"Timurid . . ."

"Minister Timurid was a fool," the princess said, her voice taking on a cold edge he had not heard before. "But like all fools, he must be allowed to bring about his own ruin. It is always so. He only interfered a little with my plans."

"*Your* plans? I never even heard of you. How have you managed to bring me here? And where are my friends? My cousin—"

"Do not worry about your cousin," Tsingsia said, smiling her lotus smile. "In due time I shall take care of her."

There was something ominous in the musical voice. Rhys began to feel uneasy, anxious to get up and get away. Again, as though she could read his thoughts, the princess smiled and refilled his goblet with the wine.

"Drink a little more. It restores the blood. And do not be anxious, my Captain. All will be well."

"I wish I could be so certain. Nothing has been well until now."

"That is because you were without my help. You see, I am one of the emir's wives. My father, four years ago, sent me to this barbaric country to marry this barbaric prince, in an effort to assure safe passage of his trade

319

routes to the west. While I had no choice but to comply, I likewise have no intention of spending my days languishing here as just another creature to warm the emir's bed. Harems, like palaces everywhere, are places of intrigue and treachery and power struggles. I find them most stimulating."

I'll bet you do, Rhys thought. This delicate, petal-like creature, with the voice like a wind chime, had the character of a well-honed sword. Though he did not fully understand the complexities of the situation, he was beginning to have a growing respect for the slight, gorgeous woman before him.

"I understood Zenobia was the emir's chief wife," he said casually.

Tsingsia's narrow eyes grew cold, though her lotus smile never altered. "Zenobia is an aged, stringy cat. A bigger fool even than Timurid. She will not be difficult to supplant. Indeed, I could do it now, but I prefer to move cautiously, languidly, leaving nothing to chance. You have come along at just the right time, dear Captain. You are the opportunity I was waiting for."

"And that is why you saved my life?"

"But of course. Now, I can see that the wine is making you sleepy. Rest for a while, Captain. You are safe here. We will talk again."

It was true. He could barely hold his eyelids open, so heavy were they. For an instant he thought perhaps the wine had been drugged. Yet his great fatigue seemed more the last dregs of his blow on the head. His mind was not clear, and somehow he knew that in dealing with this woman his mind should be very clear indeed. He slumped back against the pillows.

"Justine? Collie . . ." he murmured.

The soft hand with the ferocious talons stroked his forehead, light as feathery down.

"We will talk further," was all she replied.

After the horrors of the midnight streets of Samarkand, Justine was almost relieved to find herself deposited back in her rooms in the palace. She was still weak from her race through the streets, and so submitted quietly to the ministrations of her servants, as they washed away the offal from the canal, anointed her body with scented oil, washed and braided her hair, and laid a flowing mantle of gauzy silk over her shoulders. She even slept, though fitfully, waking to the bright sunshine of the morning streaming through the open arches to the gardens.

Trays of food appeared accompanied with goblets of tea. She ate little, but drank the tea hoping it would revive her flagging spirits. But there was no way that mere tea could blot out the dreadful certainty that both Collie and Rhys were dead, hacked to pieces on the square in front of Tamerlane's huge mausoleum. Tears lay choked within her, unable to flow since she needed all her strength to face her own predicament. Without her friends, what hope was there that she would be rescued from a life of eternal imprisonment within this golden cage, the wife of a man she found horribly repulsive. No, she would die by her own hand first. That would be her last hope. Between that end and her present isolation lay only one possibility—Col. Hughes. *If* she could get to him, *If* he could somehow persuade the emir against this marriage, *If* he could help her to escape. So many *Ifs!*

Her servants dressed her in the usual jewels and

finery, taking, it seemed, more care than necessary. She understood the reason why when, a little later, she was summoned by the guard along the empty halls toward the public rooms. They left her inside a small antechamber, alone and anxious, hoping only that perhaps Col. Hughes would join her as he had once before.

Her heart sank as a curtain on the far wall was pulled aside and Ulugh Khan walked into the room. One manservant shuffled behind him carrying a large ornate enameled box, which the emir motioned him to set on a low table. The servant then backed out of the room. It was the first time Justine had ever been alone with the prince of Bokharta, and her anxiety rose accordingly. She looked frantically around, noting the guard with his back to the door. Unlike so many rooms in the palace, this one did not open onto the gardens. She was enclosed in a tiny space with no exit, trapped with this fat man with the blubbery lips whose eyes deprived her of every stitch. She had a flashing mental image of a delicate bird caught in the jaws of a great predator.

"I am not accustomed to having women stare at me so boldly," Ulugh Khan said in careful English. "It is also customary for them to be on their knees in my presence."

"I wish to return to my rooms," Justine said as haughtily as she could make it sound.

He went on as though she hadn't spoken. "My wives grovel before me. They would not dare to address me to my face, certainly not so openly. I find it . . . refreshing, up to a point."

"In my country only slaves grovel," Justine answered, her eyes flashing.

"Ah, but my wives ARE my slaves."

"I demand to be released. This is intolerable. I'm little better than a prisoner here."

322

Ulugh Khan's eyes narrowed dangerously. "I do not think prisoners in your country are dressed in silk and adorned with jewels. Nor are gaols so beautiful as my palace."

"Nevertheless, I am not free. I want to go home to America. You cannot keep me here—it is against every principle of international law."

The emir gave a low humorless chuckle. "America is too far away for international law to matter overmuch in Bokharta. Yes, I think it would be refreshing to have a Caucasian wife. It would give me stature among my fellow rulers."

Justine's jaw dropped. "You can't be serious!"

He lifted a corner of her drapery off her arm, fingering it lightly. Though she shrank from his touch, there was a magnetism born of fear that prevented her from tearing her arm away. "You will come to like it here in time. I can be most generous when I am pleased."

"This is absurd. I am an English citizen. I will not be treated this way!"

With a sudden motion he reached to grip her arm, squeezing the flesh painfully. Bending into her face, his tiny, slanting eyes grew hard as agate. The thick lips, framed with the trailing greased mustachios, no longer smiled. A terrible fear swept over Justine. "Foolish woman, hush your tongue. You will do exactly what I wish, or your head will be severed from your beautiful body and fed to the birds."

As swiftly as it had come, his mood altered back to the supercilious friendliness of the moment before. His fingers relaxed and stroked her flesh as easily as a feather. Though her knees trembled, Justine fought to appear unaffected by his sudden threats and the evil mask of a face so near her own.

"Surely you realize I only came to this country in hopes of taking the money sent by Prince Tai back to my government. I am your guest. I believed the emir to be conscious of the rules of hospitality."

Ulugh laughed and turned away. "There is no treasure. I have told all you English that. There never was. It was only a foolish story. But it was not entirely useless, since it brought you here. Allah may be thanked for that."

"I don't believe you. My government believes in it. That is why Col. Hughes followed me here."

"Col. Hughes is nothing but a pawn in this game. I find it useful for the moment to keep him here. You English are very busy in the Mogul provinces, and until I know what you are about, it pleases me to have the colonel around. In due time he will have served his purpose and will be disposed of. Do not expect him to help you. He is not as clever as he appears, the colonel."

Justine turned away from the emir who was fussing with the enameled box, her mind working furiously. Should she appear to go along with his horrible plans for her, in order to seek a means of escape? She had a feeling he would see right through such a ploy, her revulsion was so great. Her anger and defiance seemed only to amuse him all the more. And it was all too true that there were no people of her own who might help her. It might be years before any other Englishmen worked their way across this country. What chance would she have—imprisoned in a harem—to even reach them if they did come to Bokharta. All the stories she had heard of life in such a place came roaring back. Never allowed to step outside, surrounded by eunuchs and women all the rest of her life, not even permitted to speak to or be seen by any other man other than this gross tyrant until she withered and died an old woman! No, she would kill herself before accepting such a fate.

She heard him step up behind her and turned swiftly to face him. He loomed over her, reaching out to grasp her throat in his hands. Stifling a scream, she backed against the wall.

"There," Ulugh Khan said with satisfaction. "Yes, it suits you perfectly. Its beauty is enhanced by yours."

All her breath went out in relief, as she realized he had draped a chain around her neck. Looking down, she saw dangling at the end of it the most enormous black pearl she had ever seen, like a huge teardrop. It was of a translucent ebony that gleamed with the light, like the waters of a dark pool.

"I don't want this," she muttered.

"You would refuse my gift? It is very valuable. I think you shall keep it nevertheless. You must wear it for the wedding."

"How many times must I tell you, there isn't going to be any wedding!" she spluttered, pulling at the chain that seemed welded to her throat.

"Perhaps you have visions of escaping again, as you tried to do once before. It cost your friends their lives, and a second attempt will cost you yours. There is no escape. I know everything and I am always ready. Perhaps you would prefer that I give you to my soldiers for *their* use. Those women grow old very quickly. Your beauty would not survive long. It would be a shame, I think."

Justine gripped the wall, all hope fading. "You wouldn't?"

"Who is to stop me? I do what I wish with my own people. Though your defiance is amusing, even now I grow weary of it. You shall have time to yourself to think

325

on these things we have discussed. Then we shall talk
again."

Justine, for the first time, looked at the emir, and
really saw him. He was barbaric, cruel, a figure out of a
nightmare. But he was not merely the ridiculous fool she
had thought him up until now. The sensuousness was
gross, but not without intelligence. There was power
under the surface and cruelty, ready to crush what did
not please him. He was as lethal as a wild boar and just
as crafty. She felt absolutely helpless to defend herself
without Rhys and Collie to help her.

She had a sudden realization of the pearl, cold against
her skin like a knife thrusting its point into her breast.
Ulugh waved a hand, and the guard stepped into the
room, taking Justine's elbow none too gently.

"We shall talk again," the emir said, and moved behind the curtain with a swiftness unexpected in a man of
his bulk. Fighting back her tears, Justine followed the
soldier back to her room and threw herself on the divan,
more despondent than she had ever been in her life.

The serving girl had just left after depositing her tray
of stewed mutton and flat bread—the same meal she had
brought for days now. Rhys tried to keep count, but it
was difficult since they all seemed so much the same,
each one flowing into another without interruption. He
felt suspended in time, not knowing where he was or why.
Even the vivid face of the Chinese princess was beginning
to seem more like a dream than reality. Perhaps he *had*
dreamed it, a strong image dredged up out of his longing
to find a powerful ally. And yet, it was true that he was
alive, he was here in this small but pleasant room,
servants came several times a day bringing him food and

drink and seeing to his comfort. There had to be some kind of intelligence behind all this, and it did not appear to be a malevolent one.

Now that he was feeling stronger, he was also more bored. There was an element of being in gaol in being confined to this tiny room, no matter how pleasant.

Princess Tsingsia had not visited him since that shadowy night when he woke in her beautiful rooms. He had seen no one but servants, since fainting dead away that night, and it was getting more and more difficult to believe there was some reason to his confinement. Once or twice he had tried to leave the room, only to find his way blocked by armed men, obviously Chinese and in the pay of the princess. They did not harm him, but they made it very obvious that they would if he persisted in leaving the room. And so he waited.

A sudden glaring light brought him up out of a lethargic doze. Rubbing at his eyes, he fought to recall where he was, and remembered having gone to bed hours before. Surely it was not morning yet.

"I'm so sorry to disturb you, Capt. Llewellyn," said a cool voice. Rhys's vision cleared, and he saw the beautiful white face of Princess Tsingsia bending over him. A sense of *déjà vu* brought him sitting up on the divan.

"Is this another dream?" he muttered.

She gave a musical laugh and stood upright, a dazzling vision of gold and blue shimmering in the light of the lamp held by her servants. "It is unfortunate that our only opportunity to talk must be in the middle of the night, but you can understand that your presence here must be kept secret."

Rhys sat on the edge of the bed and tried not to let his annoyance show. "You have certainly kept your distance. I was beginning to think I dreamed our first meeting."

"I was not able to come to you before tonight," the princess said coolly. "You did not want for anything, I trust."

"Nothing. Your hospitality has been most gracious. It was only my wits that were left dangling."

"That could not be helped. However, soon your enforced detainment will be at an end, I assure you. I had to await the most propitious moment, as I'm sure you can understand. Failure is not something I will tolerate, not even to satisfy your curiosity or impatience."

Rhys nodded at her reprimand. "I understand," he said. She had all the cards, and he had better accept that if he wanted her help. No more annoying little digs.

With a motion of her hand, the princess had her servants produce an exquisite silk-covered stool. She took her place upon it with an almost motionless effort and watched Rhys, a little smile still hovering on her brilliant red lips. "Exactly why are you here in Bokharta, Captain?"

Rhys studied her inscrutable face a moment, wondering what the best reply would be. She was likely to see through any lie he might invent so he decided on the truth.

"I was sent here by the United States of America, to bring back a large sum of money your father has promised to my government. In Baghdad I was told that the emir of Bokharta was holding that money in trust for me. That is why I came to Samarkand."

The princess nodded. "You have done well to speak the truth, Captain. I rather expected some farfetched tale. It would have warned me not to trust you. And yet, these United States as you call them—is it not true that they are actually rebellious colonies of Great Britain? Their little independence hangs on a delicate balance right now, as I understand."

"I am amazed, Princess, that you should know or even care about my little country, so far away from this section of the globe."

"We are not all barbarians in this part of the world, Captain."

This princess certainly was not. She was the most sophisticated person he had met since leaving Philadelphia. And yet, there was in her a self-contained iciness that he would not wish to explore. "It is true that my country is fighting for its very life right now, Princess. But independence will come, if not now, certainly in the future. Britain is too far away and too selfishly stupid about her colonies to contain them. Also, we have great men of character guiding our destiny. Our country is rich in natural resources, and its people have a stubborn determination to be free. Your father's loan will make a great difference to us, but with or without it, we shall gain our liberty."

"You speak eloquently, Captain. My father knows something of what you have said. He feels that trade with America will benefit China as well as your country. He also fears and resents the attempts by Great Britain to monopolize commerce between China and the West. That is why he offered this loan to your countrymen."

Rhys shrugged. "It has all been rather useless, hasn't it? There is no money. The emir told me that it was captured en route here and stolen by bandits. Of course, I'm not certain I believe him. From what I've seen of Ulugh Khan, he might well have taken it for himself and made up that tale of bandits to throw us off."

Tsingsia folded her long talons, silvered today, in her

lap. "That is quite true. Ulugh Khan hoped from the first to get his greedy hands on that treasure. He cares nothing for your country's concern or any wider trade beyond Mogul India."

"He is your husband. Why do you call him greedy and work behind his back?"

"How little you know of women, Captain. There is only one consolation for a wife of the emir—to be the power behind the throne. I intend to be that power. Ulugh Khan is much struck by my beauty, but he distrusts my intelligence. I must prove to him that my wits serve his ends."

"And Zenobia . . ."

The red lips turned downward for an instant in contempt. "Queen Zenobia has passed her days of glory. She is not wise, that woman. She thought that by giving your cousin a valuable ring that was once a gift from Ulugh Khan, she could convince him of her sympathy. In fact, she sees your cousin as the rival she is, and hates her for it. She would do your cousin great harm, but that she fears the wrath of Ulugh Khan."

Rhys—helpless to defend her—had a momentary pang for Justine's life. What was she enduring now?

As though she had read his thoughts, Tsingsia said: "Of course your cousin is not quite so clever either. It was she who told Col. Hughes of Timurid's clumsy attempt to help you escape. He went straight to the emir with the plan, and you saw what happened. Had I not sent my soldiers, your head would now adorn the gates of the palace alongside Timurid's."

Rhys stared at the princess. "Justine told Hughes of our escape! She couldn't have been so stupid. I don't believe it."

"You have allowed your feelings for her to cloud your

330

judgement. I assure you, I do not make such statements lightly. Why should she not trust Col. Hughes? He is a compatriot of hers. They are both after the same thing, my father's treasure."

Rhys turned away from the princess's knowing eyes, trying to sort out his feelings. Of course, he had suspected it all along and never wanted to face the truth. What other reason would Justine have for coming all this way to this strange part of the world? Her story of traveling had never rung true. She must have seen Collie in Baghdad after he did, and accepted his offer to accompany her. And Collie. Surely he wasn't traveling this backward way back to England for nothing. He also wanted to get his hands on that money.

Tsingsia's cool voice went on ruthlessly. "The emir's arm has a long reach. He learned that your cousin's father was entrusted to make this journey, in order to prevent this loan from being given to you. He sent an assassin to dispatch the man, never realizing his daughter would take on the assignment. I do now know quite how the colonel fits into the plan, but I suspect that when he learned of the death, he must have followed."

"How do you know all this?"

Tsingsia shrugged. "My arm, too, has a long reach. It is assisted by my father's position in Tsinghai. The emir plans to marry your cousin, you know, and make her another of his wives. He is intrigued with the thought of a red-haired Caucasian beauty in his bed. While I do not fear your cousin, since her capacity for intrigue does not seem threatening, yet to have a favored wife even for a short time does not suit my plans. That is why I intend to help you."

So that was it. He knew there would be some selfish reason behind the princess's attempt to save him. "I am most grateful," he muttered, hoping he sounded sincere. His feelings toward Tsingsia seemed to undergo a metamorphosis every few minutes—admiration for her great beauty and intelligence, respect for her knowledge of the situation, horror at the cruelty and great ego behind that cool, flower-delicate exterior, even fear of making a wrong step that might send her off on some other tangent which would better serve her interests.

"What will the emir think if his intended bride is spirited away?"

The princess laughed. "I can handle the emir. I shall convince him that her escape was necessary to his interests. Ulugh Khan is not without intelligence, but his wits are not sharp. Now, come close, Captain, and listen very carefully."

Lifting her hand, Tsingsia sent the servants gliding silently from the room. Rhys shifted to the floor and moved to sit at her feet, wondering *what now!*

Her voice was low and cool, her beautiful face as impassive as a dance mask. She might have been recounting the latest recipe for mutton stew.

"It is true that my father, Prince Tai, sent a loan of money across the Celestial Mountains for safekeeping into Samarkand. However, it was to me that it ought to have come. The emir, hearing of it, reasoned that since I was his wife, the money belonged to him.

"The treasure was entrusted for safeguarding to my Uncle Chai Wang, a faithful and valuable relative of my family. Its journey was supposed to be a great secret, but treachery and greed are everywhere apparent. Not only the emir knew of its passage, but others, not so easily handled, also learned of it. Bandits in the Tien Shan attacked the small caravan, killing the guards and the ambassadors who were traveling with the train. My uncle

Chai Wang managed to escape with the treasure. Before he died, he hid it well, then sent word to me in a coded message of its place."

Rhys's hopes revived to sudden life. Hiding his excitement under a mask as inscrutable as Tsingsia's, he asked quietly: "How did your uncle manage to carry away such a large chest?"

She leaned closer. "There were chests in the caravan, but they were mere decoys. The actual treasure consists of a small urn, a soldier's war canteen which once belonged to the great Timur the Lame. It is formed of pure gold, and is completely encrusted with precious stones—a rare and beautiful piece. In addition to its value, my father filled it with gold pieces. The bandits, of course, fell on the chests, never suspecting that the injured man who managed to slip away might have secreted the treasure under his robes."

Rhys could barely suppress his pleasure at hearing this news. His trip was not in vain after all! In spite of all the obstacles and delays, he might still manage to salvage his country's effort to win independence. "And you know where it is hidden?"

"I know only what my uncle wrote me—that the treasure lies near the Waters of Heaven, where 'wind and rain are gathered in and earth and sky meet.' That last part is taken from an ancient Chinese text regarding the harmony and center of the universe. However, in this instance, I feel my uncle meant it to have a more specific meaning."

"But you're not sure what it is?"

"No. That is for you to discover. I can tell you this much. There is a large fall of water, south of the Muzart Pass, which is sometimes referred to as the Celestial Falls. I believe the treasure to be hidden near it. It will be up to you to find the meaning for the rest of the message. It means nothing to me."

Be careful, Rhys thought, as he stared up into her white face. She has admitted that she wants power. Who knows what is behind these confidences? What might be her ultimate plan for Justine and himself? This was a weighty secret indeed for her to entrust to him, and he could not quite make out her motive.

"Princess, you have saved my life, and now you give me this information which any number of men around me would kill to obtain. I am profoundly grateful to you . . ."

One long silver talon reached out and gently raked his shoulder. "But you wonder why I should do this."

"As a matter of fact, yes. Could you not earn the emir's everlasting gratitude by giving him this information? You might well become the power behind the throne at once, without having to play these devious games."

"And how much should I ever see of this wealth once Ulugh Khan got his hands on it? One does not build power from the ground up with one small generous act. My enemies would convince him that I was trying to keep it for myself and was forced to admit where it was. No, it suits my plans better to have the treasure far away from this country. Just as it is better for me to have your cousin far away, unable to influence events in Bokharta."

Somehow he could not see Justine influencing anyone in this country, certainly not Ulugh Khan whom she could barely force herself to look upon. Better not to tell Tsingsai this, however. Let her think Justine would be a great rival. It increased their chances of receiving her help.

He had a moment's anger when he remembered that it

334

was Justine who brought about the ruin of their first attempt at escape. It would serve her right if he did leave her to deal with this dangerous woman and the repulsive emir. She deserved life in a harem!

Remembering her lovely face—so open and honest, so English—in comparison to the strange, inscrutable princess whose mind always seemed to be leaping behind her impassive face, he shook off his anger with Justine. That rounded, soft body that had brought his own to the brink of ecstasy so often, those sculptured lips, so ready to meld with his own, her joyous laughter, her courage in sailing halfway around the world to carry out what she thought was a righteous mission—there was no escaping the fact. He loved her and wanted her, and would no more leave here without her than he would discard his soul.

"I shall not come to you again," he heard Tsingsai saying and shook off his reverie.

"Then how—"

"All will be well. At the proper time, my soldiers will lead you and your friends out of the city and set you on your way. Follow their directions without fail. This is very important. If you do not and are captured, I will not lift a finger to help you. Please be sure of this."

"I understand, Princess." He would have to trust her. What other choice did he have?

Tsingsai rose from her stool, drawing in a swarm of servants in motion around her. At the door she paused and looked back. "However, I do not think it necessary any longer that you wait in solitude for that moment. My servant, Mei Lai, will conduct you to your friend. Farewell, Captain."

Rhys gave the princess his best bow as she disappeared. His heart was pounding a little too hard at the thought that she must have meant Justine. Was he to see her at last, hold her in his arms again? Share the long frustrating wait with her until they could leave together? It would be a great consolation!

The young serving girl waited by the door until he noticed that she wanted him to follow her. Rhys stepped into a long hall, this time with no soldiers in sight, and moved cautiously after the servant who glided with mincing little steps down the corridor. There were no windows and no doors, just a long dark tunnel with a dim light at the end. Hardly knowing what to expect, Rhys moved silently behind the girl until she stopped by an open door. From inside he could hear the soft giggling laughter of women, while fragrant spices and the delicious scent of roast meats wafted into the hall. He stepped inside, allowing his eyes to become accustomed to the glaring light as Mei Lai pulled a curtain back across the opening and disappeared behind it.

Across the room he saw a huge pile of cushions arranged haphazardly on a bed. Three young girls lounged among them, giggling and laughing as they played with a large swatch of silk cloth. Incense clouded the room from brass braziers, and trays laden with fruit and meats sat on either side alongside silver jugs and an elaborate water pipe. The girls grew silent as they noticed him, and moved away from the center of the bed where the blue silk undulated and rolled. Then it was thrown back and a figure emerged from beneath. Long straggly hair dangled from beneath a turban askew on the head. A short dark beard covered the narrow chin, while the eyes, staring back at Rhys, grew wide with surprise and embarrassment.

Rhys sucked in his breath.

Collie!

Fourteen

"I don't believe it!"

Collie's lips slid into the familiar lopsided smile. More than ever before he looked like the cat caught in the cream jar. "I knew ye'd show up eventually to spoil my fun. Come, my lovelies. Scoot now. I'll see ye all later."

Pushing the girls off the bed, Collie crawled out from under the covers, wrapping the silk coverlet around his thin frame. Recovering from his shock, Rhys walked over and pulled up one of the hassocks.

"By all that's holy, you ought to be dead," he said.

"You sound disappointed."

"Of course not. But how on earth did you survive those scimitars? The last I saw of you, you were buried beneath them."

"You can thank the princess that I'm still around. That and the fact that they struck me with the flat of the blade instead of the cutting edge. I was more than a little surprised myself, when I realized they intended no more than to beat me insensible. Which they did, by the way. I've still got the bruises to show for it."

337

"But why . . ."

"It was all an act, don't ye see. We stumbled into the guards loyal to the princess, and they made sure it looked like they were doing away with us, when actually all they wanted was to get us hidden here. We were very fortunate, my friend."

"Then why not bring Justine here, too?"

Collie scratched underneath his blue silk turban. "I suppose it was because the princess did not want the emir to be completely disappointed. As long as he had her, he might not look too closely into what happened t'us. I don't know how it's been for you, but personally I'll take this kind of imprisonment any day."

"Yes, you appear to be enjoying yourself. I've been bored to death. No nubile young fillies for me, although it's just as well. I was too worried over Justine and the end of our hopes to be able to appreciate them."

"I worried, too," Collie said, reaching to pluck a stem of fat grapes from the tray beside the divan. "I just didn't allow it to interfere with me pleasure. One doesn't get a chance like this too often."

"Be serious, Collie," Rhys snapped. "Tsingsia tells me we're to be allowed to escape. Can you travel, or do you require more 'recuperation'?"

"I'm all but healed. And pleasant as it is here, I do not think much more time spent in Bokharta is going to be good for our health, not for any of us. What about Justine?"

"She's coming, too, I'm told. If she isn't married to Ulugh Khan before the princess decides it is expedient for us to leave. It's all so fantastic. I wonder if that Chinese princess can be trusted."

"Don't ye underestimate Tsingsia. From what I've been able to learn, she sits like a gigantic spider at the

338

center of this place, spinning her webs of intrigue. We can thank our stars that it suited her to keep us alive. Otherwise we'd all be under the sod by now."

Collie pushed the tray toward Rhys, who turned away from it, still too preoccupied to enjoy the comforts of the room. "Did you know it was Justine who ruined our escape?" Rhys said with an edge of bitterness in his voice. "She told Col. Hughes about it and, of course, he went straight to the emir. Half the time I want to wring her neck for it, but the other half, I cringe to think where she is now and what she must be feeling."

"She probably believes we're both dead."

"Let her think it. At least until it's actually time to go. I don't want Col. Hughes ruining things again. The colonel is playing a peculiar game. He's after the treasure, of course, but why he thinks Ulugh Khan will help him to get it is beyond me. Of course, he'd like to eliminate us as rivals."

"With any luck, he may possibly eliminate himself. Ulugh Khan is an unlikely ally."

Too restless to sit, Rhys jumped up and prowled the room. No windows and no door other than the one that he had entered earlier. He lifted the curtain that covered it and peeked into the corridor. The guards had returned, standing watch a short way down the hall. No doors appeared to open off the corridor, except the one far down where he had been. The room they occupied also served as the end of the hall.

"I think we're under the palace," he whispered to Collie. "This place appears to be part of an underground complex. Feel how damp it is. And there's no light but the lamps. There's no way out but the hall where the guards are."

Collie sprawled back on the bed. "Tsingsia's guards,

I hope."

"For God's sake, Collie! How can you be so . . . so cavalier about all this? We're prisoners here, at the mercy of a Chinese dragon who could change her mind and snuff us out in the blinking of an eye. We've got to do something."

"And what do ye suggest, my Captain?" Collie replied sarcastically. "The truth is there's nothing we can do but wait and hope that the princess will abide by her word. Meanwhile, why not enjoy what the place has to offer?"

"You enjoy," Rhys snapped, pacing the room. "I'm going to find a way out of here, just to keep from going crazy!"

The time that had seemed to drag so slowly for Rhys, seemed to Justine to speed with increasing momentum, propelled by her fear and worry over what lay ahead. Even her solitude increased her concern. She saw no one but her ladies, and could not talk to them because they could not understand her language. As day rolled into day, she grew increasingly depressed and fearful. Even the grief she felt over losing Rhys and Collie only served to accentuate how alone she was. She had no help now and must depend only on her own wits, which at times she felt she was in danger of losing. That the emir did not come to see her was the only consolation of her long days.

She knew the proposed wedding must be drawing nearer by the way her women giggled and gestured, more silly every day. Each morning there was a parade of fabrics the like of which she had never seen—silks, damasks, embroidered satins, gauzy scarfs where the colors blended like a rainbow into one another, cloth of gold, silver lamé. If Ulugh Khan thought she was to be wooed by such finery, he was mistaken. She pushed them all away with an icy disinterest. In the afternoon came the goldsmiths with ropes of pearls and bracelets, earrings and necklaces of gold and silver shimmering with precious stones. These, too, she sent away, unimpressed. Her only obsession was how to find a way out, or, failing that, what best means she might use for killing herself during or before the marriage. Even that was not going to be easy, for she had not been able to secrete so much as a fruit knife without her women knowing.

One morning her dull routine was broken when she had a visitor. Col. Hughes walked into her apartment, bowing over her hand as nonchalantly as though they had met the day before.

"You look pale, my dear," he said, lifting his long face from her fingers. "You should get out more."

"Where have you been?" she snapped. "Why haven't you come to see me before? If you only knew how worried and frightened I've been . . ."

Hughes lowered his voice. "It wasn't safe to come before now. I was not certain that your efforts to escape might not have a disastrous effect upon me as well. Fortunately, I still enjoy the trust of the emir. I meant what I said about getting out. How would you like to go riding?"

Justine's heart gave a leap. "Are you serious? I'm never allowed to leave this room."

"I have convinced Ulugh Khan that confinement is not conducive to good health or beauty. He has graciously allowed me to ride out with you, if you wish it."

341

Justine was already halfway across the room, discarding her flimsy harem scarfs. "Just try to get away without me!"

She could not believe how sweet it was to be in the fresh air with a beautiful gray Arabian filly underneath her. Though the ever-present soldiers followed at a distance, and Hughes's two repulsive henchmen were not two lengths behind, still the sun on her face and the brisk canter of her superb mount more than made up for their watchful presence. They made their way through the city streets and beneath the gates into the gardens on the other side. Men were working in the fields, urging their plow oxen, working the waterwheels, carrying bales, and heaping grain onto flat wagons. The sight of such ordinary people doing such ordinary things had never seemed so beautiful to Justine. They were almost enough to make her forget the strange and dangerous turns her life had taken.

They did not ride far enough to suit her. Hughes turned their mounts around before they even reached the outer gates, taking a different road back into the city. He had been very quiet during most of their ride, but Justine had been too happy to be back out in the world again to notice. Now, all at once, her attention was drawn to the man riding alongside her. He looked around at the fields and the people with none of her enthusiasm. In fact, there was more than a little contempt in the way he stared down his long nose at the peasants working the fields and canals on either side of the road.

"You don't like these people," Justine said, more of a statement than a question.

"They are peasants. Good for this kind of backbreaking work, but little else."

"Perhaps you prefer the emir? That gross tyrant who cares for nothing except his own pleasure."

"No. He is not much to be admired either."

Justine gave a bitter laugh. "Is there anyone you do admire, Colonel?"

Hughes shrugged imperceptibly. "I do not see much that is admirable among the ruling factions of the world. To the north of us sits Queen Catherine of Russia, a monstrous woman with a capacity for cruelty and egocentricity unparalleled among your sex. The king of France is an idiot who cares for little beyond his own aggrandizement, and is henpecked by his wife to boot. Even our own King George would be better suited to running a farm than a great empire."

Justine gasped. "That is treason!"

"Perhaps, and certainly I would not speak my mind so openly were we not in this backwater of the world. But the truth is, a better king would have solved this problem with the Colonies long ago. A firm hand in the beginning would have prevented a deal of mischief. Riffraff must be severely and swiftly dealt with, if one wishes to have stability in government."

Justine bristled with resentment. "Surely you do not consider all Americans riffraff? I admit there are some troublemakers, but most of the men who are committed to this rebellion are both honorable and sincere."

Hughes laughed. "A typical woman's view."

"It happens to be true. And truth contributes more to stability in government in the long run than arrogance and pride." She was amazed at her own words. And yet she realized as she never had before, that Col. Hughes represented all the wrong thinking that had brought the Colonies to openly defy their mother country. Why had

343

she ever thought she could depend on this man for anything!

"Besides," she went on, "you look with disdain on these poor peasants, but you tolerate those two ruffians behind us as companions. It makes little sense to me."

One eyebrow on Hughes's aristocratic face inched upwards. Only a twinge in his narrow cheek revealed how furious he was at her comments. "Those men are my bodyguards," he snapped. "And better-suited to the role, I might add, than your late captain and his Arab servant."

An ugly feeling was beginning to grow between them. Justine ignored the instinct that warned her to tread carefully and went on. "They are horrible. It would not surprise me to learn that they were the ones who told the emir of our plan to escape. His soldiers were waiting for us the moment we stepped outside the palace. Someone had told him."

"Very discerning of you, my dear, but you do them an injustice. I was the one who told the emir of your plans."

He took some satisfaction at the shock on her face.

"You! But why? You might have gone with us."

"To a certain death? Timurid was a fool. Ulugh Khan had been watching him for months, waiting for the opportunity to pounce. He could not have been given a better one."

"You traitor!" Justine exclaimed. "I trusted you, and you betrayed me and caused the death of my friends."

"May I remind you that your friend the captain was in Bokharta only to get his hands on the money the emir was holding. Once he had it, he would have returned it to finance a rebellion that is ruinous to our country. And yet you call *me* traitor!"

"There is no treasure. The emir told Rhys so himself."

"I do not believe the emir. You have allowed your feelings for the rebel captain to cloud your judgment and your patriotism."

Sensing her mounting anger, Justine's little mount began to dance nervously. She concentrated on the reins, trying to steady her horse and, at the same time, gain control of her seething emotions. There was too much truth in the colonel's scathing comments for her to shake them off. Her love for Rhys and her grief at his death had almost completely diminished any fire she had once felt for supporting the Loyalists of her country. Hughes, with his arrogance and pride, represented the worst of that condescending attitude she had often encountered in Englishmen toward Americans. And America was her country, she saw with a new clarity. Not England.

"You are despicable," she muttered. "I want nothing to do with you."

In a sudden motion Hughes reached out and grabbed her arm, his fingers digging into her flesh forcefully enough to bruise it. "You had better learn to depend on me," he said through tight lips. "This is not a kind part of the world, Justine. Look up there, then tell me where safety lies."

Justine tried to pull her arm away, but he held it fast. Almost against her will, her eyes were drawn upward toward the gate that towered over them. Impaled on a sharp prong, Timirud's sightless eyes stared back at her. There was enough left of the minister's head to recognize, though the birds had pecked at it for days. Justine gasped and fought against giving way as her stomach turned over. Beneath the gate men and women, soldiers and civilians, horses and cattle went milling

345

about, entering and leaving the city, oblivious to the obscenity above their heads.

"You have no one but me to turn to now that your friends are dead," Hughes went on relentlessly. "It would be wiser to curb your sharp tongue."

Justine smoothed her mount's sleek neck, fighting to regain control of her anger. She no longer felt she could trust the colonel to protect her, and yet there was no one else. How was she going to escape being buried in a Mongol harem unless he helped her? She glanced back at the other two Englishmen who sat their horses, waiting dumbly for the colonel to move on. The smaller one examined the roadside, his crafty little eyes darting among the people moving about, as though seeking some way to take from them the little they possessed. The big man was even less hopeful. He sat watching her, his blubbery lips near to drooling, his dim eyes focused on her breasts. He was so huge he almost dwarfed his little horse, and his muscles bulged beneath the short sleeves of his tunic. He looked as though he could break her in half with a flick of his wrist.

"I want to go back," Justine said quietly.

"Of course." Hughes motioned her to move ahead through the gate, then followed, smiling with satisfaction. Silently she rode through the streets and back inside the palace. Without a word she dismounted and made her way back to her rooms, where she threw herself down on the divan, fighting back her tears. Though her solitude was oppresive, for the first time she realized she would rather have her own company than that of anyone else in the palace. It was a small comfort, yet she still found that she could not hold back the tears that washed the sorrow from her heart. She cried with a hopelessness so terrible, it caused her chest to ache. Folding her arms under her, she sobbed into her sleeves, hoping to soften the sound of her crying. She did not hear the quiet steps of her women, and only knew they were there when she felt a gentle hand on her arm.

"Not cry," a young girl said, her eyes full of compassion. She was one of the more quiet of the serving girls, a pretty young thing barely more than fifteen. Justine had hardly noticed her before, except to regard the serious way she went about her duties. She sat up, wiping at her eyes.

"You speak English?" It was the first time any of the women had said a word in her language. The girl shrugged.

"Little," she answered quietly. "Please not cry." The affection in the way the girl looked at Justine awakened for the first time a sense that the serving women around her might actually feel something for her. She had taken it for granted that they were forced into her service and disliked her for it.

"You don't understand," Justine answered bitterly. "I hate this place. I don't want to marry the emir. And there is no one to help me."

The young girl regarded her seriously, painstakingly working out the sense of her words. "Queen Zenobia?" she said brightly.

"Zenobia hates me. She would kill me, if she dared."

The girl slowly nodded her head. "That is true," she replied in careful English. "Too bad you not see Princess Tsingsia."

"Princess who? Who is she?"

The young girl spoke haltingly and very softly.

"She Ulugh Khan's Chinese wife. Very strong,

347

Princess Tsingsia. She help."

"Another wife! No, she would hate me, too. There is no hope for me," Jess said, her eyes filling again. "I'll be entombed here in this wild, crazy place with no hope of getting home ever again! I could die when I think of it!"

The girl knelt in front of Justine. "Very pretty lady, I serve you well. Make you nice bath now. Feel better."

Justine smiled down at the girl's sweet face. So young, so eager to be of help and comfort. Perhaps she would not be completely friendless in this horrible palace after all. "What is your name?"

"Zada, madam."

Justine tipped up the girl's chin. "You are very young, Zada. Very well. I will allow you to make my bath and pamper me until I feel better. It will be small comfort, but something is better than nothing."

Zada touched her head to the floor in submission, then rose on her knees to smile up at Justine. "All will be well, madam. You see."

During the following days the preparations for Justine's wedding began to leap ahead at a frantic pace. She could barely wait to get Zada alone, to ask her if she knew when the ceremony was to take place. Her heart sank when the girl confided that it was only two days away.

"What am I going to do?" Justine wailed. She even briefly considered approaching Col. Hughes, but quickly ruled that out. She could never trust him again.

Her frantic concern and worry took its toll, and although she found it hard to get to sleep, once she dropped off, she slept as one drugged. It was in one of the early hours of the day before the ceremony was to take place that she felt a gentle shake on her arm that gradually brought her up out of blessed oblivion.

"What's the matter?" she murmured, shielding her eyes from the piercing glare of a small lamp that was pushed into her face. Behind it she made out Zada's grim features.

"Come, madam," the girl whispered. "Come now."

Justine looked around anxiously, wondering if she was being lured into another ambush. There were no soldiers that she could see. There was no one but Zada and her lamp. "I don't understand . . ."

Zada put a finger to her lips. "Please to come with me," she whispered again, with an urgency in her voice Justine had not heard before. "And hurry."

There was nothing to do but trust her. Justine slipped from the bed and took the clothes Zada handed her. Even in the dim light of the lamp, she could tell they were not her usual attire. The fabric was coarse and rough, and the several skirts and thick tunics were more the clothes of a peasant than a bride. Justine's heart gave a little leap of hope.

"Why?" she whispered.

"No talk," the girl whispered back. Justine hesitated only a second before pulling on the clothes. Whatever all this meant, it promised more than anything else that had happened to her over the past weeks.

Once Justine was dressed, Zada extinguished the lamp and took her hand, leading her out into the passage. The torches that burned at intervals on the walls lit their way and warned them of an occasional guard, several of whom were sleeping soundly in the corridors. Darting from shadow to shadow, hardly daring to breathe, Justine

349

followed the girl, having no idea where she was or where they were headed. They soon left the familiar passages alongside the gardens and moved quietly down several short flights of stairs to an underground section Justine had not even known was there. The halls were narrow and cramped, and there was a dampness that suggested they were below the canals. Justine fought not to let her imagination run riot, and stir up hopes that might not be realized. For all she knew, she might well be on her way to an encounter with another minister or wife. But oh, she hoped not!

They heard the tramp of soldiers' boots before they saw them ahead. Zada pulled Justine back into a darkened alcove, and they both pressed against the stone, holding their breaths for fear of being detected. The soldiers passed close enough to leave a strong odor of horses and leather in the air, but they moved on without incident. Justine let her breath out slowly.

"We go now," Zada whispered, and grabbed Justine's hand to dart down the hall away from the soldiers. It was a dark corridor with a dim light at the end, drawing them like a beacon. Zada stopped in the shadows, looking back. "You go up," she whispered to Justine and pushed her ahead. Jess saw that the light came from a tiny lamp in the wall, giving a faint glimmer to a flight of stone steps that led upward into darkness. Justine hesitated, realizing that Zada was leaving her to go up the stairs alone. She looked a question at the girl.

"Go, madam," Zada smiled. The light glistened on her dark eyes. "Go and good fortune."

"But . . ."

The girl was gone, swallowed in the darkness, before Justine could stop her. Just as well, Justine thought, since she did not yet know what lay at the top of those stairs. And yet, if it really was freedom, she would have liked to express her gratitude.

Cautiously she inched her way up the stairs, feeling for any unexpected barriers. The cool air on her face told her she was coming up outside, perhaps in the gardens. As she reached the top however, the pungent odors of the canal gave rise to hopes that she was outside the palace. Inching her way along the wall, she peered around the opening. Certainly this was a street outside the palace. She recognized the murky outline of houses, and the torches set in the walls far down the street. Their fluttering light was blocked by a group of dark shadows. With a start Justine realized there were men standing against the wall, swathed in cloaks and hoods. She froze, her heart in her throat. Were they soldiers waiting for her? Was she meant to walk out into their trap? Were more men waiting behind her, hoping she would try to find her way back and run into their hostile arms?

"Justine!"

She gasped as she recognized that whisper. One of the shadows moved toward her, reaching down the steps to gather her in its arms. She pulled back, trying to scream, but a hand was placed over her mouth.

"For God's sake, don't call out!" Rhys said, drawing her close into his embrace. He had to support her as her knees gave way. Still in shock, she clung to him, not believing what her senses told her.

"Is it really you?" she finally gasped against his chest.

"Yes, it's me right enough." His fingers laced her thick hair, his lips caressed her cheek. "Oh, my dear, are you all right?"

"I thought you were dead . . ." she cried as she

fastened her arms around him, reveling in the feel of his strong, solid body. "I thought you were dead!"

He stroked her back and kissed her cheek, her neck, her lips, wondering how he had managed to exist so long without her. "We must go," he whispered and began kissing her again. A thin hiss from down the street brought him to his senses and he stepped back, cradling her face between his hands.

"No time for this now," he whispered. "Later. Come, my love. And don't talk!"

Though she felt weak, Justine followed Rhys back into the street, holding tightly to his hand. The shadows ahead materialized into three men. She recognized one of the slight, smiling figures before he stepped forward to grasp her hand.

"Collie! Oh, Collie!"

"Ssh," he warned, but he lifted her fingers to his lips in the warmest greeting he had ever given her. Her heart was near to bursting as she looked at the two of them. Then she recalled the other two men. Surely they were soldiers, but in the strangest uniforms she had seen yet! Pointed helmets and leather tunics and faces with crevices heightened by the glare of the torches down the street. They spoke softly to Rhys and handed over several items wrapped in cloth. Then they moved briskly off, leaving the three of them by the wall.

"What now?" Collie whispered to Rhys.

He didn't answer, but stood against the wall in the shadows, waiting. Collie wisely kept quiet, hoping Rhys knew what he was doing. The soldiers were barely out of sight before a stooped, slight figure of a man came shuffling toward them. He stopped, looked directly at Rhys, then took off again. Without a word, Rhys followed, pulling Justine by the hand, with Collie hurrying along behind. Justine had glimpsed enough of the man in the shadows to be sure that he was Chinese. Hoping he was to be trusted, she darted alongside Rhys down dark, narrow streets and along the fetid canals, keeping always in the shadows of houses or trees, until they came at last to a long, stone wall, so ancient that the signs of its crumbling were obvious even in the dark. Their guide paused, dropped to his knees, and began removing several large boulders from the base of the wall. "Keep watch," Rhys whispered to Collie, and knelt to help remove the stones. In a few short minutes, a hole appeared, large enough for a man of Rhys's size to squeeze through.

Their Chinese guide stood and beckoned them through the hole. Rhys, still not certain of what they would find on the other side, sent Collie first, then Justine. He silently thanked the guide, then followed, squirming through the opening which, with his bundle, was a tight fit.

They were waiting for him on the other side, huddled against the wall. The fragrant sweet odors of grasses and trees told them at once they were outside the city, and all three of them breathed deeply with relief and renewed hope. They had little time to enjoy it. Almost immediately they were aware of a group of men and horses standing beneath a tree nearby. One of the men beckoned, and Rhys moved swiftly over to them, Justine and Collie reluctantly following. The horses' hoofs had been covered with sacking to muffle their steps, and the group was so quiet that Justine realized she had only sensed they were there. Once she was near them, she could see that there were several horses, but only three men. The leader spoke one word softly to Rhys and handed him a small dark bundle. Then he abruptly thrust her at one of the smaller horses. Before she was in the saddle, Rhys and Collie were also mounted and they started off, led by one of the men, but leaving the other two behind. The whole thing had happened so easily, so efficiently, and so quickly, that Justine still could not trust her senses. She was outside the palace, free, and with the two people she felt closest to in all the world— two people she had given up for dead. It was almost too much to take in. She blocked out all thoughts of anything but the purpose at hand, and concentrated on following Rhys's dark pony. If all went well, there would be time enough later to think and wonder about it all.

It seemed as though they rode for hours, yet she knew it had not been nearly that long. Though she did not know where they were, she recognized the familiar outlines of fields, orchards, and canals that filled the area between the city's inner and outer gates. And she knew enough about the people who lived among them to be certain that she could not breathe easily until they were actually through the outer walls.

When at last she saw those walls looming up out of the darkness, her heart turned over. Their mounted guide pulled to a halt and dismounted, and all her hopes congealed to fear. Then she saw that he was opening some kind of ancient door in the wall. It squeaked piercingly on its rusty hinges, as he pulled it back and waved his arm at them to hurry them through.

"Wait!" Rhys whispered. Justine had heard it, too, the sudden clatter of horses coming toward them. Swiftly the soldier who was their guide stepped away from the door, motioning them back into the shadow of the wall, while he stood beside his pony waiting. Rhys looked around frantically. If they rode back down the road they had come, it would be an obvious sign that they were up to no good. They might be able to dart through the gate, but that would be an invitation for the soldiers to follow them, and if they were caught, that would be the end of everything. He sat, fighting down panic and praying that their guide was actually to be trusted. Quickly they all three pulled their hoods over their faces and waited in the dark, their anxiety a live thing between them.

The mounted men galloped up, and Rhys was relieved to see there were only two of them. They had made enough noise for five.

There was a guttural exchange between the three soldiers, one on the ground, the other two on their mounts, while the three fugitives waited silently, guardedly in the background. "What's he saying?" Rhys managed to whisper to Collie when the exchange had gone on for several moments. He did not like the way the two mounted soldiers kept looking their way.

"We're peasants, trying to get back to our village."

One of the soldiers walked his pony over to them and barked a command. Rhys looked at Collie, who began to dismount. Hoping he knew what he was doing, Rhys followed and motioned for Justine to do the same. They hunched in their heavy clothes, hiding their faces in the shadows of their hoods, and praying they would not be examined closely.

Collie bowed up and down, as humble a peasant as an arrogant officer could want. Though Rhys could not understand the few words Collie exchanged with the man, he had never been so grateful for the little Englishman's talent for languages. One of the newly arrived soldiers fastened his gaze on Justine, apparently only beginning to realize that there was a woman beneath the dark billows of her cloak. He had leaned forward in his saddle and reached out to throw back her hood, when he was stopped by Collie suddenly shouting several sentences in his language. The man turned and spoke to the guide, who answered nodding his head up and down. The soldier peered at Justine, gave a sharp laugh, and turned away.

They waited, holding their breaths while the guide spoke again, rummaged in his tunic for a small leather bag which he handed over to the soldiers, then got back on his horse. The two guards gave the 'peasants' one more glance, then turned their mounts and galloped off. Hardly daring to breathe, Rhys watched them leave, then looked back at the guide.

The man's face was a mask of fury and concern. Nodding toward the open gate, he slapped the rump of Justine's horse sending it through. Rhys went next, ducking to avoid cracking his head on the low frame, then pulled up to wait for Collie.

"What did you say to them?" he whispered to Collie.

"Never mind. Let's just get away from here," Collie answered, kicking at his pony's sides. "Do ye know the way?"

"Toward those hills."

It was all they needed. They cantered off down the road, aware of the squeaking metallic groan of the door closing behind them, fast but not too fast to attract attention, leaving the dreaded city and its armed men behind. Almost at once they were enveloped by the darkness.

Justine could hardly believe it. Free! Free! Still

fighting down her exhilaration, she cantered along behind Rhys, her hair flying in the wind, the clean, cool air against her face, and a triumphant smile on her lips. She had no idea at all where they were going, but she no longer cared. As long as it was away from Bokharta and Ulugh Khan, hell itself would not be unwelcome.

Princess Tsingsia had not been able to sleep, and when the princess could not sleep, neither did anyone who served her. She had ordered soft music on the harps, and soothing drinks. One serving girl rubbed her forehead, another waited to massage her back. Two stood over her with fans, creating a gentle breeze that modified the hot night. Others waited on the fringes of the room, stifling yawns, ready for any command the princess might wish to give them.

Tsingsia was quite annoyed with herself. Ordinarily she never allowed emotions to interfere with the careful execution of her plans. Order, precise planning, every detail anticipated—that was the way to proceed. Feelings, fears, and worry all got in the way of the cool, step-by-step achievement of her intentions.

Yet she could not shake the concern that this time she was dealing with more complicated people—crazy Westerners whose emotional reactions could not always be anticipated. It made her task far more difficult.

And yes, she must admit to herself that even the Ulugh Khan himself was more like the English in this respect than the cool Chinese. She was not so certain that his response would be the expected one. And great things rested on that response.

She was startled out of her reverie by a stirring near

the door. One of her soldier guards—a young man she had first known in her father's court—stepped up to her bed and fell on his face. Tsingsia sat eagerly forward.

"Well . . ." she said quietly.

The man sat up far enough to speak, though still considerably below her level. "It is done, Princess."

"And did they get safely away?"

"They are beyond the outer wall and on the road to the Tien Shan."

"What of the map?"

"It is in their hands."

Tsingsia allowed her fragile lips the smallest smile. She sat back against the cushions, folding her gilded taloned hands one over the other, and sighed. "Was there any trouble?"

"Only once, Princess. But we avoided it without incident."

"Good." She leaned forward, close enough to whisper in the soldier's ear. "You know what to do. That girl, that peasant, the other horsemen—all must be eliminated. They must not be questioned."

The soldier bowed to the ground. "It will be done, my Princess."

He backed away while Tsingsia lifted a hand to bring her serving women to her side. "I am feeling better. Prepare my bath. Make ready my most elaborate and beautiful garments. Send for the goldsmiths and their chests, and warn my hairdressers they must accomplish the most exquisite work of their lives. Then send word to Ulugh Khan that his wife, the Princess Tsingsia, wishes an audience tomorrow morning."

Fifteen

The ledge was little more than a short shelf extending like the palm of a hand from the vertical thickets of the mountainside. Collie cautiously eased his slight body out along it, hoping it had enough support underneath to take his weight. Lying flat he wiggled forward inch by inch, until he could peer over the rim down to the valley below.

The air was thin and cold, making it difficult to breathe. He had never liked heights anyway, and having spent the last ten years in flat desert lands only served to sharpen his terror of being suspended in air with nothing solid underneath. His fingers dug into the rock as he tried to concentrate on the scene below. At least from here you could see the valley without your sight being blocked by the side of the mountain. The vista of jagged mountainside, plunging steeply downward to thrust sharply upward again, must be beautiful to someone who wasn't so terrified, he thought. Good country for eagles! Then, as movement in the green foliage of the valley below became more certain, the beauty of the scene was forgotten. A thin procession, some on horseback with others walking behind, was working its way along the path through the high grasses of a meadow. It did not take Collie long to recognize who they were and mark where they were headed. Satisfied, he scrambled backwards until he was on the narrow path again, and took off up the mountain.

It was an almost vertical walk, along a track half-overgrown with thickets and choked with those few hearty weeds that could manage to struggle in the thin air. Ten minutes brought him to the narrow meadow where Rhys and Justine waited. He threw himself down on the grass beside them, wheezing for breath.

"They're there right enough. I saw them."

"Are you sure?" Justine asked as she pulled her short cloak closer around her shoulders.

"A bird circling overhead couldn't have seen them any better. It was the emir's soldiers, for certain. And Col. Hughes, and those two thugs of his are with them."

Rhys pounded his fist on his knee. "I don't understand it. How could they be so close on our heels so quickly. We ought to have been far ahead of them. Unless . . ."

". . . the good princess set them on us," Collie finished for him. "It's possible, ye know. That might have been her plan all along. It would raise her standing considerably in the emir's eyes to return his fugitives to his prison."

"After helping us to escape? I don't think so. She could have turned us over to Ulugh Khan anytime when we were secreted beneath her palace. No, whatever she's up to, I don't think she wants us brought back to Samarkand."

"Perhaps that story you gave those soldiers at the

outer gate about my having an advanced stage of the French Pox didn't hold up once they knew we were missing," Justine said acidly to Collie. "I may never forgive you for that!"

"It got us away, didn't it? I had to think of something fast, and it happened that syphilis was one word I knew in their language."

"Well," Rhys murmured to Justine, rubbing the stubble on his chin, "at least we know that this time you didn't say anything to the colonel. Ulugh Khan must have sent him along in order to get rid of him. If the colonel should be fortunate enough to kill us and find the treasure, Ulugh Khan's soldiers will promptly dispatch the colonel. The emir wins again."

Justine rummaged around in the bundle of food they had bought off a farmer two days before. It was almost gone now and they would have to parcel it out sparingly, unless they came across another nomad family driving their flocks to high ground for the summer. Trying to forget how hungry she still was, she stood up and walked over to the edge of the path, looking at the jagged peaks of the Tien Shan. The Celestial Mountains, they were called. It was an apt name, though whether they were named thus because their beauty was so heavenly scenic or because their peaks appeared to touch the heavens, she couldn't tell. She might have appreciated their beauty more had the change to thin, cold air not been so sudden. And if they had been able to keep to the well-worn pass through the peaks, instead of hiding among the vertical paths that clung to the mountainsides. Her muscles ached from the constant climbing, and her body shuddered from the constant cold. She had to remind herself that at least she was free and on her way home.

Once over these wild, rugged, impossible mountains, it would probably all seem worth it.

Rhys got to his feet, pulled his pack over his shoulder, and yanked his felt hat down over his ears. "We'd better keep going," he said, almost as though he wished they would disagree with him.

After climbing in serpentine fashion around the granite boulders and sparse forests, the path brought them out on a broad plateau. The grass was breast-high and waved like feathers in the gentle breeze. Even the sun seemed stronger here. Halfway along they stumbled on a small hut where a nomadic family had made their summer home. The horses had been sold almost from the moment they started through the Tien Shan, and Rhys had enough money left now to purchase a new supply of food. Using Collie's brief stock of native words, he inquired as he had at each stopping place about the "celestial waters" and the place "where earth and sky meet."

"They don't know anything about that last part," Collie reported, "but the celestial waters are the Celestial Falls."

"The same answer we always get. Ask them if they know where the falls are."

One of the older men in the group, a grandfather whose face was a mass of lines and whose tiny eyes looked out at them with the wisdom of the ages, spoke haltingly to Collie. "I couldn't understand much of what he said, but I think he meant the falls are over there, among those peaks."

"That means tackling the Muzart Pass," Rhys muttered. Justine dropped her head in her hands. Another climb! "Well, give him the money and our

362

thanks, and let's be going," Rhys added, pulling Justine to her feet.

"Why couldn't we have stayed and rested?" she complained as they struck out through the sea of high grass once more.

"The less people know of us, the less they'll be able to tell if Hughes and his guards question them. Besides, it's a long way across that pass, and the sooner we get there, the sooner we'll get away."

She did not see the wisdom in this explanation until later that afternoon, when, near evening, they heard a distant rumble on the road. Collie dropped quickly down, his ear against the earth. "Horses!" he said, sending the three of them into the high grass. Justine and Rhys crouched and huddled together, while Collie came behind them covering their progress as much as possible. They did not dare stand up far enough to see who was thundering by, though they could hear them and feel the earth shake. Justine nestled close to Rhys, hardly daring to breathe until the horde had passed.

"Was it Hughes?" Rhys whispered to Collie.

"Without question. Who else would send an army tramping around in these impossible mountains?"

"Damn. They're closer to us than I thought. We'd better try to find another way."

To Justine's disappointment they struck out away from the plateau, climbing again along the vertical woodlands and high meadows of the steep hills. They had to stop when darkness fell, or risk tripping and falling in the rough terrain. Luckily they happened on a rocky depression, almost a cave, where they could build a small fire and huddle out of the wind.

"I never thought I would think longingly of the emir's

palace," Justine said as she nestled down for the night in Rhys's arms. It was curious to her that his physical nearness—usually so intoxicating as to drive out all other sensations—now was primarily a comfort and a refuge. They were both too weary and cold and encased in too many layers of clothing to think of anything but sleep when night came.

In the morning they were up with the sun, had a hasty breakfast, and started once more up the slopes which would eventually bring them to the glacial plateau that formed the Muzart Pass. As they traveled higher the path grew ever more rugged and steep, rising like a wall in places, and causing them to dig at the rough surface for handholds as they climbed. Justine's only consolation was that surely they must have evaded the emir's guards by following this terrible, almost unusable track. Then they rounded a bend to see the path widen into a narrow road curving upward. What had appeared to be a walkway, she saw on closer inspection, was actually a platform six feet wide, built straight out from the face of the mountain and supported by planks set at an angle into the rock. This man-made ledge curved around the mountain peak, rising ever higher until it was lost in a swirl of mist above them.

"I'm not walking on that!" Justine breathed.

Even Rhys hesitated. "Someone built it, and it shows signs of use."

"I think I agree with Justine," Collie murmured. "It looks like a fragile kind of floor, and even though there's a handrail, there's also a lot of open space below it."

"Come along, you two," Rhys snapped, every inch the captain. "We cannot go back, so we must go forward. This path looks as though it will take us around the mountain at least."

"If it doesn't fall apart!"

He took Justine's hand, leading her forward, testing the plank floor carefully at first. Justine followed, then Collie, all of them encouraged by the way the path seemed sound beneath their weight. As they gripped the rail and climbed upward, they soon noticed the face of the cliff falling away below. From a gentle slope beneath the road, the rubble-strewn rock soon gave way to steep inclines, falling off in places into a straight drop of several hundred feet. The wooden ledge itself was firm and in good condition, and soon Justine fought down her fear and walked briskly, just not daring to look down.

For nearly an hour they traveled along this ledge, at times marveling at the great sweeping vistas of jagged peaks spread out around them. There was little time to rest except on those infrequent spots where the ledge gave way for a short space to a fairly flat piece of ground. After several of these respites, the cliff face began to grow even more steep, and the ledge curved around its high peak with a dizzying serpentine sweep. It was as they came around one of these, that they found they could see far below the road which they had traveled earlier. And spread out along it were the mounted men of the emir's calvary, their metal breastplates glistening in the afternoon sun.

"How did they get so close!" Rhys muttered. "They'll be on us within the hour, unless we can find some way off this ledge."

"Whose idea was it to sell our horses?" Justine said sarcastically. "We can never keep ahead of them while they're mounted and we're not."

Collie made a soft clucking noise with his tongue. "Has

it occurred to you two that we are in a bad position here? We cannot go back without running into their hands, and if we go forward, they're bound to catch up with us. There's not even a place to hide on this ledge."

Rhys refused to be panicked by the situation. "We must keep going ahead. If we can get around this cliff, the road may broaden out onto another plateau, and we can find a place to hide."

"The eternal optimist."

"Do you have a better solution?" Rhys snapped. Collie grinned at him, knowing full well he did not, and reluctantly they began climbing again, a little more hurriedly this time.

Yet each curve of the narrow trail seemed only to lead to another. After an hour of difficult hiking, holding on to the handrail and gasping for breath in the cold, thin air, even Rhys admitted they had to find a better solution. They could hear the faint sound of voices behind them and the occasional neighing of a horse. "A little more time, and we might have made it around this thing," he said when they stopped to catch their breath. "We've got to think of something."

Justine could feel her panic rising, but she fought it down. They had come this far, they must find a way to go on. She and Collie both looked trustingly at Rhys, who returned their stare, then went back to searching the road that wound around the cliff face behind them. All at once he dropped to his knees, flattened down on the ledge, and, holding tightly to the sides, peered underneath.

"Oh, no!" Justine cried. "Not me! Not under there!" Collie turned white, but said nothing.

"It's our only chance," Rhys said, sitting up again.

"The timbers are strong. I think they'll hold us."

"You *think!*"

"Will they hold us and the horses and men passing by above us?" Collie muttered, hoping to discourage Rhys.

"Can you think of a better solution?"

"Rhys," Justine cried. "It's a long way down if we fall!"

"Don't think about that. Just hold on for dear life."

She couldn't believe he was serious. Yet as the sounds of the pursuing soldiers behind them grew louder, even she knew they must do something. Rhys went over first, to see if it could be done. Then with Collie's help, she was eased down over the rim of the ledge and onto one of the wide timbers that supported the road. Her perch was seven feet long and nearly a foot in width. Smaller supporting framework extended from it near the road's edge, while the other end appeared to be embedded in the face of the cliff. She opened her eyes long enough to see Collie squirm down along another timber ahead of her, and Rhys ensconced on one behind her. Only once did she glance down. When her stomach turned over, she looked quickly up. The ground did slope slightly, but it was still a steep drop of sheer rock. Far below she glimpsed the green of the valley floor before she shut her eyes and buried her face on the timber's rough surface, not even caring about the splinters she picked up. They were barely in place before the first of the soldiers rode by above them, setting the wooden road swaying and shaking with their movement. Justine did as Rhys had told her—she held on for dear life, praying the supporting buttress of the ledge would hold. Time seemed to grind to a halt as they clung to their fragile support, while the road above them shuddered with the passing men and horses. When at last the movements ceased and the road steadied, they waited still, not daring to move too quickly from their hiding place.

Getting back up to the surface of the ledge proved to be harder than getting down. Collie went first, squirming like a worm along the timbers, using all fours to cling to them. Even then he slipped once and slid backward, dangling from the supporting beam until he could drag his body back over it. Both Justine and Rhys gasped as they watched him ease back up and over the rim of the road, not daring to breathe until he was safely on top. Then he leaned over to give Justine a hand as she scrambled up. Last of all came Rhys to join them, sprawled flat on the surface, reveling in the solid floor beneath them.

But Rhys knew they could not afford the luxury of a rest. He drove them to their feet, and they started back down the ledge, away from the soldiers and over the track they had taken earlier. Going down was much swifter than the trip up had been. The first plateau they reached they struck out away from the cliff, hoping to find a route to the next mountain through the valley floor instead of around the peak. By the time darkness fell, they were far enough away from the circular ledge to feel safe. They were so tired and still so shaken that they did not bother with a fire, though the sharp air was very cold. They picked at the food they had bought from the nomads, and fell into a drugged sleep where Justine dreamed of falling.

The following afternoon Justine and Rhys rested in the crevice of a boulder, while Collie left to scout the area. He returned an hour later, scrambling down to the shadowed depression where they lay propped against the granite wall, his lopsided grin wide across his face.

"I am the bearer of both good news and bad," he said as

368

he sat down beside them.

Justine put the comb she had been using to groom her hair back inside the small bundle of her personal effects. "I could use some good news. And judging from the look on your face it promises to be very good indeed."

Collie could barely hide his excitement. He leaned forward, spreading out the crude map the princess had given them and which they had been following since leaving the palace. "I came across another of those traveling families making their summer home in the mountains. They told me we are right here," he said pointing a stubby finger at the map. "And they knew of the falls. They are just about here, on the other side of the Ice Pass. Once through that we shouldn't be more than a few miles from them. That should get ye both on your feet."

Rhys bent to study the parchment, rubbing his hand along his chin. "Yes, but where are Hughes and his men? It won't do us any good to find the falls, if they're still breathing down our necks."

Collie sat back, leaning his elbows on his knees. "That's the bad news. They're still in the area. I saw signs of them in the neighborhood, though I didn't glimpse them. They must have picked up our trail again."

"What about 'where earth and sky meet'?" Justine asked. "Did your nomads know what that meant?"

"Unfortunately, no. It meant nothing to them. But if we find the falls, surely the rest of the puzzle will unravel itself. We'll just have to have a good look around."

Rhys got to his feet and pulled the pack with their supplies over his shoulder. "We ought to be moving along, if Hughes is somewhere about. At least we know we're going in the right direction. Good work, Collie."

Collie and Justine exchanged glances. Rhys almost

never complimented Collie, or in any way acknowledged how dependent both he and Justine were on his cleverness. The little Englishman could not hide his satisfaction. He smiled broadly at Justine when Rhys turned away to stride back toward the trail.

The air grew steadily thinner as they climbed, making exertion more difficult. Justine had no way of knowing how high up they were, except for the occasional vistas of soaring peaks, clouded with a lacy film of mist. The air grew colder as they moved ever higher, so that even the efforts of her climb could not keep her completely warm.

They stumbled on the Muzart or Ice Pass as evening was beginning to fall. It spread out before them, a huge glacier surrounded by peaks sheeted with ice. That night they camped on the glacier's edge, building a fire of wood they had gathered from the last few trees they passed, and fashioning a tent from some of their blankets, while wrapping themselves in the ones that were left. The next morning, in the brilliant air, Justine was able to appreciate the beauty of the bright light on the marble peaks and the glowing blue-tinged whiteness of the flat glacial plateau.

They climbed on to the glacier and stumbled along it for miles, keeping to the edges as much as possible. The map was very vague at this point but it was obvious they had to work their way between the peaks in order to reach the Southern slopes. Often their way was hidden by clinging mists rising from the surface of the ice, mists which occasionally cleared to reveal looming cliffs of white marble or red porphyry.

Frequently the glacier was cut with crevices and chasms filled with beautiful blue water. There was a strange exotic beauty in the sharp ice blue vista around them, but it made for difficult going. They were not far into it when Collie, looking back over the valley, spotted dark figures on the trail behind them. In the distance they appeared little larger than ants scurrying along the surface.

"Hughes?" Rhys asked when he pointed them out.

Collie nodded. "It must be. But it's a smaller party than before. He must have sent some of the soldiers another way trying to trap us in a vise."

Justine shivered in the cold air. "Do you think we can get through the Pass before they reach us?"

"We can't go in any other direction," Collie mumbled. "We'll just have to hurry."

"I wonder if they spot us as frequently as we spot them," Rhys asked. "Perhaps that is why we haven't been able to shake them off."

"I shouldn't wonder if it was," Collie replied as he tucked the ends of a blanket around his shoulders under his belt. "We'd better cover all the ground today we can, because once we light a fire tonight, we've as good as sent them a signal where we are."

But they did light a fire once night came, both against the cold and to ward off any strange animals that might be prowling about. They made camp behind a ledge, using it as a windbreak and a cover, and were up with the first rays of dawn to start off once more, confident they were nearing the southern slopes.

The air was sparkling and clear, and so cold Justine could feel it chilling her lungs when she breathed deeply. But the sun as it rose higher seemed stronger than the day before, and she savoured the warmth of it on her cheeks. They stopped before noon to rest at a rubble-strewn stretch of ground bordering the ice-crusted water, where tiny clumps of stubborn grass struggled up out of the thin crust of snow. Once she was rested, Justine

371

wandered a little ahead around a jutting ice cliff, to find an edge of the stream where the ice was thin enough to get to the water underneath. It was freezing cold, of course, but it had been so long since she washed her face and hands, that it was refreshing to dabble it on them. She was on her knees leaning over the water, when she heard a noise behind her. She turned, gazing at the cliffs, her breath in her throat. Collie had warned her of possible predators—snow leopards, wild boars, elk, and ibex. Yet somehow she knew it was not an animal. She could feel the eyes, the breathless waiting, waiting to pounce.

She stood up, calling, "Who's there? Collie? Rhys?"

A cold silence. The hairs on the back of her neck came alive. She began to inch her way back around the cliff, gingerly at first, and then breaking into a run. A dark hulking form loomed up in front of her and she stumbled straight into it, her arms gripped suddenly in an iron vise.

A scream tore from her throat as she looked up at the thick, smiling lips of Colonel Hughes's huge bodyguard. He lifted her off her feet as he might throw a doll under his arm. Screaming, Justine flailed wildly at the crushing grip around her waist. Fear and revulsion merged as he broke into a run, thumping along the rocky terrain. She could not see Rhys cut him off ahead, but she realized the monster gripping her had turned, pausing only an instant before starting out over the frozen river.

"Jess!" It was Rhys's voice. With her nails she scratched at the arm around her waist and he shifted, half-slinging her across his chest. She dug at his face, raising a thin red welt. The man cried out and tried to slap at her with a hand as huge as a bear's paw. But he was running too fast, and the blow only glanced off her head.

"Rhys, help!" she screamed again. Then she heard the

sharp, splitting crack underneath.

Rhys was running toward her with Collie fast on his heels. "The fool's on the ice!" Rhys saw what was happening before the big, slow-witted man realized it himself.

"Justine, jump!" he called. With a splintering roar the ice gave way, disintegrating beneath the giant's feet. Justine felt herself falling. The grip around her waist eased, as she was suddenly swamped in water so cold it almost stopped her heart beating. She went under, too stunned for a moment to move, then fought her way back to the light above her. The big man was thrashing near her, showering her with spray. She could not feel the lower half of her body. But she managed to push herself away from the giant's frantic flailing and grip the edge of the ice, holding on for dear life.

With her vision clouded, she could just make out Rhys stretched flat on the ice, extending his arm toward her.

"Reach!" he cried, then looked behind him to see Collie running toward them. "Don't come out here!" he yelled. "I can't save both of you."

Collie stopped, feeling the ice move beneath his feet. He retreated, helplessly watching as Rhys inched closer to Justine. Her face above the ice was almost as white as the glacier.

With a great effort Justine reached out, her fingers just touching Rhys's splayed hand. He inched closer and gripped her wrist. Holding firm with one hand, he tore away the belt at his waist with the other, and flipped the end over to where she could grab it.

"Collie!" he cried. "Pull us away from here. But watch you don't break the ice, or we're all gone."

Collie gingerly tested the ice around his feet until he found an area strong enough to support his weight. Then stretching flat on the ice, he managed to squirm close enough to Rhys to grap his ankles. Very carefully he began sliding backward. It was hard going once Justine's weight was felt on the other end, but finally he felt sure enough of the ice to get up on his knees and pull. When he and Rhys together had her clear of the water, they slid her along the ice and into their arms, half-carrying her back to shore. Behind them the water had settled, quiet and still with only small ice floes floating on its crystal surface. "We've got to get her out of those clothes," Rhys said as he began throwing the last of their wood together to build a fire. Her teeth were chattering so hard she could not speak, and most of her body felt as though it was not there any longer.

"But if Hughes is around—"

"God's teeth, man! It doesn't matter. We've got to warm her up. If we're caught, well, we're just caught, that's all."

Rhys began stripping Justine's soaked clothes away and rubbing her arms and legs. Together, he and Collie wrapped her in the extra blankets, then took off the ones they wore over their clothes and added them. When Collie had the fire going, he broke some of the ice and melted it to make a thin tea, then forced her to sip it. At every moment they expected the rest of Hughes's party to come sweeping down on them. When nearly an hour had passed with no sign of their pursuers, they all three began to breathe more easily.

"Could that oaf have been alone out here?" Rhys wondered aloud.

"I was wondering the same thing," Collie said. He was vastly relieved to see the color returning to Justine's cheeks, though her hands still seemed as blue as the water in the distance. "It's possible, ye know. He was so big, the colonel might have sent him one way while they went another."

"But he was not very bright, to put it mildly. Perhaps he took off on some whim of his own. He might have just stumbled on Justine and not been able to resist carrying her off."

"Whatever the reason, we have one less enemy to fear," Collie said nodding at the still water. "We'd better stay the night close by and be off with the dawn."

"I'd prefer to leave now, if Justine could travel. I suppose that's out of the question."

"Let's go a little way," Justine murmured. "I'd as lief not spend the night here."

In the end, they followed her suggestion and moved down the river nearly a mile to a sheltered cove with an overhang they could use as a makeshift cave. By the next morning Justine was feeling almost normal again, except for an involuntary shudder when she thought of Hughes's manservant lying beneath the ice.

By noon they were through the Pass and ready to begin the trek down the south slopes of the Tien Shan. There was an abrupt, startling change in the climate and the terrain as they moved lower. The glacier gave way to barren slopes of rock and stark valleys covered with a coarse brush. The air was bright, the sky dazzling, but as they descended the heat was suddenly as constricting as the cold had been earlier. They were traveling through a completely new kind of country. On the northern slopes of the Celestial Mountains, there had been high grassy plateaus and lush forests. Now, where the jagged upward thrusts of rocky peaks announced the western borders of China and swept on to the barren desert of the Taklamakan, the land was far more dry, the rock ledges and crevices more daunting and rugged, the lines of trees

375

fewer and more stark. It was as though the mountains themselves blocked any life-giving rains and winds from the north, bathing the one slope with verdure and leaving the other to a stark, moistureless existence. The farther they traveled into this inhospitable country, the more Rhys despaired of finding a river, much less a waterfall. With Tsingsia's map and the peaks to guide them they pressed on, relieved at least that they saw no further sign of the emir's soldiers or Col. Hughes.

They heard it long before they saw it. A faint, distant murmur in the background, almost drowned out by the chattering of the birds and the winds singing in the occasional grove of fir trees. Rhys, attuned as he was to the murmur of the sea, heard it first. He stopped, listening, studying the rocks ahead.

"I could swear that is water," he said quietly, "though where it could come from in all this dry barren rock, I can't imagine."

"Can ye tell the direction?" Collie asked, trying to hide his excitement.

"It's difficult to say, but I think . . . up that way," Rhys answered, pointing to a long bare face of rock above them.

"There's no water there," Justine said, dreading another difficult climb. "I haven't even seen a creek, much less a stream or a river. You must be wrong."

Rhys hitched his pack off his shoulder and tied it around his waist. "Well, one thing is for sure. I'm going to find out if I'm wrong or not before I go any farther."

To Justine's dismay he began to climb the face of the rock. It was not particularly steep, but the surface was slippery and smooth, making it difficult to find places to pull himself up. She and Collie both followed Rhys's lead, avoiding treacherous spots and using the hand supports he found for them. Though the sound of the water grew louder, she could still not believe it could exist in this barren mound of granite. They clambered over the face of the boulder and into a line of trees that marched almost in single file down the hill. A little beyond came a narrow forest of firs where the ground leveled out and became thickly covered with brittle, dry leaves. At least the tiny forest offered them shade and something to hold on to, but Rhys pushed through it to a spot where the rocks lay heaped as though scattered by some giant hand into haphazard mounds of granite.

"Look!" Rhys cried.

Justine gripped one of the tree trunks and peered at the rocky ledges, dappled by the fringe of trees that grew around it. No stream or river was anywhere in sight but there it was. A sheet of water, spewing from the rocks and falling in a column of spray and white water, straight down at least fifty feet to disappear again into the rocks below.

"I've never seen anything like it," she cried. "Where does it come from? Where does it go? It ought not to be here at all!"

Collie rubbed at his chin. "She's not very grand, is she. Compared to what I've heard of other great falls."

"It's amazing," Rhys said. "It must come from a stream buried in the rocks, and it probably disappears into one as well."

Collie looked down at the narrow opening between the steep sides of granite, hidden under the vaporish mists from the falls' spray. "Would that be where earth and sky meet, do you suppose?"

"I don't know," Rhys answered, "but I intend to find out."

"Rhys, you can't," Justine cried. "There's no way to

get down there. Look at the sides of those rocks. They're straight down."

"We'll find a way," he said, shaking off her hand to begin the descent. Going down was more difficult than climbing up, Justine soon found. Once more she and Collie followed in Rhys's footsteps, letting him search for the crevices in the rocks, the occasional small tree growing between the boulders, or the small stands of pines that would give them a handhold. Before they were halfway down, they were drenched from the constant spray.

"This is insane!" Justine cried when her foot slipped on a wet boulder and she went sliding in a sitting position into a pine tree. "We'll never make it, Rhys," she called, but he ignored her. Collie, as he climbed down the rocks, kept a wary eye out for anything that might fit the description they'd been given, but there was nothing that he could see that remotely suggested "where earth and sky meet." The farther down they went, the more he was inclined to agree with Justine.

They were almost three-fourths of the way down when Rhys fell. With a loud cry he went sliding on the surface of a large wet boulder and out of sight down the falls. Justine screamed and grabbed for him, but her motion only sent her careening after Rhys. She felt her body slipping along the surface and into the void. Over the rocks she went to hurtle down through the air, gasping as the water hit her face, her arms flailing wildly. She had a dim realization that her life might be over when she hit the water, plunged down deeply below the surface, and began to fight her way back toward the light over her head.

Choking, she broke the surface of the water and gasped for air as she was caught in its currents and pulled along.

378

Though she could barely see, she knew she was floating in some kind of a stream that churned and roared along the floor of a narrow canyon. She was caught in the grip of a downdraft that dragged her under, only to send her bounding, choking for air, back to the surface. She was dimly aware of trees flying by, of a shore not far away, but too far to reach. Blindly she fought to keep her head above water as she was swept along like a leaf in the swirling, streaming water.

Then, so gradually she was not aware of it at first, the churning eased and the current calmed. Exhausted, she went limp, floating along the stream until she realized she could actually make it to the shore. Although her arms felt like leaden stumps, she was able to move them enough to propel her toward the water's edge, where up ahead she saw Rhys dragging himself from the stream.

Abruptly she felt gravel beneath her. She dragged her body up along it until she was able to pull herself up onto the sandy bank. Her heavy, woolen waterlogged clothes dragged her down. She pushed back her hair streaming around her face, and clawed her way up along the bank to fall exhausted on the grass. Dimly she was aware of Collie, dragging up the bank behind her, water running from his soaked tunic.

Justine rolled over on her back on the grass, her arms spread out at her sides, breathing heavily. "I can't believe I'm still alive," she muttered.

Beside her Rhys raised up on one elbow. "What happened? All I remember is falling."

"Ye slipped," Collie said, wringing out his sleeve. "Justine tried to grab ye, and she slipped, too. I wasn't going to be left back there alone, so I followed. I must have been out of my mind."

Rhys was beginning to get his senses. He sat up, resting

his arms on his knees, and dug at his ears which still sounded as though he was underwater.

"We were lucky there was really a stream there. I thought I was going over some kind of precipice. I certainly couldn't see it up above."

Justine sat up and began wringing out her long, streaming hair. "We're nowhere near the falls now, are we?"

"After that ride? I don't see how we could be. In fact, I have no notion of where we actually are."

She felt Collie freeze suddenly beside her. Following his gaze, she turned toward the thick fringe of trees. "Don't look now," Collie muttered, "but we are not alone!"

Rhys turned and tried to rise to his knees as a swarm of men broke from the trees, running straight at them, howling as they waved their scimitars above their heads. Justine gasped as she was grabbed by her arms and dragged to her feet. A babble of foreign voices exploded around her. She was too startled to notice anything except that they were little men with fierce faces, slanted eyes, and armed to the teeth with knives and spears. One of them threw his arm around her neck, pulling back her head. They were obviously soldiers, wearing tunics of hard leather and metal breastplates. Some wore helmets with long pieces that fitted over their heads and hung halfway down their noses.

Rhys never had time to reach for his knife. "Run, Collie!" he yelled, as his arms were caught behind him and he was pushed to the ground. Collie's face appeared suddenly in front of him, a soldier's boot pressing his head into the grass.

"I'm in no position to run anywhere," he muttered. "Justine, are you all right?"

She could not answer. Horrible visions flew through her mind, but though the men held her immobile, they made no attempt to hurt her.

"Collie," she breathed. "Who are they? The emir's men?"

Collie and Rhys were both rudely yanked to their feet and ropes trussed around their necks and arms linking them together. "Hardly," Collie said quietly. "Unless I'm mistaken, that babble they're speaking is Chinese."

"You mean we've crossed into China?" Rhys muttered to him as one of the men shoved him ahead.

"Carried by the stream," Collie managed to say, as he and Rhys were shoved along a trail that wound into the woods. Justine hurried to stay near them, her hands bound in front of her but with no other restraints. She was too terrified of the fierce-looking armed men around her to think of anything except hovering close to Rhys and Collie. She hardly noticed where they were stumbling, except to be aware that the trees were thick around them and they were climbing again. They walked all afternoon, until the sun was dropping behind the peaks, dappling the forests with somber shadows. Only once did they rest, and by then the three of them were so weary they fell in their tracks to lie on the dried leaves, breathing deeply of the thin air.

"If they are not the emir's men, then why are we captives?" she whispered to Rhys when she thought they were not being observed.

"We're as strange to them as they are to us. Collie, can you understand anything they're saying?"

"A word now and then. Do you have something from the princess that might impress them?"

"Only the map, and I've no intention of sharing that with anyone. At least not until I know more about all this."

With a sudden burst of guttural commands, the soldiers roughly pulled them to their feet and started off once more. They pushed ahead even as night draped its ebony mantle over them. Justine was too weary to care anymore where she put her feet as she stumbled through the underbrush, shoved rudely by the nearest soldier when she lagged behind. At last when she thought she could go no longer, they spotted fires in the distance, glimmering among the trees like stars fallen to earth. They stumbled into a clearing dotted with small bonfires and backed with a large wall of rock that held a deep indentation where torches spluttered along the inside walls. There were others there, the same kind of rough armed men as those who had brought them. They clambered around the captives, laughing and touching them and prodding the two men with the points of their primitive spears. Justine had an impression of dirty faces, ragged grins and missing teeth, slanted eye-slits, and the oppressive, unpleasant odor of bear grease. She clung to Rhys as much as possible, pulling back when they reached to run their rough hands along her hair or slide their hands over her body. Huddled together, the three of them did not at first notice the sudden presence of a man who emerged from the cave. The soldiers eased back, leaving them room to examine the figure who stood at the cave's entrance.

"God's blood!" Rhys muttered under his breath. "What now?"

Collie slipped up behind him, whispering into his ear: "We've fallen into the hands of the Philistines, my friends. If that's anything other than a bandit chieftain, I'm the prime minister of England!"

382

Sixteen

He was the ugliest man Justine had ever seen. His face
was a mass of scars, the puffiness heightened by its
cruelty. He was large and beefy, his hands on his hips,
thick feet wide apart. He wore some kind of tunic made
of skins, and his legs were wrapped in leather tied with
thongs. His arms were bare and looked like tree stumps,
except that they glistened with oil in the flickering light.
His hair was pitch black, pulled back into a long pigtail,
and greased to the contours of his skull. He stood
appraising them with as much interest as he might give a
side of beef.

Except for her. The thin eye-slits, unsoftened by the
presence of any eyebrows at all, glinted with an evil light
when they fell upon Justine. She inched closer to Rhys,
trying to hide behind his body as Collie had.

Rhys decided to take the bull by the horns. He stepped
bodly forward. "I am Capt. Rhys Llewellyn of the Colony
of Pennsylvania in North America," he said arrogantly.
"This is my . . . er, wife, Mrs. Llewellyn, and this
worthless creature behind me is my servant, Yarmid Ali.

We demand you free us at once and allow us to go on our way unmolested."

Not a flicker passed across the face of the bandit chief. "Do you think he understood me?" Rhys whispered to Collie.

"Who's to know? There's more expression in those rocks than on that face."

The chieftain lifted his arm in an abrupt gesture, sending his soldiers rushing around them once more, dragging them to one side of the clearing. They were roughly shoved and locked inside a small cagelike square made of thin reeds. There were dirty rushes on the floor of the cage, and just room enough that Justine and Collie could stand upright though Rhys could not. He slumped on the floor, Justine beside him.

"At least we're together," Rhys breathed as he sat back against the bars. Justine leaned against him. She was famished, tired, and afraid, but at least for the moment the three of them could take comfort from each other.

Justine nestled in Rhys's arms. "Why did you tell them that I am your wife?" she asked, looking up at him with eyes that showed delight even through fear and concern.

"I thought it might deter them from taking advantage of you. It didn't work too well, did it, since they didn't understand a word I said."

She buried her head in the comforting valley where his shoulder joined his neck. Somehow she could not say how much the idea pleased her. If they were ever lucky enough to get out of all this, lucky enough to get back home, having Rhys as a husband would make her life complete. She smiled to herself, remembering how once the difference in their respective loyalties had seemed a chasm nothing could breach. Even now, if Rhys should actually find Prince Tai's money, she wasn't certain she would not try to take it from him. And yet, they had gone through so much together, that somehow the rebellion of the Colonies seemed very remote and meaningless. She shuddered to think of the heresy in that idea, and Rhys tightened his arms around her.

"Don't be afraid, my girl. We'll find a way out somehow."

She reached up and kissed his cheek, grateful for his concern. "I'm not afraid," she lied. "I was just thinking how I never thought I'd find anyone more repulsive than the emir of Bukhara. But this chieftain has surpassed even him!"

They spent a fitful night, unable to sleep for the noise around them and the fear that any moment it might erupt into violence directed their way. It was a relief when the first gray threads of dawn began to weave through the woods and the camp began to stir. When one of the soldiers opened the door and shoved a round bowl inside, they all hoped it might contain food. Instead it was half-filled with water, dingy and gray with the flotsam of the forest floor floating on the surface.

A short while later a different man approached, opened the door to their prison, and beckoned them outside. Stooping slightly from the cramped sleeping quarters, Rhys followed Justine and Collie into the clearing where once again they were tied together and led into the cave. To their surprise this vaultlike indentation went far back into the face of the mountain, one room leading to another until they stood in a high, damp, domed hall. Square in the middle was a beautiful Chinese woven rug, and on that a squat chair in which the chieftain of the night before was sprawled, examining them curiously. He sat scooping up handfuls of his breakfast of rice and meat with his hands, wiping them on his leather tunic and taking long draughts from a wooden jug on a small table at his side.

Justine felt her mouth begin to water at the sight of the food and the pungent aroma of the meat. The chieftain appeared to be amused at the way all three of them eyed the food, naked hunger on their faces.

"So," the chieftain said in Turki. "You intruders come into my home carrying nothing to rob. What shall I do with you?"

Collie breathed a sigh of relief to recognize a language he could manage. He dropped quickly to his knees, pulling Rhys and Justine down with him. They watched in amazement as he bowed his head to the ground in front of the chief.

"Oh, Great Leader," he intoned, raising his head only high enough to be heard. "We ask only for passage through your kingdom. We mean you no harm. We are travelers from a far-off country."

A quick look of amazement settled on the chief's face to hear his language being spoken so well. It disappeared almost immediately. His words were careful. "Travelers from a far country usually come with many camels and horses and goods. Something useful!"

"But we are not merchants," Collie quickly explained. "We only travel to cross the Tien Shan and reach Canton on the sea."

A quizzical expression danced on the chieftain's face. "Canton, in China," Collie added, thinking that this stupid bandit captain probably had no idea where Canton was.

386

"China is a big country. To the other end of the earth. It would take a lifetime to cross. Bah! What use are you to me? You do not even have anything worth stealing. I shall have you all killed—all but the woman. I'll keep her for my own use, even though she is ugly—too pale and too thin!"

Collie bowed to the ground again and Rhys followed suit, whispering, "What did he say?"

"He'll have us killed, all but Justine. We don't have anything worth stealing."

Rhys glanced at the crude face of the chieftain. Rice lingered on his wide chin, and his drink dribbled down from his thick lips. His clothes were filthy and his greased hair smelled so strongly it offended Rhys's nose. Why was he groveling before such a loutish brute?

He jumped to his feet, dragging Justine and Collie with him. "Do you know what you're doing?" Collie said in a panic.

"Tell this gorilla that we demand to be released."

"Captain, you can't talk that way. This man is a bandit. He would kill us with no more concern than he would squash a flea!"

The chief's little eyes had narrowed dangerously when Rhys stood up. Now he watched the two men, not understanding what they were saying, but curious at Rhys's bravery.

"I cannot converse with a nonentity. What is this brigand's name?"

"Oh Great Leader, my Master would know how to address you," Collie said bowing as low as the rope around his neck would allow.

The chieftain's eyes darted between the three captives. "I am Wusu, the most feared man in all Sinkiang. And

387

who is this who dares to stand before me, as though I did not have the power to pull his head from his neck!"

Collie bowed lower. "My master is Capt. Llewellyn, from America. And the woman is his wife, Justine. They mean you only respect, Great One."

Rhys threw Collie a quick glance, then said in his most pleasant voice: "Tell this scummy pile of rotting compost that we come with the blessings of Princess Tsingsia and her father Prince Tai. That if any harm comes to us, he will answer to both the princess and her father."

Rhys was pleased to see a slight recognition at the sound of the princess's name. This oaf might not know English but he knew Tsingsia's name well enough. He smiled benignly at Wusu as the chieftain leaned forward in his chair, taking in Collie's translation.

"How do you know Tsingsia?" he asked in his guttural voice.

"How do we know her, Master?" Collie asked in English. The sarcasm in his voice was heavy. He felt certain Rhys was gambling with all their lives for the sake of his inexcusable pride.

"We were sent by her from her court in Samarkand, you stinking bag of rotten bones," Rhys answered, warming to his task. It was a release of sorts to be able to speak his mind to this loutish thief and not be understood.

Collie respectfully translated. Wusu, he noted, appeared to be a little confused. His outright hostility had been tempered by the thought that these three nuisances might be useful after all.

Justine, who had been listening to all this while trying not to concentrate on the heady sight and aroma of Wusu's breakfast, suddenly felt her knees give way. She slumped and was caught in Rhys's arms. "She's weak from hunger," he said angrily. "Explain that to this brigand."

Collie translated so effectively that the chieftain waved a hand, summoning a woman whose presence they had not even noticed, so skillfully had she blended into the wall. She hurried forward with a second bowl of rice, generously supplemented with chunks of boiled meat and broth. Rhys lowered Justine to the ground and sat beside her, as all three dipped into the bowl greedily.

"Not too much," he warned. "You'll make yourself sick. And a little less enthusiasm, Collie. Otherwise the Great Wusu might wonder that we allow our servants to eat from the same bowl."

Collie shoved the rice into his mouth. "I'll explain that ye're from America and believe in equality and all that. I wonder what this meat is."

"Don't ask. I don't think we want to know."

Justine did not care. Nothing had ever tasted so delicious, whatever it was. Revived by the food and the sweet, strong drink that was provided with it, she leaned against Rhys, hoping she looked adequately wifelike.

"Will he let us go, do you think?"

"It's not likely," Collie muttered between mouthfuls, "unless we can make it worth his while. What do we have to bargain with?"

"Only one thing," Rhys answered. "And I'd rather cut off my head than let this bastard in on it."

Collie knew he meant the treasure. "If ye don't let him in on it, ye may well get your head cut off for you."

Rhys struggled with his thoughts for a moment. "Oh, all right. We can't very well find the money if we can't get away from here. But be careful. Only tell him as much as you need to, to whet his appetite. And don't mention the map!"

Rejuvenated by his breakfast, Collie threw himself into the business of bargaining with Wusu. It turned out to be not as difficult as he thought, since Wusu already knew of the money Prince Tai had sent his friend, Robert Morris.

"Is there anyone in the whole world who hasn't heard about this money!" Rhys commented dryly when Collie translated. The Englishman went on: "He wants to know how ye intend to find it. Are ye certain I shouldn't mention the map."

"Don't you dare. Without that we have nothing to bargain with. Tell him that the princess told me where it was. Only me."

Rhys could see from the way Wusu studied him with his narrow, cruel eyes that he was not sure whether or not to believe this. Rhys went on. "Tell him that if he will allow us to go search for the treasure, I will give him a percentage of it. A quarter. That should be generous enough."

"He wants half," Collie explained after conveying this to Wusu.

"That's too much. Tell him that it is so great a treasure, that a quarter is more than he could steal from forty caravans. And stress I was sent to carry it back for my country."

Collie translated Rhys's words, trying not to sound as uneasy as he felt. When he had finished, Wusu roared to his feet, flinging a string of incomprehensible invective at all three of them. Collie cowered, but Rhys stood firm, staring the furious chieftain down.

"I can't translate that," Collie whispered. "It's Chinese."

Three soldiers came rushing up to shove the prisoners back toward the entrance of the cave. Prodded by spears, they were driven out into the clearing to be dumped back in the bamboo cage. Justine stretched out on the dirty floor, weary from lack of sleep and feeling a little drugged from the food and drink.

"I don't think he liked yer terms," Collie said bitterly, resting his arms on his knees. He was much more anxious about all this than Rhys, having heard many tales of the viciousness and cruelty of these Chinese mountain bandits. And Wusu appeared to be one of the more notorious of the clan.

Even Rhys was disappointed, since things had seemed to be going his way quite nicely before Wusu's sudden temper tantrum. Yet they had given the chieftain something to chew on. He hoped Collie had convinced Wusu that he knew where the treasure was for it meant he had one thing the filthy robber wanted. As long as the bandit chief did not discover the map, or resort to torture to get the information from him, he felt they might be able to work out a bargain.

All day Wusu's men went about their various, undemanding duties in the clearing, with their eyes on the prisoners in the cage. Often they formed small groups around it, taunting and poking at Rhys and Collie, and trying to fondle Justine. Though Rhys felt certain they would not dare harm them without Wusu's permission, nevertheless, as evening came on, he grew more and more anxious. By nightfall, with a roaring fire going nearby, the soldiers began to pass around jugs of *kumiss*, a fermented drink made from mare's milk. As they grew more drunken and rowdy, his fears increased. The more inebriated of the soldiers danced toward the cage, poking spears through the bamboo bars, occasionally even drawing blood from the two men imprisoned there. A contest developed with bows and arrows, using the top of the cage as a target. The wicked-looking shafts thumped on the roof of the cage, setting up great hilarity among the soldiers, while the three prisoners huddled near the rear, hoping no one would decide to see if they could shoot between the bars.

A few of the men had already passed out in a drunken stupor when several of the more aggressive decided to examine Justine more closely. Working the door open, they rushed inside, pulling her out of Rhys's arms. As Rhys and Collie both went tearing into the mob, one of the soldiers knocked Collie on the head, sending him sprawling unconscious in a corner. Rhys clung to Justine as they were dragged into the clearing, vowing that they would have to kill him to get her away. Her screams brought the chief, Wusu, to the door of the cave, where he stood impassively staring down the drunken men. With a brief gesture of his hand, he sent two of his more sober followers to take Justine from the others and bring her toward the cave.

"Oh, no," Rhys exclaimed, yanking his arms away from those who were trying to hold them. "She's not going without me!"

Wusu stared through his slitted eyes at them a moment, then shrugged. After growling a furious reprimand at his soldiers, he turned to reenter the cave. Rhys and Justine were led inside after him, but not before Rhys noted that the door to the cage where Collie still lay unconscious was being locked again. Afraid to think of what lay ahead, he followed the two men while Justine clung to him, trembling. They went far back into the cave, down one of the passageways off the main room where they had been taken earlier. It ended in a dead wall of rock, before which stood a wall of bamboo bars. Thrusting the two of them inside, the soldiers tied the door shut and left them.

Rhys helped Justine to the end of the room and sat her against the granite wall. Though the tiny space was cool and damp, it was also quiet and dark, and, for the moment at least, safe. There was a thick mat of old straw on the floor which he heaped into the semblance of a bed. Then spreading his coat over it, he helped her to lay down, scrunched down beside her, and held her in his arms until the tremors grew still.

"I've never been so frightened," Justine whispered against his chest. "Not even in Ulugh Khan's palace. Do you think we will be safe here?"

"I think so. Wusu obviously wants to protect you, and he may have let me come along because I'm supposed to be your husband. What he'll do in the morning is anyone's guess."

"Poor Collie. I hope he's all right."

Rhys pulled her close against him. "He's very good at taking care of himself. And he has an advantage over us in that he speaks their language. I'm more worried about what will happen in the morning than about Collie."

Justine nestled her head against the hollow of his shoulder. "Rhys, do you really think Wusu would dare to kill us?" she asked softly, as though afraid to hear his answer.

Rhys hesitated. He was not going to tell her that his greatest fear was that Wusu would kill him and Collie, leaving Justine at his mercy. Yet he refused to gloss over the truth. They were facing possibly the greatest danger of their entire trip, and they would need all their wit and courage to get through it.

"It's not unusual among bandits, I'm afraid," he

whispered, lightly kissing her silken forehead. "On the other hand, we have the lure of the treasure and the map to tempt him. He may want to keep us alive for that, if nothing else."

Justine's arms went around his neck, and they pressed their bodies together against the cool rock, wrapped in the darkness and the quiet. Far away they could hear the occasional sound of laughter echoing through the passageway. Tiny pinpricks of light from torches set in the walls near the end of the tunnel glimmered like stars in blackest night.

"Oh Rhys," Justine breathed against his ear. "This might be our last night together. Ever!"

He didn't answer, for it was working on him, too—the relief after an all-consuming fear, the darkness and quiet after that terrible scene in the clearing, the nearness of her supple body, the thought that indeed they might never share such a night together again.

"After all, you are my husband," Justine said, laughter in her voice. Gently she slipped her hands inside his tunic and underneath the coarse shirt he wore. His chest felt warm and furry beneath her fingers.

"That was only a ploy," Rhys answered, flicking his tongue in the shell pink cavity of her ear. He felt her tremble in his arms, not with fear this time but with sheer delight. "What would I really want with a Tory wife?"

At another time Justine might have bristled at those words. Now she was far too consumed with a rising warmth and need swelling inside her, working its magic like the growing crescendo of an ocean nearing its demise on the shore. Her reply strangled in her throat as Rhys's hands worked at her clothes, not to remove them, but only to bare those parts of her body where his need drove him. He was quickly beyond thought or finesse himself.

He forced her on her back, bending over her, tearing her breast from the confines of her jacket, and lifting it with his hands into his mouth. Her back arched against his probing, thrusting lips as he pulled the taut nipple ever higher. Thrusting his other hand beneath the waist of her skirt, he searched her thighs, finding the moist warmth between her legs, and thrusting, massaging, working at her until she was writhing in an ecstasy of sheer need. Back and forth she slipped along the straw, until the rock behind her left her helpless against his driving manipulations, while her cries, muffled by his body, grew in intensity.

Her fingers, which had been digging into his back, sought out his body instead. Slipping her hands around his waist, she forced them underneath his belt, down the wide trousers, until she found the pulsating, hard shaft she sought. While he pulled at her crested nipple, she pulled at his manhood, feeling it swell and grow beneath her hand. His own need grew like a storm within him at her deft manipulations. Throwing up her skirt, he fell over her, driving into that yielding, beckoning grotto of delight. Justine clasped her arms around his hard body, moving rhythmically with him as together, their cries muffled against each other, they went soaring on a wild wave of passion, crashing against the unyielding shore, poised for an instant in timeless ecstasy.

They lay for several long minutes clasped together, allowing their pounding hearts to gently ebb. At length Rhys lifted his head and kissed the tears off her cheeks, holding her tightly to him. "My dearest love," he said, still wrapped in the glow of a few moments before. "If we do manage to get out of this mess safely, I'll marry you, Tory or no."

"Oh, you will," Justine answered, laughing. "I always

395

understood the girl had something to say about marriage."

"That's one of the few unenlightened reforms of this enlightened age. Do you mean you aren't interested in marrying a Rebel?"

"I might be persuaded, *if* we get out of this mess. But a girl likes to be asked."

"You want me to go down on my knees?"

"Well . . ."

For an answer he rose on all fours over her, looking down in her face.

"That's not what I meant!" Justine cried, pulling him down in her arms again. He smoothed away the long strands of hair that had become loose in their love-making. "We're very good together, aren't we?" he said.

"In so many ways. Rhys, if we don't get out of this alive, I want you to know that the times I've had with you have been worth more to me than all the treasure of Asia. I love you, even if you are a Rebel."

He kissed her without answering.

They lay clasped together, sleeping fitfully until one of the soldiers came to open the cage and pull them out. After straightening her clothes and smoothing her hair, Justine followed Rhys and the guard through the cave and out into the clearing. Dawn was just breaking, bathing the woods in a shroud of gray, but she was able to make out Collie's hunched form standing near the charred embers of last night's bonfire. She ran to him.

"Are you all right?" she said, helping him to stand.

"I've the granddaddy of all headache's," he moaned. "Otherwise, I guess I'll do. I'm that glad to see ye both. I feared ye'd been dragged off to some horrible doom."

"No. We were safer in there than out here."

They broke off their whisperings as Wusu came

striding out of the cave, kicking his corsairs back into consciousness. He stood before the three prisoners, hands on his hips, laughing at the pitiful sight they presented. Groggy from lack of sleep, they faced him with visions of some horrible death plucking at their minds. Then he rattled off a long diatribe in Turki.

Suddenly Collie dropped to his knees and bowed to the ground, pausing only to drag Rhys and Justine down with him.

"What is he saying," Rhys whispered an aside.

"He's letting us go! For God's sake, be grateful!"

Rhys looked up in surprise. Wusu, catching his eye, smiled his evil, sly smile, and Rhys was more certain than ever that this was not an act of generosity. "What's in it for him?"

Collie and the chieftain exchanged a few more sentences. "He is allowing us to go, so we can find the money Prince Tai sent his daughter," Collie explained. "When we've found it, he gets half. That is the bargain. Otherwise he'll have us skinned alive and find the treasure himself."

"Suppose we find it for him, and *then* he has us skinned alive!"

"Does the captain suggest any other alternative? Personally, I will take any solution that allows us to leave this camp."

Rhys forced himself to smile, and even bowed slightly to the chieftain. "Tell him we appreciate his great generosity."

"I already have," Collie exclaimed, bowing to the ground once again.

Having once made up his mind, Wusu acted quickly. To the disappointment of his soldiers, he had Rhys, Collie, and Justine all led from the camp back to the river where they had been found. There they were untied and abandoned, while the soldiers disappeared back into the forest.

"He might have given us a few provisions," Justine complained, aware of how little they had eaten in the last twenty-four hours.

"Think of the alternative," Collie exclaimed, "and be glad we're here. We can find something to eat along the way. At least we're free. I was beginning to think we wouldn't be alive by sundown."

"I admit I was thinking the same," Rhys added. "But let's hurry. The sooner we get away from this place, the better. We'll follow this stream back up to the falls. I have a hunch the rest of that message refers to something close around there, and I intend to find it."

Going back upstream proved to be much more difficult than the wild ride down. They steered clear of the water and clung to the banks. Along the way they foraged for berries and nuts, which took the edge off their hunger. The fringe of trees followed the narrow stream as though given life from its waters, for beyond them all was barren rock and gravel. With the shade and cover of the spruce and poplar forest, they all found their spirits and hopes growing as they worked their way upstream. By evening they could hear the falls in the distance.

After camping under the trees that night, they worked their way up the falls early the following morning. They stood at the bottom, looking up at the narrow plunging water, getting damp from its spray. On both sides the rocks and boulders formed a wall.

"We'll never be able to climb up that," Justine said, hoping Rhys would agree, but doubting that he would.

"Take courage," Rhys answered dryly. "We may not have to go all the way up, but I want to see what's behind all that water."

"You have some theory, *effendi*," Collie intoned.

"As a matter of fact, yes." He was already searching for a handhold and, having found one, hoisted himself up on the rocks. "Ready for a little climbing," he said gaily, reaching down for Justine.

"Rhys, it's straight up!" she moaned. "I don't think I can do it."

"Nonsense. Collie will come behind you and catch you if you fall."

"Wonderful," Collie muttered. "And who catches the two of us?"

Justine took Rhys's hand and pulled herself up. The rock surface was very smooth and slippery, but there were crevices among it that Rhys had used to begin his climb.

"I'll go ahead and make sure it's safe," Rhys said as he pulled himself up higher. His confidence was assuring, and Justine bravely followed, even while telling herself this was insane. As they moved ever higher up the wall of rock, even Rhys's confidence could not convince her this climb was a good idea. Unable to look down, soaked from the constant spray of the water, exhausted from the steepness of the climb, she doggedly followed Rhys, searching for his handhold to pull herself up yet another two or three feet. Then she realized he had stopped.

"It was about here, I think," Rhys muttered. "Wait where you are a moment, and let me look around."

Justine clung to the face of the rock she had just pulled up to. They were only halfway up the length of the falls, she thought, but she didn't dare look below to make certain. She leaned against the hard surface of the boulder, clutching at its slippery sides, and waited. Above her Rhys disappeared, and she caught at her breath.

"What is he up to?" she heard Collie say from below.

"I don't know, but I'm not moving from this spot until he gives me his hand."

"There's nothing around here. We've got to get to the top. Tell him to hurry."

Justine recognized a note of panic in Collie's voice, and remembered his fear of heights. This was probably harder on him than it was on her, she thought, but somehow that didn't help.

Rhys's face appeared over the edge of her rock, smiling down on her. "It's just as I thought," he said, an edge of triumph in his voice. "Here, let me give you a hand up."

With his help she hoisted herself up to the next level, and found she was standing on a small ledge nearly three feet wide. It was the most solid floor she had touched since they began their climb. She sat against the rock and rested, while Rhys pulled Collie up to join them.

"Why did ye stop?" Collie muttered, sinking to his knees on the ledge. "This is no time to rest."

Rhys answered, "See how this ledge extends behind the falls. There's an opening there behind the waterfall. I thought I spotted it when we were here before, but I wasn't sure. But the more I thought about it, the more I felt certain it might be important."

"God's blood, Captain, that ledge is barely as wide as me foot. Ye expect to follow that behind all this water! It's crazy!"

"I've already done it. And it widens as you get behind the falls."

"Oh, well then, that makes it safe," Collie muttered, his voice dripping sarcasm. "And even if there is a cave there, how do we know it's the one where the treasure is hidden?"

"We don't. But it is the most likely place to look.

400

'Where wind and rain are gathered in,' remember? 'And earth and sky meet.' The problem is the opening narrows down to a kind of tunnel. We'll need someone smaller than me to go in there."

"I notice ye're not looking at Justine," Collie moaned.

"Only because it might not be safe. Who knows what you'll find in there."

"I don't mind," Justine offered tentatively.

"No, no," Collie said, hoisting himself to his feet. "I haven't left the precepts of a polite society so far behind as all that. Very well, Captain, let's get on with it."

"Good fellow!" Rhys cried. He flattened against the rock to allow Collie to pass by him, then followed along the ledge with Justine right behind. The narrow footpath edged its way behind the falls, soaking them thoroughly. It was eerie once they edged behind the wall of water. The light filtered blue and shimmering and the roar of the water was so loud that they could not hear each other speak. Collie came to the opening first, a concave black hole in the wall, large enough for the three of them to crouch inside and away from the worst of the spray. "I suppose it's too muddy to find any footprints," Rhys said, searching out the floor of the small cave. "But it does appear that there might have been others here before us."

"It could be anyone, Captain. These nomads know all the caves in these rocks. They probably have their winter supplies stored in this one."

"I don't think so. It's too inaccessible for one thing. Anyway, let's see where it leads."

Collie eyed the tiny opening at the back of the cave. It was just large enough to wiggle through, and it did not look promising. "I'm not even sure I can turn around in that thing," he muttered.

"Then back out. Here, tie one end of my sash around you. We'll yank you out if we have to."

"Seeing as how I don't know who or what I can expect to meet in there, ye'd best be prepared to yank away at the first holler from me."

"You can count on it."

Collie fastened the sash around his waist and disappeared into the black space that was all Justine could see of the opposite end of the cave. She sat with her knees drawn up, resting against the damp rock, and waited with Rhys. They could hear Collie's restless swishing as his body slid along the tunnel. Once when these comforting sounds grew quiet, Rhys knelt at the opening and called to ask if Collie was all right.

After a long silence—during which the two of them stared anxiously at each other with suspended breath— there came a muffled voice: "So far . . ."

Justine rested against the rock wall, watching the end of the tether jiggle as Collie moved deeper into the cave. It felt so good to sit and quietly relax after the rigors of their climb, enjoying the coolness of the spray off the waterfall and not moving at all. Then, all at once Collie came wiggling backwards out of the hole. He scrambled to his feet, his voice full of excitement.

"There's something back there, right enough. Come and see."

Rhys was already on his feet. "Do you think we can fit through the tunnel?"

"It's going to be tight for you, but ye'll make it. Hurry!"

Like an agile mole, he had already turned and climbed back inside the dark depths of the opening. Rhys dropped to all fours and started after him, then stopped to look back at Justine. "Do you want to wait here?"

She knelt beside him. "Alone? Never! I'll be right

402

behind you."

With a reassuring smile he was gone. Jess swallowed and then climbed in behind him, wiggling along the narrow tunnel. At once she regretted it. It was like being buried alive, swallowed into a black void with the oppressive knowledge of solid rock on all sides. She had more room to maneuver than Rhys, but was besieged by the falling dust and gravel debris his body dislodged ahead of her. Doggedly squirming on, she was reassured by the sounds of Rhys's struggle and tried not to think of all the things that could happen to imprison them there forever.

At last she caught a faint glimmer of light. It had been blocked by Rhys's body, but when he dropped suddenly out of sight she found herself facing daylight. The tunnel must lead outside, she thought, as she poked her head through.

Immediately she saw she was wrong. There was a drop of about four feet from the lip of the tunnel into a small cavernlike area. From high above, sunlight fell gently through an opening in the earth, filtered with dust, filigreed by vines around the top, and giving the cavern an ethereal beauty. But they were still below ground, Justine thought, disappointed. The walls were damp from several thin trickles of water seeping from above, and were thick with lichen and the long fingers of creepers and vines. The three of them stood looking up at the light, admiring the quiet serenity of the cave.

"Are ye thinking what I'm thinking," Collie said, his voice whispery, as though they were standing inside a cathedral.

"It's the perfect spot," Rhys answered quietly. "Where wind and rain are gathered in, and earth and sky meet. Chai Wang must have stumbled on it when he was trying to outrun those brigands. Now all we've got to do is figure out where he buried the canteen for safekeeping."

Collie walked slowly around the middle of the cave. "Look how the light falls directly here in the center of the floor. Could that be what he meant by a meeting of earth and sky?" He dug into the packed earth with the heel of his boot. "It seems awfully firm to have been recently disturbed."

"I think that's too obvious," Rhys muttered. "Too easy."

Justine ran her hand along the rough, damp walls. "We've always assumed that 'waters of heaven' referred to the falls. What about these trickles of water here in the cave? Perhaps he meant to guide us to them."

Rhys began working around the edges of the cave before she finished speaking. At the base of each thin stream, the earth was a pool of mud. "It wouldn't be difficult to bury something here," he said. "And we know this thing isn't very large." Kneeling down, he shoved up his sleeve and thrust his arm into the ooze. "The water must run through this and down into some deeper passage."

"Let's all pray he did not discover his way to another tunnel!" Collie breathed. "Can you feel anything?"

There was a sucking woosh of a sound as Rhys pulled his arm out of the mud. "No. Nothing. Try the next one."

Gingerly Collie knelt and began probing the mud at the base of another of the thin streams. Without being asked to, Justine went to the third one, the smallest of them all. In fact it was so thin she thought she really needn't bother. Her hand went in as into warm butter, slipping down into the mud. It was necessary to pull it out and try another spot several times, but all to no avail. Pushing her sleeve up higher, she extended her arm into the mushy earth nearly to her armpit.

"I think I feel something!" she cried as her fingers just touched a firm surface.

"Are you certain?" Rhys said, hesitantly.

"Yes, yes. There's something substantial here where nothing else is. But I can't reach it."

Both Rhys and Collie hurried over to her. Rhys, with the longest reach of the three, forced his arm in beside hers, carefully and slowly. "I feel it, too," he breathed. "Slowly now. Too much motion might send it farther down."

"It may be a rock," Collie muttered, bending over the two of them.

"Wait now," Rhys said, forcing his arm deeper. "I think . . . I've got . . . it. I've got something, anyway."

Very cautiously he dug his fingers around an object deep in the mud. It was much larger than he had thought, too big to hold in one hand. He grasped his fingers around it as tightly as he could, got underneath, and began working it slowly to the surface. Beside him both Justine and Collie were beginning to dance with excitement.

"What does it feel like?" Justine cried. "It's not another rock, is it?"

"I don't think so. Rhys was half-lying on the ground now, his arm imprisoned in the earth. He refused to be hurried by their elation, so afraid was he that he might lose the object and cause it to slip away. Slowly, deliberately, he worked it toward the surface.

Then, as Justine and Collie bent closer over him, he got it free. With his other hand, he grasped it and pulled it from the sucking mud.

"It doesn't look like anything," Justine muttered.

"It's a bundle of some kind," Collie said, reaching for it. Rhys yanked it away.

"Hold on. I dug it out. I'll open it."

Laying the muddy object on the ground, Rhys began working away the outer wrappings. They were thick with mud and difficult to separate. Very carefully he pulled them apart, peeling one strip of cloth from another until he revealed a globe-shaped straw basket tied round and round with thin strands of twine.

"Well, one thing's certain," Collie breathed. "It's not a rock, anyway."

"Oh, do hurry," Justine cried, bending over the basket. "Untie it."

Rhys yanked at the strings. "This will never come untied. It's too tight and too strong. I don't suppose you'd have a knife hidden away somewhere, Collie."

"Wusu's barbarians took it from me. Try this." He picked up a thin slice of granite that somewhere in time had dislodged from the wall of the cavern. One edge was roughly hewed and thin enough to serve as a slicing mechanism, though it was nowhere near sharp enough to cut. Rhys rubbed it across the strands of twine and was encouraged to see some of the threads begin to fray apart. "This may do it, but it will take time. Control your excitement, Justine."

"Let me help," she said, anxious to do anything to unwrap the bundle. In the end they all three took turns, each slicing away until their arms gave out. It seemed that as soon as one strand was loosened, there were three more to take its place. But at last they wore them down to the last layer, where Rhys could begin to pull the ties away. He laid the globe on the ground, staring at it for a moment.

"Well, go ahead," Collie breathed.

"I'm almost afraid to. It might be just some shepherd's lunch, stashed away here years ago."

"Tied up like that?"

"I'll do it," Justine said, and pulled the basket in front of her. She felt certain this object was significant, and that there was a good chance it was the money they had come so far to find. Her breath felt tight in her chest as she reached out to pry apart the two sections of the basket. They broke in her hand, revealing a round object wrapped in dark blue lapiz-colored cloth.

"It's very heavy," she said in a whisper.

"And that's silk, isn't it? No shepherd ever wrapped his lunch in that!"

"My turn," Rhys said, gently taking the object from her. He pulled it from the basket and laid it on the ground. Then he carefully began unwrapping the blue cloth.

Justine and Collie both bent close. The light from the opening above them filtered down, evoking a glossy shimmer from the silk as Rhys laid it aside, like waves of the sea in his hands.

The first inkling Justine got of what lay inside was when a shaft of sunlight caught ruby fire and it flashed in her eyes. She gave a short gasp as the silk fell away, revealing a rainbow of glistening colors, wavering on the walls of the rock. She heard Collie's quick intake of breath beside her. Rhys pulled away the last of the cloth, and they all three stared down at the thing in his hand, unable to speak.

It was symmetrical in shape, about the size of a large melon, and undoubtedly fashioned of gold. But the surface was difficult to see for it was completely encrusted with precious and semiprecious stones. Pearls, emeralds, rubies, and sapphires marched in rows around its perimeter, bordered with more mundane jade, lapis lazuli, and carnelian. Rhys reached out a finger to touch it, as though it were not actually there in his hands.

"I've never seen anything so beautiful!" Justine gasped. "It must be worth a fortune."

"If it really belonged to Timur the Lame," Collie breathed beside her, "it would be worth a fortune for that. But with all those jewels . . ."

"That's not all," Rhys said quietly. With careful precision he maneuvered the top of the jug. It came off in his hand, leaving an opening nearly three inches across. He tipped the jug and shook it, and a shower of gold fell into his hand.

"Medallions," Collie said, taking one and turning it over. "They are struck by the Emperor of China for use on the trade routes. How many are in there, do you think?"

"My guess would be close to one hundred, anyway." Mentally Rhys was calculating that this jug and its contents would be enough to finance the revolution for the next ten years. His heart soared with the thought.

"All we have to do now is get it out of here," he added, becoming briskly practical. "Enough admiration. Put back the gold, Collie, and let's bundle this thing up and leave this place. It's a little too confined for comfort."

Grudgingly Collie dropped the gold piece back in the jug, and Rhys wrapped it all up again in the silk, and put it back in the basket. Using some of the longer pieces of the twine that still remained he began to tie it up while Collie was looking around the cavern.

"Has it occurred to you that Wusu's men might have followed us to the falls," Rhys said as he knelt by the basket. "If we go back that way, they may be waiting for us."

"But what other way is there?" Justine asked, peering down the narrow dark hole that had brought them into

408

the cave.

Collie looked straight up. "We could go out up there."

"Climb that wall! I'd rather go back through the tunnel."

Rhys was on his feet, the basket under his arm secured within his coat. "Collie is right. The safest way out would be up there. It's not completely sheer. I think we can make it."

"I'll go first and see," Collie said, reaching for the creepers that tangled the side of the cave. "After some of the places we've climbed, this shouldn't be half-bad. Just don't be under me if I fall."

Agile as a monkey and careful not to look down, he began working his way up the chimneylike opening, scrambling for handholds and footrests, and using as much of the vines as would take his weight. When he reached the top, Collie pulled himself over the rim, then flattened out to look back down on them.

"You're next," Rhys said to Justine. She threw him a hopeless glance and carefully began searching for a foothold in the rocks. "I'll try to catch you if you slip," Rhys added as she started up.

"If that is supposed to be comforting, it isn't," she retorted. As Collie had found, the wall appeared to be more steep than it actually was, yet it was sheer enough to give her palpitations when she first glanced down. After that she kept her eyes on the bright opening above and tried not to think about falling. Only once did she slip, but was able to catch herself on the creepers long enough to fit her foot into a crevice in the rocks. Once she was close to the top, Collie reached down to pull her out. She heaved her body over the edge and fell exhausted on the ground, while Collie bent to help Rhys when he reached the top. Years of climbing yardarms on ships served Rhys in good stead, and he was over the edge before Justine had had time to completely catch her breath.

"Which way?" Collie asked as the three of them clambered to their feet. Rhys adjusted the basket under his coat.

"The opposite direction from Wusu's camp," he answered as they took off, half-running away from the sound of the water in the distance. There was a sense of urgency in their steps, as though having found the treasure, it was now necessary to get as far away as possible. Collie was in the lead, hurrying ahead of the others. Justine was sprinting to catch up with Rhys when she saw Collie go sprawling, falling face-first on the ground. Crying out, she rushed forward to try to reach him, but her feet shot out from beneath her and she fell with a thud just behind him. Rhys went down on top of her. A piercing pain blinded her as she smacked her head against a jutting tree root. She heard a loud woosh, then felt more than saw the crazy-quilt pattern of a hemp net that swung over the three of them, imprisoning them on the ground.

They rolled and pulled at the thongs of the net, struggling to collect their wits as a tall man stepped from the trees and spoke in a cool voice over them.

"I'll just trouble you for whatever it was you found in that cave, Capt. Llewellyn, if you please."

Her head cleared. Stumbling to her knees she clutched at the edge of the net, threw it back from her face, and looked up into the cold, dispassionate eyes of Col. Augustus Hughes.

Seventeen

Rhys could not answer. His fingers tightened around the basket even as he stared in disbelief at the smirk on the colonel's face. All kinds of alternatives raced through his mind: Brazen it out. Pretend there was nothing of value in the bundle. Claim right of ownership by virtue of having found it. He knew by looking at Hughes's triumphant, determined face that they were all useless.

But he'd be damned if he'd give up without a fight.

"How did you find us?" Justine stammered, stalling for time. The disappointment and anger on Rhys's face raised chills on her spine.

Hughes could not resist the temptation to brag. "Oh, it wasn't difficult. These Mongol barbarians are quite good at tracking. We've been on your trail ever since you left Samarkand, except for the past day or two. I've been watching and listening above that cave for the last half hour. Your servant here is not especially quiet."

"We were hiding from robbers in the area," Collie muttered, trying like Justine to gain a little time.

"I don't think so. I know what you were after and what

411

you found, though it seems uncommonly small to be what I think it is. Nevertheless, I'll have a look. Give it to me."

Rhys glanced around. He could see a few of the emir's guards standing behind Hughes, as well as that small English bodyguard of the colonel's. At least they no longer had to fear the big, beefy one. A long, wicked-looking sword gleamed in Hughes's hand, but the soldiers behind him looked on almost objectively. Was there a chance they wouldn't interfere?

"One more time, Captain. Hand it over or I'll run you through with no compunction at all. Your death might easily be considered an unfortunate accident of war."

Rhys thrust the basket forward. "Take it from him, George," Hughes said, never taking his eyes from Rhys's face. Sporn jumped forward to pull the net away from the prisoners and grab the basket. At the colonel's direction, he laid it on the ground, forced it open, took out the blue silk, and began to unwind it. Once the beautiful canteen lay on the folds of blue silk, even Hughes could not resist staring at it.

"A king's ransom," he muttered, his tongue sliding across his thin lips. "Worth all the effort . . ."

Rhys's glance was drawn to the side where one of the soldiers had stepped closer. He had pulled his scimitar out of his wide sash, and it rested lightly in his hand. His eyes met Rhys's, and he smiled very slightly.

It was worth a chance. Leaping up, Rhys jumped at Hughes, catching him off guard long enough to grip his sword wrist. At the same time Collie reached for the canteen, bundling it in the silk under his arm, and trying to run back through the trees. Almost at once he was stopped by a wall of guards. Rhys and Hughes fell

412

wrestling to the ground, rolling over one another. Twisting Hughes's hand, Rhys forced him to drop his sword, but with a surprising strength, Hughes was then able to shove Rhys backward, throwing him onto the ground with a thud.

The breath was knocked from Rhys's body for an instant, while Hughes scrambled to his feet and raised his sword to pin him to the ground. In that instant the soldier moved, throwing his scimitar to Rhys, who rolled away from the thrust that sent the sword tip three inches into the ground. Rhys nimbly scrambled to his feet, grasping the scimitar. Hughes pulled his sword from the earth, and they went at each other, metal clanging against metal. It was like no fencing Rhys had ever done. He was unused to the short curved sword and could use it mostly to deflect the blows from Hughes's blade. Leaping and scrambling around the small area, while Justine hovered near Collie who was held firmly by one of the emir's corsairs, the two men went at each other with plunging, flailing blows. Rhys could not get close enough to Hughes to cut him, but he was agile at blocking the deadly thrusts of the colonel's sword.

Then he stumbled, falling backward. The scimitar rolled from his hand, and he lay looking up at Hughes who raised his sword to strike.

"No!" Justine screamed. "Colonel, no!"

Hughes paused, his blade upraised. "You've got what you wanted," Justine cried, tears in her voice. "What use is it to kill him. Hasn't there been enough blood shed over this damned treasure!"

Slowly the colonel lowered his sword as something of the honor involved in years of life as a British officer took effect. "All right," he muttered. "For your sake and your father's sake, I'll let him live. Hold him, you men."

Several of the soldiers stepped forward to grip Rhys's arms. The colonel sheathed his sword. "You can all three go back to Samarkand and live as the emir's guests the rest of your lives. That should be punishment enough."

He made certain that the three of them were firmly secured by the emir's soldiers, then ordered Sporn, "Bring that thing here. I want a closer look."

Rhys was yanked to his feet and stood with the others, while George Sporn laid the blue silk on the ground and pulled away the folds to reveal the jeweled canteen. The light filtering through the trees caught the brilliant stones, and threw the ruby, green, and blue colors—like a cathedral window—around them in a rainbow. For a moment Hughes forgot all else as he knelt to examine the canteen. He turned it over in his hand, he shook it, he rubbed his fingers along the rows of precious jewels. Then, carefully working away the lid, he poured two of the gold pieces into his palm.

"God's teeth, Colonel. That ought to make us rich for life," Sporn breathed beside him. "Never did I see such gold."

Hughes was thinking how this precious thing by rights belonged to His Majesty's government. And yet . . . who was to say that some of these gold pieces might not be lost along the way . . .

A sudden flash of movement. A streak of light. Justine screamed, her voice searing the quiet of the forest.

The soldier who had thrown Rhys his scimitar leaped forward and buried it into the colonel's back with a horrible thud. Hughes's head shot back and he gave a ghastly cry of surprise. Then he fell forward over the canteen.

414

"No!" Sporn yelled. His cry became a gurgle as a second soldier stepped behind him and yanked a thin cord around his throat, garroting him on the spot. Justine heard herself screaming and screaming before Rhys was allowed to reach her and pull her into his arms. She buried her face in his shoulder, trembling with shock and horror.

Rhys's glance moved across the faces of the Mongol soldiers, fighting a fear like none he had ever felt before. The man in charge kicked Hughes's body away with his boot and bent to pick up the canteen. He held it up, laughing as the others joined him. With much gaiety they waved the blue silk like a flag before wrapping it once again around the canteen. Then bundling it under his tunic, he directed the others to move off, dragging Rhys, Justine, and Collie with them. Rhys kept tight hold of Justine. It was a small encouragement that the soldiers had not dispatched them as easily as they had Hughes and Sporn. Perhaps the emir had ordered them to be returned alive. If so, it was their only hope.

They stumbled off down the mountainside. Rhys was not certain of the direction, but he thought it was toward the pass leading back into Bokharta. The sounds of the falls grew more faint and were soon gone, while the vegetation and warmer air suggested they were leaving the stark southern reaches of Tien Shan. Beside him Justine stumbled, half-supported by his grip. All she could think of was that she was walking back into Samarkand to a life of hopelessness in the emir's harem. And there was not a shred of hope that this time she would escape. There would be no one to turn to. They had no weapons, no friends, no help at all. She wished they had never found that terrible treasure.

They walked the rest of the day, until the sun slipped behind the mountains towering above them. Darkness came suddenly, and with it the cold. Rhys had begun to think they would walk all night, when at last a halt was called. They fell exhausted on the ground, while around them the soldiers—who never seemed to weary—built a fire and pulled out their rations. This turned out to be an unappetizing mess of dough and bread-sauce, and although she hadn't eaten much all day, she was still too upset to even try it when one of the soldiers offered her a little. She sat next to Rhys, cradled in his arms, the silent tears running down her cheeks, and tried to calm the trembling which still racked her body, a combination of fatigue and memory.

"Still shaken by that scene back there?" Rhys whispered, lightly kissing her forehead. He gently stroked her hair back from her brow, and Justine, grateful for the comforting nearness of his body, buried her face in his neck.

"It was so terrible. One minute Hughes was alive, gloating over that horrible canteen, the next he was dead. Just like Timurid. Only this time I could see it all happening."

Rhys thought back to the battles he had taken part in at sea. How many times had he seen men cut down, sometimes with horrible wounds. You never got used to it. It had been one of the reasons he had wanted to escape the war. He hadn't escaped very well, he thought grimly.

"Try to put it out of your mind. You'll need to rest if we continue at this pace all the way to Samarkand."

"Oh, Rhys. I can hardly bear to think of going back to that barbaric place. Isn't there anything we can do to escape?"

Rhys glanced at Collie, who was sitting with his arms around his knees, staring at the fire. "Well, Collie," he said softly. "You're usually resourceful. Can you think of anything?"

"I've been going over the possibilities all day," he whispered back. "Not a one of them appears to give us a fighting chance. I think we'd best go on back to that loathsome emir, and see what we can do then."

Rhys shook his head. "I disagree. Once inside that place again, I doubt we'll ever get out. Princess Tsingsia isn't going to risk her neck a second time over us. Especially after she's got what she wanted in the first place. We'll have to come up with something before we reach Samarkand."

"Well, I'm blamed if I know what it's going to be," Collie muttered, sinking his head onto his arms.

Rhys leaned back against one of the spruces around the clearing and drew Justine close inside his arms. "Try to rest," he whispered again, "we'll think of something in the morning."

Although she never thought she would be able to sleep, she fell almost at once into a fitful, restless slumber teeming with disturbing dreams. It was so uncomfortable on the ground, that in spite of Rhys's reassuring nearness she kept waking, only to slip back into a kind of drugged unconsciousness brought on by sheer physical and mental weariness. The night was very cold, and the fire soon died down. All around them the dark humped shapes that were the sleeping soldiers lay scattered like boulders. Now and then one would turn restlessly in his sleep or mutter indecipherable words.

Rhys was surprised the men had set no one to stand watch, but all fell around the fire stretched out on the

417

ground as though accustomed to sleeping there every night. Occasionally one would wake and throw a few sticks on the embers, then go back to sleep again. He tried to stay awake, if only to guard Justine, but weariness finally overcame him and he nodded off, his body curled around Justine's and his face against her hair.

He never knew what woke him. Suddenly he was alert, staring into the darkness, conscious of having heard a noise back through the trees. Across Justine's sleeping body, Collie snored gently. One of the soldiers stirred nearby as Rhys listened intently, straining for any sound.

All was still. The fire was nearly gone now, red embers glowing like tiny eyes in the darkness. Was it an animal he had heard, a predator drawn by the unusual smell of humans in the area? Very carefully he moved his head, so as to be able to listen more clearly. There it was again, and not just a single murmur through the dried leaves, but several of them.

Rhys reached carefully across Justine and shook Collie. He stirred, almost crying out in surprise, but Rhys managed to shake his shoulder in time.

"Shh . . ." he hissed. He laid a finger against his lips and motioned toward the trees. Collie slowly turned over and stretched out, as though changing position in his sleep. Rhys could tell he was alert and listening.

Once again the sound came, a slipping along the forest floor. Collie heard it, too, and lifted his head. Sliding quietly along the ground, he worked his agile body away from the circle of men toward the trees. Rhys gently shook Justine awake, laying a finger over his lips as she looked up at him with questioning, bleary eyes. Then the two of them joined Collie, easing away from the fire and into the deeper darkness of the surrounding trees. They had gone only a few feet when suddenly the night was shattered by a series of piercing screams. From the shelter of the trees, bodies came careening into the camp, screaming as they fell on the startled soldiers. The whole area erupted into chaos, weapons flailing, startled cries followed by shattering screams from the soldiers who struggled up from sleep as dark monsters from some evil world fell upon them.

Rhys saw what was happening in an instant. He jumped to his feet, pulling Justine up with him, and ran from the camp. Almost at once he hit a wall of armed men who grabbed him by the collar, grasping and twisting his arms behind his body. Justine threw herself against him and buried her face against his chest so she could not see what was happening. The screams from the camp were horrible and continued for minutes, punctuated by the clanking of scimitars and the cries of the soldiers barking orders. As they slackened, he saw men running from the camp, followed by others on their heels. He heard the deadly swish of their swords and the horrible thud as they struck home. He felt his own knees giving way a little, then got hold of himself. There was nothing he could do but pray the savages would not turn on him.

It ended almost as quickly as it had begun. The ghastly screams became the laughter and gloating of victory. The man who held Rhys shoved him back toward the camp where others were throwing debris on the fire, building it up. It threw its light on a scene of carnage he could barely bear to look at. All around the fire lay the bodies of the emir's soldiers. Many were hacked to pieces. In three different places a severed head lay on the ground, the startled eyes staring up toward the night sky. Blood was everywhere, seeping into the ground around his feet.

The victors were enjoying their triumph. They pulled at the clothing and armor of the dead men, taking anything they thought of value and kicking aside the corpses. Rhys looked around dumbly, wondering when they would find the basket with the treasure and what they would make of it. If they fought each other for it, it might afford him and the others a chance to escape.

Those hopes were dashed when the men moved aside as their captain came striding into the camp. He stood by the fire, hands on his hips, smiling at the ghastly bloodshed around him.

"Wusu," Rhys muttered. "I should have known."

One of the men stepped forward and thrust Collie down in the dirt in front of the bandit. "So," Wusu said to him in Turki. "I, Wusu, must rescue you foolish foreigners once again."

Collie was encouraged by the word rescue. He bobbed obsequiously, expressing his gratitude and that of his master.

"Get up, you insect," Wusu said, kicking Collie with the toe of his boot. "And tell your master here that I intend to kill him in the most horrible, painful method I can find. He broke his word! Wusu will never tolerate that."

Collie did not even bother to translate. "But why, oh great leader? My master never broke his word. He would never do such a despicable thing."

"Then why did he make off with the treasure when he promised to give me my share!" Wusu roared. Rhys's arms tightened around Justine. He did not know what was being said, but he hoped Collie could handle it.

"No, no, Great Leader," Collie said bobbing up and down. "My master never had a chance. We no more than

420

drew ourselves from the cave where the treasure was found then we were captured by these soldiers from whom you have liberated us. The English colonel took us prisoners, and then the soldiers killed him. They were bringing us back to the emir in Bokharta."

Wusu strode over to Rhys and grabbed him by the collar, staring into his face. Rhys stared back, as defiantly as possible.

"Is this true?" the bandit yelled. Rhys turned his head from the offensive odor of Wusu's breath. "What's he talking about?" he muttered to Collie.

"I told him how you were unable to return his share of the treasure because we were captured by the emir's corsairs. He intends to flay you alive for breaking your word to him."

Rhys looked around the clearing searching for the captain of the emir's guard. He was relieved to recognize his body lying on the far side of the camp near the woods. It appeared not to have been plundered as yet.

"Tell this robber that I had no intention of making off with the treasure. In fact, if he will only search that body over there, he will find it himself."

"Are you sure you want to say that?" Collie muttered.

Rhys sighed. "Do I have a choice? They'll find it eventually. Perhaps it will soften his attitude towards us if I tell him where it is first."

"But Captain . . ." Collie said, looking a little sick. "After all we've been through . . ."

"Tell him," Rhys snapped. "It's the only way."

Collie translated the information and Rhys had the satisfaction of seeing Wusu's eyes light up. The chieftain ordered one of his men over to the body of the Mongol captain and watched eagerly as the man shoved the corpse over with his boot and began to rummage in the soldier's clothes. When he came up with a bundle of blue silk, Wusu demanded it be brought to him immediately. He took the bundle in his hands, smiling broadly.

"It is heavy, but not big enough," he rattled off to Collie. "It should be a chest or a barrel. Is this another of your English tricks?"

Collie did not bother to translate for Rhys. "Open it," he said wearily. Wusu laid the bundle in his lap and began tearing away the folds of silk. When at last he had the jeweled canteen in his hands, he was speechless. He held it up to the firelight, turned it over and over, then threw back his head and laughed.

"What is he saying," Rhys asked.

"I don't know the exact translation, but roughly it means, 'I'm rich as Croesus.' I think ye can gather that he is very pleased."

Rhys stepped toward the chieftain. "Remind him of our bargain," he told Collie, who immediately translated. Wusu ignored that as he worked away the lid from the jug and poured three of the gold pieces into his fat hand. All around him his men were bending to watch in amazement, broad grins on their faces. They all but danced with delight as Wusu rattled the canteen, laughing with pleasure at the soft chink of the gold pieces within.

"The bargain!" Rhys demanded a second time.

Collie thrust himself in front of the chieftain, falling to his knees and loudly translating Rhys's words. The chieftain frowned, turned toward Rhys, and sputtered a long diatribe in Chinese.

"Great Leader, I cannot speak that language," Collie implored. "My master has honorably told you where the

422

treasure lay. He asks that you remember the bargain you made with him in good faith."

"Ha!" Wusu said. "Bandits have no need of good faith. We take what we want. I could kill you all right here, and no one would ever know."

"This isn't going very well," Collie said, turning pale. "Have you any other suggestions, Capt. Llewellyn?"

Rhys suspected that the only thing that might save them was to hold his ground. "Tell this sneaky knave that that canteen was sent by Prince Tai of Tsinghai to my government, the Independent United States of North America. If he does not return it and allow us to go on our way, my government will send a great army to seek him out and tear his limbs from his disgusting body. And make it strong, Collie!"

Without raising an eyebrow, Collie translated as Rhys had told him. He had the satisfaction of seeing Wusu turn thoughtful over the word "army."

"You see what we have done to the soldiers of the emir," the chieftain blustered. "What fear do I have of an army?"

"This will be a very great army," Rhys answered. "It includes many, many men who will comb these mountains and seek him out. They are waiting even now to embark, and if we do not return with the treasure soon, they will come looking for us."

Justine, who had been hovering near Rhys all this time, trying not to look at the carnage around her, whispered: "Do you think he will believe that? The colonies are so far away, no army would ever be sent here."

"Yes, but he doesn't know that," Rhys whispered back. And indeed, Wusu was studying them thoughtfully, as though trying to decide if this country they came from was close enough to invade the Tien Shan and search him out. He had never heard of North America, but he vaguely knew of England—a great power over the sea whose long arm had reached even into China and farther south into India. He could not decide if this threat was a real one or not.

Suddenly Wusu's fat face was split by a huge grin. "Come," he said good-naturedly. "We are friends, are we not? We have made a bargain. I have the treasure, and you shall have your lives."

"What does he say?" Rhys asked Collie.

"I don't think ye want to hear," Collie moaned. "He gets the treasure and we get to live."

"What! God's my life, you tell this two-faced thief that I demand he return that canteen to me for my government immediately," Rhys shouted.

Collie translated and Wusu turned a coldly angry face toward him. Collie quavered a little as he translated the chieftain's reply.

"He says that your government is a long way away, but Wusu is right here. Either you accept his terms, or he will hang all our heads from these tree limbs and let the birds pick our bones along with those of the emir's corsairs. For pity's sake, Captain, tell him you agree."

"Tell the bastard to go to hell!"

"My master says Wusu is the soul of generosity," Collie cried in Turki, bowing and scraping before the chieftain, "and he gladly accepts your most kind offer." Immediately Wusu beamed upon Rhys and Justine.

"Damnit, Collie, what did you tell him!" Rhys muttered.

"I said we accept his offer. For Justine's sake . . ."

424

What could Rhys say when it was put like that. She looked up at him and he could see in her eyes the wish to be gone away from this place no matter what it took. It cost him a lot to give up the dream for which he had come so far, but he realized there was no other way out. "Tell him I hope he rots in hell!" he muttered.

Collie translated for nearly two whole minutes, extolling Wusu's generous and gracious heart. His long speech had some effect, for when he was finished, Wusu smiled broadly and motioned Collie to come to him. With his knees trembling—for he did not trust this bandit for one second—Collie rose and stood hovering before the robber chief. Wusu, still smiling, turned over the canteen and shook out one of the gold pieces. He handed it to Collie and directed him to give it to Rhys.

"This is to get you back to your North America," Collie said as he dropped the piece in Rhys's hand. "For God's sake, Captain, try to look pleased. Smile a little!"

"One whole piece of gold! That ought to just about take us to the China Sea."

"My master thanks you from the bottom of his heart, oh Great Leader," Collie said in Turki while Rhys forced a grim smile.

Wusu called one of his men up. "This warrior will conduct you to the north mountains and the caravan trail," he said to Collie. "You had all better go right away, before I change my mind about this. Right now I am feeling generous, but I might reconsider. Wusu is his own law. He does what he wishes."

There was a brisk exchange in Chinese between Wusu and his warrior, who was not happy to be chosen to lead these infidel nuisances back to civilization. Losing his patience, Wusu reached out and knocked the man on the side of the head, sending him sprawling. He scrambled to his knees, holding his head while the chieftain rose, swishing his sword around in the air.

"Please, Rhys," Justine cried, turning away, "let's get out of here while we have the chance!"

Even Rhys seemed to reconsider his former reluctance. "Collie, tell this black-hearted bastard we are ready to leave now, and we will never forget the spirit he has shown us. In truth, we will never forget!"

Collie translated loosely enough to placate Wusu, who once again resumed his seat. Their guide shuffled off through the trees and the three of them hurried after him, fearing that any moment the screaming horde would follow, scimitars waving in the air. It was just beginning to get light enough so that they could see their guide ahead of them, a shadow in the forest. He moved quickly, obviously not caring if they followed or not. They ran to keep up, wanting only to put as much distance between themselves and the bloody camp as possible. For Rhys, at least, the vigorous hike had the advantage of keeping his mind off the jeweled fortune that lay behind them clasped tightly in Wusu's fat hands.

Neither Rhys nor Collie had any idea how far they were from the north side of the mountains. Rhys was sure that if they were more than two or three days away, they would never be able to keep up with their guide. Nor did they trust him. He was so unhappy with this job that it was not unlikely he would lead them into some kind of disastrous terrain and leave them there to wander until they died. Or he might even try to kill them himself, and go back to make some excuse to his chieftain. They put nothing past him.

Their relief was thus great when by evening of that day

426

their guide paused on the brink of a high hill and waited for them to catch up. He pointed below and rattled off a long diatribe in Chinese.

Far below they could just make out a road. "The caravan route?" Rhys asked Collie.

"He doesn't appear to speak Turki," Collie answered. "But I think that's what he's trying to tell us. That must be the southern road along the Tien Shan. This is much more settled country. We ought to find a village around somewhere, and houses where we can buy some food."

"Apparently he was more afraid of Wusu than I realized," Rhys answered. "Tell him we appreciate his help."

Collie spoke in Turki to the man who, in reply, spit on the ground and took off in the opposite direction. "Lovely fellow," Rhys muttered.

"Forget him," Justine said, staring at the green fields far below them with a thin ribbon of white road wandering along their boundaries. "We're out of there! Safe at last. Thank God!"

Collie's broad smile shared something of her relief. "And with any luck we'll find a caravan on its way into China that we can join. Come along, Captain. Let's leave these mountains and start back to civilization."

"Yes, with any luck," Rhys said quietly, and took off after Collie and Justine who were already working their way through the trees toward the meadows below.

Eighteen

She was drawn on deck at first light by the squawking of a sea gull circling the ship. Without bothering to tie up her hair, Justine threw on her clothes, tied a shawl around her shoulders, and climbed to the fo'c'sle, straining to see through the dim gray shroud of the morning. The sailors were already busy in the rigging, shouting to one another as they unfurled the sails to catch the rising wind. The great ship gave a series of groans, as though just waking to the day, then plowed down into the froth of the waves to rise like a phoenix on the breast of the sea. Justine clung to the railing, her hair swirling around her face, and peered at the sapphire horizon. Surely there was land over there, just beyond the distant edge of ocean. She could almost smell it.

"You're up uncommonly early," came a friendly voice from the other side of the deck. She turned, pushed aside her streaming hair, and smiled at First Mate Rogers, who was standing halfway up the rope ladder where he had been watching the sailors working above.

"I thought I heard a herring gull," Justine said, raising

her voice against the wind. "That means land is near, doesn't it?"

Rogers jumped nimbly down from the ladder and walked over to her. "You heard one right enough. There should be several of them by now, and more as the sun rises. But, though I hate to disappoint you, it doesn't mean land is just over the horizon."

"Mr. Rogers, not only do you disappoint me, you break my heart! After all this time, I was so certain we were nearing land. Listen, there it is again. And I see it, too. Three of them, in fact."

As if in confirmation of her words, the screeching birds swooped around the jib to dive at the water's surface. Her eyes shining with excitement, Justine pointed at them. "There they are!"

"Yes, Ma'am, but I only caution you that we won't be nearing port today, even though we've come close enough to attract the gulls. They fly miles out to sea, you know. However, by tomorrow perhaps . . ."

Justine plopped down on a three-foot high coil of rope and began pulling her hair into line. "I wish it was today, but tomorrow will do. I've waited long enough to see Philadelphia again. I can wait one more day."

Pulling a length of ribbon from the front of her bodice, she caught the wide strand of her hair and tied it up at the nape of her neck. Rogers, his eyes straying back to the sails above, hoped he had not been overly optimistic in predicting landfall by tomorrow. It all depended on whether or not this wind stayed strong.

"You have come far, Ma'am, that is for certain. I don't think I ever knew anyone to go so far around the world and come home again. It boggles my mind to think on it."

"Well, we would not be about to come home again had

it not been for you, Mr. Rogers. To find you waiting with the *Boedecia* in Canton was a miracle. We thought you would have left long before."

"I did leave once on a short voyage to New Zealand. But somehow it didn't seem right to return to America without the captain, so I just kept waiting and hoping. And then one day, by God, you both turned up! I was as glad to see you, as ever you was to see me and this ship."

Justine thought back to that evening, when the Chinese junk had carried them up the Pearl River to the town of Canton. The harbor had been lined with foreign ships of all flags crowded among the hordes of Chinese boats sandwiched in the harbor, but Rhys had picked out the *Boedecia* almost at once. It had seemed like a benediction at the end of all they had endured. Yet there was no adequate way to explain that to Rogers without detailing all the hardships of their journey, and that she could still not do for anyone. So she gave him her brightest smile and pulled her fingers through her hair. He seemed to recognize that distant look that came into her eyes whenever her experiences in Persia and China were mentioned, and tactfully touched his cap and left her there gazing out over the taffrail.

Justine was barely aware that he had left. How far she had come since stumbling with Rhys and Collie out of the Tien Shan and onto the Great South Road! They had been fortunate enough almost at once to join up with a caravan that was headed for the larger trading cities along the northern border country. It had taken a large slice of Rhys gold medallion to pay their way, but they managed to stay with the main group of the caravan until they reached Peking near the China Sea. And what a harrowing trip it had been! Skirting deserts, crossing mountains, dealing with peasants in the towns to whom the sight of a Westerner evoked horror as well as curiosity, and, all along the route, paying out tribute to warlords for safe passage. None of them turned out to be as bad as Wusu, but several came close. It was amazing that Rhys had been able to manage it all with one gold piece.

And then the emperor's court with its sumptuous palace and thrones, gilded courtyards and jeweled robes. Never had she seen so much wealth concentrated in one place. They had been treated politely, but as little more than prisoners before being escorted onto a Chinese junk for the voyage by sea to Canton. It was obvious the emperor and his mandarins were relieved to be rid of them, and probably hoped they would perish in one of the fierce storms so prevalent in the area.

She still recalled those frantic days in Peking with a shiver. The emperor, the "Great Sun of Heaven," was all for bundling them across the wall into Russia, for no foreigners were allowed anywhere in China except within a few blocks in the port city of Canton. It had taken a lot of persuasion and a few well-placed bribes to gain permission to go south by sea. Somehow Rhys and Collie between them had managed, and they were dispatched on a rickety, basket-shaped boat that had, thanks be to God, carried them safely to Canton.

Once there they had seen little of the city since they embarked almost at once on the *Boedecia*. Yet Justine had an impression in her mind that never dimmed—rows of two-story buildings along the shoreline with narrow arched windows, that caught the last rays of the sun on their white facades. Rhys had explained that these were the European offices and storehouses from which spices,

431

silks, porcelains, and jade were sent to adorn the houses and persons of Caucasians halfway around the world. Behind them lay the tangled low sloping roofs of the Chinese sections of the city, dark and somber after the whiteness of the European compound, and the colorful flags that snapped in the breeze in front of it.

Their joy at finding a ship to carry them home had only been tempered by having to say good-bye to Collie. There had been so many English ships in the harbor however, that she felt certain he would be able to find passage on one of them before the *Boedecia* was well out into the China Sea. She hoped so, anyway. Her thoughts had often gone to him during this long voyage home, and many times she had whispered to the wind, "Godspeed, Collie."

She was startled out of her reverie by two arms that slipped softly around her shoulders and the butterfly flutter of lips on her neck. Murmuring, she stirred dreamily against them. "I didn't hear you come up behind me."

"I took care that you shouldn't," said Rhys, nibbling at her ear lobe and tightening his embrace. "Mmmmm, you taste delicious. Better than any breakfast ever devised."

Justine nestled into the circle of his arms. "Didn't you have enough of this last night? All that wonderful privacy in your cabin brings out the beast in you."

"I'll never have enough," he replied, darting the tip of his tongue into the silken cavity of her ear. "Besides, I have a lot of abstinence to make up for. All those long nights on the caravan when we were almost never alone. And the emperor's palace where we had separate rooms. Not to mention those awful days running from the emir and your Col. Hughes, when fear and worry drove everything else from my mind."

Justine gave a little shiver, though she couldn't be sure whether it was from the memory of those terrible days in the Tien Shan, or from the delicious waves of pleasure that his tantalizing lips sent through her body.

"Well, it's nice to know that something can drive thoughts of making love from your mind," she said giggling. "But the sailors, Captain. Remember, we have an audience." Rhys slid his hand lightly up her waist to cup her breast. "Mmmmm," he murmured against her cheek. "Audience or not, I may not be able to stop myself."

Justine pulled abruptly away, holding him at arm's length. "Rhys! You may not mind, but I do! Control yourself." The mischievous gleam in her dancing eyes belied the sharpness of her words. He pulled her into his arms again and kissed the nape of her neck. "Oh, all right. I'll behave while we're up on deck. But just wait until tonight when I get you below!"

"We may be in Philadelphia tonight. Look there on the horizon. Sea gulls. That means we're nearing land at last. Just think, Rhys. We'll be home again, among our own people. After all this time, it brings my heart near to bursting just to think of it."

He watched the swooping gulls then looked up at the cloud of sails ballooning above them. "I doubt we'll make land today. But if this wind keeps fresh, we may see Delaware Bay sometime tomorrow. That means I'll have a lot to make up for tonight."

"Oh, Rhys, be serious. Aren't you happy to finally be nearing home again? Aren't you excited at the thought?"

He moved to stand next to her at the rail, one arm

433

around her shoulders. His profile, chiseled and more sharply tuned than she remembered when she first met him, was dark against the lightening sky. The wind caught a strand of his dark hair and laid it against his broad forehead, emphasizing the frown of his eyes.

"Happy? Yes, I suppose so. Only sometimes I feel as though we will be saying farewell to one set of problems, only to face a parcel of new ones."

"You mean the war," Justine said, snuggling against him. "But has it occurred to you that it may be over by now? We've been gone so long, that perhaps the Rebels have worked out some kind of solution with the Crown."

"I doubt that. The mood among the men I knew was independence or nothing. And I don't see England giving in graciously. No, my love. I fear that coming home is going to force us to make a lot of adjustments we have been able to avoid in this idyllic sea journey. But, why think of that now. It promises to be a beautiful, bright day with a good wind and a steady sea, and that is all a ship's captain can ask for. That, and a beautiful girl beside him. Now, I hear Rogers having a dispute midships and I sense an adjustment is needed at the wheel. I'd better get about my duties, or we'll end up in Savannah instead of Pennsylvania." He kissed her lightly on the lips. "I'll see you later in my cabin!"

Justine watched him go nimbly down the steps from the fo'c's'le deck to speak to the first mate. She settled once more on the coil of rope and pulled her thick strand of hair over one shoulder, staring over the railing toward the horizon. Somehow her mood was not as euphoric as it had been a few moments before. She was still thrilled to be nearing Philadelphia again after so long a time away, and yet, Rhys was right. Coming home meant that a lot of changes might be in store for them both. How would they be able to ignore their strong political differences once they were back in the middle of the war? Even though neither of them had been able to bring back Prince Tai's treasure for their respective sides, yet both would undoubtedly have demands made upon them to support the people who believed as they did.

Even more disturbing was the thought that once back in the city, they could never live as they had on this journey. Though they had tried to be discreet, she was certain everyone on the ship knew their true relationship. The men on the ship still treated her with respect for the captain's sake, but she knew she would not have that respect in Philadelphia, a city of strong moral principles. She had hoped perhaps Rhys would keep his promise and marry her in Canton, but they had left the city so quickly there had been no time to find someone who could perform the ceremony. Justine felt a shiver as the wind quickened, and she hugged her arms around her chest. In fact, Rhys had not mentioned marriage at all since that awful night in Wusu's camp. Perhaps he had no intention of tieing himself to a girl so loyal to the Crown and so against everything he believed in. They had both been half-convinced they were going to die back there in the bandit's cage. Rhys's talk of marriage probably came from that conviction, and once he actually had time to think about it, he regretted every word.

And what about her own convictions? Somehow they did not seem so important compared to what she felt for this rebel captain. He had become her whole life, almost her reason for being. Yet how was she going to explain that to the British army officers who had come to expect

435

loyalty and support from her family? How would her father have felt, were he still alive, to know that she had thrown her hat over the windmill for a detestable traitor to the Crown?

The ship rose suddenly on a high wave, and Justine jumped up as she thought she spotted a thin dark pencil line of land on the edge of the sea. A thrill went through her body to think America was over there, her country, her homeland. What did it matter who won the war, it was still her country either way. All she wanted was to set her foot on its soil once again. These other problems would sort themselves out somehow.

The wind did not hold, and it was actually two days later that the *Boedecia* glided smoothly up the Delaware to her mooring near the foot of Market Street. It was early morning by the time they docked, and the rosy rays of dawn were just tinging the spires and cupolas of the town with rouged gold. Justine sat in the longboat that carried her to the dock, her hands clutching her cottage cloak around her, her heart almost audible with anticipation. The ships in the harbor were clustered so close together that their thin, jutting masts made a filigreed pattern against the sheen of gray water. Beyond them the sun glinted on the brick houses of the city, turning them a soft pink. As she drew nearer, she could see that the docks were more bustling than ever. Crowds of men in somber blue and black coats mingled with sailors whose faces were tanned by days in the sun. Women and children created splashes of color among the throngs of merchants, ships' officers, seamen, and longshoremen. There were more Negroes than she ever

436

remembered—women in brightly colored turbans, men working the docks in shirtsleeves and vests.

The dock was a jumble of crates, bales, boxes, and barrels, stacked in places as high as the roofs of the stores and grog shops that lined Water Street. Even the odors seemed more pungent than she remembered. Tar, seaweed, spices, tallow, rum, wet wood, and canvas, coffee, all mingled in the air, often heightened by the scattered piles of garbage along the wharf and in the water close to shore.

Justine collected her portmanteau and made arrangements for her other boxes—carrying what she had been able to salvage from her long trip—to be sent to the house on Fourth Street. She bade Rogers a warm good-bye, fully expecting not to ever see him again, though she extended him a warm invitation to call on her. Then, unwilling to take the first carriage or sedan chair available, she decided to walk down the wharf and into the city. Somehow she did not want to go back to her former home just yet. Rhys had arranged to meet her within the hour at the London Coffeehouse after he took care of a few business matters, so she decided to wander leisurely around the town until then. Afterwards she would go home, face Moriah and her memories, and try to decide how she was going to get on with her life.

It was minutes before it finally dawned on her what it was that was so very different from the city she remembered. Of course! There was no profusion of scarlet coats everywhere she looked. Where had they gone? There were not even the customary bright fabrics among the civilians. It seemed as though a more somber and dignified populace had taken over from the one she had left. That, or they had all become Quakers in the time

437

she was gone!

Then she spotted a familiar face. Justine ducked her head to hide beneath her bonnet, for she did not wish to be recognized yet and Henry Laurens had been a close friend of her father's before the war and conflicting loyalties had divided them. Since he was also a member of the Continental Congress, a dreadful suspicion began to grow in her breast. She glanced around and spotted a merchant looking over a manifest three feet away.

"I wonder, sir, if you could tell me where the British Headquarters are located in this city." Might as well let him think she was a stranger.

"British headquarters, Ma'am? Oh, you won't find them here no more. Gone to New York they have over a year ago."

"Oh. Then, the rebellion? Is it over?"

The man pulled at his ear, anxious to get back to his business. "It's not over, Mistress, if you mean has we won independence. But most of the fighting now's in the south. Or up around the neutral ground near New York town. I reckon we'll have won presently."

So that would explain Laurens' presence. Philadelphia was controlled by the rebels once again and, no doubt, the Continental Congress was sitting there once more. Somehow it did not hurt as much as she had thought it would.

Justine picked up her portmanteau and resumed her stroll down the wharf, thinking she might even walk up to Second Street and around the town. She was about to turn away from the busy waterfront, when she was stopped by a quarrel going on behind her. There was so much noise around her, that she almost did not catch the shouted epitaphs the two men were hurling at each other.

438

Glancing around she saw that one of the men was a large, fleshy workman in a leather apron that engulfed his huge stomach. He had a club of some sort in his massive hand, and was shaking it threateningly at the other man, who was much smaller. The short fellow had his back to her, but she could see he was wearing a gray bagwig under a tricorn hat, a shoddy black frock coat, buff breeches, and sagging worsted stockings.

And there was something very familiar about that stance.

And that voice!

Justine dropped her portmanteau and stood rooted to the ground as the shorter man flayed the larger one with his angry words.

"Ye great, galumping oaf! I've seen elephants with more grace. Aye, and more intelligence, too. I've seen camels that look like kings beside you. And don't come at me with that poker, or I'll flay the hide off ye with my knife before ye even know ye've been skinned!"

"Collie!" Her voice startled him out of his furious invective. Turning, his mouth gaping, he was all at once at a loss for words. Taking advantage of it, the large man reached out to grab him by the frayed stock at his throat.

"I'll teach you to go around nipping my rum and not paying. Have the constable on you, I will!"

Justine threw herself between the two of them, clutching at the larger man's arm. "Wait, please. I know this gentleman. What's the trouble?"

Startled at the sight of a gentlewoman coming to the thief's defense, the big man lowered his cudgel. "He drank my rum and tried to sneak out without paying. Can't have that, Mistress. Where's my custom if I don't get my coin?"

439

"Now, Justine," Collie said, straining against the grip on his collar. "I was going to pay him. It's just that I don't have much with me yet. As soon as I got a little work, I'd have come right back here and settled. Tell this great oaf that I would."

Justine dug into her reticule. "Here," she said, handing the barkeep a coin. "And if this is not enough, send round this evening to the Maury house on Fourth Street for the rest. Is that sufficient?"

The barkeep thought this over. Maury was a familiar name in the city, and the lady appeared to be trustworthy. He released Collie—almost dropping him on the pavement—and pocketed the coin. Justine lost no time dragging her old friend back to where her portmanteau was waiting.

"Collier Rigby, I cannot believe it! What are you doing here in America? I thought you took ship for England."

Collie straightened his stock, trying to look dignified, though Justine could barely suppress a laugh at how uncomfortable he appeared in European dress. She was certain she'd never get used to seeing him that way.

"It's a long story," Collie mumbled. "And I'm too hungry at the moment to go into it. This city of brotherly love does not always live up to its name when a poor man arrives without a means of taking care of himself. I'm forced to admit, I was never so glad to see anybody, Justine, as you just now."

Justine stopped, not caring how the crowd had to mill around the two of them. Throwing her arms around Collie's neck, she hugged him fiercely. "Oh, Collie, my dear old friend. And I, you!"

Taking Collie's arm in hers, Justine led him straight to

the London Coffeehouse where she ordered a small private room and a substantial breakfast for them both. Although she had little money with her, she knew she had only to see the Hon. Brewster Chapman—who had been handling matters while she was gone—to obtain more. They had been there half an hour, laughing and talking between mouthfuls of ham, salted herring, and a pigeon pie, when Rhys walked in. At first he did not recognize the small man in the shaby frockcoat and ill-fitting wig who was sharing a private meal with Justine. Then his eyes grew wide, his mouth hung open, and he stood by the door unable to move.

"God's my life, I don't believe it!"

"Close yer mouth, Captain. You look like ye've seen an apparition," Collie intoned.

Rhys walked to the table and clapped Collie on the shoulder. "You look like an apparition yourself in those clothes. Merciful heaven, will we never be rid of this fellow, Justine?"

"Isn't it wonderful, Rhys! I was never so surprised in my life when I ran across him on the wharf this morning."

Collie rose and made Rhys an elaborate leg. "And may Allah bless you also, *effendi*," he said, sweeping his hand through the air. "The truth is, this lady saved me from a horrible death by starvation. Imagine coming all this way, only to waste away on the Carpenters Wharf from lack of vittles. Allah be praised, I'd of been better off in Baghdad."

Rhys pulled up a chair to the table and poured himself a tumbler of Madeira. "I always told you, you should have stayed there. But how on earth did you get here?

441

And why? I thought you were so homesick for England."

Collie resumed his seat, picked up his fork, and jabbed at what was left of his pigeon pie. "Well now, that was a subject I had been giving a deal of thought to, even before we reached Canton. Once there, it just didn't seem such a good thing for me to return to England. After all, they might still want me for desertion, and I've no mind to survive Wusu and Ulugh Khan just to rot in an English gaol."

"You never said anything to us," Justine said.

"No, because I wasn't sure. But when I saw ye both sail away for America, I got to thinking how I might find a place there meself. It would be the next best thing to England, but without the threat of gaol. And it wouldn't be the Far East! I took the next ship out for Philadelphia, a trim two-masted schooner that near flew across the Pacific. I've been here a week, looking the wharfs over everyday, hoping I'd see the both of ye."

"Well, I think it's wonderful the three of us are together again," Justine exclaimed. "We crossed the world together, braved death, starvation, captivity, heat, and cold. You saved my life at least three times over." She raised her pewter tumbler. "I think we should toast to being together again. Friends forever!"

Rhys and Collie joined her in the toast, after which Collie bent and fastened his gaze on his plate, more moved than he wanted to admit. "Of course," he said casually, "I have no idea what I'll do over here. Is there much need for tailors in this Colony?"

Rhys reached out and turned over the frayed collar of his friend's coat. "I don't think your calling is plying a needle, Collie, judging from the fit of these clothes. But you know the world and you know ships. I'll wager there

442

is a place for you somewhere in the mercantile profession."

"I thought about that. But without Prince Tai's treasure, I haven't got a shilling to buy a stake in any venture.

"If I had the money to finance another ship, I'd take you on."

"No thank you, Captain. I've no wish to become a common seaman again. But I'm told there are a lot of opportunities in this country. I'll find something."

Justine looked from one man to the other. "Rhys," she said thoughtfully, "do you mean that you could buy a ship and sail it on a trading voyage, while Collie managed its affairs back home?"

An excited glint deepened the green of Rhys's eyes. "Something like that. We could form our own company. Once this war is over, and independence is a fact, there will be a need for all kinds of goods. With Collie's knowledge of the world and my sailing ability, we might make a fortune one day."

"Do you really think so?"

"I'm certain of it. But what's the use of dreaming. While the war still lasts, there isn't going to be any extra capital to finance new ventures of that sort. The best I can hope for is to be given another ship and reap a few profits."

Justine jumped up abruptly and rushed to the corner where her portmanteau sat against the wall. Rummaging around she pulled out a small pair of scissors, returned to the table, turned her back on the two men, and pulled up her skirts. They watched curiously as she dug at the fabric at her waist.

"You're not trying to plunge those things into your

443

ribs, are you, Justine?" Rhys said laconically. "The situation's not that bad."

"Of course not." Throwing her skirts down, she turned and laid a small piece of cloth on the table, carefully laying back the overlapping edges. When she had finished, a luminous, glossy black pearl lay on its bed of cloth, a long gold chain woven around it.

"Merciful God!" Rhys breathed, bending toward the jewel. "Where did you get that?"

Justine picked up the chain and waved the pearl under his nose. "It was a gift from the emir of Bokharta. I've been hoarding it all this time, so I could bring it back and give it to the British authorities, as my father would have wanted. But now that the British have abandoned Philadelphia, and I've come to be so involved with a damned rebel, well, I suppose the British will just have to win the war without my help."

Collie took the pearl from her hand and held it up to the light, smiling his crooked smile. "It's beautiful. Worth a fortune. Would you really want to part with it?"

"I never wanted anything that reminded me of Ulugh Khan, yet I couldn't bear to just throw it away. It ought to do some good for someone. Why not us? It would serve the emir right if his money financed our future."

"Justine, I love you!" Rhys cried and bent over the table to kiss her soundly. Then, just as quickly, he pulled away, took the pearl, laid it on the table, and addressed them soberly.

"Before we go any further, I've a confession to make, too. And, considering the nature of it, we'd better have it out before we make any plans. In fact, you may not want to make any plans that include me, when you hear what I've got to say."

444

Collie and Justine looked at one another quizzically. Justine sat back in her chair and clasped her hands on the table. It was not like Rhys to be this sober.

"The truth is . . . well." Rhys rubbed at his chin. "The truth is, I did bring back that treasure. Some of it anyway."

"You what!" Collie exclaimed. "And ye never said a word—"

"But how," Justine finally managed to get out. "There was no way—"

"Yes there was. After Collie went up the wall of the cave and while you were following him, I shook out most of the gold medallions and slipped them into my boots and my pack. Then I filled the canteen with rocks and gravel, and put a few back on top. I gambled on the fact that you would be so frightened of heights you'd never look down and see me. I was also holding my breath both times Col. Hughes and Wusu shook out some of the gold."

"Now I understand how you managed to make that one little gold medallion go so far," Justine said. "But why didn't you tell us?"

Rhys spread out his hands in a hopeless gesture. "I was afraid you'd want to give it to the Crown, or that Collie would take it for himself."

"Think on that, Justine," Collie said. "All this time, and all we've been through, and still he didn't trust us. I believe I'm insulted."

"No," Justine said evenly. "You were right, Rhys. I would have wanted to bring at least part of it back to help my country."

Rhys laid his hand over hers on the table. "You see, I felt so strongly that I had been entrusted with a mission,

445

and I simply had to fulfill it. Not just for my country's sake, but for my own peace of mind. I knew you felt that way, too."

Collie broke in. "But God's life, man. Where is it now? Why, surely there must be a little left over to help us get started in business."

"No," Rhys said. "I went straight to Robert Morris this morning and gave it all to him. I didn't even take my commission."

Justine fastened her large eyes on his face. "Why not?"

He stared back at her, lost in the depths of her gaze. "Because I didn't think it was right that I should profit when neither of you did."

"Oh, Rhys," she cried, throwing herself into his arms. "What a perfectly splendid man you are! And how I love you! Love you! Love you!"

He nearly went over in the chair. Laughing, he hugged her tightly. "And do you forgive me, too?"

"Of course I do," she said sitting on his lap and kissing him. "You oaf. We don't need that gold. You can use my pearl to buy a ship and start a business. It would have only prolonged the war longer had it gone to the Crown."

Rhys jumped up and swung her around, whooping with joy. "Justine, you're a priceless pearl yourself. And now we can get married, right away. Today, in fact."

It was Justine's turn to stop, startled. "Married? But . . ."

"You still want to marry me, don't you? I recall asking you quite clearly."

Justine threw her arms around his neck. "Of course I do. But I thought you had forgotten . . . or changed your mind. You never mentioned it after that night."

He took her face between his hands. "That's because I was afraid you would never forgive me for hiding the treasure and returning it to the American government. My dear, beautiful, Tory sweetheart!"

He kissed her, a long, savouring, blissful kiss.

"Ahem," Collie coughed quietly. "I hate to interrupt this tender scene, but ye might recall there's a third party here. I haven't heard ye ask if I forgive ye!"

Justine linked her arm through Rhys's and smiled up at him. "What do you think, Capt. Llewellyn? Should we ask this shoddy fellow for his forgiveness. Or do you think we may be able to get through the rest of our lives without him to show us how?"

"Well, considering how he brought us through several frightening scrapes, I suppose I must. Collier Rigby," he intoned, "I humbly ask your pardon for not sharing Prince Tai's treasure."

Collie smirked and jabbed at Rhys's chest with a long finger. "Well, you won't get it. Oh, not because I care a fig about the gold—I can understand your thinking about that right enough. But I'll never forgive ye for not allowing me to see Wusu's face when he discovered there was rocks and gravel in that canteen!"

Rhys grinned with relief. "All things considered, I don't think you would have wanted to be there. In fact, I was anxious for us all to get as far away as possible, before he realized he'd been tricked. I didn't breathe easy until we reached Canton."

"He had Tamerlane's jeweled canteen," Justine said. "That should have been some consolation."

"And now that all that is out of the way, Collie, I'd be honored to have you stand up with me at the ceremony today."

447

"Today!" Justine cried. "But Rhys, so soon?"

"Why not. We've waited long enough. I'm not even going to seek out a clergyman, for he would want to cry the banns. We'll find a ship's captain here on the wharf, and get the deed done at once. What do you say, Collie?"

The little Englishman could not hide his pleasure. "I say this calls for another toast." He reached for the neck of the green bottle on the table, shook it, and upended it. "Look at that. It's full out. Well, you two lovebirds wait here, and I'll go get another. Your credit is good, ain't it, Captain?"

"It's good," Rhys said laughing. He waited until Collie disappeared through the door, then turned and grabbed Justine to plant a long, warm kiss on her smiling lips.

Breathless, she broke away to slip her arms around his waist and lean against his firm, hard body, her heart swelling.

"Happy, my love?" Rhys whispered.

"Oh, yes. So happy."

Gently Rhys smoothed her silky hair away from her brow. "And you really don't mind that I kept you from bringing back Tamerlane's treasure for the Crown?"

Lifting her face, she studied the strong line of his jaw. Then reaching up, she kissed him lightly on the cleft of his chin. "My darling Rhys, I've got all the treasure I ever want right here in my arms!"